In Vector Prime, *based on a story line approved by George Lucas,* New York Times *bestselling author R. A. Salvatore takes the* Star Wars *universe to previously unscaled heights of action and imagination, expanding the beloved story of a galaxy far, far away . . .*

Twenty-one years have passed since the heroes of the Rebel Alliance destroyed the Death Star, breaking the power of the Emperor. Since then, the New Republic has valiantly struggled to maintain peace and prosperity among the peoples of the galaxy. But unrest has begun to spread and threatens to destroy the Republic's tenuous reign.

Into this volatile atmosphere comes Nom Anor, a charismatic firebrand who heats passions to the boiling point, sowing seeds of dissent for his own dark motives. And as the Jedi and the Republic focus on internal struggles, a new threat surfaces from beyond the farthest reaches of the Outer Rim—an enemy bearing weapons and technology unlike anything New Republic scientists have ever seen.

Suddenly, Luke Skywalker; his wife, Mara; Han Solo; Leia Organa Solo; and Chewbacca—along with the Solo children—are thrust again into battle, to defend the freedom so many have fought and died for. But this time, the power of the Force itself may not be enough . . .

Also by R. A. Salvatore

THE DEMON WARS

THE DEMON AWAKENS
THE DEMON SPIRIT
THE DEMON APOSTLE

STAR WARS

THE NEW JEDI ORDER

VECTOR PRIME

R. A. SALVATORE

LUCAS BOOKS

DEL REY

A Del Rey® Book
THE BALLANTINE PUBLISHING GROUP • NEW YORK

A Del Rey® Book
Published by The Random House Publishing Group

www.starwars.com
www.delreybooks.com

ISBN 0-345-47933-5

Map design by Daniel Wallace
Map by Chris Barbieri

Manufactured in the United States of America

First Edition: July 2000

OPM 9 8 7 6 5 4 3 2

To Diane, with all my love, and to my kids,
Bryan, Geno, and Caitlin,
who make it easy for me to empathize with Han Solo!

ACKNOWLEDGMENTS

This, as much as anything I've ever done, was a team project, and I'd be remiss if I didn't give credit where credit was due. First, to Shelly Shapiro, for holding my hand through the *Star Wars* maze, and for bringing a fresh vision to an old story. To Jenni Smith, for her support, enthusiasm, and knowing eye. To the folks at Lucasfilm—Sue Rostoni, Lucy Autrey Wilson, and Howard Roffman—who brought an honest and un- yielding concern for quality that forced me to stay at my best. And to two fellow authors: Mike Stackpole, for giving me in- sights about this world I was entering, and Terry Brooks, who reminded me that it would be incredibly stupid to say no to *Star Wars*!

TINGEL ARM

EMPIRE

BELKADAN
(HELSKA) (SERNPIDAL)
BASTION
DUBRILLION
MUUNILIST
DANTOOINE
YAGA MINOR
GARQI
AGAMAR
DATHOMIR

HYDIAN WAY

CORPORATE SECTOR

ALMANIA

YAVIN
ITHOR
MERIDIAN
SECTOR
WAYLAND
MYRKR
ORROA-SKAI

PERLEMIAN TRADE ROUTE

TION CLUSTER

HAPES CLUSTER
CRON
DRIFT CLUSTER

MON CALAMARI

KASHYYYK
HOLATIN
BIMMISAARI

HUTT SPACE
KESSEL

NAL HUTTA
HONOGHR
YLESIA
BARABI

GAMORR

ZOB

HYDIAN WAY

PERLEMIAN TRADE ROUTE

RALLTIIR
RHINNAL
ESSELES
BRENTAAL

CHANDRILA

CORULAG

THE STAR WARS NOVELS TIMELINE

ONE

Fraying Fabric

It was too peaceful out here, surrounded by the vacuum of space and with only the continual hum of the twin ion drives breaking the silence. While she loved these moments of peace, Leia Organa Solo also viewed them as an emotional trap, for she had been around long enough to understand the turmoil she would find at the end of this ride.

Like the end of every ride, lately.

Leia paused a moment before she entered the bridge of the *Jade Sabre*, the new shuttle her brother, Luke, had built for his wife, Mara Jade. Before her, and apparently oblivious to her, Mara and Jaina sat comfortably, side by side at the controls, talking and smiling. Leia focused on her daughter, Jaina, sixteen years old, but with the mature and calm demeanor of a veteran pilot. Jaina looked a lot like Leia, with long dark hair and brown eyes contrasting sharply with her smooth and creamy skin. Indeed, Leia saw much of herself in the girl—no, not girl, Leia corrected her own thoughts, but young woman. That same sparkle behind the brown eyes, mischievous, adventurous, determined.

That notion set Leia back a bit, for she recognized then that when she looked at Jaina, she was seeing not a reflection of herself but an image of the girl she had once been. A twinge of sadness caught her as she considered her own life now: a diplomat, a bureaucrat, a mediator, always trying to calm things down, always working for the peace and prosperity of the New Republic. Did she miss the days when the most common noise around her had been the sharp blare of a blaster or the hiss of a lightsaber? Was she sorry that those wild times had been replaced by the droning of the ion drives and the sharp bickering of one pride-wounded emissary after another?

Perhaps, Leia had to admit, but in looking at Jaina and those simmering dark eyes, she could take vicarious pleasure.

Another twinge—jealousy?—caught her by surprise, as Mara and Jaina erupted into laughter over some joke Leia had not overheard. But she pushed the absurd notion far from her mind as she considered her sister-in-law, Luke's wife and Jaina's tutor—at Jaina's own request—in the ways of the Jedi. Mara was not a substitute mother for Jaina, but rather a big sister, and when Leia considered the fires that constantly burned in Mara's green eyes, she understood that the woman could give to Jaina things that Leia could not, and that those lessons and that friendship would prove valuable indeed to her daughter. And so she forced aside her jealousy and was merely glad that Jaina had found such a friend.

She started onto the bridge, but paused again, sensing movement behind her. She knew before looking that it was Bolpuhr, her Noghri bodyguard, and barely gave him a glance as he glided to the side, moving so easily and gracefully that he reminded her of a lace curtain drifting lazily in a gentle breeze. She had accepted young Bolpuhr as her shadow for just that reason, for he was as unobtrusive as any bodyguard could be. Leia marveled at the young Noghri, at how his grace and silence covered a perfectly deadly fighting ability.

She held up her hand, indicating that Bolpuhr should remain out here, and though his usually emotionless face did flash Leia a quick expression of disappointment, she knew he would obey. Bolpuhr, and all the Noghri, would do anything Leia asked of them. He would jump off a cliff or dive into the hot end of an ion engine for her, and the only time she ever saw any sign of discontentment with her orders was when Bolpuhr thought she might be placing him in a difficult position to properly defend her.

As he was thinking now, Leia understood, though why in the world Bolpuhr would fear for her safety on her sister-in-law's private shuttle was beyond her. Sometimes dedication could be taken a bit too far.

With a nod to Bolpuhr, she turned back to the bridge and crossed through the open doorway. "How much longer?" she asked, and was amused to see both Jaina and Mara jump in surprise at her sudden appearance.

In answer, Jaina increased the magnification on the forward screen, and instead of the unremarkable dots of light, there appeared an image of two planets, one mostly blue and white, the other reddish in hue, seemingly so close together that Leia wondered how it was that the blue-and-white one, the larger of the pair, had not grasped the other in its gravity and turned it into a moon. Parked halfway between them, perhaps a half a million kilometers from either, deck lights glittering in the shadows of the blue-and-white planet, loomed a Mon Calamari battle cruiser, the *Mediator*, one of the newest ships in the New Republic fleet.

"They're at their closest," Mara observed, referring to the planets.

"I beg your indulgence," came a melodic voice from the doorway, and the protocol droid C-3PO walked into the room. "But I do not believe that is correct."

"Close enough," Mara said. She turned to Jaina. "Both Rhommamool and Osarian are ground based, technologically—"

"Rhommamool almost exclusively so!" C-3PO quickly added, drawing a scowl from all three of the women. Oblivious, he rambled on. "Even Osarian's fleet must be considered marginal, at best. Unless, of course, one is using the Pantang Scale of Aero-techno Advancement, which counts even a simple landspeeder as highly as it would a Star Destroyer. Perfectly ridiculous scale."

"Thank you, Threepio," Leia said, her tone indicating that she had heard more than enough.

"They've both got missiles that can hit each other from this close distance, though," Mara continued.

"Oh, yes!" the droid exclaimed. "And given the proximity of their relative elliptical orbits—"

"Thank you, Threepio," Leia said.

"—they will remain within striking distance for some time," C-3PO continued without missing a beat. "Months, at least. In fact, they will be even closer in two standard weeks, the closest they will be to each other for a decade to come."

"Thank you, Threepio!" Mara and Leia said together.

"And the closest they have been for a decade previous," the droid had to slip in, as the women turned back to their conversation.

Mara shook her head, trying to remember her original point to Jaina. "That's why your mother chose to come out now."

"You're expecting a fight?" Jaina asked, and neither Leia nor Mara missed the sparkle in her eye.

"The *Mediator* will keep them behaving," Leia said hopefully. Indeed, the battle cruiser was an impressive warship, an updated and more heavily armed and armored version of the Mon Calamari star cruiser.

Mara looked back to the screen and shook her head, unconvinced. "It'll take more than a show of force to stop this catastrophe," she replied.

"Indeed, it has been escalating, by all reports," C-3PO piped up. "It started as a simple mining dispute over mineral rights, but now the rhetoric is more appropriate for some kind of a holy crusade."

"It's the leader on Rhommamool," Mara remarked. "Nom Anor. He's reached down and grabbed his followers by their most basic instincts, weaving the dispute against Osarian into a more general matter of tyranny and oppression. Don't underestimate him."

"I can't begin to give you a full list of tyrants like Nom Anor that I've dealt with," Leia said with a resigned shrug.

"I have that very list available," C-3PO blurted. "Tonkoss Rathba of—"

"Thank you, Threepio," Leia said, too politely.

"Why, of course, Princess Leia," the droid replied. "I do so like to be of service. Now where was I? Oh, yes. Tonkoss Rathba of—"

"Not now, Threepio," Leia insisted, then to Mara, she added, "I've seen his type often."

"Not like him," Mara replied, somewhat softly, and the sudden weakness in her voice reminded Leia and Jaina that Mara, despite her nearly constant bravado and overabundance of energy, was seriously ill, with a strange and thankfully rare disease that had killed dozens of others and against which the best doctors in the New Republic had proven completely helpless. Of those who had contracted the molecular disorder, only Mara and one other remained alive, and that other person, being studied intently on Coruscant, was fast dying.

"Daluba," C-3PO went on. "And of course, there was Icknya—"

Leia started to turn to the droid, hoping to politely but firmly shut him up, but Jaina's cry stopped her abruptly and swung her back to face the screen.

"Incoming ships!" Jaina announced, her voice full of surprise. The telltale blips had appeared on her sensor viewer as if from nowhere.

"Four of them," Mara confirmed. Even as she spoke, the warning buzzers began to go off. "From Osarian." She turned her curious expression up to Leia. "They know who we are?"

Leia nodded. "And they know why I've come."

"Then they should know to leave us alone," Jaina reasoned.

Leia nodded again, but understood better. She had come to

the system not to meet with the Osarians—not at first, at least—but with their principal rival, Nom Anor, the cult figure stirring up trouble on Rhommamool. "Tell them to back off," she instructed Mara.

"Politely?" Mara asked, smiling, and with that dangerous twinkle in her eyes.

"New Republic shuttle," a halting voice crackled over the comm. "This is Captain Grappa of Osarian First-Force."

With a flick of a switch, Mara put an image of the captain on the viewscreen, and Leia sighed as the green skin, spiny head ridge, and tapirlike snout came into view.

"Wonderful," she remarked sarcastically.

"The Osarians have hired Rodians?" Jaina asked.

"Nothing like a few mercenaries to quiet things down," Leia replied dryly.

"Oh, dear me," C-3PO remarked, and he shuffled aside nervously.

"You come with us," Grappa insisted, his multifaceted eyes sparkling eagerly. "To Osa-Prime."

"Seems the Osarians want to talk with you first," Mara said.

"They're afraid that my meeting with Nom Anor will only heighten his stature, both among the Rhommamoolians and throughout the sector," Leia reasoned, a notion not without credence, and one that she had debated endlessly before making the decision to come here.

"Whatever the reason, they're closing fast," Mara replied. Both she and Jaina looked to Leia for instructions, for while the *Jade Sabre* was Mara's ship, this was Leia's mission.

"Princess Leia?" an obviously alarmed C-3PO asked.

Leia sat down in the chair behind Mara, intently studying the screen, which Jaina had switched back to a normal space view. The four approaching fighters were clearly visible.

"Lose them," she said determinedly, a request that neither of the pilots needed to hear twice. Indeed, Mara had been eager to put the shuttle, with its powerful twin engines and state-of-the-art maneuvering systems, through a real test.

Green eyes sparkling, smile wide, Mara reached for the controls, but then retracted her hands and put them on her lap. "You heard her, Jaina," she said.

Jaina's mouth dropped open; so did Leia's.

"You mean it?" Jaina asked.

Mara's only reply was an almost bored expression, along with a slight yawn, as if this whole thing was no big deal, and certainly nothing that Jaina couldn't easily handle.

"Yes!" Jaina whispered, clenching her fists, wearing a smile nearly wide enough to take in her ears. She rubbed her hands together, then reached out to the right, rolling her fingers over the floating-ball control of the inertial compensator. "Strap in," she ordered, and she dialed it down to 95 percent, as fighter pilots often did so that they could gain a tactile feel to the movements of their ships. *Reading the g's,* Jaina had heard it called, and she always preferred flying that way, where fast turns and mighty acceleration could push her back in her seat.

"Not too much," Leia said with concern.

But her daughter was in her element now, Leia knew, and she'd push the shuttle to its limits. Leia felt the lean as Jaina veered right, angling away from the approaching ships.

"If you run, we shoot you down!" came the uneven voice of Grappa.

"Z-95 Headhunters," Mara said derisively of the closing craft, an antiquated starfighter, and she flipped off the comm switch and looked back at Leia. "Can't shoot what you can't catch," she explained. "Kick them in," she added to Jaina, motioning to the primary thrusters, thinking that a burst of the powerful engines would shoot the *Jade Sabre* right past the befuddled Rodians and their outdated starfighters.

Even as she spoke, though, two more blips appeared on the sensors, streaking out from the shadows around Rhommamool, angling right in line with the *Jade Sabre*.

"Mara," Leia said with concern. At that, Mara did reach for the controls. But only for a moment, and then she looked

Jaina right in the eye and nodded for the young woman to proceed.

Leia lurched forward in her seat, held back only by the belt, as Jaina reversed throttle and kicked the etheric rudder right. There came a metallic thump behind them—C-3PO hitting the wall, Leia guessed.

Even as the *Jade Sabre* came to a sudden halt, nose turned starboard, Jaina pumped it out to full throttle and kicked the rudder back to the left, then hard right, fishtailing the ship about in a brutal one-eighty, then working the rudder hard and somewhat choppy in straightening out her direct retreat. As they turned, a laser cannon blast cut across their bow.

"All right, the first four are on our tail," Mara instructed calmly. The *Jade Sabre* jolted, hit aft, a blow the shields easily held back.

"Try a—" Mara started to say, but she lost the words, and nearly her lunch, as Jaina pulled a snap roll right, and then another right behind it.

"Oh, we'll be killed!" came C-3PO's cry from the doorway, and Leia managed to turn her head to see the droid leaning in against the metal jamb, and then to see him fly away, with a pitiful cry, as Jaina kicked the etheric rudder again, putting the ship into another sudden fishtail.

A pair of Headhunters streaked past the viewscreen, but just for a split second, for Jaina vectored away at a different angle, and at single-engine full throttle, pressing Leia back in her seat. Leia wanted to say something to Jaina then, some words of encouragement or advice, but found her words stuck in her throat. And not for any g forces.

It was the sight of Jaina, the fire in her brown eyes, the determined set of her jaw, the sheer concentration. At that moment, Leia knew.

Her daughter was a woman now, and with all the grit of her father and mother combined.

Mara glanced over her right shoulder, between Jaina and Leia, and both followed her lead long enough to see that two of the initial four had altered course accordingly and were fast closing, laser cannons blasting away.

"Hold on," a confident Jaina warned, and she pulled back the stick, lifting the *Jade Sabre*'s nose, then shoved it forward, dropping the shuttle into a sudden, inverted loop.

"We're doomed!" C-3PO cried from the hallway—the hallway ceiling, Leia knew.

Halfway around, Jaina broke the loop with a snap roll, then kicked her into a fishtail and a barrel roll, bringing her about to nearly their original course, but with the initial four behind them. Now she did kick in both ion drives, as if to use sheer speed to split the gap between the two incoming fighters.

Both angled out suddenly, then turned back in, widening that escape route but giving them a longer shooting angle at the shuttle, and an easier turn to pursue.

"They're good," Mara warned, but, like Leia, she found her words lost in her throat, as Jaina, teeth gritted to fight back the g's, reversed throttle.

"Princess—" The plaintive cry from the corridor ended abruptly in a loud crash.

"Coming in hot!" Mara cried, noting the fighter fast approaching to port.

Jaina didn't, couldn't even hear her; she had turned inward now, was feeling the Force coursing through her, was registering every movement of her enemies and reacting instinctively, playing the game three moves ahead. Before Mara had even begun to speak, Jaina had hit the forward attitude adjustment jets, lifting the nose, then she pumped the throttle and kicked the rudder, lifting the *Jade Sabre* and bringing her nose about to starboard, to directly face the other incoming Headhunter.

And that eager Rodian did come in at them, and hard, and the *Jade Sabre*'s defensive array screeched and lit up, warning of a lock-on.

"Jaina!" Leia cried.

"He's got us!" Mara added.

But then the closer ship, coming from port, passed right under the *Jade Sabre*, and Jaina fired the repulsorlifts, bouncing the *Jade Sabre* up and sending the poor Headhunter into a wild, spinning roll.

The closing ship from starboard let fly its concussion missile, but it, and the Headhunter, zipped right underneath the elevated *Jade Sabre*.

Before the three women could even begin to catch their breath, another ship streaked in, an X-wing, the new XJ version of the starfighter, its own laser cannons blasting away from its wingtips. Not at the *Jade Sabre*, though, but at the Headhunter that had just gone past.

"Who is that?" Leia asked, and Jaina, equally curious, brought the *Jade Sabre* about hard.

The Headhunter snap-rolled left and dived, but the far superior X-wing stayed on her, lasers scoring hit after hit, depleting her shields and then blasting her apart into a million pieces.

"A Jedi," Mara and Jaina said together, and Leia, when she paused to collect the Force sensations about her, concurred.

"Fast to the *Mediator*," Leia instructed her daughter, and Jaina swung the *Jade Sabre* about yet again.

"I didn't know there were any Jedi in the sector," Leia said to Mara, who could only shrug, equally at a loss.

"Another one's out," Jaina informed them, watching the blips on her sensor screen. "And two others are vectoring away."

"They want no part of a Jedi showing a willingness to shoot back," Mara remarked.

"Maybe Rodians are smarter than I thought," Leia said dryly. "Smooth it out," she instructed her daughter, unbuckling and climbing unsteadily to her feet.

Jaina reluctantly dialed the inertial compensator back to full.

"Only one pursuing," Jaina informed them as Leia made her way to the door.

"The X-wing," Mara added, and Leia nodded.

In the hallway outside the bridge, Leia found C-3PO inverted and against the wall, his feet sticking up in the air, his head crunched forward so that his chin was tight against his chest.

"You have to learn to hold on," Leia said to him, helping him upright. She glanced across the way to Bolpuhr as she spoke, to find the Noghri still standing calmly in the exact spot she had assigned him.

Somehow, she wasn't amazed.

Jaina took the *Jade Sabre* at a swift but steady pace toward the distant *Mediator*. She checked often for pursuit, but it quickly became obvious that the Rodians in their outdated Headhunters wanted no part of this fight.

Leia rejoined them a short while later, to find Jaina in complete control and Mara resting back in her seat, eyes closed. Even when Jaina asked her aunt a question about docking procedures, the woman didn't respond, didn't even open her eyes.

"They'll guide you in," Leia interjected, and sure enough, a voice from the *Mediator* crackled over the opened comm, giving explicit directions for entry vector.

Jaina took her in, and Jaina took her down, easily—and after the display of flying she had just given them out with the Headhunters, Leia wasn't the least bit surprised by her ability to so smoothly tight-dock a ship as large as the *Jade Sabre*.

That final shudder as Jaina eased off the repulsorlifts and settled the shuttle onto the docking bay floor stirred Mara from her rest. She opened her eyes and, seeing where they were, rose quickly.

And then she swayed and seemed as if she would fall.

Leia and Jaina were there in an instant, catching and steadying her.

She regained her balance and took a deep breath. "Maybe next time you can dial down the inertial compensator to ninety-seven instead of ninety-five," she said jokingly, straining a smile.

Jaina laughed, but Leia's face showed her deep concern. "Are you all right?" she asked.

Mara eyed her directly.

"Perhaps we should find a place where you can rest," Leia said.

"Where we all can rest," Mara corrected, and her tone told Leia to back off, a reminder that Leia was intruding on a private place for Mara, a place she had explicitly instructed all of her friends, even her husband, not to go. This disease was Mara's fight alone, to Mara's thinking, a battle that had forced her to reconsider everything she thought about her life, past, present, and future, and everything she thought about death.

Leia held her stare for a moment longer, but replaced her own concerned expression with one of acceptance. Mara did not want to be coddled or cuddled. She was determined to live on in an existence that did not name her disease as the most pressing and important facet of her entire life, to live on as she had before, with the illness being relegated to the position of nuisance, and nothing more.

Of course, Leia understood it to be much more than that, an internal churning that required Mara to spend hours and tremendous Force energy merely holding it in check. But that was Mara's business.

"I hope to meet with Nom Anor tomorrow," Leia explained, as the three, with C-3PO and Bolpuhr in tow, headed for the lower hatch, then moved down to the landing bay. A contingent of New Republic Honor Guard stood waiting there, along with Commander Ackdool, a Mon Calamarian with large, probing eyes, a fishlike face, and salmon-colored skin. "By all reports, we should all be rested before dealing with him."

"Believe those reports," Mara said.

"And first, it seems I get to meet with our savior Jedi," Leia added dryly, looking back behind the *Jade Sabre* to see the X-wing gliding in to rest.

"Wurth Skidder," Jaina remarked, recognizing the markings under the canopy on the starfighter.

"Why am I not surprised?" Leia asked, and she blew a sigh.

Ackdool came over to them, then, and extended his formal greetings to the distinguished guests, but Leia's reaction set him back on his heels—indeed, it raised more than a few eyebrows among the members of the *Mediator*'s Honor Guard.

"Why did you send him out?" Leia snapped, motioning toward the docking X-wing.

Commander Ackdool started to answer, but Leia continued. "If we had needed assistance, we would have called for it."

"Of course, Princess Leia," Commander Ackdool said with a polite bow.

"They why send him out?"

"Why do you assume that Wurth Skidder flew out at my command?" the cool Commander Ackdool dared to respond. "Why would you assume that Wurth Skidder heeds any order I might give?"

"Couple o' ridge-head parachutes floating over Osarian, if those Rodians had any luck," came the singsong voice of Wurth Skidder. The cocky young man was fast approaching, pulling off his helmet and giving his shock of blond hair a tousle as he walked.

Leia stepped out to intercept him and took another quick step for no better reason than to make the Jedi stop short. "Wurth Skidder," she said.

"Princess," the man replied with a bow.

"Did you have a little fun out there?"

"More than a little," the Jedi said with a wide grin and a sniffle—and he always seemed to be sniffling, and his hair always looked as if he had just walked in from a Tatooine sandstorm. "Fun for me, I mean, and not for the Rodians."

"And the cost of your fun?" Leia asked.

That took the smile from Wurth Skidder's face, and he looked at Leia curiously, obviously not understanding.

"The cost," Leia explained. "What did your little excursion cost?"

"A couple of proton torpedos," Wurth replied with a shrug. "A little fuel."

"And a year of diplomatic missions to calm down the Osarians," Leia retorted.

"But they shot first," Wurth protested.

"Do you even understand that your stupidity likely escalated an already impossible situation?" Leia's voice was as firm and cold as anyone present had ever heard it. So cold, in fact, that the always overprotective Bolpuhr, fearing trouble, glided closer to her, hanging back just behind her left shoulder, within fast striking distance of the Jedi.

"They were attacking you," Wurth Skidder retorted. "Six of them!"

"They were trying to bring us down to Osarian," Leia harshly explained. "A not-so-unexpected response, given my announced intentions here. And so we planned to avoid them. Avoid! Do you understand that word?"

Wurth Skidder said nothing.

"Avoid them and thus cause no further problems or hard feelings," Leia went on. "And so we would have, and we would have asked for no explanations from Shunta Osarian Dharrg, all of us pretending that nothing had ever happened."

"But—"

"And our graciousness in not mentioning this unfortunate incident would have bought me the bargaining capital I need to bring some kind of conciliation from Osarian toward Rhommamool," Leia continued, anger creeping in thicker with each word. "But now we can't do that, can we? Now, so that Wurth Skidder could paint another skull on the side of his X-wing, I'll have to deal with an incident."

"They shot first," Wurth Skidder reiterated when it became apparent that Leia was done.

"And better that they had shot last," Leia replied. "And if Shunta Osarian Dharrg demands reparations, we'll agree, with all apologies, and any monies to be paid will come from Wurth Skidder's private funds."

The Jedi squared his shoulders at the suggestion, but then Leia hit him with a sudden and devastating shot. "My brother will see to it."

Wurth Skidder bowed again, glared at Leia and all around, then turned on his heel and walked briskly away.

"My apologies, Princess Leia," Ackdool said. "But I have no real authority over Jedi Skidder. I had thought it a blessing when he arrived two weeks ago. His Jedi skills should certainly come in handy against any terrorist attempts—and we have heard rumors of many—against the *Mediator*."

"And you are indeed within striking distance of surface missiles," C-3PO added, but he stopped short, this time catching on to the many disapproving looks that came his way.

"I did not know that Jedi Skidder would prove so . . ." Ackdool paused, searching for the right word. "Intractable."

"Stubborn, you mean," Leia said. As they all started away, Leia did manage a bit of a smile when she heard Mara behind her tell Jaina, "Maybe Nom Anor has met his match."

C-9PO, a protocol droid, its copper coloring tinged red from the constantly blowing dusts of Rhommamool, skittered down an alley to the side of the main avenue of Redhaven and peeked out cautiously at the tumult beyond. The fanatical followers of Nom Anor, the Red Knights of Life, had gone on the rampage again, riding throughout the city in an apparent purge of landspeeders on their tutakans, eight-legged lizards with enormous tusks that climbed right up past their black eyes and curled in like white eyebrows.

"Ride the beasts given by Life!" one Red Knight screamed at a poor civilian as the wrinkled Dressellian merchant was dragged from the cockpit and punched and pushed to the ground.

"Perversion!" several other Red Knights cried in unison. "Life-pretender!" And they set upon the landspeeder with their tubal-iron pummelstaves, smashing the windshield, bashing in the side moldings, crushing the steering wheel and other controls, even knocking one of the rear drive's cylindrical engines from its mounts.

Satisfied that the craft was wrecked beyond repair, they pulled the Dressellian to his feet and shoved him to and fro, warning him to ride creatures, not machines—or, better still, to use the legs that nature had provided and walk. Then they beat him back down to the ground and moved on, some climbing back atop the tutakans, others running beside.

The landspeeder continued to hover, though it had only a couple of repulsors still firing. It looked more like a twisted lump of beaten metal than a vehicle, tilting to one side because of the unequal weight distribution and the weakened lift capacity.

"Oh, dear me," the protocol droid said, ducking low as the contingent stormed past.

Tap, tap, tap came the ringing of metal on metal against the top of the droid's head. C-9PO slowly turned about and saw the fringe of the telltale black capes, and the red-dyed hides.

With a screech, the droid stood up and tried to run away, but a pummelstave smashed in the side of his leg and he went facedown in the red dust. He lifted his head, but rising up on his arms only gave the two Red Knights a better handhold as they walked past, each scooping the droid under one shoulder and dragging him along.

"Got a Ninepio," one of the pair called out to his lizard-riding buddies, and a cheer went up.

The doomed droid knew the destination: the Square of Hopeful Redemption.

C-9PO was glad that he wasn't programmed to experience pain.

* * *

"It was a stupid thing to do," Leia said firmly.

"Wurth thought he was helping us," Jaina reminded, but Leia wasn't buying that argument.

"Wurth was trying to find his own thrills," she corrected.

"And that hotshot attitude of his will reinforce the ring of truth to Nom Anor's diatribes against the Jedi," Mara said. "He's not without followers on Osarian." As she finished, she looked down at the table, at the pile of leaflets Commander Ackdool had given them, colorful propaganda railing against the New Republic, against the Jedi, and against anything mechanical and technological, and somehow tying all of these supposed ills to the cultural disease that engulfed the society of the planet Osarian.

"Why does Nom Anor hate the Jedi?" Jaina asked. "What do we have to do with the struggle between Osarian and Rhommamool? I never even heard of these planets until you mentioned that we'd be coming here."

"The Jedi have nothing to do with this struggle," Leia replied. "Or at least, they didn't until Wurth Skidder's antics."

"Nom Anor hates the New Republic," Mara added. "And he hates the Jedi as symbols of the New Republic."

"Is there anything Nom Anor doesn't hate?" Leia asked dryly.

"Don't take him lightly," Mara warned yet again. "His religious cry to abandon technology and machines, to look for truth in the natural elements and life of the universe, and to resist the joining of planets in false confederations resonates deeply in many people, particularly those who have been the victims of such planetary alliances, like the miners of Rhommamool."

Leia didn't disagree. She had spent many hours before and during the journey here reading the history of the two planets, and she knew that the situation on Rhommamool was much more complicated than that. While many of the miners had traveled to the inhospitable red planet voluntarily, there were quite a number who were the descendants of the original "colonists"—involuntary immigrants sent there to work the mines because of high crimes they had committed.

Whatever the truth of the situation, though, Leia couldn't deny that Rhommamool was the perfect breeding ground for zealots like Nom Anor. Life there was tough—even basics like water could be hard to come by—while the prosperous Osarians lived in comfort on white sandy beaches and crystal-clear lakes.

"I still don't understand how any of that concerns the Jedi," Jaina remarked.

"Nom Anor was stirring up anger against the Jedi long before he ever came to Rhommamool," Mara explained. "Here, he's just found a convenient receptacle for his wrath."

"And with the Jedi Knights scattered throughout the galaxy, and so many of them following their own agendas, Nom Anor might just find plenty of ammunition to add to his arguments," Leia added grimly. "I'm glad that my brother is thinking of reestablishing the Jedi Council."

Mara nodded, but Jaina seemed less convinced. "Jacen doesn't think that's such a good idea," she reminded her mother.

Leia shrugged. Her oldest son, Jaina's twin, had indeed expressed serious doubts about the course of the Jedi Knights.

"If we can't bring some sense of order to the galaxy, particularly to isolated planets like Osarian and Rhommamool, then we're no better than the Empire," Mara remarked.

"We're better than the Empire," Leia insisted.

"Not in Nom Anor's eyes," Jaina said.

And Mara reiterated her warning to Leia not to take the man lightly. "He's the strangest man I ever met," she explained, and given her past exploits with notorious sorts like Jabba the Hutt and Talon Karrde, that was quite a statement. "Even when I tried to use the Force to gain a better perspective on him, I drew . . ." Mara paused, as if looking for some way to properly express the feeling. "A blank," she decided. "As if the Force had nothing to do with him."

Leia and Jaina looked at her curiously.

"No," Mara corrected. "More like he had nothing to do with the Force."

The perfect disconnected ideologue, Leia thought, and she expressed her feelings with a single sarcastic word: "Wonderful."

He stood on the platform surrounded by his fanatical Red Knights. Before him, ten thousand Rhommamoolians crowded into every open space of the great public square of Redhaven, once the primary trading spaceport of the planet. But those facilities had been leveled in the early days of the uprising, with the Rhommamoolians declaring their independence from Osarian. And more recently, since the coming of Nom Anor as spearhead of the revolution, the place had been renamed the Square of Hopeful Redemption.

Here, the citizens came to declare freedom from Osarian.

Here, the followers came to renounce the New Republic.

Here, the believers came to renounce the Jedi.

And here, the fanatics came to discredit progress and technology, to cry out for a simpler time, when the strength of a being's legs, and not the weight of his purse, determined how far he could travel, and the strength of his hands, and not the weight of his purse, allowed him to harvest the gifts of nature.

Nom Anor loved it all, the adulation and the fanatical, bordering on suicidal, devotion. He cared nothing for Rhommamool or its inhabitants, cared nothing for the foolish cries for some ridiculous "simpler time."

But how he loved the chaos his words and followers inflicted upon the order of the galaxy. How he loved the brooding undercurrent of resentment toward the New Republic, and the simmering anger aimed at the Jedi Knights, these supercreatures of the galaxy.

Wouldn't his superiors be pleased?

Nom Anor flipped his shiny black cape back from his shoulder and held his fist upraised into the air, drawing shrieks of appreciation. In the center of the square, where once had stood the Portmaster's Pavilion, now was a huge pit, thirty meters in diameter and ten deep. Whistles and whines emanated from that pit, along with cries for mercy and pitifully polite words of protest—the voices of droids collected by the folk of Rhommamool and dropped into the hole.

Great cheers erupted from all corners of the square as a pair of the Red Knights entered from one avenue, dragging a 9PO protocol droid between them. They went to the edge of the pit, took up the poor 9PO by the arms and the legs, and on a three-count, launched him onto the pile of metal consisting of the astromech and mine-sniffer droids, the Redhaven street-cleaner droids, and the personal butler droids of the wealthier Rhommamoolian citizens.

When the hooting and cheering died down, Nom Anor opened his hands, revealing a single small stone. Then he clenched his fist again, squeezing with tremendous power, crushing the stone in his grasp so that dust and flecks of rock splinters slipped out the sides.

The signal to begin.

As one the crowd surged forward, lifting great chunks of stone, the debris from the wreckage of the pavilion. They came to the edge of the pit one after another and hurled their heavy missiles at the pile of droids.

The stoning went on for the rest of the afternoon, until the red glare of the sun thinned to a brilliant crimson line along the horizon, until the dozens and dozens of droids were no more than scrap metal and sparking wires.

And Nom Anor, silent and dignified, watched it all somberly, accepting this great tribute his followers had paid to him, this public execution of the hated droids.

TWO

Intergalactic Eyes

Danni Quee looked out from the western terra-tower of ExGal-4, a solitary outpost on the Outer Rim planet of Belkadan in the Dalonbian sector. Danni came here often at this time of day—late afternoon—to watch the Belkadan sunset filtering through the thirty-meter dalloralla trees. Of late, those sunsets had been more spectacular for some reason, with tinges of orange and green edging the typical pinks and crimsons.

She had been on Belkadan for three years, an original member of ExGal-4, and traced her roots to the always under-funded ExGal Society back another three years before that, to when she was only fifteen. Her homeworld, a Core planet, was badly overcrowded, and for independent Danni, even trips to other nearby worlds didn't seem to alleviate the feeling of being squeezed by too many people. She wasn't a fan of the government, be it the Empire or the New Republic; she wasn't a fan of anything bureaucratic. In fact, she considered the "ordering" of the galaxy a terrible thing, robbing people of excitement and adventures, burying cultures beneath the blanket of common civilization. Thus, the notion that there might be life beyond the galaxy, the thought of something undiscovered, excited the young woman.

Or once had.

Now, standing there, staring at the same landscape of towering trees and unbroken green canopy, the young woman wondered again if she had chosen her life's path correctly. At twenty-one, she was one of the youngest members of the fifteen stationed on ExGal-4, and one of only four women. She had developed into a very attractive young woman, small of frame, with long curly blond hair and green eyes that always seemed to be asking questions of everything they surveyed, and of late, it seemed as if she had spent more time resisting the advances of several young men than in staring out at the galactic rim.

In truth, Danni didn't blame the young men, though. They had all come out here full of hope and adventure, pioneers on the edge of the galaxy. In short order, they had established a base, a walled fort, actually, to hold out the savage wildlife of Belkadan, and had set up their listening and looking equipment: great dishes and telescopes, including orbiting scopes. That first year had been full of dreams and hard work, and danger—two of the original members had been seriously wounded when a redcrested cougar had leapt over the wall from a nearby tree.

And so the work had continued, clearing the trees back thirty meters, further securing the outpost.

All that work was done now, with ExGal-4 secured and self-contained, with an abundant clear-water well right below them and multiple gardens. A smoothly functioning, scientific outpost.

Danni missed the old days.

Even the faces of those around her had become stale, though half the members were not original colonists, but had rotated in from other ExGal satellite stations, or from the independent ExGal Society's home base.

The bottom rim of the sun dipped below the distant horizon, and the orange and green tints spread wide from north to south. Somewhere unseen in the jungle, a redcrested cougar gave a long and low growl, heralding the onset of twilight.

Danni took it all in and tried to dream, but given the reality of her current tedium, the endless listening for signals that never came, the endless staring at the same intergalactic haze, she wasn't quite sure of what she should dream about.

Behind her, from one of the windows of the station's center structure, Yomin Carr watched the young woman's every move. He was new to the station, the most recent to join the crew, and it hadn't taken him long to recognize that many of the others looked up to Danni Quee, and that many of the men were obviously attracted to her.

Yomin Carr didn't understand that sentiment at all. He found Danni, as he did all humans, quite repulsive, for while Yomin Carr's people, the Yuuzhan Vong, resembled humans in form—though they were on average a dozen or so centimeters taller and quite a bit heavier and had less hair on their heads, both face and scalp—their ways were hardly similar. Even if Yomin Carr might admit that Danni was somewhat attractive physically—though how could she be, with not a single scar or tattoo to mark her rise toward godhood!—those tenet differences, attitude differences, made him consider any union with her with disgust. He was Yuuzhan Vong, not human, and a Yuuzhan Vong warrior. How ironic then that the pitiful humans thought him one of them!

Despite his revulsion, he did watch Danni, and often, for she, above all others, was the leader of this democratic group. According to the others, she had been the one to kill the cougar that had slipped into the compound that first year; she had been the one to take the creaking old Spacecaster shuttle into orbit to repair the damaged orbiting telescope only a couple of months earlier, and she had been the one to figure out how that scope might be repaired in the first place.

They all looked up to her.

She was the one Yomin Carr could not ignore.

"Early again?" came a voice behind Yomin Carr.

He turned to regard the speaker, though he knew from the voice, particularly the teasing tone, that it was Bensin Tomri.

"Or is it that you're still here from last night?" Tomri went on, and he gave a chuckle.

Yomin Carr smiled, but did not reply—no answer was needed, he understood, for these people often wasted words merely to hear the sound of their own voices. Besides, there was more truth to the words than Bensin Tomri could ever guess. Yomin Carr had not been in here straight through since his shift the previous night, but he had been present more often than not. The others of the station thought it was simply "newbie" excitement, the feeling they had all shared when they had first arrived that the elusive extragalactic signal could happen at any time. In their eyes, Yomin Carr had taken that excitement to the extreme, perhaps, but he had done nothing, he was confident, to arouse any real suspicion.

"He'll get bored with it soon enough," Garth Breise said, another of the night-shift controllers, sitting up on the wide room's higher level, where the comfortable chairs, the gaming table, and the food could be found. The room was elliptical, with a wide viewscreen on the front wall, seven control pods in a three-one-three pattern before it, and the raised galley area taking up the rear quarter.

Yomin Carr forced another smile at the remark and made his way down toward the front of the room, to his usual position at Pod 3, the left-hand one of the first row. He heard Garth and Bensin whispering some remarks about him from above, but he ignored them, taking the attack on his pride—normally a call for a death duel—in stride with the knowledge that soon enough they would know better.

Danni Quee entered next, moving down to Pod 4, the central pod, the one whose viewing scan overlapped the quadrants scanned by all six of the others. Then came the last member of the night shift, Tee-ubo Doole, the Twi'lek woman—the only nonhuman, as far as the others knew, among the fifteen at the station.

Tee-ubo gave Yomin Carr a sly look, almost a wink, and stretched languidly and shifted her lekku, the twin tentacles that grew out of the back of a Twi'lek's head. She had made no secret of her interest in the newcomer, which amused Yomin Carr greatly. For he was coming to understand these people, and their constant insecurities. Normally a Twi'lek woman, with her exotic lekku and greenish skin, and typically scarce clothing, would be the center of male attention anywhere outside her home planet of Ryloth—and Twi'lek women were known to enjoy such attention greatly!—but Tee-ubo had found more than her match in Danni.

Still looking at Yomin Carr, the Twi'lek held up a small vial and gave it a shake.

Ryll, Yomin Carr knew, a recreational intoxicant that several of the compound members used to alleviate the boredom.

He noted, too, that Danni crinkled her nose in disgust at the sight and even shook her head in disapproval. For a long while, Danni had forbidden Tee-ubo from bringing the stuff anywhere near the control room, but even the resolute Danni had relented—though her motion to Tee-ubo now made it clear that she wanted the intoxicant off the main floor.

Both Bensin and Garth were more than happy with that request. Tee-ubo was running low of the ryll now and had become stingy about handing any out. They weren't expecting any cargo shuttles for several months, and despite the Twi'lek's best efforts, there was no guarantee that any of the illicit drug would even make it aboard the next shuttle.

They settled in then to their usual positions. After a quick check of all systems from the central pod, and setting the forward screen to cycle through the smaller viewers of each individual pod, Danni joined the others, who were done with the ryll and were all laughing, in the galley area. On her suggestion, they began a four-way game of dejarik, a board game where holographic monsters of varying strength traveled specified paths along the rows of squares, vying for tactical advantages against their opponents.

At his post, Yomin Carr, as he did every night and most days when he could inconspicuously hang out about the pod, dialed down the volume so that only he would hear any tell-tale signals, and covertly locked his dish on sector L30, the location he knew to be the entry point: Vector Prime.

"You want to play?" came Bensin Tomri's call an hour later, his tone making it clear to Yomin Carr that Tomri was not faring well in the strategic battle.

A part of Yomin Carr wanted to go up there and engage in the game, particularly waging against Danni, who was a strong strategist. Such competitions were good; they kept the warrior mind sharp and focused.

"No," he answered, as he had for every night in the last few weeks. "Work to do."

"Work?" Bensin Tomri scoffed. "Like the greatest scientific discovery of the last millennium will happen at any second, to your waiting eyes."

"If you feel truth to that, on the next shuttle you should go?" Yomin Carr politely returned, and he saw by their curious expressions that he had mixed up his sentence structure again. He made a mental note to review with his tizowyrms later on.

"Newbie," Bensin muttered sarcastically under his breath.

"He's got a point," Danni said, and Bensin threw up his hands and turned away from the table.

"Are you sure?" Danni asked Yomin Carr.

"I enjoy this," he replied haltingly, paying careful attention to every word, then settling comfortably into the pod's chair.

Danni didn't argue; in fact, Yomin Carr understood that she respected his dedication, that she wished some of the others would follow his example.

And so it went as the night lengthened. Bensin Tomri was soon snoring contentedly, while Tee-ubo and Garth Breise argued and tittered about everything and nothing at all, and Danni continued to play dejarik, but against three computer opponents.

Then it happened.

Yomin Carr caught the slight blip on the very edge of the pod's viewscreen out of the corner of his eye. He froze, staring intently, and dialed up the volume just a bit.

It came again, accompanied by the rhythmic signal that could only emanate from a ship.

Yomin Carr could hardly find his breath. After all the years of preparation . . .

The Yuuzhan Vong warrior shook such distracting thoughts from his head. He waited a moment longer, to confirm the positioning, Vector Prime, the predetermined entry point into the galaxy, then he quickly shifted his dish all the way over to Sector L1. That would buy him a couple of hours on this screen. He looked up at the main viewer, repeating the image of the central pod, and breathed a sigh of relief to see that it had already cycled past Pod 3 and wouldn't be back for at least an hour—and even then, it would not overlap past L25, and the signal would be long past that point.

With the dish angle changed, Yomin Carr dialed his volume back up to normal, then stood up and stretched, his movement attracting Danni's attention.

"Walk I—" he started to explain, and realized that he was confusing the sentence structure once more. "I need to take a walk," he corrected.

The woman nodded. "It's quiet enough," she replied. "You can knock off for the rest of the shift if you want."

"No," he answered. "I need jus—jus—only to stretch out a bit."

Danni nodded and went back to her game, and Yomin Carr walked out of the room. As soon as the control room's door was closed behind him, he removed his hard boots and broke into a dead run.

He had to pause for a long while when he got into his private quarters, forcing himself to steady his breathing. It would not do for the executor to see him so obviously rattled.

Nor would it do for the executor to see him in this horrid human disguise, he reminded himself. Never mind that humans did not typically appropriately paint their skins or mutilate any part of their bodies to show their worship to a worthy pantheon—human eyes did not droop with the appealing bluish sacks beneath them, as did Yuuzhan Vong eyes, and the human forehead was flat, not enticingly sloped, as were those of the Yuuzhan Vong. No, even after these months as an advance agent of the Praetorite Vong, Yomin Carr could hardly stand the sight of the infidels.

He stripped off his clothing and moved to the full-length mirror at the side of his room. He liked to watch this, to use the visual stimulation to heighten the sensation of exquisite agony.

He moved his hand up beside his nose, to the little crease beside his nostril, his fingers working at the obscure seam at the side of his left nostril, the contact point for the ooglith masquer. Sensitive to his touch, and well-trained, the creature immediately responded.

And Yomin Carr clenched his teeth and fought hard to steady his trembling as the thousands of tiny grappling tendrils pulled free of his pores, the ooglith masquer rolling back over his nose and separating across his cheeks. The seam widened down his chin and neck and the front of his torso, his fake skin peeling back, rolling down until he merely stepped out of it.

The ooglith masquer shuffled across the floor toward the dark closet, making slurping, sucking sounds as it moved, and Yomin Carr stood at the mirror, regarding his true form admiringly, his taut, strong muscles, his tattoo pattern, nearly complete upon his body, a sign of high rank in the warrior class, and mostly, his intentional disfigurements, the oft-broken nose, the extended tear to his lip, the split eyelid. And now, showing his ornamental disfigurements and tattoos, he was ready to address the executor on this most important matter.

He moved to the side of the room, to his locker, and he was trembling so badly that he could hardly work the combination. He finally did manage to open it, though, and as the top rolled back, the platform inside raised up, showing a brown cloth covering a pair of ball-like lumps.

Gently, Yomin Carr removed the cloth and considered the lumps, his villips. He almost went to the one on the left, the one joined with Prefect Da'Gara's villip, but he knew the protocol and wouldn't dare disobey.

So he went to the one on the right and gently stroked its ridged top until the single break in the membranous tissue, a hole that resembled an eye socket, puckered to life.

Yomin Carr continued to stroke the creature, to awaken the consciousness-joined villip more than halfway across the galaxy. He felt the pull of that creature a moment later and knew the sensation to mean that the executor had heard his call and was likewise awakening his own villip.

Yomin Carr moved his hand back fast as that central hole puckered and then opened wide, and then rolled back over itself, the villip inverting to assume the appearance of the head of the executor.

Yomin Carr bowed respectfully. "It is time," he said, glad to be using his native language once more.

"You have silenced the station?" the executor asked.

"I go now," Yomin Carr explained.

"Then go," the executor said, and with typical discipline, not even inquiring about the details of the incoming signal, he broke communication. In response, Yomin Carr's villip rolled back in on itself to once again appear as a nondescript ridged membranous ball.

Again, the warrior resisted the urge to utilize the other villip, reminding himself that he had to move fast, that the executor would not tolerate any failure from him at this critical juncture. He rushed across the room, back to his closet, and took out a small coffer; he kissed it twice and muttered a swift prayer before opening it. Inside sat a small statue of a creature, the most beautiful creature of all to Yomin Carr and to all the warriors of the Yuuzhan Vong. Its mass resembled a brain, with a single huge eye and a puckered maw. Many tentacles extended from that bulk, some thick and short, others fine and long. This was Yun-Yammka, the Slayer, the Yuuzhan Vong god of war.

Yomin Carr prayed again, the entire litany of Yun-Yammka, then kissed the statue gently and replaced the coffer in his closet.

He wore only a skin loincloth, as it had been in the purer days of his warrior people's dawn, showing all of his remarkable tattoos and his rippling muscles, and he carried only his coufee, a crude, but ultimately effective, large double-edged knife, again, a ceremonial throwback to the early days of the warrior Yuuzhan Vong. Yomin Carr thought all ceremony appropriate for this particular mission, the linking salvo between the advance force and the actual invasion. He poked his head out into the hall, then moved through the complex, his bare feet making not a whisper of sound. He knew that getting out of the place without his human disguise might be difficult, but realized also that if he was discovered without the masquer, no one would recognize him as their associate. Besides, he figured, if he was discovered, that would only be an excuse to kill someone, an appropriate sacrifice to Yun-Yammka on this momentous night.

The night was chill, but that only invigorated Yomin Carr. His blood pumped furiously from the excitement, from the danger of this mission to the understanding that the Great Doctrine was at last under way. He ran to the wall and sprinted up a ladder, scrambling over the top and dropping, with hardly a thought, to the cleared ground outside.

The distant roar of a redcrested cougar gave him no pause. He was in that creature's element now, but he, too, was a hunter. Perhaps one of those 140-kilogram animals, with 10-centimeter fangs, huge claws, and a tail that ended in a lump of bone as solid as any crafted cudgel, would provide him good sport this night. And Yomin Carr was ready for such a challenge. His blood pounding, his strong heart racing, a terrific fight would be a wonderful release.

But not now, he reminded himself, for he was indeed drifting toward the thick jungle canopy in anticipation of meeting a redcrested cougar. He straightened his line and ran flat out to the tall girder-work tower, the only structure outside the compound. He considered the thick cable that crawled out from the compound to the base of the metalwork, and almost started for it with his coufee.

Too easy to repair, he realized, and his gaze drifted up, up. Fortunately, the gridwork pattern of the girders was not wide spaced, so up Yomin Carr went, hand over hand, his strong, toned muscles working furiously, propelling him fast to the top of the hundred-meter tower. He didn't look down, was not afraid, was never afraid, and focused solely on the junction box and the cable.

Chill winds buffeted him, giving him an idea, so he went to work on the connection between cable and box gently, easing out one rivet, turning open one screw. The others, if they ever managed to get this far along in their repairs, would think this damage to be the result of the constant wind and the often harsh Belkadan weather.

Secure that the connection was broken, Yomin Carr started down the tall tower, again working fast, reminding himself that the incoming signal was likely nearing L10, and that he had a long way yet to go. He dropped the last few meters, landing in a roll and coming up right beside the cable. This time he couldn't resist; he knew that these were just communication wires and nothing carrying substantial power. He brought the cable to his mouth and chewed it viciously, taking perverted pleasure in the tingle of pain as he got through the insulation and sparks erupted all about his mouth and face.

Let them find this break and repair it, he thought, and then return inside to learn that the system still would not function!

Mouth, cheeks, and chin bloody, his nose—already permanently misshapen and flattened to one side—torn along both nostrils, the warrior started back for the compound, but he stopped fast, noting a movement along the ground not far away. He hustled over and fell to his knees, and then smiled widely as he held up a reddish brown beetle with hooked mandibles and a single protruding tubular tongue. "My pet," he whispered, for he had not seen any of the beetles since coming to Belkadan, since bringing them to Belkadan, and he was glad to learn that they had already traveled this far across the planet's surface.

Danni Quee would soon learn the reason that her precious sunsets were becoming somewhat tinted.

Yomin Carr set the dweebit down again and, reminding himself of the dangers of delay, sprinted back for the compound, catching the top of the three-meter wall in one great leap, then running on, back into the main structure, padding quietly along darkened, silent halls. In his own room, he went to the closet, bidding the ooglith masquer back to him.

The pain as the creature enveloped him, thousands of tiny tendrils boring into his skin, was perfectly exquisite, bringing shudder after shudder of edgy pleasure to Yomin Carr. A quick trip to the mirror showed him that the disguise was complete.

Then he took out another small coffer and carefully removed the top. Inside was a single wriggling creature, a small worm. Yomin Carr eased the coffer up near to his ear and tilted it, and the worm responded, crawling forth and burrowing right into the Yuuzhan Vong's ear cavity. Yomin Carr put his finger up there a moment later, to ensure that the tizowyrm had crawled all the way in, and also to signal the creature to begin its work. He felt the low vibrations a moment later. Tizowyrms were decoders, a creature bred by the Yuuzhan Vong alchemists to translate other languages. Despite their diminutive size, they could store enormous amounts of information and could emit that information subliminally. Thus, as Yomin Carr left his room, he was getting yet another lesson in the language most commonly used in this galaxy.

A few minutes later, he was back in the control room, to find Tee-ubo and a very unsteady Garth huddled about Pod 3, with Danni working to reposition Pod 4 to the same alignment.

"Yomin," Danni called, noting his return. "Come here, quick. I can't believe you missed this!"

"Missed?" Yomin Carr echoed.

"A signal!" Danni explained breathlessly.

"Static," Yomin Carr offered, running to her side.

And there it was, on the screen and through the audio lead, the clear signal of something—something very large—crossing through the galactic rim, into the galaxy.

"Extragalactic," Danni said seriously.

Yomin Carr bent low over the instruments, studying the data, calculating the vector, though he knew, of course, that Danni's description had been accurate. He looked up at her solemnly and nodded.

Bensin Tomri burst into the room then, along with several other members of the team, and soon enough, all fifteen were present, angling the pod viewers, computer-enhancing the signals, running comparisons of this signal to all the millions of others in their data banks, trying to gain as many perspectives as possible on whatever had just streaked into their galaxy.

Then, predictably, the debate began. It never ceased to amaze Yomin Carr how endlessly these humans could debate and argue about practically anything, an observation that merely reinforced his belief in the strict hierarchical structure of his own society. He would never question a prefect, a prefect would never question a high prefect, as these fools were arguing with Danni now.

Never—and that, he believed, was the weakness his masters would come to exploit.

At first, the debate centered on the composition of the incoming asteroid. As it was transmitting no apparent technological signals, there was little argument for its being a vessel. An asteroid, then, somehow finding its way through the great emptiness between galaxies, somehow penetrating the turbulence some scientists theorized existed beyond the small band of empty space surrounding the galaxy, and obviously getting some sort of a boost in speed—perhaps from crossing too near a tremendous gravity field—in the process. That belief, that this was merely an extragalactic lump of rock, perhaps even a lump of rock from their own galaxy that had somehow escaped and then got pulled back in, did little to temper the excitement, though. Before this moment, no one had ever witnessed evidence of, let alone the actual event of, an extragalactic breach. Many scientists argued that such a breach could not even be accomplished. Certainly several brave explorers, and a couple of desperate outlaws being chased by the authorities, had gone into the turbulence of the galactic rim over the last few decades, but none had ever been heard from again. Here might be the answer. And the questions. What materials might this asteroid contain? What signs of life? Would this asteroid, once they caught up to it and examined it, provide new answers to the questions of the universe, perhaps even to the creation of the universe, or would it simply raise many, many more questions, perhaps some that went to the very root of their understanding of physics?

And then the debate shifted to a less profound, though certainly no less contested, matter. It started when Bensin Tomri remarked that he would put together the announcement, to be broadcast back to ExGal Command.

"Not yet," another of the scientists strongly argued.

"We have to tell them," Bensin replied. "We have to get some ships out here fast enough to catch the thing for study."

"Where's it going?" the other man came back sarcastically.

"It's in our galaxy now, and we can track it to the other rim, if necessary," another added.

"We're not an autonomous unit," a woman, Lysire, reminded.

"Aren't we?" another argued.

"But do we really know what we're tracking?" Yomin Carr asked, and all eyes turned toward him, most expressions incredulous.

"Do we?" he asked again, in all seriousness.

"Something extragalactic," another answered.

"Never did I agree to that," Yomin Carr said, and again, the curious expressions turned his way.

"We don't know that," Danni put in, apparently taking Yomin Carr's side. "We've already agreed that it's just as likely an asteroid from our own galaxy that escaped, or nearly escaped, and was pulled back in."

"It could indeed be something from our own galaxy," Yomin Carr went on, smiling inwardly at the irony of that statement, at the secret double meaning of *our own galaxy*. "In fact, I think it very likely that it is just that."

"Then what's your point?" Bensin Tomri asked rather indignantly.

"My point?" Yomin Carr echoed, mostly because it bought him the time to figure out the meaning, with help from the tizowyrm, of that curious expression. "My point is that we do not even know if it was ever extragalactic," Yomin Carr answered.

"You saw the vector," Bensin argued.

"I did indeed," Yomin Carr said. "A vector that could reflect a rebound."

"That's absurd," Bensin retorted.

"How come we didn't track it out there, then?" another asked.

"We do not know that we didn't," Yomin Carr said. He held up his hands to deflate any further attacks. "All that I am saying is that we should be absolutely certain before alerting the rest of the galaxy."

"And any call we make will be public information before it ever gets to ExGal Command," Danni agreed.

"Yes," Yomin Carr said, "and then we may discover the signal to be no more than a failure of one of our tracking systems, or a piece of useless space debris bouncing back in from our own galaxy, and how intelligent we shall look in the eyes of the judging ExGal commanders."

"This is bigger than us," Bensin Tomri replied.

"It is," Danni agreed. "But we were put out here to function independently. Maybe Yomin Carr's right. If we go prematurely alerting the whole galaxy, we could look like fools."

"And any such error, rousing half the fleet, could hurt the funding of ExGal," Tee-ubo added with a nod.

"Even if we are correct, if this is something that escaped and returned, or even something from another galaxy or from the supposed emptiness between galaxies, are you ready to announce it?" Yomin Carr asked Bensin directly.

Bensin looked at him as if he did not understand.

"Do you want a host of New Republic scientists, and perhaps even a couple of Jedi Knights to show up?" Yomin Carr asked sarcastically. Some of the expressions coming back at him showed that others hardly saw any connection between this and the Jedi, but Yomin Carr didn't let that slow him. "This is our moment. This is what we have earned from our sacrifice of months—for most of you, even years—of our lives, toiling in this wretched place. At the very least, we owe it to ourselves to prevent embarrassment, or to ensure our proper credit if it does show to be extragalactic. To begin the first formal study. To chart where it came from to make sure it's not a rebound. To chart its current path, and to try to gain as many insights as possible."

"Way to go, newbie," Garth Breise remarked with a grin.

The debate ended as abruptly as it had begun. Danni backed Yomin's argument completely, and even Bensin didn't disagree.

Yomin Carr smiled inwardly once again. If practical arguments didn't work against these often stubborn inferior heretics, then appealing to their overblown sense of pride always did. He looked about at the working scientists, at their excitement and sense of relief and accomplishment. If only they knew.

More than halfway across the galaxy, Nom Anor sat quietly in front of his villip, considering the words of his agent, Yomin Carr.

It had begun.

THREE

The Role of Politics

With a hesitation in his step that betrayed his uncomfortable feelings, Jacen Solo followed his uncle Luke into the council chamber. Jacen knew the new chief of state and his six councilors, of course, but his dealings with them had been primarily restricted to social events. This was business, serious business, judging from the tense nature of Luke Skywalker's stride. They had come to Coruscant so that Luke could accept an invitation to address the New Republic Advisory Council concerning his plans to reestablish the Jedi Council, but there was no doubt in Luke's mind that he would face some tough opposition on that matter, even from some councilors he considered his friends.

What made it all the worse for Jacen was the fact that he hoped his uncle Luke's opponents proved victorious in this matter.

The six councilors, Chief of State Borsk Fey'lya in the middle, sat at a semicircular table facing the doorway. Two chairs had been set before the long table—down lower, Jacen noted, and it seemed to him a rather thinly veiled attempt to elevate the stature of the councilors above their invited guests.

In this particular instance, that seemed utterly ridiculous.

Especially in the case of Borsk Fey'lya. Jacen had been

with his uncle Luke and his mother, Leia, when the news had come through that Borsk, as the longest-serving member of the council, the "elder statesman" of the New Republic, had been elected chief of state, a position the conniving Bothan no doubt relished.

Just a few years before, Borsk had escaped a lengthy prison sentence only through a generous pardon. Ever was he the consummate politician, who leaked information to weaken his opponents, once nearly unseating Leia as chief of state with damaging, and ultimately untrue, allegations. Despite getting caught in such an unseemly situation, Borsk, as always, found a way to land on his own political feet. He had climbed within a handbreadth of the top, serving the council as Chief of State Mon Mothma's trusted adviser, and then he had crashed to the bottom, facing charges that could have landed him in prison, or even, if the charge of treason had been pushed, a sentence of permanent exile.

And yet, here he was again, lingering on like the Findris flu, seated between a new generation of councilors, who looked upon him as an age-wizened statesman and hero of the New Republic.

On the day when the news of his latest ascension had come down, Jacen's mother had honestly wondered if she had done right in resigning as chief of state. Leia had even openly remarked that she might go back into politics.

It was Luke who had dissuaded her, reminding her that more than the mood of the government had changed greatly in the year since she had resigned, that familiar and friendly faces had walked away. Even respected and dutiful Admirals Drayson and Ackbar had taken the apparent firming of the New Republic as their signal to retire, and neither had shown any inclination to remain politically active.

As Borsk called the meeting to order, offering a polite recitation of the agenda and a welcome to their guests, Jacen looked around at the members, viewing their respective expressions in light of the information his uncle Luke had given

him regarding their positions toward Luke and the proposed
Jedi Council. At the far end to Jacen's right sat Niuk Niuv of
Sullust. With his Sullustan features, the oversize, rounded
ears and ample jowls, Niuk Niuv appeared more like a child's
cuddle toy than a councilor, but Jacen knew Sullustans better
than that, knew that they could be steadfast allies and dangerous foes. Niuk Niuv, according to Luke, would be among
his most vocal detractors.

Next to Niuk Niuv sat Cal Omas of Alderaan, a man sympathetic to Luke's plans, possibly Luke's strongest ally on the
council. After his homeworld had been destroyed by the Empire, Cal Omas had fought with the Rebel Alliance through
all the trials, and he knew well the value of the Jedi.

The Wookiee, Triebakk, another potential ally for Luke,
sat between Cal and Borsk, but the squid-headed creature on
Borsk's other side, the Quarren, Pwoe, was perhaps Luke's
greatest enemy of the group. Dour, like most of his water-
dwelling brethren of Mon Calamari, Pwoe was the first
Quarren ever to serve on the Advisory Council, and certainly
an unexpected choice. The planet of Mon Calamari would, of
course, always hold a seat, since their star cruisers and their
support had proven so valuable in overthrowing the Empire
and establishing the New Republic, but always before—and
it was commonly assumed that the tradition would continue
in perpetuity—it had been a Mon Calamarian, and not a
Quarren, to serve on the council. Indeed, Admiral Ackbar
had seemed the logical choice to represent Mon Calamari on
the Advisory Council, as he had done back when the first Pro-
visional Council was formed, but when the push for Pwoe—a
push Luke suspected orchestrated by Borsk—had become
serious, Ackbar had waved away all thoughts of rejoining the
council and had retired.

The remaining two members were both human, Fyor
Rodan of Commenor and Chelch Dravvad of Corellia. It was
Fyor Rodan who had requested Luke at council, Jacen knew,

and according to his uncle, Rodan was no friend and not to be trusted.

With all of that in mind, with all the insights Luke had given him about these councilors, Jacen sat back and observed very carefully.

After the somewhat hypocritical pleasantries and formalities that seemed to Jacen to go on and on, Borsk Fey'lya looked Luke right in the eye and asked, in the gravest of tones, "You have heard the initial reports from the *Mediator*?"

"Leia will be meeting with Nom Anor soon, I am told," Luke replied, avoiding the obvious.

"A meeting complicated already," Borsk said.

"Would all councilors who are surprised please raise their hands," Fyor Rodan put in, and even to sixteen-year-old Jacen, his sarcasm seemed rather juvenile, and certainly out of place in the somber hall.

"I heard of the . . . intervention," Luke admitted.

"The Osarians were wrong to try to intercept a New Republic envoy," Cal Omas remarked.

"A convenient excuse for our Jedi hero to rush to the rescue," Fyor Rodan shot back.

"Quick to the trigger, they are," Pwoe said, his accusing stare falling over Luke.

Jacen could hardly believe the lack of respect, and the obvious thinly masked intentions behind it all. The New Republic was having growing pains, with minor squabbles erupting throughout the galaxy, many of them age-old conflicts that had been buried under the blanket of the Empire for years and years but now, with the new freedoms afforded to individual planets and species, rising up once again. So of course, the New Republic and its councilors and representatives had been taking many verbal hits of late, as had the Jedi Knights, and thus the finger-pointing between the two groups had escalated.

On it went, one recounting after another of a civil war here, a vendetta there, grievances from one agriculture planet, and a workers' strike that had spread to several mining planets, with even the Wookiee Triebakk howling out some complaints at Pwoe about a failure in one of the nav systems of the newest Mon Calamari battle cruisers.

It all seemed like so much nonsense to Jacen, a bunch of talking heads full of complaints and short on solutions, and yet another reminder of his fears concerning his uncle's schemes for enacting some control over the Jedi. He tuned right out of the meeting for many minutes, falling into some silent meditative techniques he had been trying to perfect, until Borsk again looked Luke in the eye and bluntly asked him his plans concerning the Jedi Council.

Luke paused for a long while. "I haven't made any final decision," he replied, which took Jacen somewhat by surprise, since his uncle had seemed fairly certain that he would indeed reestablish the council.

"Whether with council or by yourself, you must rein in these wandering Jedi," Councilor Niuk Niuv said with uncustomary passion.

Triebakk howled in protest, and Cal Omas gave words to the sentiment. "Rein in?" he echoed incredulously. "Need I remind you that you speak of the Jedi Knights?"

"A dangerous group," Councilor Pwoe remarked gravely, the watery essence of his voice only adding weight to the statement.

"Causing disturbances throughout the galaxy," Fyor Rodan was quick to add.

Jacen noted that his uncle was watching the quietest member of the council, Chelch of Corellia, one he believed might be the swing vote on any resolutions concerning the Jedi, and one who was now giving no outward hint whatsoever of his intentions.

"Why, I have heard of battles along the Outer Rim, as far out as the Angor system," Fyor Rodan went on, standing up and waving his fist. "Jedi swooping in, torpedoes flying, against innocent citizens."

"Smugglers, you mean," Cal Omas retorted.

"Many who aided in the overthrow of the Empire!" Fyor Rodan shot back.

"And you take that as an excuse for their current illegal activities?"

"The Jedi Knights are not the law," Niuk Niuv pointed out.

"So they should be told," Fyor Rodan said. "Chief Fey'lya, perhaps we should consider a resolution against the Jedi. A strong statement from this council demanding that they end all policing efforts that have not been explicitly authorized by this council or by regional ambassadors."

Borsk Fey'lya turned to meet Luke's stern gaze, blanched, and rubbed his hairy face. "Let us not be premature," he said.

Jacen did not miss how the Bothan seemed to shrink back from his uncle Luke's powerful presence.

"Premature?" Fyor Rodan echoed with a laugh. "These wild ones have become a bit inflated concerning the policymaking role of the New Republic. Are we to tolerate that?"

"Are we to deny their help in those areas where they are best qualified?" Cal Omas retorted angrily, bringing a derisive snort from Fyor Rodan, a shout of agreement from Triebakk, a groan from Pwoe, and a stream of retorts from the ever more impassioned Niuk Niuv.

And so the shouting began again, at new heights, and Jacen quickly backed away from it all. The Jedi, it seemed, were to be judged on every move, and by people who, in Jacen's estimation, had no right to judge them.

He and Luke left the council chamber a short while later, the war of words, about nothing and everything all at once, raging behind them. To Jacen's surprise, Luke was wearing a satisfied smile.

"Both Fyor Rodan and Niuk Niuv tipped their hands in the last part of the exchange," he explained to the obviously confused Jacen.

"With the smugglers?"

Luke nodded and smiled.

"You think they're tied to smugglers?" Jacen asked incredulously.

"It's not so uncommon," Luke said. "Ask your father," he added with a grin that set Jacen back on his heels. The roots of Han Solo were no secret to the young man.

"So you think their complaints about the Jedi have to do with their own profits?" Jacen asked. "You think some of the councilors are working with smugglers that some Jedi are giving a hard time?"

Luke shrugged. "I don't know that," he admitted. "But it seems to fit."

"And what are you going to do about it?"

Luke stopped. Jacen did, too, the pair turning to face each other directly.

"We have a hundred Jedi Knights setting their own agendas throughout the galaxy," Luke explained. "That is the problem."

"You don't think these Jedi at the Outer Rim are justified in going after smugglers?" Jacen asked.

"That's not the point," Luke replied. "Not at all. The point is that the scattering of Jedi Knights prevents any cohesive movements."

Jacen's gaze seemed distant, as if Luke had just lost him.

"We have Wurth Skidder acting foolishly defending Mara's shuttle and the Osarians over here, other Jedi apparently going after smugglers with a vengeance at the Outer Rim, and I've heard stories of still other problems in other sectors," Luke explained. "It's hard to keep up with it all, and sometimes it feels like I'm fixing symptoms without ever getting to the real disease."

His choice of words gave Jacen pause, and Luke, too, when he thought about them in the context of his wife.

"That's why we need the Jedi Council," Luke pressed on a moment later. "A singular purpose and direction."

"Is that what it means to be a Jedi Knight?" Jacen asked bluntly, a question Luke had been hearing many times in the last few months—from Jacen, and not from his other apprentice, Jacen's younger brother, Anakin.

"Why do you care what the councilors think?" Jacen asked, as much to change the subject as out of true curiosity. "You don't need them to reestablish a Jedi Council. Why would you want anything from them and their foolish arguing?"

"I don't need them," Luke admitted. "The Jedi, despite what Fyor Rodan and Niuk Niuv and even Borsk Fey'lya might think, don't answer to the council. But if I don't have their agreement in this matter, my plans, as I develop them, both for the academy and for the Jedi Council, might prove more difficult to implement, at least in the public relations department. You learn to play along, Jacen. That's the game called diplomacy."

But that was just the point, Jacen thought, though he kept it to himself. Any formalities concerning the Jedi, from the academy to any new councils, seemed to him to be layers of bureaucracy added to something spiritual and personal, something that should not be governed. In Jacen's idealistic sixteen-year-old eyes, the individual Jedi Knights, by their mere acceptance of the philosophy necessary to sustain their Force powers, should be self-governing. A properly trained Jedi Knight, who had been taught to avoid the dark side, who proved he could resist the temptations associated with such power, needed no bureaucrats to guide his actions, and putting that governing layer there, he feared, would steal the mystery.

"We know that Rodan and Niuk Niuv are against us," Luke went on, walking again as he spoke. "I doubt that Pwoe will be receptive to anything that he feels will threaten the power of his position—the Quarrens have waited a long time for a seat on the council. Triebakk will be with me on whatever I decide, as will Cal Omas, who learned long ago to trust me and the Jedi. That makes Chelch Dravvad the key vote, and I think I'll have him if I can answer the concerns of some of these problems that Rodan and Niuk Niuv are pushing."

"What about Councilor Fey'lya?" Jacen asked.

Luke waved his hand, as if the Bothan was irrelevant. "Borsk wants whatever is best for Borsk," he explained. "If Chelch goes over to side with Rodan and his group, making it four to two against me, then Borsk will back them. But if the others are split, three to three, Borsk will lead them either to inaction, not wanting to risk a fight with me and Leia, or he'll back us, hoping we'll return the favor."

"Mom would never back Borsk for anything," Jacen said dryly, and Luke didn't disagree. "Borsk Fey'lya would be a fool to think that she would."

"He lives in a world where alliances shift by the moment," Luke explained. "Borsk does what Borsk needs to do, at any given moment, to benefit Borsk. And he's so jaded by that personal philosophy that he thinks everyone else plays by the same rules."

Now it was Jacen's turn to come to an abrupt halt. "And these are the people you want to please?" he asked skeptically. "These are the people you seek to emulate with your own council?"

"Of course not," Luke replied, taken aback.

"But that's what will happen," Jacen argued.

Luke stared at him long and hard, and Jacen more than met that stare. They had been around this route so many times of late, without resolution. The paradoxes within Jacen's own mind kept him somewhat impotent against his uncle. Jacen had been trained as a Jedi Knight at the academy, yet he had become convinced that the academy was not a good thing, that it was too formal and structured, and that growth within the Force was a much more personal experience. Actually, though the academy remained, Luke had come to somewhat agree with that perspective. He felt that the academy had been a necessary stepping-stone back to the old ways, where Jedi Knights in training worked with Masters one-on-one, as Jaina was with Mara, and Jacen and Anakin were with him. This arrangement would not have been possible before now, for Luke had long been the only Jedi close to attaining the status of Master. Now there were others, and the old ways were being rediscovered, a process that Luke understood would take some time.

Still, Jacen had begged his uncle to go further and faster, to bring the Jedi back to the one-master-one-student model of old, but to improve even upon that model. Instead of finding Force-strong youngsters to train in the ways of the Jedi, Jacen wanted such promising students to find their way to the Jedi. Luke thought his arguments a play of semantics, but to Jacen they went much deeper—they went to the core of what it was to be a Jedi Knight.

"I have not even put my ideas on solid footing yet," Luke said, and Jacen knew that to be as polite a reply, and as much a concession, as he would ever get. He knew what it was that his uncle feared: that Force-strong potential Jedi Knights might be ensnared by the dark side before they ever found their way to the Jedi Masters. But still, to Jacen, this internal strength in the Force remained a personal thing and, ultimately, a personal choice.

They said no more as they left the senate building, making their way down to the docks where Han, Anakin, and Chewbacca were working on the *Millennium Falcon*.

FOUR

Seeds Planted

"The *Jade Sabre* has made orbit," Shok Tinoktin informed Nom Anor that night. "Leia Organa Solo is aboard her, along with her daughter and Mara Jade Skywalker."

"And a Noghri," Nom Anor added. "Always at least one Noghri if Leia Solo is about."

"The Noghri are worthy adversaries," Tinoktin agreed. "But I fear the others more. So should you."

Nom Anor turned a glare upon the man, reminding him of who was the boss here, and who the mere attendant. And Shok Tinoktin did shrink back, the blood draining from his face. He had been around Nom Anor long enough to fear that glare as much as, perhaps even more than, he feared death itself.

"They are Jedi," he stammered, trying to clarify his warning, trying to make certain that Nom Anor did not note any lack of confidence in him. Speaking doubts about Nom Anor had proven a fatal flaw for several previous advisers.

"Leia is not true Jedi, or at least, she has not embraced her Jedi powers, from what I have been told," Nom Anor replied with a sly grin, one that allowed Shok to relax a bit. "Nor is her daughter a proven Jedi."

"But Mara Jade is counted among the strongest of the Jedi Knights," Shok Tinoktin pointed out.

"Mara Jade has her own problems to consider," Nom Anor reminded.

Shok Tinoktin didn't take comfort in that; in fact, the reminder of Mara's disease only heightened his trepidation about letting her see Nom Anor at this time.

"She should be long dead," he dared to say.

Nom Anor smiled again and scratched his head. He had been wearing his ooglith masquer for a long while and was literally itching to take the thing off. But he hadn't the time, of course, and in truth, he didn't want even the trusted stooge Tinoktin to see his true, self-disfigured face, with its strange eye, a reflection of Nom Anor's highest show of devotion on the day he was awarded the position of executor among the Yuuzhan Vong, and first advance scout for the Praetorite Vong invasion force.

He had taken the eye out with the sharpened end of a burning stick. Of course, he had filled that hole in his face with yet another marvelous organic innovation, a plaeryin bol, a creature that looked much like a normal Yuuzhan Vong eyeball, but its pupil was really a mouth, and one that could spit a venomous glob accurately across ten meters at the command of its host, by a simple twitch of Nom Anor's eyelid.

"I am impressed with Mara Jade's ability to resist the spores," he admitted.

"Everyone else you tested them on was dead or dying within a few weeks," Shok Tinoktin replied. "Most within a few days."

Nom Anor nodded. His coomb-spore formula had indeed proven wonderfully effective, breaking down the victim's molecular structure and causing horrible death in short order. If only he could find a way to make the not-so-subtle shift from simple poison to disease, where the spores could become self-propagating, spreading on their own from being to being and thus infecting large populations.

Nom Anor sighed and scratched his head yet again. The

spores—coomb, brollup, tegnest, and a dozen other varieties—
were but a hobby, one that he had been able to insert into his
official duties in attempting to develop some method for
easily killing the supercreatures, the Jedi Knights. Also, such
alchemical work, if successful, could prove critical in Nom
Anor's ascension to the rank of high prefect. But in those en-
deavors and aspirations, to date at least, it appeared as if he
had failed, for Mara Jade Skywalker had somehow defeated
the spores, or at least had held them at bay.

"Do you have the shlecho newt?" he asked.

Shok Tinoktin nodded and reached into his pocket, producing a small brown-orange lizard.

"Make certain that it gets near to Mara Jade's mouth,"
Nom Anor explained, and Shok Tinoktin, who had heard the
explicit instructions several times already, nodded. The coomb
spores Nom Anor had used in his lethal blend were the favored delicacy of the shlecho newt, and if there was any trace
of them at all on Mara Jade's breath, the little creature would
surely detect it.

"I shall escort them in," Shok Tinoktin offered, and after a
confirming nod from Nom Anor, the man turned on his heel
and walked from the room.

Nom Anor rested back in his chair, considering the upcoming meeting and the potential gains he might find. He
thought it quite humorous that Rhommamool's enemies on
Osarian were so fearful of the meeting that they thought
Leia's recognition of Nom Anor in such a manner would
strengthen his prestige and, therefore, power. For, in truth,
Nom Anor hardly cared for any such gains in prestige at this
time. In fact, his thinking went to quite the opposite. He carried all the emotional weight and influence he needed to control the weak people of Rhommamool, or of any other planets
on which he planned to stir up trouble, but beyond that immediate sphere of influence, Nom Anor preferred anonymity.

For now.

No, Nom Anor was looking forward to this meeting simply

so that he could gauge the effect of his infection upon Mara Jade, and so that he might learn more of the Jedi in general, including Leia, a woman he knew would prove pivotal in the upcoming events, and Jaina, who might prove to be a weak link to get to Leia Solo, perhaps even to Luke Skywalker and Mara Jade. That was one of his missions here, to identify those most dangerous foes and to find some way to minimize their effectiveness. Occasions such as the Osarian-Rhommamool conflict, where Nom Anor could also further the effects of the internal squabbles among the humans and their allies, could *bruk tukken nom canbin-tu*, or "weaken the hinges of the enemy's fort," as went the common saying in his native tongue, were then all the better. There were other agents doing that very same thing, after all, though in Nom Anor's estimation, it wasn't even a critical component of the Yuuzhan Vong's overall plan. These humans and their pitiful allies would propagate their own problems by their very nature, he knew. They had no sense of structure and order, not in terms of the regimen and hierarchical code to which his own people adhered, at least. He had witnessed disinformation campaigns waged against political enemies, even one that had basically accused Leia Organa Solo of treason. He had witnessed coup attempts on many, many worlds and had seen supposed authorities profiting many times from the activities of less-than-legitimate business contacts. These infidels did not understand the law, or the need for unbending adherence to it.

That would make it all the easier for the disciplined Praetorite Vong, he knew, and all the more justifiable.

Nom Anor noticed on one of his many security holocams then that Shok Tinoktin was returning, with Tamaktis Breetha, the former mayor of Redhaven and now a member of Nom Anor's independent senate, and Leia, Jaina, and Mara. He noted the movements of two others, as well: a golden droid—and he would have to remember to punish Shok Tinoktin for allowing a droid into his complex!—and a ghostly gray creature seeming almost to float behind the others, hanging close to Leia, as if it was nothing more substantial than the woman's shadow. The expected Noghri bodyguard, Nom Anor knew. He nodded at the sight and made a mental note to keep careful watch on that one. In many ways, Nom Anor held much more respect for the Noghri, those deadly warriors, than for any humans, even Jedi.

Then he let his gaze shift back to Mara, studying her every movement, trying to discern some hint of instability, some hint that the infection was fighting on. He did see Shok Tinoktin's shlecho newt on the man's shoulder, eyeing Mara directly, its eyes wide, its tongue darting, and its head a brilliant shade of crimson, a clear sign of excitement.

So, he mused, the coomb spores, at least, continued their assault on the woman, and Nom Anor's respect for Mara heightened even more.

He went to his closet then and took out his great black cape, throwing it about his shoulders, pulling the hood up over his head, cowl low and concealing, then reaching in and lifting the black screen he used to completely cover his already-masked face. Though this was his usual public dress, Nom Anor chuckled as he completed the outfit. He knew the history of his guests and understood that the sight of him dressed like this might play interestingly upon them, particularly upon Leia, for it was hard to miss the likeness of Nom Anor to another foe Leia had once battled.

In a box on a shelf hidden deep in that closet, Nom Anor kept his remaining infectious agents, and it occurred to him, though only briefly, that he might use this opportunity to infect the other two, as well. How crippled might the New Republic become if Leia Organa Solo suddenly succumbed to the same disease Mara Jade Skywalker was fighting? How debilitated might Leia and Luke, Mara and the always dangerous Han Solo become if Jaina Solo fell ill and died?

Pleasant thoughts, no doubt, but Nom Anor couldn't take the chance of linking himself so obviously to the deadly infection. Along that same line of thinking, particularly given the sensory powers of the Jedi and the evasive nature of Noghri, Nom Anor realized that it would be a mistake to allow Leia and the others into these private quarters. He hustled to his door and pushed out into the hall, arriving just as Shok Tinoktin led the group around a bend in the corridor.

He saw the spark of recognition on Mara's face, and he knew as she turned quickly to Leia that she was informing the other woman of his identity. In the back, Tamaktis Breetha bowed and held his position.

Nom Anor nodded to Shok Tinoktin, and the man moved out of the way, allowing Leia a clear path to Nom Anor.

She sucked in her breath; Nom Anor saw the recognition, the surprise, even horror, upon her face. He looked like Darth Vader!

"I bring greetings from the council of the New Republic," Leia said in formal greeting, and the fact that she spoke so quickly, and with her voice controlled and even, offered Nom Anor a bit of insight into the strength of this woman. She was one to respect.

"You bring interference where it is not wanted," he countered. Tamaktis Breetha gasped, and even Shok Tinoktin was a bit taken aback at Nom Anor's sudden surliness and brusque attitude.

"We have come as arranged," Leia said. "An agreement between you and Borsk Fey'lya, I believe."

"I agreed that an emissary could come," Nom Anor admitted. "To what end, I do not know. What can you contribute, Leia Organa Solo, to the dispute between Rhommamool and Osarian? What flame of hope can you light within the Rhommamoolians that their desperate cry for independence shall not be ignored by the New Republic, who speak of freedom as the greatest of all virtues?"

"Perhaps we should retire to more private chambers," Leia suggested. Tamaktis Breetha seemed about to agree, but a look from Nom Anor cured him of that suicidal urge.

"What have you to hide?" Nom Anor mocked her.

"More comfortable quarters, then," the woman persisted.

"Will a chair make you more comfortable?" Nom Anor asked. "Physically, perhaps, but will it make you more comfortable with the truth?"

Leia looked at him incredulously.

"For that is all that I have to offer you," Nom Anor rolled on. "The truth that Osarian has no claim over the people of Rhommamool. The truth of the frailties and failings of your New Republic. The truth of the false heroes, the Jedi Knights."

"*Your* truth," Mara interjected, and Leia glanced back at her.

Glad of the confirmation that his little tirade was wearing thin on them, Nom Anor didn't even try to hide his smile, though it was hardly visible through the black face screen.

"There is only one truth," he said calmly. "It is when one does not like to hear it that one concocts other, more palatable versions."

"If I may, Princess Leia," C-3PO began, moving forward. "There is ample history of the Jedi Knights to show them as true—"

"Silence!" Nom Anor growled at the droid, and the powerful being trembled visibly, as if he was about to explode into murderous action against poor C-3PO, who was also trembling, though hardly in a threatening manner.

"Are we to discuss the situation between Osarian and Rhommamool?" Leia asked, her tone diplomatic and soothing. She moved as she spoke to gently push C-3PO back, and nodded to Jaina to collect the droid and to keep him quiet.

"I thought we were doing just that," Nom Anor said, under complete control once more, as Leia turned back to him.

"This is not a meeting," Leia countered. "It is a lecture in a hallway."

"And even that is more than Borsk Fey'lya deserves," Nom

Anor was quick to answer. "Would you not agree, former Councilor Solo?"

"This is not about Borsk Fey'lya," Leia retorted, keeping her calm, though Nom Anor saw the fringes at the edge of that calm beginning to unravel. "This is about the fate of two worlds."

"Who need nothing from the hypocritical New Republic," Nom Anor added. "The New Republic that speaks of peace and prosperity, when it means peace in terms of the lower classes having no power to gain wealth or power, and prosperity only for elite friends of the New Republic."

Leia shook her head and sputtered a few undecipherable words.

"Order your battle cruiser to destroy the Osarians' ability to attack Rhommamool," Nom Anor said in all seriousness. "Shoot down their starfighters and cripple their missile pads, and forbid them to rebuild such offensive weapons."

Leia stared at him hard, and the depth of her expression, he knew, carried more than the frustration of the immediate circumstances, carried in it the remembered weight of long-ago enemies.

"And when they leave us alone, the conflict will be at its end," Nom Anor went on. "Peace will prevail. And so will prosperity." He paused and brought a hand up to his black-masked face and struck a pensive pose. "Ah, yes, then prosperity will prevail, but it will be prosperity for Rhommamool and not Osarian, not the favored elite of the New Republic."

"You can't believe what you're saying," Leia returned dryly.

"Can't I?" Nom Anor asked, his voice dripping sarcasm. "A plausible read of the situation. Go out yourself among the streets of Redhaven and ask."

"If you cared for the people of Rhommamool, you'd sit down and negotiate away this budding war," Leia said bluntly.

"I thought that was what we just did," Nom Anor said.

Leia's expression again turned incredulous.

"I told you how to stop it," Nom Anor went on. "A simple call to the commander of your intervening terror weapon . . ."

Leia looked back at Mara and Jaina and shook her head.

"Not what you expected?" came Nom Anor's sarcastic, taunting reply. "But more than you, or the New Republic, deserved. I think our positions are clear, and so I bid you turn about, back to your silly little flying box, and away from Rhommamool. I am afraid that I have lost patience with your foolishness."

Leia stared at him long and hard, then turned on her heel and stormed away, sweeping up Jaina and Mara in her wake. Bolpuhr, too, turned about, but not until he had given a long and threatening stare at Nom Anor, who merely smiled widely in reply.

C-3PO, too, turned to leave, but he lingered there a moment, wilting under Nom Anor's glare, perhaps the coldest stare he had ever felt.

"Excuse me, sir, but may I inquire if there is a problem?" the droid gingerly asked.

"One I could easily rectify," Nom Anor answered ominously, coming forward a step, his stance threatening.

"Have I somehow offended you?" the droid politely asked, although he was quaking with fear.

"Your mere existence offends me!" Nom Anor growled, and C-3PO, having heard enough—too much, actually—wheeled about and hustled away, calling for Princess Leia.

"I did not expect such an encounter," Tamaktis Breetha dared to say, moving to stand beside Nom Anor.

"Nor did I," Nom Anor replied. "I had thought the meeting would be boring, and hardly that much fun." He looked at his former mayor and recognized the doubts on the man's face.

"Speak your mind," Nom Anor bade him. "Your questions will only strengthen me."

"Rhommamool will indeed need the help of the New Republic," Tamaktis Breetha said after a long pause.

Nom Anor chuckled. The man didn't understand. This

wasn't about Rhommamool—Nom Anor would hardly care if he left the place and then later learned that Osarian had completely obliterated it. Of course, he would never go on record making such a statement.

"Our cause is bigger than the civil war between a pair of planets," he told Tamaktis. "It is about the basic freedoms of citizens of the New Republic and basic fairness to the exploited masses everywhere. When that truth comes out, then Rhommamool will find all the allies it needs to crush the thief-lords of Osarian."

The former mayor squared his shoulders as Nom Anor spoke, taking pride in the cause—the greater, if impractical, cause. "I will see that our guests depart promptly," he said, dipping a bow and, after Nom Anor motioned for him to proceed, starting away.

Nom Anor went to Shok Tinoktin and gently patted the head of the still-excited shlecho newt.

"The scent of the coomb spore was strong on her breath," Shok Tinoktin remarked.

"And she wasn't as strong," Nom Anor added. "I could see it in the way she walked and held herself." Supremely pleased with himself, the executor headed for his private quarters, Shok Tinoktin moving to follow.

"Make sure that their course away leads them past the square," Nom Anor said to him on sudden insight. "I want them to witness the devotion."

Shok Tinoktin bowed and turned away.

Nom Anor went into his room. He started for the two villips he had concealed in his closet, but changed his mind and went to his viewscreen instead, staring up at the images of the stars that were just beginning to peek out as the sun disappeared. Had they made contact? he wondered. Had the yammosk set up the controlling base?

"He looked like Darth—" Jaina started to say.

"Don't even talk about it," Leia cut her off, her tone leaving no room for debate. "Try to keep up, Threepio," she said, more sharply than she had intended, when the droid came bounding around a rounded corner in full flight, nearly crashing into one of the metal support girders that lined the hallway like a giant rib cage. "And try not to get lost."

"Oh, never that, Princess Leia," C-3PO said, as sincere as he had ever been, and he glued himself to Leia's side.

They continued along the winding maze of corridors, up stairwells and through heavy doors, and it occurred to all of them how defensible this place truly was, a bunker more than a statehouse. Also, given the number of stairs they climbed, and where they eventually came out, they realized that Nom Anor's private chambers were quite far below ground, something that had been lost on them in their trip down, a journey that had followed a more meandering route, along corridors they now understood to be gently, almost imperceptibly, sloping.

They arrived at the *Jade Sabre* without incident, and the guards standing before the shuttle's hatch briskly stepped aside.

"I wish that it could have gone better," Tamaktis Breetha remarked to Leia after Jaina, Mara, and C-3PO went aboard to begin departure preparations.

"Perhaps you should tell that to Nom Anor," Leia replied, and the gentle-eyed old man bowed.

"You must understand that Osarian has been ruling us as a virtual slave colony for decades," Tamaktis began.

"I know the history, and the current standing," Leia replied. "Your intractable leader does not help the situation."

Tamaktis, obviously unconvinced, didn't respond.

Leia shook her head and moved into the ship, Bolpuhr gliding in behind her, the Noghri never taking his wary gaze from Tamaktis or the two sentries.

"We've got a course change," Mara informed Leia as soon as she joined the others on the bridge, taking her customary seat behind Jaina.

"They want us to fly low across the city, then vector out from the west," Jaina explained.

"A trap?" the wary Leia asked.

"I don't see the point," Mara said. "They could have taken out the shuttle while we were with Nom Anor, and could have easily captured us inside the complex."

"Unless they're trying to make it look like an accident," Jaina put in.

Leia nodded, reflecting her similar concerns.

"They haven't got a thing that will take us out of the air once we're up and fully powered," Mara said firmly.

"Nothing that we know about," Leia added, and that truth gave Mara pause.

"We could signal the *Mediator* for an escort," Jaina offered.

Leia shook her head. "Just follow their course," she offered. "But be ready to blast out of here at the slightest sign of trouble."

They heard Bolpuhr give a low hiss in the hallway, apparently not pleased with that choice.

"Maybe your Noghri noticed Nom Anor's resemblance to Darth Vader, as well," Mara said with a tension-breaking grin.

But Leia shuddered visibly at the awful thought.

The *Jade Sabre* lifted off and skimmed across the city, barely above the rooftops, as the departure controller ordered. A few moments later, Leia understood the design of this course change, as the great square of Redhaven came into view, where a celebration was in full swing, great bonfires burning.

"What is that?" Jaina asked, pointing down at the huge pit, and Mara, equally curious, brought the *Jade Sabre* in for a low flyby.

C-3PO wailed and the three women crinkled their faces when the truth of that pit became apparent, when they saw the battered, pitiful droids, some still moving or sparking, and every motion invariably drawing a new volley of stones from the crazed crowd that ringed the pit.

"Barbaric!" C-3PO cried. "The inhumanity!"

"Get us out of here," a disgusted Leia instructed, but Mara was already spinning the *Jade Sabre* up on end and punching full throttle, the roar of the twin engines making many of the fanatics in the square dive for cover. A squawk of protest came over the comm, but Mara just clicked it off.

"Well," she said as they soared far, far away, "I warned you about Nom Anor. Still think I was exaggerating?"

"He is about as infuriating as any being I've ever met," Leia agreed.

"And once again, my sensitivity to the Force revealed nothing about him," Mara added. "Nothing. I even tried to silently call to him, just to get a reaction, but he didn't respond at all—I don't even know that he heard it—and so completely did he ignore me that there was little I could learn about him."

"Same with me," Jaina admitted. "It's like he was totally devoid of the Force. I didn't like the feel of that other one, Shok Tinoktin, either."

Mara nodded. "But I don't have the feeling that there was any hint of a bluff in Nom Anor's rebuttal," she said. "He brought us here for no better reason than to snub us, and even if Osarian puts the pressure on, I doubt that one will ever negotiate."

Leia got up and rubbed her eyes, shook her head in utter frustration, and gave a helpless sigh. "I admire you," she said to Mara. "Truly. You met him once and agreed to do so again. You're a braver person than I."

Luke and Jacen found the *Millennium Falcon* right where they left it, Docking Bay 3733, and judging from the sounds coming from the bay, the clank of metal wrenches, the hum of turbo drivers, and the stream of muttered curses, they figured that Han and Chewie were still trying to figure out how to fix the thing.

On the way to Coruscant, Han had given the controls over to Anakin, who was more than a bit jealous that Mara often let Jaina fly the *Jade Sabre*, and the fifteen-year-old, predictably, pulled a few hotdogging maneuvers on the way down. But while the *Millennium Falcon* was surprisingly agile for a ship that looked more like an old garbage scow than a starfighter, she was also much, much more powerful. The *Falcon* had the agility to pull the turns Anakin put her through—though with his inertial compensator dialed down only 2 percent, everyone on board had nearly passed out from the g's—but the boy had apparently throttled up a bit too hard coming out of more than one. By the time Han had managed to take back the controls for the last remnant of the flight to dock, the *Falcon* was listing badly, with one engine and several repulsorlifts firing intermittently and unpredictably. Even now, secured in the bay, one of those repulsors popped off now and again, jolting the ship's edge up a few degrees, to bounce back down as the repulsor sputtered back out.

Luke and Jacen exchanged a smile as the *Falcon* went up yet again, higher this time, nearly onto its side, then dropped fast to horizontal, slamming down against the floor.

"Weeow!" came the screech of R2-D2.

"Chewie!" Han cried, from somewhere above the open lower landing ramp, followed by a thud, a swear or two, and a wrench bouncing down the ramp to clang out into the docking bay.

Han staggered down behind, covered in grease and sweat, muttering every step of the way. He bent to retrieve the wrench, but stopped and glanced up at his returning son and brother-in-law.

"Teenagers," he muttered.

"I thought you'd have it fixed by now," Luke replied.

"All but that number-seven repulsor," Han explained.

"Something crossed and shorted in one of the kid's rocker-rolls. Keeps firing off and on even if we power her down. Artoo got a bit of a shock when he plugged into the nav computer."

Luke smiled widely. Ever since he had met Han and set eyes on the *Falcon*, he considered the two, pilot and ship, to be almost spiritually linked. Both were a patchwork of seemingly unrelated skills, and both were far more formidable than they appeared. And both, Luke thought now, always seemed to be breaking down and defying logic in the repair mode.

"Try it now!" came Anakin's voice from within, answered by a Wookiee wail.

The *Falcon* hummed to life, repulsorlifts firing in testing sequence: one-ten, two-nine, three-eight, four . . . seven.

And seven fired beautifully.

"Kid's got talent," Han remarked, but even as he said it, something inside the *Falcon* exploded and thick smoke poured down the landing ramp, accompanied by another R2-D2 "Weeow!"

Chewie wailed again.

"You pushed it too fast!" Anakin yelled at the Wookiee, and Chewie's wail became a growl, and a moment later, Anakin came running down the ramp, waving the smoke from his face, as filthy as if he had just dived face-first into a Tinuvian tar pit.

He skidded to a stop before his glowering father.

"He pushed it too fast," Anakin sheepishly tried to explain.

"You pushed it too fast," Han countered, anger rising.

"You said I—"

"I said you could fly it," Han interrupted, poking his finger at the boy. "I didn't say you could try to outdo your sister, because you can't, you know. And you can't turn the *Falcon* the way you turn a landspeeder!"

"But—" Anakin paused and looked to his uncle and brother for support, but while the two weren't smiling any longer, neither did they have anything to offer against Han's assessment.

With a sigh that sounded more like a snarl, Anakin waved his hands in frustration and stormed back up the landing ramp.

"Teenagers!" Han cried.

Now Luke did smile again, for he could envision a young Han Solo in exactly the same situation, hearing the exasperated cry of "Teenagers!" from every adult around him. There were many differences between Anakin and Han, with the son seeming far more introspective. But concerning many matters, like flying the *Falcon*, apparently, Anakin Solo had his father's unbridled spirit. In cases like this, it almost scared Luke how much Anakin was like Han, in appearance and in temperament.

Chewie greeted the returning Anakin with a disapproving growl.

"We'll fix it!" the boy replied with a sigh. "It's just a stupid ship."

Even before those last words had left his mouth, Anakin found himself up in the air, his head uncomfortably close to the myriad of wires in the *Falcon*'s main power grid. The powerful Wookiee held him there easily, with just one hand, while his other hand reached down to Anakin's belt and pulled free his lightsaber.

"What—" Anakin started to ask, but then his surprise multiplied many times over and he yelled out, "Hey!" as Chewie brought the lightsaber into his mouth and made a move as if he meant to bite the thing.

Aside from the risk of blowing his head off if he released the energy within that hilt, Chewie's threats to scratch or damage Anakin's precious instrument unsettled the boy profoundly. He yelled at Chewie again and reached up for the lightsaber, but the Wookiee elbowed his hand away and scolded him profoundly.

"Okay, I get it," Anakin replied, head down, for the Wookiee's comparisons between Anakin's feelings for the lightsaber and Chewie's own for the *Falcon* certainly hit the point. "I get it," he said again.

Chewie howled, hardly seeming satisfied.

"We'll fix it!" an exasperated Anakin assured him.

For a few moments, Luke continued to envision the problems a younger Han might have caused to those adults around him. Han cocked his head at Luke, apparently noting his expression, and smirked. "How'd your meeting go?"

"Wonderful," Luke answered sarcastically. "How else could any meeting chaired by Borsk Fey'lya go?"

"They've got their problems," Han said. "Borsk and his friends are finding that managing a galaxy isn't as easy as they believed."

"So they find scapegoats," Luke said.

"Such as . . . ," Han prompted.

"A problem along the Outer Rim," Luke explained. "Someone's banging blasters with smugglers. Jedi, they believe, and that's not to the liking of Fyor Rodan or Niuk Niuv."

"Probably costing them a fortune," Han reasoned with a wry grin.

"Whatever the reason, the council's not happy about it."

"Which means they're laying it on you," Han said. "Well, what are we to do about it?" Han's tone made it pretty clear that he didn't think highly of intervening.

"Didn't you tell me that Lando was out there, mining asteroids or something?" Luke asked, and Han's expression soured.

"He's out there," Han replied. "Pair of planets called Dubrillion and Destrillion, near an asteroid system he modestly named Lando's Folly."

"I need a thread to hang on," Luke explained. "Maybe a little insider information."

"That'd be Lando," Han agreed. He didn't sound particularly enamored of the idea.

Luke understood the man's apparent reticence and recognized it for pure bluster. Han and Lando were friends—dear friends—but there always seemed to be a reluctance from both to publicly admit it. "Maybe," Luke said. "Lando always seems to know what's going on, and if I find out the inside story, I might be able to use it to persuade a couple of councilors to see things my way."

Han started to nod, then blinked and stared at Luke curiously. "You've been hanging around me too long," he remarked. "What are you smiling at?" he asked Jacen, who was beaming at Luke's side.

"The belt," Jacen said. "Jaina's going to be pretty happy about this."

"The belt?" Luke asked.

"Running the belt," Jacen explained, but Luke's expression remained curious.

"Lando's got an operation going on the side," Han explained. "Calls it *running the belt*. It's a game—and there's probably more than a little betting going on around it—where pilots test their skills by zipping around the asteroids, seeing how long they can stay in the place before getting bumped away."

"Blasted away, you mean," Luke said. "Into little pieces. Doesn't sound like a promising career."

"Only one pilot's been hurt," Jacen interjected, drawing a surprised look from Luke. "Jaina told me," he explained. "Lando modified some TIE fighters with walls of repulsor shields so that they can take a hit, or two, or ten, and just bounce away."

"It's supposed to be one of the highlights of the galaxy," Han replied. "But I'm betting there's more to it than just a game."

Luke nodded and didn't have to ask for clarification. He

had heard a couple of reports of smugglers diving into asteroid belts to evade pursuit. Perhaps Lando's game was providing some interesting training.

"You want to go and visit him?" Han asked. "He's not on especially good terms with the New Republic these days."

"Is he ever?"

"He's likely running a few side businesses the New Republic would see as less than legitimate," Han added.

"Isn't he always?"

That brought a chuckle from Han, but just for a moment. "What about Mara?" he asked seriously. "They'll be back soon, and from what I hear, things didn't go very well."

That hit home to Luke, a reminder, as everything seemed to be a reminder, that his beloved wife was not well. The best doctors in the galaxy were shaking their heads helplessly, able to do nothing but watch as something inside Mara continually altered her molecular structure. No medicine, no therapy, had come close to treating the rare disease, and only her own internal strength, her use of the Force, was somewhat keeping it in check. Those others who had contracted the disease had not been so fortunate.

So what would a trek across the galaxy do to her? Luke had to wonder. Would it be too much? Would it put her in a dangerous position?

"Aunt Mara just went to Rhommamool," Jacen reminded. "That's three days' travel, and she didn't find any vacation once she got there."

"True enough," Han said. "Maybe a run to the Outer Rim, far away from the council, will do her, and my wife, good."

Luke shrugged and nodded, and so it seemed settled.

They heard R2-D2 beeping wildly then, Chewie wailed, and the number-seven repulsorlift coil fired to life.

And then there came another explosion from inside the *Falcon*, and the lift coil sputtered out.

Anakin came storming down the landing ramp. "That's it!" he grumbled. "I'm done."

Before Han could even begin to yell at him, though, a huge, hairy paw landed on the boy's shoulder and yanked him back inside, and Anakin's feeble attempt at any protest was blasted away by a tremendous Wookiee roar.

Han blew a sigh and tossed his wrench over his shoulder, to clang on the metal floor.

"Teenagers," Luke remarked, tossing a wink at Jacen.

FIVE

The War Coordinator

Danni Quee pored over the charts again and again, checking coordinates and vectors. She was in the control room. Most of the scientists were spending the whole of their waking hours and some of their sleeping ones in there, now that they had something interesting to watch. Nine of the fifteen were in the room now.

"In the Helska system," Garth Breise said to her. "The fourth planet."

Danni nodded; it did indeed seem as if their incoming asteroid, racing along faster than any natural object they had ever witnessed, would soon enough sail into the Helska system. There, given its present course and speed—and there seemed to be no reason to expect either to change—it would collide with the fourth planet.

"What do we know of that planet?" Danni asked.

Garth Breise shrugged. "There isn't much in the data banks about the Helska system. There's not an easily inhabitable planet among the seven, and no one's taken the time or trouble to build one up. None of them even have names—just Helska 1 to 7."

"Point the orbiting scopes toward that fourth planet then," Danni instructed. "Let's find out what it's made of."

"Ice," Yomin Carr said from Pod 7, the one now showing the clearest tracking of the asteroid.

The other scientists in the room turned to regard him.

"I did some research, and some personal viewing," Yomin Carr explained. "Once we determined that the asteroid would make a close pass, or a hit, I took some shots from our orbiting scope."

"So it's just a frozen ball of rock?" Garth asked.

"Or a ball of frozen water," Yomin Carr replied. "I could detect nothing more substantial than ice and vapor. No sign of minerals at all." Of course, Yomin Carr knew much more about that planet, the fourth in the Helska system. He had been there; he had studied it. He had left the villip beacons out by the galactic rim to steer the incoming brethren, the glory of the Praetorite Vong, to it.

"And you're sure it's going to hit it?" Tee-ubo asked.

"Looks like it," Danni replied.

"How big's that planet?" Tee-ubo asked.

"Not big," Yomin Carr replied. "A few thousand kilometers in diameter."

"If it's nothing but ice, then that asteroid will disintegrate it," Bensin Tomri remarked, and a grin widened on his face. All of them had been excited when they discovered that the incoming asteroid was on a path for a collision, for none had ever witnessed that rare event. Now, if Yomin Carr was right about the composition of the planet, the show might be amazing indeed!

"Let's try to get a better reading on that planet," Danni suggested. "And I think it's time we send out the word so that ExGal and the New Republic can get some scientists out there."

"And fast," Bensin Tomri added. "They've only got a few days before—" He paused and smiled widely, then threw his hands out wide as he finished suddenly. "—boom!"

Tee-ubo went right to the transmitter in the raised section

of the chamber and clicked open the normal channel for accessing the galactic net and contacting ExGal.

It didn't work.

"Have the dovin basals tighten their lock on the planet," the huge and powerful Prefect Da'Gara told his crew—his crew on the asteroid, which wasn't an asteroid at all, but rather a huge, ten-kilometer chunk of yorik coral, a living worldship.

"You wish more speed, Prefect?" another of the tattooed warriors asked.

Da'Gara, not used to being questioned, looked at him curiously.

"Belek tiu," the other said, snapping his fists against opposite shoulders, the reply and signal for both apology and permission to continue.

Da'Gara nodded. This one, Tu Shoolb, had proven resourceful and cunning in their trip across the galaxies.

"A change in speed might alert all those watching," Tu Shoolb explained. "For natural bodies would not so obviously accelerate."

"Those watching?" Da'Gara questioned. "Do you doubt that Yomin Carr has performed?"

"No, Prefect," Tu Shoolb said, and he signaled his respect again and reiterated, *"Belek tiu."*

Da'Gara motioned him off on his task to the dovin basals, the organisms that propelled the worldship. Possessed of the ability to lock on to specific gravity fields, to the exclusion of all others, even to gravity fields millions of kilometers away, the adult, three-meter spherical dovin basals worked like perpetual thrusters. And the more they focused their line, the greater the pull. Now they were locked on a planet, the one the inhabitants of this galaxy called Helska 4, as per the instructions of Yomin Carr's villip beacon, which had been left out at Vector Prime, the breach point of the galactic rim, with specific directions.

Da'Gara almost reconsidered his order to Tu Shoolb then,

for the instructions of Yomin Carr had called for a steady run to the fourth planet, but the prefect was anxious, and if Carr had done his job correctly, no one would be the wiser. Of course, the acceleration might force some last-minute course corrections to properly intercept the planet, but so be it. For the prefect wanted to be on with it. He had been back to the main holding compartment to communicate with the great yammosk, the war coordinator; and the gigantic creature, its bulbous head glowing red with eagerness, its many tentacles—some thick and others filament-thin but a hundred kilometers long—coiled and twitching, had clearly revealed to him its desire to begin.

Da'Gara was a prefect, no minor title, and this was his ship to command, but the greater mission was the province of the war coordinator, a creature, a tool, genetically engineered over centuries to serve his people in just this conquering capacity.

The yammosk was eager.

So was Da'Gara.

"A tail," one of the scientists at ExGal-4 announced, and he stood up and slapped the edge of the console. "I knew it!"

Danni, Bensin, and several others rushed over to the Pod 7 viewer, nodding as they acknowledged the visible tail of the asteroid. "Not much of one," another remarked, but a trailing line of something was indeed visible.

"A comet, then," Bensin Tomri mused, and several conversations erupted all at once, mostly concerning the apparent lack of heat beyond the galactic rim, for if there was indeed sunlike heat and energy out there, as many scientists had theorized, then no comet could have come through with any ice intact.

Danni and Bensin exchanged sincere smiles. This had been a day of unexpected discoveries, always a delight to the scientific mind. First, they had noted that the streaking asteroid was significantly accelerating, though they hadn't yet

determined whether that was due to some galactic rim rebound, or some gravitational force they had not yet dis-
cerned, and now they learned that it wasn't an asteroid at all,
but a comet, trailing a small, but undeniable, tail.

"Has Garth got that comm system fixed yet?" Danni asked.

"He's working on it," Bensin Tomri replied. "Something
chewed right through the cables, and he's got to build a connector big enough to sort them all."

Across the room, Yomin Carr watched it all with amusement. That was no comet coming in, and no tail behind it.
The trailing tendrils of the worldship were huge membranous
creatures anchored at the end by piloted coralskippers,
smaller, starfighter versions of yorik coral. At times of weak
gravitational-pull fields, those membranes would be extended wide as cosmic sails, riding interstellar winds.

Garth Breise entered the room then, lugging a large metal
box. "Two days," he said to Danni.

"Make it tomorrow," she answered. "We want to give them
time to get on the spot."

Garth sighed, but nodded and hustled away.

Yomin Carr only smiled, knowing the futility of it all.
Garth Breise would fix the cables, only to find that the system
wouldn't work anyway. How long would it take them, the
Yuuzhan Vong warrior wondered, to find out the next problem: the subtly disconnected cables at the top of the tower?

Yes, these foolish beings were in for many surprises over
the next few days, and they'd never get the word out to their
fellows, and then their planet would burn down around them.

The sunset that night was thick with green and orange, a
clear sign that Yomin Carr's little dweebits were working their
deadly magic.

Da'Gara sat in his multicolored compartment and felt the
vibrations and the less-subtle movements about him. It was
all in place now, for he had ordered the slowdown to intercept

the fourth planet, the place he and the yammosk would make their base of operations.

Out behind the worldship, dozens of single-piloted coralskippers fanned out, carrying with them the huge membranous sail. They inverted that sail into a semicircle, with the worldship at its apex; the dovin basals, at the commands of the helmsmen, released their grip on the planet's gravity and focused instead on opposing fields, slowing the huge, living vessel.

The coralskippers brought it in, and it contacted with the planet, not with the great explosion those watching from afar had expected, but with a dull splat, the membranes shielding and buffeting the impact like a gigantic mattress.

Da'Gara, like the other five thousand Yuuzhan Vong aboard, moved to his locker and coaxed out a fleshy, membranous creature, a variation of the ooglith masquer called an ooglith cloaker. With help from the prefect, the creature rolled up over his legs and enveloped him, and then began the stinging ecstasy of the joining, its millions of connecting tendrils slipping into Da'Gara's pores. Unlike the masquer, the cloaker's facial mask was transparent, showing the glory of its host's disfigurements. After a short pause to fully experience the connection, Da'Gara scooped a soft star-shaped creature from the water tank beside him and held it up to his face, where it latched on. The prefect gagged a bit as the central tendril of the gnullith snaked down his throat, and he had to put a finger to either side of his nose to keep the pincers there from closing off his air supply.

But then the connection was complete and the creature understood. Now it breathed from the water within Da'Gara's body, while he pulled in needed oxygen through his nose.

The prefect made his way along the rough-walled corridors to the lowest level, where his many soldiers, and the great yammosk, waited.

The yammosk led the way out of the worldship, its thicker tentacles spreading wide to get a solid grip on the icy surface.

Then the creature exposed its huge central tooth and, with the force of an ion cannon, drove it down into the ice, battering repeatedly, digging down, down, and secreting a liquid from that single fang to further erode the crust.

After nearly an hour, the tooth broke through, and the yammosk wasted no time in contorting its huge and boneless body, sliding down, down, into the watery world below.

Da'Gara and his crew went next, fast down the long slide to slip under the water, where the gnullith they had latched upon their faces would do the breathing for them and the ooglith cloakers would protect them from the freezing temperatures.

Soon enough, the yammosk's secretions wore away, and the ice fast covered the hole. But not before another gigantic creature, a brownish tubular worm, had slipped one end out from the worldship, down the hollowed chute, and into the water. The air inside this tubular creature was too warm for the ice to re-form, making it the lifeline and communications line for Da'Gara and the others back to their vessel.

The pilots of the coralskippers went to work next, carefully overlapping the membrane and then releasing it. They flew to the higher docking bay on the ship, and there they awaited the orders of the war coordinator.

"The gravity of the planet got it anyway!" Bensin Tomri announced excitedly. All fifteen were in the control room then, hoping for just such an event, hoping that the acceleration of the comet would not allow it to get past the fourth planet.

They all watched intently as the small blip approached the planet, and then . . .

Nothing. Not an explosion, not the vaporization of the ice planet.

Nothing.

"What the heck?" more than one confused scientist asked, and every one of them was scratching his or her head. All the data coming back from this comet had been inconclusive, showing them no signs of anything familiar in its composition, and now this.

"Did you get that communications tower fixed?" Danni asked Garth rather sharply.

"The only thing I haven't tried yet is climbing up the thing to check the connections on that end," the man replied in the same frustrated tone.

Danni's look showed no compromise.

"I'll do it. I'll do it," he said, throwing his hands up in defeat, and he stormed out of the room.

"Does anyone have any idea of what we just saw?" the frustrated Danni asked, turning her attention back to the viewscreen.

No answers came back at her.

"We've got to contact ExGal," Bensin remarked. "Either with the tower, or from space."

"You want to take the Spacecaster up?" another asked doubtfully.

"That's just what we'll do," Danni interjected. "We'll take it up and all the way to the planet, and we'll give a call out to the galactic net on the way."

There came no arguments, but neither did anyone in the room seem overly thrilled with that prospect. The last time the aging Spacecaster had been used, it had barely made orbit, and the prospect of flying it all the way to the Helska system was more than a bit intimidating.

Except to Yomin Carr, who thought the whole scene of bumbling, undisciplined scientists rather enlightening.

SIX

Take Me Far, Far Away

The *Jade Sabre* came out of hyperspace for the last leg of its journey to Coruscant. Jaina handled all the plotting, engaging and disengaging the hyperdrive, with Mara watching over her, and now, back at sublight, Mara was so confident in the girl that she gave her the bridge alone.

Leia was surprised when she entered to see her daughter sitting comfortably at the controls, with Mara nowhere in sight. "Where's your aunt?" she asked.

Jaina turned, her smile wide. "She said she was tired."

Leia moved to take the seat beside Jaina. "How long to Coruscant?" she asked.

"Two hours," Jaina replied. "Mara told me to come out of lightspeed early because of the heavy traffic in the region. She wants me to wake her up before the final approach."

Leia nodded and sat back. She, too, was tired—tired of it all. Over the last years, she kept resigning her posts, and then allowing herself to be dragged back in, often poignantly reminded, or reminding herself, that a million lives could hang in the balance. Leia was considered among the finest diplomats in the New Republic hierarchy, the one person whose heroic reputation, negotiating skills, and true empathy would allow her to intervene in pending crises.

She closed her eyes and gave a self-deprecating chuckle,

reminding herself that all those skills and reputation had done absolutely nothing to help the Osarian-Rhommamool situation. The Rhommamoolians had many legitimate complaints against Osarian. The Osarians lived much better than their Rhommamoolian counterparts, relaxing in luxury off the labors of the miners, and it was no secret that the Rhommamoolians were greatly underrepresented in the Osarian government. Now, though, those complaints had been compounded and exploited, turned into something zealous and religious in nature, and what should have been a workers' arbitration was in danger of becoming a holy war.

In great danger, Leia now understood, for in all her years, she had rarely dealt with anyone as intractable as Nom Anor, or at least, as intractable as Nom Anor given the fact that the man and the people he was supposedly representing were likely going to get annihilated in a war they could not win. After the disastrous meeting, Leia had made many calls to him from her post on the *Mediator*, and he had answered every one.

Usually just to tell her that he had no time to speak with her.

With those annoying thoughts in mind, Leia drifted off to sleep.

"Wow," Jaina breathed, and Leia popped open her eyes, thinking there might be trouble.

"What is it?" she asked with obvious alarm.

"Mon Calamari Star Defender," Jaina answered, pointing toward the upper left quadrant of the screen. With a flick of her other hand, she angled the viewer to bring the beautiful ship into complete view.

And it was spectacular. Like all the Mon Calamari ships, this one was unique, an artwork, sleek and flowing, and ultimately deadly. It was the largest ship ever produced on that watery world, nearly twice the size of the battle cruiser they had left behind between Osarian and Rhommamool, and the first Mon Calamari Star Defender produced for the New Republic fleet.

"The *Viscount*," Leia remarked. "Just commissioned two weeks ago. It must be making a flyby for the approval of the council."

"Wow," Jaina breathed again, those brown eyes sparkling.

Leia silently laughed at herself. When she had heard Jaina's gasp, she had immediately assumed there was trouble, and she had worried that Jaina couldn't handle it. She examined her apparent lack of confidence in her daughter then, and for a moment believed she must be a terrible mother to think so little of the proven girl.

No, not girl, Leia reminded herself. Young woman.

When she had first come in, after finishing the report of the brewing disaster on Rhommamool, and seen Jaina alone, her heart had skipped a beat. Yet Mara, as competent a pilot and responsible an adult as Leia had ever known, had seen fit to leave Jaina on her own.

Why couldn't Leia hold that same confidence in her own child?

She studied Jaina carefully, the sureness of her movements, the calm expression on her face.

"How close now?" she asked.

Jaina shrugged. "You were asleep for over an hour," she explained. "We've got another half hour, maybe, depending on the course they tell us to follow."

"I'll go get Mara," Leia offered, climbing out of her chair and stretching away the last remnants of sleep.

"You could let her rest," Jaina suggested. "I can bring the *Jade Sabre* down."

Leia thought it over for a moment. Yes, Jaina could land the shuttle with no problems, and Leia was an experienced pilot and could watch over her all the way, and Mara could certainly use all the rest she could find. She almost agreed.

Almost—and again came those nagging doubts about the way she mothered Jaina.

"It's Mara's ship," she said. "To land it without her explicit permission would be a slight against her."

Glad for the etiquette dodge, Leia smiled and patted Jaina's shoulder. "I know you'd put it down so softly that Mara wouldn't even shift in her bed," she said, and she winked at Jaina when the young woman looked up at her.

That brought a smile to Jaina's face, and Leia patted her shoulder again and left the bridge, heading for Mara's room.

She paused outside the door and lifted her hand to knock, but then hesitated, hearing quiet sounds coming from within. Leia put her ear to the door and listened carefully.

She heard only an occasional sniffle, and Leia understood that Mara was crying.

"Mara?" she called softly, and knocked on the door.

No reply, and Leia pushed the button and let the door slide away. Mara sat on her bed, her back to Leia, her shoulders hunched slightly, as if she had just gotten control of her emotions.

"Are you all right?" Leia asked. Mara nodded.

Leia moved over and sat on the bed beside her, draping her arm across Mara's shoulders as soon as she recognized the moistness rimming the woman's eyes.

"What is it?" she asked softly.

Mara sat up straighter and took a deep breath, ending in a forced smile. "Nothing at all," she answered.

Leia stared at her skeptically.

"A dream," Mara clarified. "And when I woke up, I was just being foolish."

"Do you want to talk about it?"

Mara shrugged.

Leia waited a moment longer, but the other woman apparently would not offer anything more. "We're nearing Coruscant," Leia explained. "Would you like me to help Jaina bring her in?"

"I can do it," Mara assured her. She rose and started for the door, a step full of stiffness that brought a wince to her face.

Leia was up in an instant, hooking Mara under the arm for support.

"I just slept in a twisted position," Mara tried to explain, but Leia, not buying that for a moment, didn't let go. She came around Mara's side and gently forced her to sit back on the edge of the bed.

"It's not the way you slept," she said. "It's the disease, isn't it?"

Mara looked up at her, successfully fighting back any trace of tears. "It came on again a little while ago," she admitted.

Leia sighed and shook her head, wishing there was something, anything, she could do to help her sister-in-law, her dear friend.

"That's fairly common, you said," she prompted. "Is there something different about the attack this time?"

Mara looked away.

"You have to tell me," Leia said, more sternly than she had intended, and the look Mara returned to her, not of anger or violation, but more of incredulity, set Leia back. Why did Mara have to tell her, after all? It wasn't as if she could do anything to help the woman. All of the others who had come down with this disease had told their doctors and had subsequently been referred to the best physicians in the New Republic. All of them had detailed every twinge, every ache, and had begged for any help at all. They were all dead, or soon would be.

"I'm sorry," Leia said, that disturbing thought hanging thick in her mind. "You don't have to tell me anything." She leaned forward and kissed Mara on the cheek, then rose to leave, offering the woman her hand.

Mara took that hand, but instead of getting up, she pulled Leia back down to the bed beside her. Then she stared long and hard into Leia's eyes. "My womb, this time," she said.

Leia crinkled her face, not understanding.

"This illness," Mara explained. "It came to me again while I slept, this time attacking my womb."

Leia's eyes widened with fear. "Did you defeat it?"

Mara nodded, and managed a slight smile. "It won't kill me yet," she replied with a less-than-comforting chuckle.

Leia nodded, full of admiration for this strong and stoic woman. Every time the disease had cropped up, Mara had focused her strength, had focused the Force inward, and beat it back. "But it was more difficult this time," Leia remarked, thinking she had the answer to Mara's uncharacteristic tearful reaction.

The woman shook her head. "Not so bad an attack," she replied.

"Then what?" Leia asked.

Mara took another deep breath. "My womb," she said solemnly.

Then it hit Leia fully. "You're afraid you might not be able to have any children," she said.

"I'm not so young anymore," Mara answered with a self-deprecating chuckle.

It was true enough—Mara, like Leia and Luke, was past forty, but except for the disease, she was very healthy and, as far as Leia knew, still able to have kids. Leia surely understood the woman's concerns, though, given the disease's attack on her very core of womanhood.

"When I married your brother, we talked about having kids," Mara explained. "He had watched your three grow so strong and wonderful, and more than anything in the world, we both wanted our own."

"You can still have them," Leia assured her.

"Perhaps," Mara answered. "But who knows, Leia? I'm growing tired of fighting, and this disease shows no signs of letting up."

"Nor is it gaining any ground," Leia reminded.

"I haven't given up," Mara assured her. "But I can't have kids now—I don't even know if I'd pass this along to them, or if they'd be killed by it inside of me. And who knows when it will be over, or if it will have caused too much damage for me to ever have them?"

Leia wanted to say something reassuring, but how could she possibly dismiss Mara's obviously well-grounded logic? She put her arm on the woman's shoulder. "You have to keep hoping," she said.

Mara managed a smile. "I will," she promised. "Besides, I've got Jaina under my wing now, and that's almost as good."

A quick flash across Leia's face betrayed her.

"What?" Mara asked with concern.

Leia blushed and laughed out loud.

"What?"

"There have been times when I've been so jealous of you and Jaina," Leia admitted, smiling with every word. "I see the bond between you, and I feel both wonderful that Jaina has found so inspiring a friend and mentor, and awful. When I see the two of you working together, I want to rush over and hug you and choke you all at once!"

Mara's expression revealed true concern, until Leia fell over her, wrapping her in a tight hug. "Oh, you'll beat this," Leia said. "You will. And you'll have babies, and maybe soon after you, Jaina will have her own." She pushed Mara back to arm's length. "And won't that be fun?" she asked. "The three of us sitting around, trading stories, while Luke gets to baby-sit them all."

It was the perfect thing to say at that moment, and the edges of Mara's lips turned up, just a bit, into a smile, and a flash of hope crossed her vivid green eyes.

Leia knew, though, as she and Mara headed back to the bridge, that it might well be a fleeting hope, and an image of herself and Jaina sitting and talking to Jaina's babies about their brave, deceased great-aunt Mara nearly broke her down at that moment.

Nearly, but she held back the tears. She had to, they all had to, for Mara's sake.

* * *

Jacen heard the telltale hiss and electric snapping as he approached the main chamber of the *Millennium Falcon*. Anakin was in there, he realized, and practicing with his lightsaber again.

Always practicing.

Normally, Jacen would leave his little brother alone, knowing that the two of them simply couldn't come to any philosophical agreements in their present states of mind. This time, though, after the spectacle of the council meeting, Jacen was in the mood for a good argument, and so he moved through the hatch.

There was Anakin, soaked in sweat, dodging and turning, his lightsaber flashing to parry each of the many energy zaps of the small remote as it floated all about him, seeking a hole in his defenses.

His little brother was getting good, Jacen had to admit, as Anakin brought the glowing blade down in a cross to the left, up high to the left, and back over to the right in flashing sequence, each movement neatly picking off an energy missile.

The sequence ended, and Anakin clicked his blade off and stood breathing heavily.

Jacen started a slow, almost mocking, clap.

"Could you do as well?" Anakin asked, before he had even turned around to face his brother.

"Does it matter?" Jacen replied.

Anakin crinkled his face in disdain and snorted.

"You spend half your life dancing around with that thing," Jacen commented.

"We're Jedi Knights, or soon to be," Anakin replied.

"And all the Jedi should spend all their waking hours alone, dancing about with remotes," Jacen said sarcastically.

"You practice," Anakin retorted.

"And I spend more time alone than you do," Jacen agreed.

Anakin looked at him skeptically, as if to ask, given that admission, what the problem might be.

"There is a reason for the solitude, and the practice," Jacen tried to explain.

"To hone our skills," Anakin replied.

Jacen was shaking his head before his little brother had even finished that expected response. "To deepen our understanding," he said.

"That again?"

"That, always," Jacen said firmly. "When you are practicing, what are you thinking about?"

Again, the skeptical expression.

"Are you fantasizing that you're hunting outlaw Gamorreans?" Jacen asked. "Saving the galaxy, as Dad once did?"

"When I'm in the practice regimen, my mind is clear of clutter," Anakin replied, but again, Jacen shook his head, unsatisfied with the answer.

"Right before you fall fully into the Force," he clarified, "and right after. What are you thinking about?"

Anakin's expression turned to one of anger.

"What are you thinking at those times?" Jacen pressed. "What fantasy battles do you wage in these sessions?"

"Why does it matter?" Anakin snapped.

"Because that's not the truth of the Force," Jacen answered, just as sharply. "You keep thinking of it as a tool, a weapon in your war against everything you see as bad. But that is such a limiting philosophy."

"It *is* a weapon," Anakin replied slowly. "A powerful weapon and a great responsibility."

Jacen shook his head. "Those are the minor truths of the Force," he said. "The ones that so many like you focus on to satisfy your personal hunger for glory."

Anakin seemed as if he was about to spit.

"The Force is a method of serenity and truth, not an outward-projecting tool to be used to further any single person's perception of good," Jacen lectured.

"Do you think the New Republic is evil?" Anakin scoffed.

"Neither good nor evil," Jacen explained, taking no offense. "But I don't agree with all of their actions. Certainly individual communities have suffered at their hands, just like during the reign of the Emperor."

"But this time, in actions taken for the greater good," Anakin argued vehemently, obviously not pleased with hearing any comparison between the New Republic and the old Empire.

Jacen merely chuckled, the simple, mocking reaction having the effect of turning Anakin's words around so that the younger brother had to recognize the subtle truth in them.

"I'm getting sick of hearing all of this," Anakin remarked.

"You'll hear it until you learn the truth," Jacen replied immediately. "That is my responsibility."

"Uncle Luke told you that?"

"This isn't about him," Jacen replied. "It's about you and me."

"He's going to put the Jedi Council back together," Anakin said, as if those words gave him a victory.

"He has to," Jacen said, his tone making it clear that he wasn't happy about the admission. "Or risk disaster because of the other Jedi Knights like you, running through the galaxy, righting every wrong." He waved his hands dismissively at his brother and turned to leave, but before he had gone two steps, Anakin grabbed him by the shoulder and pulled him about.

Anakin held up the pommel of his lightsaber. "This," he said emphatically, "is an instrument of law."

"No," Jacen snarled in his face. "That is a tool through which a Jedi might look inside himself and find his inner peace, a measuring stick for his acceptance of the Force."

Anakin's expression revealed clearly that he didn't get the point at all.

"To deny full entrance of the Force during such a practice session will weaken your parries and get you stung, and often," Jacen replied. "It's not about waging war, Anakin. It's about finding peace, and your place in the galaxy."

"Pretty words that mean nothing when the fighting starts," Anakin retorted.

"A Jedi at peace is a better warrior by far," Jacen said.

"Prove it." Anakin accentuated his challenge by turning on the blade, causing it to flash and hum to life right before Jacen's face.

"If I must, to get the point through your thick skull," Jacen answered, calmly walking by. He turned to face Anakin and brought his own lightsaber to glowing life before him.

Anakin closed the hatch—Uncle Luke wouldn't be happy to find them sparring in here, nor would their father!—and turned back to face his brother, who was already moving in closer with deliberate, measured steps. "Maybe you'll admit the truth when I beat you," Anakin said, but it was apparent that Jacen wasn't listening, was already falling into the levels of deepest concentration, the preface to the conscious emptiness that was pure Force acceptance.

Both paused for a long while, and then, suddenly, Anakin came rushing ahead, lightsaber twirling up and around, slicing down for Jacen's shoulder, and when Jacen easily parried, Anakin sent it around the other way, diving along the opposite angle.

Jacen parried that, too, catching Anakin's weapon with his own and bringing both around and down, back out to Jacen's left, and then around some more. When the blades were each out straight between the brothers, Jacen rolled his wrist, looping his blade further about Anakin's.

But Anakin was up to the measure, and he snapped his blade straight downward to break it free of the dangerous tangle, then brought it up again fast enough to knock Jacen's blade aside before his brother could put it point-in at his throat and score a quick victory.

Anakin brought his blade back past one shoulder and slapped it out, sparks flying as it connected with Jacen's parry. Again, Anakin attacked, and then again, as if he meant to beat his brother back right through a wall.

"Anger betrays you," Jacen said, and the words sent a chill through Anakin, words that spoke of the truth of the moment, and of the dark side of the Force, a place no Jedi could ever afford to visit.

Anakin's attack mellowed, went more to finesse, subtle thrusts and slashes, and deceptively slight movements to parry Jacen's every attack.

And so they went for many minutes, back and forth across the room, each seeming to gain a momentary edge only to lose it again through the other's quick response. They had to trust in themselves, and in each other, for there were no practice modes on their lightsabers. The slightest miss, or wrong deflection, or too-far thrust, could bring serious harm.

But they went on anyway, their philosophical differences playing themselves out through sword fighting, and before long, Jacen's warning notwithstanding, both were into it viciously, swiping and dodging, thrusting low and high, and more than parrying, batting each other's blade aside. Jacen came out of that fit first, mellowing his parries to those subtle and beautiful shifts and turns, and offering few offensive routines at all.

That sudden passivity only spurred Anakin on to greater intensity. His lightsaber slashed once, twice, and thrice from the left, then he spun about a complete circuit, reversing his grip as he went, and slashed, once, twice, thrice, from the right.

Jacen parried the first three from his left, then parried again and again from the right, and then . . . ducked.

And Anakin, so into the flow, thinking to take the third parry and spin back the other way, swooshed his blade right over his ducking brother and overbalanced as the weapon hit nothing but air.

Up Jacen came behind it, a sudden, subtle stab, that sent Anakin's lightsaber flying away and made the younger boy leap back and grab his stung hand.

Jacen clicked off his blade. "The Force is a power within, for the good of within," he said. "We're not a galactic patrol."

Anakin stared at his brother long and hard, clearly surprised that Jacen, who practiced far less than he, had so cleanly beaten him.

"Uncle Luke used the Force to destroy the Death Star," Anakin reminded.

"And Mara uses it now to battle her disease," Jacen replied. "Only when we are at peace within can we think of acting properly upon battles in the wider galaxy."

Anakin didn't reply, just stood clutching his hand and staring at his brother as a long, quiet moment slipped past.

"You're getting better," Jacen offered, and he winked at Anakin and headed for the door.

"I'll beat you next time," came Anakin's predictable call behind him, and Jacen smiled all the wider as he stepped out into the corridor leading to the ladder. Down below, he heard a clank of metal and a few more curses from his frustrated father, who was still hard at work.

"You're going to cross the lines!" Han yelled.

Chewbacca howled, and there came a sharp, sparking retort, followed by Han's "Yow!"

Chewie's head popped up through the open service panel.

"Get back here, hairball!" Han cried.

Chewbacca came out of the hole in a single, graceful spring—or at least, it seemed that way to Jacen until he noticed his father's arm sticking out of the hole behind the Wookiee, a sparking cable in hand, and the wisps of smoke wafting off of Chewie's bottom.

He couldn't help but chuckle, but he tried very hard to suppress it when the Wookiee stormed up to him, rubbing his bottom. "Aaaah, aeeeaaah!" Chewie scolded.

"I didn't do it," Jacen exclaimed. "It was Anakin."

Chewie howled again.

"No, we're not all the same," Jacen protested.

The Wookiee threw his arms out wide, covering about a

three-meter expanse, fingertip to fingertip, and shook his huge hairy head, growling and roaring.

"I never said you could snap-turn the *Falcon*," Jacen argued. "And I never did snap-turn the *Falcon*. Talk to Anakin."

"Aaaahh-aaah-aaa!"

"You think you might wander over and help me with this compensator?" Han asked dryly, turning the Wookiee about. He held a pair of cables in his hand, one of them throwing the occasional spark, and his face was covered in grease so that his eyes and teeth shone brightly in contrast.

Jacen laughed again—or started to, until Chewie spun back around and glowered at him. Nothing like a Wookiee glare to sap the mirth.

"Well?" Han asked, and with a resigned roar, Chewie turned about and headed back for the opened service panel.

A short time later, Mara, Jaina, and C-3PO found their friends at work on the *Falcon*, while Leia headed off to issue her full report to the council.

Jaina wasted no time in pulling her brothers aside and dazzling them with her tale of evading the Z-95 Headhunters. Anakin puffed up with satisfaction as she recounted the story, taking it as proof of his understanding of the Force.

Jacen didn't bother to start up the argument again.

Similarly, C-3PO rushed to R2-D2 and began spewing every detail of the adventure with Nom Anor, "a most disagreeable person."

R2-D2 clicked and whistled, seeming impressed, especially when C-3PO told of his final encounter with the Rhommamoolian leader, one in which he had faced down the mighty Nom Anor.

Mara, meanwhile, filled in Luke about the deadly intervention by Wurth Skidder.

"He's a hair trigger," she explained.

"You're sure he wasn't just trying to help?"

"We didn't need his help," Mara answered resolutely. "And

he knew it, too. The *Jade Sabre*'s got more than enough fire-power to blast a few Headhunters. Besides, by the time he got near to us, we were breaking clear. No, Wurth just wanted some kicks, and to add a couple of kill markers under his canopy."

Luke shrugged, feeling more than a little helpless. A hundred Jedi Knights roamed the galaxy now—how could he keep them all under wraps?

"One at a time," Mara said, and when Luke looked at her curiously, she merely returned a wistful smile. "You're hearing all the problems, and they seem like they'll overwhelm you, but that only means you have to deal with them one at a time. Your sister put Wurth in his place—for now, at least—so I don't think you need to worry about him for a while."

"How do you feel about a trip to the Outer Rim?" Luke asked her, and now it was Mara's turn to offer a curious expression, and Luke's to give a wry grin.

He fell over her, then, in a great hug and a heartfelt laugh. He always felt so much better when his wife was around.

Chewie stood quietly outside the council chamber, leaning back against the wall, his hands behind his head. When Mara and Jaina had come to the *Falcon*, Han had sent the Wookiee here to escort Leia, but Chewbacca understood that he had really been sent here just to get him away from Han and the *Falcon*. The repairs weren't going so well, and Han and Chewie had spent the bulk of their last hour together just howling at each other. They both needed a break, and Chewie was glad for it.

But when one of the councilors, Fyor Rodan of Commenor, came out of the room unexpectedly and began wagging his finger at Chewie and grumbling about some intractable argument over certain trade privileges with Chewie's home planet of Kashyyyk, the Wookiee realized that he hadn't been away from the yelling Han for long enough.

Leia came out of the council chamber a few moments later and dropped her head in her hands. There, across the hall and in a closet, hung Fyor Rodan, his collar hooked on a coatrack.

"Let me compliment you on your choice of friends," the councilor said dryly.

"Chewie, take him down," Leia instructed.

Chewbacca growled and shook his head.

"Councilor Triebakk will hear of this," Fyor Rodan threatened. "You know Triebakk, don't you?" he taunted Chewie.

Chewie closed the closet door.

"You can't go around treating councilors like that," Leia scolded, coming forward. But then she stopped, considering the meeting she had just walked out of, the unending squabbling over minor details, the open disdain two of the councilors had shown to her concerning her failure at Osarian-Rhommamool, the obvious posturing for political reasons.

"Let's go," she said, turning down the corridor, Bolpuhr gliding behind her.

"Aaaaah?" Chewie asked, and when Leia turned back, the Wookiee motioned for the door.

"With any luck, they won't find him until after we've left," Leia explained. Chewie gave an assenting howl, and off they went.

Leia's mood improved immediately, and greatly, when they finally reached the *Falcon*, when she saw again that glimmer in her husband's eye. After all these years, the fire remained between Leia and Han, a deep and honest love and respect.

"Chewie found you," Han remarked, moving to give Leia a big hug. "Probably heard you yelling from six levels away."

"Mara told you about Nom Anor," Leia reasoned.

"And about Wurth Skidder," Luke added, coming down the landing ramp.

Leia sighed and shook her head. "You've got to do something about that one," she replied.

"One problem at a time," Luke explained.

"What now?" the exasperated Leia asked.

"Well, we're going on a little trip," Han told her.

"Far away, I hope," Leia added.

Han laughed. "About as far as you can get."

"And it still won't be far enough for me," Leia said, turning back to glower in the general direction of the senate building. "Could anyone do enough to satisfy that group?"

Luke chuckled, knowing the answer. "No one point of view would ever satisfy so—" He paused, looking for just the right word. "—eclectic a group."

"How diplomatically put," Leia said. "So what's the problem now?"

"I'll fill you in on the way."

"Jedi?"

Han's chuckle told Leia that she had guessed correctly, and in light of that, she was even more eager to go. A big part of her wanted a vacation from all the turmoil, but after the incident with Wurth Skidder, Leia was beginning to take these Jedi problems personally. She hadn't given much thought to Luke's plans about re-forming the Jedi Council, hadn't really considered it her problem, given all the responsibilities the formal authorities of the New Republic kept laying on her, but now she was beginning to see the whole picture, and better that image would be if Luke could put the Jedi Knights in order.

"We'll get to see an old friend," Han offered, and Leia looked at him curiously.

"Lando," Han explained.

So much for any thoughts of vacation, Leia realized, for anytime Lando was involved, even peripherally, situations seemed to get very complicated, and usually dangerous. In truth, she wasn't particularly thrilled with her husband having any dealings with Lando; the man always seemed to pull Han into something on the very edge of disaster. Of course, that only strengthened her resolve to go along.

"What about Mara?" she asked Luke, working hard to keep the signs of her deep concern only minimally on her expression.

"She's coming," Luke replied. "She and Jaina are plotting the course even now. Assuming we can get the *Falcon* flying again."

Leia looked at Han.

"Anakin," he explained, and somehow, Leia wasn't surprised.

"Are you sure Mara's up to it?" Leia asked Luke.

"Try to stop her," Luke replied.

Leia managed a smile. For all the pain and the impending threat of death, Mara was determined to live her life fully, to live without this unknown disease being the center of her existence.

That truth only made Leia even more glad to have Mara as Jaina's mentor.

SEVEN

Launch

"Was there ever any doubt?" Bensin Tomri asked sarcastically when Danni announced that she would go on the Spacecaster shuttle to the frozen fourth planet of the Helska system.

"You're not going alone," Tee-ubo put in, and Danni didn't disagree. In the end, they decided that three should go, including someone with a geological background and with Danni captaining the mission and piloting the rickety old ship.

A short while later, Yomin Carr answered the knock on his door to find Danni standing in the hall, her smile coy.

"You have come to ask me to volunteer," Yomin Carr reasoned.

"I thought you should be rewarded for your diligence and hard work," Danni replied. "You should have been the one to spot the comet."

"So now you offer me the scientific chance of a lifetime?" Yomin Carr asked in all seriousness.

Danni nodded and smiled at him, as though he should be pleased.

"I am afraid that I must refuse," the Yuuzhan Vong warrior went on. Inside his ear, the little tizowyrm continued its vibrations, and Yomin Carr fell into them for a moment, recognizing that it might be time for a bit of levity. "You're asking

94

me because no one else is crazy enough to go along on that broken-down garbage scow you call a shuttle," he said, and forced a grin.

Now Danni was laughing, and not disagreeing.

"But that would not be proper," Yomin Carr said a moment later, again in all seriousness. He understood the implications here. According to his instructions, under no circumstances was he to go anywhere near the base planet. On pain of death, and a dishonorable death at that, Yomin Carr was to have no physical connection to the war coordinator, and no contact at all other than the secure villip-talk. "I am not long in ExGal," Yomin Carr elaborated. "Most of the others have been on Belkadan longer than I have been in the organization. I could not usurp their opportunity."

"You already said it," Danni replied. "Most of the others don't even want to go."

"Ah, but they do," Yomin Carr assured her. "They are afraid of the craft, as am I, and as you should be, but in truth, any scientist would be eager for this opportunity."

"Any scientist other than Yomin Carr," Danni said sarcastically.

"I believe in propriety," Yomin Carr answered, and he took some satisfaction in the fact that Danni, based on all of his actions since he had arrived on Belkadan, could not dispute the claim. Yomin Carr was always on time for his shift. Yomin Carr stayed true to his post, hour after hour, day after day, week after week, while all of the others—including, to a lesser extent, Danni—had eased around the edges of their responsibilities.

"Find your crew among those who have better earned the right," Yomin Carr said.

They were both all smiles when Danni left him, accepting his polite refusal, but as soon as she had gone, as soon as he had closed the door of his private room, Yomin Carr's expression turned to a concerned scowl. He wondered then if he should just kill them all in their sleep and end the potential threat of discovery. He fell to his knees and bent over quickly, smacking his forehead against the floor, calling out to Yun-Harla, the Cloaked Goddess, and Yun-Yammka, the Slayer, for guidance. His fingers whitened from the press he put on the floor, playing out his warrior urges against the unyielding surface.

And then Yomin Carr was calm once more and in control of his thoughts. He had to weigh the threat against the potential disaster and to help the scales balance. He went and retrieved the small coffer, for the tizowyrm had been in too long and was getting dangerously close to exhaustion. If the creature was left in too long, it would literally vibrate itself to death.

The warrior went out from his room soon after, again in the dark of night, stealthily to the small Spacecaster.

Truly this was the most distasteful part of Yomin Carr's extensive training, this working with machines, abandoning the living tools his own people employed. He reminded himself of the importance to the greater good, stoically accepting his role, as he had during those years of training, and indeed, he did take some pride in the fact that, among the entire force of Praetorite Vong, Yomin Carr was probably the finest technician.

He set up shop openly—too many were about for him to hope to accomplish his tasks without discovery—hanging lights and making no effort to conceal the clanking of metallic tools.

Sure enough, Danni Quee came out to him within the hour, to find him hard at work on the Spacecaster's inertial compensator.

"The gasket on the pressure pump had wriggled out of place," Yomin Carr honestly explained, and indeed, the Yuuzhan Vong warrior was working to the benefit of the shuttle at that time. Had Danni come out here earlier, when Yomin Carr had been disconnecting the final signal initiator on the communications port, she might have figured that something was amiss.

"I'm leaving in three hours," she informed him.

"Just checking the vital systems," Yomin Carr replied. "The hyperdrive is not up to standards, but it will get you there, though it will not be a fast journey. The ion drive is running efficiently."

Danni nodded, for she had just done the same checks.

"What about that compensator?" she asked.

"It was only the gasket," Yomin Carr replied, and he ran a laser sealer along the outside of the ring and pronounced the problem solved.

Danni came over and inspected the work, then nodded her approval. "You're sure you don't want to come along?" she asked. "I've got Bensin Tomri and Cho Badeleg coming, but we'll make room for you."

"Excellent choices," Yomin Carr said. "But, no, putting another in the Spacecaster would jeopardize the success of the mission. You will desire some time at the planet for close study, but you will not have enough supplies to take four out there and back, especially if that hyperdrive is not performing well."

"I smell a Baldavian pocket hare," Danni replied, referring to the skittish creature that was often held up as a symbol of cowardice.

Yomin Carr merely laughed, understanding that she had just kiddingly insulted him, but not getting the reference at all. "Go get your sleep," he instructed, and he turned back to his controls.

Danni put her hand on his shoulder. "I appreciate this," she said.

Yomin Carr nodded and kept his smile in check. If she only understood the irony of that statement!

A short time later, Yomin Carr clicked on the distance communicator and gave a call to the nearby ExGal-4 station. All the signals on his screens offered confirmation that the signal had been sent, but of course, thanks to Yomin Carr's efforts, it had not.

They would go out into space properly muted.

That only half satisfied the cautious Yuuzhan Vong agent, though, for what dangers might occur if Danni and the others happened upon another vehicle on their way to the war coordinator's base? There wasn't much traffic out here, but it was possible, especially since others might have tracked the incoming worldship.

With that in mind, Yomin Carr went straight to his villips when he returned to his room, and lifted the blanket on the connection to Prefect Da'Gara.

When Da'Gara's villip inverted, Yomin Carr recognized the gnullith attached to the prefect's face, their symbiosis so complete that the villip considered it a part of its host and appropriately reflected it in its imaging.

"Let them come to us," Da'Gara answered after Yomin Carr informed him of the mission. "And you did well to quiet them."

"Take heed of the woman called Danni Quee," Yomin Carr explained. "She is formidable."

A smile erupted on the face of the prefect-impersonating villip, one so wide that the edges of the prefect's lips showed around the gnullith. "One to convert?"

Yomin Carr considered that possibility for a long moment. Truly Danni would make a good Yuuzhan Vong warrior, but that very trait likely damned her, for he doubted that her strong will could be so bent against her own people. His expression, reflected perfectly by his villip before Prefect Da'Gara, showed his range of feelings and doubts clearly.

"A worthy sacrifice, then," Da'Gara answered. "She will be killed honorably and at the proper time."

"You honor me by accepting my words, Prefect," Yomin Carr replied, and Da'Gara had indeed done so, considering that this was an issue of sacrifice, as important a rite as could be found among the Yuuzhan Vong. While nearly all reasoning species understood that death was inevitable, the Yuuzhan Vong culture embraced it, nearly to the point of seeing life itself as preparation for death. Everyone would die, they understood, so *how* one died was the important factor. Normally, they reserved the most dishonorable deaths for their enemies.

"How long will Belkadan survive in its present state?" the prefect asked.

"Not long," Yomin Carr promised. He had taken some readings that morning and had done the calculations. "The gases will reach critical mass within a couple of days. The storms should come on strong soon after."

"You have your ooglith cloaker?" Da'Gara asked. "It would not do to have one who has performed as well as Yomin Carr die uneventfully on a distant world."

"I am prepared, Prefect," Yomin Carr answered, standing straight in light of yet another high compliment. His duties were almost at their end, sadly so, for after the transformation of Belkadan, he was merely to remain on the planet and ride out the greenhouse storms while the conquest was under way. "I only hope that you will find some use for me while I wait."

"It may well be," Da'Gara answered. "Perhaps we will use the data from your station to facilitate the arrival of the next group of worldships. More likely, Executor Nom Anor will hear of your fine work and gather you to help with his espionage."

There came a knock on Yomin Carr's door then, and he quickly covered the villip and replaced it in his closet, then pulled off his shirt and ran to the door, rubbing his eyes all the way to make it look as if he had been sleeping.

Garth Breise stood in the hallway, coils of rope looped about his shoulder. "You ready?" he asked.

"It is still dark," Yomin Carr remarked.

"I'd rather face the dangers of the forest night than the wrath of Danni Quee," Garth Breise replied.

Yomin Carr ran to retrieve his shirt. It was all going so very well.

The early morning air was chill, but not crisp, and thick with a strange sulfuric smell. Garth Breise twitched his nose repeatedly but made no comment, Yomin Carr noted with some relief. He reminded himself that he would be more sensitive to the odor, because he knew what it portended. Likely, Garth Breise hardly noticed it.

"Do you want to see them off first?" Yomin Carr asked, motioning toward the bay, where Danni and the others were preparing to leave.

"I already said my good-byes," Garth replied. "I just want to get this stupid work over with."

"The tower is only a hundred meters high," Yomin Carr remarked.

"Only," the sullen Garth echoed sarcastically. "And cold and windy up at the top."

"We may be fortunate enough to find a redcrested cougar waiting for us at the base," Yomin Carr went on, but Garth Breise wasn't smiling. "It would save us the climb."

That disturbing notion in mind, Garth Breise paused at the outer perimeter control tower and redirected the nearby spotlights to brighten all the area around the base of the tower. Then he took a blaster from the weapons locker, securing it on his belt, and pulled out another one, offering it to Yomin Carr, who politely declined.

They exited the compound, closing the door behind them, and started for the tower. As they approached, both noticed movement around the base of the tower, almost as if the very ground had come writhing to life.

"What the heck are these?" Garth Breise asked, bending low to inspect the source of the strange movement: a swarm of reddish brown beetles.

"Perhaps the cause of our transmitter problems," Yomin Carr offered.

"The cable was chewed by something bigger than beetles."

"But if some of them climbed inside after it was broken . . . ," Yomin Carr said, and he left the thought to Garth's imagination. He knew that wasn't the case, of course, or at least, not the only source of the comm trouble, but Garth did not—and if some of the beetles actually *had* crawled inside, the damage to the cable could be complete.

"I didn't see any out here when I found the break," Garth said.

Yomin Carr looked up, up, up. "Do you still think it worth the climb?" he asked. "Or should you first inspect the length of cable?"

Garth paused a long while before answering, and Yomin Carr thought he had convinced the man to abandon the climb. "Up," Garth said, pulling the coil from his shoulder. "Let's get it over with."

Yomin Carr started to argue, then stopped. It might indeed be better for the mission to dissuade Garth from going up now, but personally, Yomin Carr was growing more agitated, more eager for action, by the minute. He wanted to make this climb.

And so they did, hand over hand, securing each foothold, securing each length of rope, and then climbing on to the next level. It was still dark when they made the top, Garth Breise leading the way.

"There you have it," he announced, grabbing the disconnected junction box. "The wind."

Yomin Carr stepped up beside him. "Perhaps," he agreed.

A thunderous roar from behind signaled that Danni and the other two were on their way, and the pair looked about to see the Spacecaster soaring into the dark sky, her fiery plumes blotting out the stars.

"I'd rather be up here than up there," Garth noted.

"But a threat up here are you," Yomin Carr said.

"What?" Garth asked, turning about, his expression curious. Yomin Carr stole that look, and stole the man's breath, by stiffening two fingers and stabbing them hard into Garth's windpipe. The man gasped and grabbed at his throat with one hand, and Yomin Carr, with those same two fingers, struck him a blow on the wrist that broke his grasp on the tower.

Garth flailed wildly, trying to catch a hold, but Yomin Carr's hands were always in the way, deflecting him, keeping him at bay. And then, out of nowhere it seemed, the Yuuzhan Vong warrior produced a small, shining blade and thrust it menacingly at Garth's face. That was only to pull the man's arms in, though, for Yomin Carr fast reversed his attack, slashing the sharp blade upward, catching the taut rope right where it looped over one of the tower cross poles.

Garth's arms worked in wild circles as he tried desperately to hold his balance. "Why?" he gasped.

Yomin Carr could have finished the task with a simple push, but he held back, thoroughly enjoying the look of the sheerest horror on the man's face, the frantic and futile efforts.

And then the scream as Garth Breise tumbled over backward, plummeting down the side of the tower, striking one cross pole and launching into a somersaulting fall.

Yomin Carr was glad that Garth had redirected all the floodlights—they gave him a better view of the final descent and the bone-smashing impact. Because you gave me an excuse, the Yuuzhan Vong silently answered desperate Garth's last question.

He had one moment of regret: when he considered that Garth might have crushed some of his pet dweebits.

Already far, far away, Danni Quee looked out her rear viewer at the receding Belkadan, and her expression fast changed from wistful to curious. "Bring us about," she instructed Bensin Tomri, who was at the controls.

"The straighter the line to Helska, the better," Bensin replied, obviously unsure of the craft's condition. "I was about to make the jump to hyperspace."

"No, you have to see this," Danni replied.

The third member of the team, a short, dark man with hair the consistency of wool, Cho Badeleg, came up beside her. "Heck of a storm," he remarked, seeing, as Danni had, the roiling clouds on the edge of Belkadan's rim.

Bensin Tomri gasped when he brought the Spacecaster about; then all three stared in horror when they noted the scope of the storm, and the greenish yellow tint of it, something that reminded Danni of the sunsets she had been witnessing of late.

"Call the compound and tell them to secure everything," she instructed.

"The tower's not likely fixed yet," Cho Badeleg reminded her.

Danni pulled out her portable communicator. "Bring us in close," she instructed, and Bensin Tomri agreed, though they all experienced some second thoughts when he skipped off the edge of Belkadan's atmosphere and the Spacecaster shook so violently that it seemed as if it would fall apart.

"Tee-ubo?" Danni called, and she winced at the amount of static on the normally clear communicator. "Can you hear me?"

"Danni?" came a broken reply, and then Tee-ubo said something. The three thought they heard mention of Garth Breise, but they couldn't make it out.

"There's a storm south of you," Danni said slowly and distinctly. "A big one. Did you hear?" She repeated it several times, and Tee-ubo replied as much as she could, though only single words, sometimes only single syllables, came through the increasing static.

"Probably from the storm," Cho Badeleg remarked, and Danni gave up and clicked off the communicator.

Danni let her questioning gaze fall over each of the other two.

"You want to go back," Cho Badeleg reasoned.

"If we go back down there, we probably aren't coming back up anytime soon," Bensin Tomri put in. "Especially if that storm rolls in. We're lucky this thing broke orbit in the first place."

Cho Badeleg spent a long moment staring out at the spectacle of the storm. "It doesn't seem well developed," he noted. "No noticeable swirl, no defined eye."

"You think they'll be all right?" Danni asked.

"Once we get away from this static, we can relay the information with the ship's communicator," Bensin Tomri offered. "You've got to make the decision. Do we go on, or go back?"

Danni thought long and hard on that one. In the end, though, she was a devoted scientist, and certainly it seemed to her as if she and the other two were taking a greater risk than any of those they had left behind. "Tee-ubo said something about Garth," she reasoned. "He's probably got the tower fixed."

"On we go, then," Bensin Tomri said, and he turned the Spacecaster about and started again to make his calculations for the jump to lightspeed.

As they left the planet far behind, Danni went to the ship's communicator and gave a detailed report of the storm in the west, then waited a moment to see if a reply would be forthcoming. When no call came back, she hoped that they had heard her, and that the repairs on the tower simply hadn't been completed to the point where they could respond.

Nom Anor's eyes twinkled with the reflections of the plumes trailing the missiles launched toward the enemy city of Osa-Prime, an extraplanetary attack he'd been planning for weeks. Tamaktis Breetha had opposed the strike, knowing it would lead to open warfare between the planets, but when several high-ranking Rhommamoolian officials had been found murdered, the former mayor had found little support for his arguments.

Nom Anor hoped that the *Mediator* wouldn't detect the launch in time to get its starfighters away to intercept the missiles, but that, too, had not been left to chance. For hours and

hours, the executor and Shok Tinoktin had studied the planetary courses and the positioning of the New Republic ship
and had launched the missiles from a point where the initial
explosive liftoff and subsequent burn would be most difficult
to detect. Once they broke orbit, the missiles would all but
shut down, seeming as insignificant specks, and by the time
their rockets fired again, entering Osarian's atmosphere, it
would be too late for the *Mediator* to get at them.

To further the probability of success, Nom Anor had spent
hours that morning talking to Commander Ackdool, acting
conciliatory and explaining that, now that the meddlesome
Leia Solo was gone, he and the commander might strike a
deal to bring an end to the conflict. They had even scheduled
a meeting on the *Mediator* between Nom Anor and his dele-
gates and a diplomatic party from Osarian.

Commander Ackdool liked the thought of scoring such an
unexpected diplomatic victory, Nom Anor knew. It was said
that Ackdool had been given the ship primarily because he
was a Mon Calamarian, who, with the retirement of Ackbar,
were underrepresented among the fleet. Ackdool had heard
the quiet murmurs of discontent concerning his appointment,
of course, and that would make him all the more eager.
Furthermore, the commander was so secure about the overwhelming power of his ship compared to the meager power of
the people on the two planets that he would never suspect
the ruse.

Of course, the fallout from this attack would be great and
would likely force Nom Anor to flee Rhommamool altogether. But that was fine with him, for his mission here was
nearly complete, and if those missiles hit Osa-Prime and
brought the war to full conflagration, then he would happily
move on. His job now was distraction, to keep the New Republic so concerned with the explosions near to the Core that
they didn't get a chance to turn their eyes outward.

The longer Prefect Da'Gara could operate in obscurity, the

more entrenched Nom Anor's people would become, and the more worldships they could get into place.

Three hours later, Nom Anor received the outraged call from Commander Ackdool. Missile plumes had been detected in Osarian's atmosphere.

Nom Anor took full responsibility, justifying the attack in response to the assassinations of several officials—officials he had secretly ordered killed. Then he curtly cut Ackdool off.

He and Shok Tinoktin focused on the video screen, tuned to an Osarian broadcast channel. They heard the frantic reporter in Osa-Prime detailing the confusion and panic and then, after a pause, solemnly reporting the sight of the missile trails.

The holocam turned up in time to catch the descending lines of fire streaking through the night sky.

Other missiles and scores of starfighters went up to meet them.

But they couldn't get them all.

Moments later, Osa-Prime was in flames.

Nom Anor thought it a particularly glorious day.

EIGHT

Layers

"You fought with Anakin again," Luke remarked to Jacen when he found his older apprentice sitting on the wall surrounding the *Millennium Falcon*'s current dock, an open courtyard on the planet Reecee. Han and Chewie had flown here from Coruscant, explaining to their passengers, Jacen, Anakin, C-3PO, and Leia, only that they needed to make one stop before bouncing out to the Outer Rim. Leia had managed to elude Bolpuhr on Coruscant, leaving the Noghri behind in a den with his kin. She didn't want his overprotectiveness—especially now, when she honestly felt that she needed a break from the layers of intrigue and bureaucracy that her standing had forced upon her. Bolpuhr, despite his good intentions—and the good intentions of the Noghri in general—toward her, could be more than a bit smothering. Getting away from Bolpuhr was a small personal victory for her, a symbol that she was breaking free of her station and responsibility, if only for a little while.

The *Jade Sabre*, with Mara and Luke aboard, had just put down in the bay next to the *Falcon*, and all of them were now awaiting the arrival of Jaina, who, to her absolute delight, was flying Luke's personal X-wing, along with R2-D2.

"I found him practicing with his lightsaber," Jacen replied honestly. "He wanted to see how far he's come, and so did I."

"I'm not talking about the sword fight," Luke explained. "Though I don't think that your father would be happy to hear that you two were wrestling with lightsabers in the main compartment of his ship. I'm talking about your war of words."

That caught Jacen by surprise, and he stared at his uncle, his mentor, looking for some sign concerning Luke's feelings on the subject.

He couldn't read the man at all.

"An honest difference of opinion," Jacen said, turning away. "That's all."

"Concerning the role of the Jedi," Luke said.

"Concerning the role of the Force," Jacen corrected, turning back to face him.

"Do you think you could enlighten me?" Luke asked. There was no trace of sarcasm in his voice, nothing mocking at all about the way he phrased the question.

But Jacen, too awed by his uncle's seeming omnipotence, didn't see it that way. He sighed and shook his head, and turned away yet again.

Luke hopped up to take a seat on the wall beside him. "You know the decision I face," he said.

"I thought you had already made up your mind," Jacen replied.

Luke conceded that with a nod. "Almost," he said. "But if you've got something to tell me, some insight about why I shouldn't reconvene the Jedi Council, then now is the time to speak."

Jacen looked long and hard at his uncle and was surprised to find honest respect staring back at him. He was a sixteen-year-old kid—so often at odds with the adults around him that he wasn't used to being valued by them. Even Luke, whom he admired so much, was in place in the role of teacher—and a teacher of often harsh lessons.

"I don't know how to tell you," Jacen tried to explain.

"Just speak what is in your heart," Luke prompted.

"It's just that . . ." Jacen paused and sighed again. He

stared at Luke intently then, seeing the calm contentment on the man's boyish face, the wistful smile. Above all else, Uncle Luke, with all of those harrowing experiences behind him, and despite the obvious trials ahead of him, seemed to Jacen to be in a place of spiritual comfort, a place of harmony. Here was this man, the epitome of what it was to be a Jedi Knight, and Jacen, though he recognized that truth, meant to argue that very philosophy against him. "The Force seems so pure a thing to me, a clean truth of who I am, of who we all are," he began tentatively. "I don't know; putting a governing bureaucracy in place for the Jedi seems kind of like putting a bluespotted preaky bird in a cage, or even like killing one and stuffing it to keep it safe so that you can continue to enjoy it."

Luke spent a long while mulling over those words. "I'm not sure you're wrong," he said. "Those are the same fears I've had. I think we feel pretty much the same way about the Force. But," he said, raising a finger to quiet Jacen before the young man could enthusiastically jump in, "the Jedi are possessed of powers beyond the understanding and control of those people around them. And with those powers come responsibilities."

"To people like Borsk Fey'lya?" Jacen asked sarcastically.

"Yes," Luke answered simply. "To the people making the decisions that affect the lives of so many others."

"Borsk Fey'lya's not deserving of your time," Jacen spat, but Luke's reaction surprised him.

"I'm afraid of your words, and the way you speak them," Luke said in all seriousness, eyeing his nephew with an expression that reflected his sincere concern.

Jacen didn't understand.

"Pride," Luke explained, shaking his head.

Jacen echoed the word aloud, and as he said it, in more of a questioning manner than a statement, he began to understand. "Pride?" By diminishing Borsk Fey'lya, he was, in effect, elevating himself above the Bothan.

"A dangerous flaw," Luke warned. "We've all got it—too

much of it, usually—and we've all got to work hard to keep it from constantly holding us back."

"I just fear—" Jacen started to say.

"Control," Luke finished for him. "The regimen. You don't even like the academy any longer, according to your brother."

"My brother's got a big mouth," Jacen replied.

Luke laughed, and certainly didn't disagree.

"I don't like the academy," Jacen admitted.

"It gave you much of what you have today," Luke reminded.

"Did it?" the young man questioned. "I was strong in the Force—it's in my blood—and how much purer might it run if I had been trained as you were trained, one-on-one with Yoda?"

Luke didn't argue the point, just looked at Jacen with admiration. It was good for a Jedi to question, he knew. Discipline was necessary, but unquestioning obedience was a limiting thing, not a growing one. And Jacen's point about the one-on-one training had hit home to Luke; even he felt that the academy had gone too far away from that, thus leaving too many potential Jedi Knights without the necessary guidance to find their full power and, even more importantly, to resist the tempting dark side. That's why they had gone back to the master-apprentice system, and Luke right now was one of only a few Masters with more than one student.

"I'm not even going to tell you that you're wrong," Luke said, putting a hand on Jacen's shoulder. "But I will assure you that, as you grow older, you'll come to see things a bit differently."

"The more complete picture?" Jacen asked, a bit of sarcasm evident in his tone.

"You think I like dealing with Borsk Fey'lya?" Luke asked with a tension-breaking burst of laughter. He patted Jacen's shoulder and started to walk away then, but as he neared the *Falcon*'s lowered landing ramp, Jacen's voice stopped him.

"Uncle Luke!" And when Luke turned about, Jacen added in all seriousness, "Choose right."

"Oh, do be careful, Lady Vader," C-3PO said, his tone, if not his wording, mimicking that of Bolpuhr, and mimicking, too, the title many of the Noghri used for her.

Leia turned to the droid and scowled fiercely, and even more so when she heard Mara laughing behind her.

"You call me that again and I'll send you into an oil bath with an open flame," she promised C-3PO quietly.

"But you informed me that I was to be your Noghri body-guard on this journey," C-3PO protested in all seriousness.

"Only to keep you quiet before you let Bolpuhr in on my plans to get away from him," Leia returned, and the droid, though he really couldn't change the metallic expression on his face, truly seemed perplexed. Leia couldn't help but laugh at it all. Sometimes—no, all the time!—C-3PO took her words far too literally.

Across the room, on the bridge of the *Jade Sabre*, Mara surely understood. "Feeling a bit trapped by the attention?" she asked.

Leia turned and nodded. "I don't know," she said with a shake of her head. "Maybe I've reached a point in my life where I want to think of myself as Leia. Not Princess Leia, not Councilor Leia, not Chief of State Leia, and not," she finished, turning to stare pointedly at C-3PO, "Lady Vader. Just Leia."

When she turned back to Mara, she found the woman nodding her agreement.

"Do you think that selfish?" Leia asked Mara.

Mara smiled all the wider. "I think it human," she answered. "Once we're past saving the galaxy, we have to spend some time saving ourselves."

Coming from Mara, the woman so obviously balancing on the precipice between life and death, that statement carried even more weight.

"But you're my age," Leia dared to remark. "Yet you want children now. I can't imagine doing that again."

"Because you've already done it," Mara replied. "Physical age and stages of life are two different things, I've come to believe."

Leia paused a moment to consider the truth of those words, to consider her own perspective of the universe around her, how she had willingly, eagerly, run away from her expected responsibilities at the Core, even leaving her bodyguard far behind, of how she wanted, truly desired, to turn down the dial of her life's work, to sit back for a while and enjoy all the prosperity that her actions and sacrifices had helped bring about in the galaxy. Then she contrasted her desires against those of Mara, who wanted to begin the adventure of children, who wanted to remain vibrant and in the middle of things, tutoring Jaina, living through Jaina.

Leia felt no jealousy at all in that moment of revelation. Just sadness, wishing there was some way she could help Mara rid herself of the dreaded disease and get all that she desired—and deserved.

"You'll get it," Leia said quietly.

Mara stared at her curiously.

"All that you want," Leia clarified. "That disease, or whatever it is afflicting you, won't slow you down."

Mara's smile showed contentment and courage. "I know."

"Watch my back," Han said to Chewie as they entered Riebold's Foam and Sizzle, a notorious drinking hole known for murder, mischief, and mayhem. The place was loud and rowdy, with thugs from several worlds—human, Bothan, Rodian, Tervig, Vuvrian, Snivvian—milling about, cutting deals and cutting each other. If you killed a rival in the Foam and Sizzle bloodlessly, and disposed of the body, nobody noticed or cared; if you made a mess in the process, you had to flip over a few coins to cover the cost of cleaning.

Han glanced up at his Wookiee friend as he spoke, and

took comfort in that old fire in Chewie's eyes, the eager light that he and his hairy friend had shared so many times in their earlier years. He and Chewie weren't strangers to places such as this, certainly, but it had been a while, and they were getting older.

A drunken Gamorrean staggered over and bumped the pair, rebounding off Han to slam against Chewie, who didn't budge a centimeter. The Wookiee looked down at the porcine creature and growled, and the Gamorrean stumbled away, tripping to the floor and not even bothering to try to get back up, just crawling away from the huge and imposing Wookiee with all speed.

Han liked having a Wookiee beside him.

Chewie looked down at him and issued a series of protesting grunts and groans.

"I know, I know," Han conceded, for he didn't like being in this place any more than his big hairy friend. "But I'm not going out to see Lando without learning a bit more about what he's got going on out there. It's got to be more than mining—with his connections, he could get mining rights to a thousand lucrative sites near the Core. No, he's up to something, and before I come bouncing in on him with my family along, I want to know what it is."

Han snapped his fingers, ending in a wide smile. "Bagy," he said, pointing to a Sullustan across the way.

Chewie recognized the target, a notorious con artist named Dugo Bagy, and gave another less-than-enthusiastic groan.

The pair bumped their way through the establishment, through the crowd, and when they finally had a straight line of sight to Dugo Bagy, and Dugo Bagy to them, the Sullustan scoffed down his drink and started to move away.

Han signaled left, and Chewie circled that way, while Han went right. Dugo Bagy, apparently focusing on Han, started right, but skidded to a stop and darted back to the left—to thud into Chewie, Dugo Bagy's face barely reaching the

Wookiee's belly, and the Sullustan's momentum not budging huge and powerful Chewie a centimeter.

"Ah, Han Solo," Dugo Bagy said, when Han moved up behind him. "So good to see you."

"Sit down, Dugo," Han replied, pulling a chair out from a nearby table.

"You be buying, I be sitting," Dugo Bagy said with an obviously nervous chuckle, and he moved to the seat even as he spoke, Han taking a chair on one side of him, Chewie on the other.

"Why are you so nervous?" Han asked after all three were in place.

"Nervous?" Dugo Bagy echoed skeptically.

Han shot him "the stare," as his kids had come to call it, that look of complete disregard for the obvious lie coming out of Dugo Bagy's mouth that shut up the Sullustan and made him glance around nervously for a waitress.

"Hey," Han prompted, pulling him back around.

"Forgive me," Dugo Bagy said somewhat calmly. "I am surprised to see you in here, as many others are. Just to talk with you makes me suspect."

"I haven't gone that far over," Han assured the smuggler. "And I haven't been giving any of these guys any trouble at all. In fact, I've gone out of my way to intervene on behalf of a few over the last couple of years." He said the last part loudly, a reminder that he wanted all the nefarious characters who knew him to clearly hear.

"And I'm not in here to give you any trouble, either," he said seriously. "I just want a little information about an old friend."

Dugo Bagy perked up his ears and leaned forward, his suddenly interested look telling Han beyond doubt that the Sullustan was expecting some reward for his cooperation.

"I'll owe you one," Han, who had little money with him, said.

Dugo Bagy leaned back and held up his hands helplessly.

"A businessman, I am," he explained, but then Chewie leaned over him and growled.

"Owing is good," Dugo Bagy readily agreed.

"I'm going to see Lando," Han explained. "I just want to know what he's doing out there."

Dugo Bagy visibly relaxed—an easy question. "Mining asteroids," he replied.

Han gave him "the stare" again.

"He is," Dugo Bagy insisted.

"And . . .," Han prompted.

"Why more would there be?" Dugo Bagy asked. "Very profitable."

"And . . . ," Han said again.

With a sigh, Dugo Bagy leaned in, and Han and Chewie did likewise, the three going into an informal huddle.

"Lando seeks new techniques," Dugo Bagy explained. "There's a lot to be taken, if they can only figure out how."

"What do you mean?"

"Kerane's Folly," Dugo Bagy said.

"The asteroid?" Han asked.

"In the Hoth system," Dugo Bagy confirmed. "Platinum pure, but too many other asteroids contacting to get to it. Many have died in trying. Lando will see the way."

"I thought they just couldn't find the thing anymore," Han remarked.

Dugo Bagy smiled wryly.

"So Lando's just using his operation way out there as a testing ground, coming up with better ways and tools to mine the asteroids so that he can franchise them out across the galaxy," Han reasoned, and that made sense, sounding more like the entrepreneurial Lando he knew.

"Other things, too," Dugo Bagy said with a wink, a too-cute expression on the face of a Sullustan.

"Running the belt?" Han asked. "Some game, right?"

"To some a game," Dugo Bagy corrected. "To others . . ."

"Training," Han finished, catching on. "So Lando's working with the smugglers, letting them use his running-the-belt game to perfect their skills at getting away from hunters."

"Hunters trained by Luke," Dugo Bagy said, and his tone revealed clearly to Han why he had been so nervous when first confronted. The smugglers were obviously getting a bit edgy about the problems at the Outer Rim concerning these predatory Jedi—and Han's connection to the Jedi, and the academy, via his brother-in-law, his wife, and even his kids, was undeniable.

"Who is it?" he asked.

"Kyp Durron," Dugo Bagy replied. "And his do-gooder buddies. The Dozen-and-Two Avengers," he said dramatically, rolling his eyes. "Problems they cause, money they cost."

Han nodded. He knew all about Kyp, and now it made sense to him. Kyp had always been a bit of a loose ion cannon, and to make matters even worse, Kyp's parents had been killed due, in part, to the actions of a notorious smuggler, Moruth Doole.

"Why are you going to see Lando?" Dugo Bagy asked.

"A vacation," Han answered dryly, and he rose, and Chewie did, too, and when Dugo Bagy started to get up, Chewie put a huge paw on his shoulder and pushed him back down into his seat.

"Well, this should be fun," Han said to Chewie as they exited Riebold's Foam and Sizzle.

Chewie gave a great howl in reply, as if to remind Han, "Wasn't it always?"

NINE

The Honor of Dying

With a heavy pack strapped across her back—what she wouldn't have given for a simple transporter disk—Tee-ubo led a team of four out of the compound. Normally, they wouldn't have left ExGal-4, for the sturdy station could handle almost any weather Belkadan could throw at it. Danni's call had made it clear that this storm was exceptional, though, and one needing some investigation.

Also, though none of the four spoke of it openly, having a mission now helped them get through their grief over the accidental death of Garth Breise. They had all known the risks when they had come out here, of course, into a wild and unexplored land, but still, losing one of the team had hit many of them hard, especially Tee-ubo. She knew that Bensin Tomri would be devastated by the news, if they could find some way to relay it to the now-distant Spacecaster.

The Twi'lek kept her blaster holstered, but the other three did not; they moved with weapons out and ready, with Luther De'Ono, a rugged man in his mid-twenties, with coal black hair and dark eyes, diligently guarding the left flank; Bendodi Ballow-Reese, the oldest member of ExGal-4 at fifty-three, but a former barnstormer search-and-destroy agent with the Rebel Alliance, guarding the right; and Jerem Cadmir, a Corellian, watching the rear, practically walking backward as the group eased through the thick jungle. Jerem was obviously the least comfortable with his weapon. Not a warrior, the slender, gentle Jerem had been chosen to go out into the dangerous Belkadan jungle because he was the most knowledgeable member of the team with regard to geology and climatology. If the brewing storm Danni Quee had called back to warn about would truly pose a danger to ExGal-4, Jerem Cadmir would be the one to give the most accurate early warning.

"The most dangerous part will be the nights," Bendodi remarked late that afternoon. The team was making painfully slow progress through the tangles. "Redcrested cougars are night hunters, and they'll be thick about us, wanting to put a face to our strange scents." The others looked at Bendodi, at his ruggedly handsome face crossed by several scars he had earned in brutal combat, and found it hard to ignore the warning.

"We can use the flight packs once we clear the jungle," Tee-ubo offered.

"Then press on," Jerem urged nervously.

"It's still going to be two days of walking," Bendodi told them.

Tee-ubo eyed him unappreciatively. They had already fought out this debate, back at the compound. Bendodi and Luther had wanted to strap on a couple of flight packs and fly off from the compound wall, despite the unarguable calculations that showed they'd fast deplete their fuel in trying to leap over the towering trees, and might have to spend a week of walking after they had left the primary canopy behind.

Tee-ubo's plan, the sensible one, the one everyone at the station except for the two would-be warriors had agreed upon, called for traversing the jungle on foot, then strapping on the packs at the lip of the great basin about twenty kilometers south of the compound. Given the angle and the calculated winds, they could cross the three hundred kilometers of the basin for roughly the same amount of fuel that would have been used flying over the trees to the lip of the basin.

With such logic on her side, Tee-ubo had won the debate, but she had known from the first grumbling steps out of the compound that Luther, and particularly Bendodi, weren't about to let the matter rest.

So they pressed on, hot and sweaty in the steamy air, and as night descended, they found a thick nook high in a tree to call a campsite.

They got little sleep, for the jungle resounded with threatening sounds, low growls and hisses that seemed to come from right beside them. Despite the threat, though, they found no open challenge, but so disturbing were those sounds that the team set off early, determined to make the basin lip before the next nightfall. And they did, arriving at the rocky precipice on the edge of the jungle overlooking the huge valley with hours to spare.

Hours they would not waste. They quickly did some last-minute checks on the flight packs—like every other piece of terrain equipment at ExGal-4, the packs weren't in the best condition—and then lifted away from the precipice, opening wings wide to catch the gusting wind at their backs.

They flew on right through twilight and into the darkness, preferring the cold winds to the sounds emanating from the trees far below. There were no great flying predators on Belkadan, as far as they knew. Tee-ubo measured their progress by the hour, not the kilometer; given the minimum fuel burn gliding with the wind, she figured they could go for about four standard hours before exhausting the first half of their fuel.

When the time came to land, Bendodi fired a portable rocket flare into the canopy below, and the group used its guiding light to put down. They landed without incident, despite some very real and well-grounded fears propagated by the tumult of roars and shrieks in the region. A quick check of their positioning system confirmed that they had nearly crossed the length of the basin. If Danni's positioning had been correct, they should be able to find this brewing storm within a couple of days' march. Hopefully, they'd be able to get the needed measurements, mostly concerning wind speed, set their instruments, and be out of there quickly. Heartened, they settled in for a short night's rest.

It was shorter than expected.

Tee-ubo opened her eyes to the sound of coughing, a thick, mucus-filled hack. At first, she thought a thick ground fog had come up, but as the stench hit her, a noxious, rotten-egg smell, she realized that it was something else.

By the time the Twi'lek managed to sit up, she, too, was hacking and spitting.

"Go to enviro-suits!" she heard Bendodi cry. Hardly able to see, her eyes teary and stinging, Tee-ubo fumbled with her pack, finally pulling out the small hood and tank.

"Gloves, too!" Bendodi barked to all of them, his voice muffled by his enviro-suit. "No skin exposed until we know what this is."

A few moments later, her eyes still burning, the sickening stench still in her mouth, but with clean oxygen flowing, Tee-ubo inched along the limb tangle they had chosen for a campsite to join Bendodi and Luther. Jerem Cadmir had moved off along one branch with a light and seemed to be studying the leaves.

"Probably a volcano," Luther remarked. "That's what Danni saw from orbit. A volcano spewing fumes; we'll have to call back to ExGal and have them lock the compound down tight."

Bendodi and Tee-ubo nodded, not overly concerned. The compound could be made completely self-sustaining, able to hold back whatever fumes Belkadan could throw at them. Several of the other ExGal stations, with the same equipment as this one, had been situated on worlds far more hostile, one on a spinning lump of barren rock that was completely bereft of any atmosphere. If the cloud was indeed volcano formed, that would be good news, for likely there would be few, if any, potentially damaging winds.

"It's not a volcano," came Jerem's voice, and the three turned to regard him sitting on a branch and holding a leaf. "It's the tree," he explained.

That brought surprised expressions, and they moved over, one at a time, at Jerem's instructions, and lifted their hoods just long enough to take a sniff of the leaf he held.

"Let's get down from here," Luther remarked.

"No," Bendodi unexpectedly replied, even as the other three began to move for the main trunk. They looked to him questioningly.

"I can't think of a safer place to be," the scarred old warrior remarked. "We'll stay up here in our suits, and where no cougars will want to go."

The logic seemed sound; in the enviro-suits the fumes couldn't hurt them.

"How long to sunrise?" Luther asked.

Tee-ubo checked her chronometer. "Two more hours."

"Then sit tight," Bendodi said.

And they did, and when the sun came up, exploding brilliantly over the eastern horizon, they grew even more alarmed. For all the forest about them seemed to be on fire, sending greenish orange smoke up into the air. And all the green leaves had turned yellow.

It wasn't fire, they soon understood, but emissions, coming straight from the leaves, filling all the air with the noxious fumes.

"How is this possible?" Tee-ubo asked, and she, Bendodi, and Luther all looked to Jerem for an answer.

The man stood holding a leaf, staring at it wide-eyed and shaking his head. "A molecular change?" he mused.

"Luther, get up high, while the rest of us go down to the ground," Bendodi instructed, and he led the way out of the tree.

The air was just as thick and wretched at ground level, for

the grasses, even the moss and flowers, were similarly emitting the thick fumes. Jerem quickly went to one small plant and dug it up, roots and all, and as he did, some curious beetles, reddish brown, scampered out of the hole.

On Jerem's order, Tee-ubo caught one of them and held it up.

"What is it?" Bendodi asked.

"Maybe nothing," Jerem replied. "Or maybe a clue."

Before Bendodi could press him further, Luther came scrambling down the tree so quickly that he tumbled to the ground in a heap, and nearly fell over again as he tried to rise.

"It's gone way past us," he explained, waving his arm back toward the north. "And it's rolling on—I could see the trees changing color and starting to smoke!"

"Let's get out of here," Tee-ubo suggested, and she popped the beetle into a belt pouch and pulled the lever control for her flight pack forward. Hardly waiting, she fired up the pack.

Or tried to.

It sputtered and coughed, even popped off enough once to jolt Tee-ubo into the air, a short hop and nothing more.

Then it went dead.

"It can't get enough oxygen," Bendodi reasoned.

Even as he spoke, they heard a rustle to the side. They all tensed—Luther and Bendodi reached for their blasters—as a redcrested cougar broke through the brush. They didn't have to shoot, they soon realized, for the great animal was gasping, its sides heaving in and out futilely, and if it even saw them, it showed no reaction. Right before their eyes, the creature staggered a few more steps and then fell to the ground, breathing its last.

"Let's get out of here," Tee-ubo suggested, staring at the poignant reminder. She started to take off her pack, but Bendodi stopped her.

"Keep it," he instructed. "We'll need them if we can get ahead of the—" He paused and looked at the others curiously. "—of whatever the hell this is," he finished.

Jerem Cadmir pulled out his comlink and tried to call out, but the static that crackled back at him was too thick for any words to penetrate.

Off they went, as fast as their feet would carry them. After an hour—and half their oxygen—they still could not see the end of the noxious fumes before them. Bendodi sent Luther up yet another tree, while he and the others took out their comlinks and spread out, trying to find some hole in the static.

Nothing. They rejoined at the base of the tree, and a dejected Luther came back down shaking his head, explaining that he couldn't see anything through the thickening gases.

Hopelessness descended upon them, as thick as the fumes.

To everyone's surprise, Bendodi Ballow-Reese pulled off his oxygen pack and tossed it to Jerem Cadmir. "Run on," he ordered. He sniffled, then crinkled his nose in disgust. "Run on. One of us has to get back and warn them."

Jerem stood dumbfounded, as did Luther and Tee-ubo.

"Go!" Bendodi insisted, and even as Jerem started to argue, the older man turned and sprinted into the brush, disappearing from sight—though the others heard his subsequent hacking coughs.

"He's gone crazy," Luther cried, and he rushed to follow. He barely got to the edge of the brush, though, before a blaster rang out and Luther tumbled backward, shot through the chest.

"Go!" Bendodi called from somewhere beyond.

Tee-ubo and Jerem rushed to Luther, but too late—the man was quite dead. Tee-ubo took his oxygen pack, grabbed the stunned and seemingly frozen Jerem by the arm and hauled him after her, breaking into a dead run to the north.

And then they heard another shot and knew that Bendodi, too, was dead.

After another hour, no end to the biological disaster in sight, Jerem had to change tanks. He motioned for Tee-ubo to check her level, as well.

The Twi'lek didn't move.

"Do you need oxygen?" Jerem asked her.

Tee-ubo tossed him her extra tank. "Run," she explained. "I've been slowing you down for the last hour. You're the only hope." Then she took off her belt pouch—the one with the beetle—and tossed it to the stunned man, as well.

"I'm not leaving you," Jerem declared, and there seemed no room for debate in his voice. The extra tank in hand, he started for the Twi'lek, but stopped fast as Tee-ubo's blaster came up, leveled at him.

"One of us has to continue with the remaining tanks," she explained. "You're faster, and—you're better trained—to figure out what's—going on, so I—made you the offer." Already, from the gasps she took between her words, it was evident that her oxygen was waning. "Last chance," she said, waving the blaster toward the north.

"Both of us," Jerem insisted.

Tee-ubo pulled off her hood and threw it far to the side. Then, to Jerem's absolute horror, she took a deep breath of the noxious fumes about them. Immediately, her eyes turned reddish yellow, and foamy liquid began running from her nose.

"You're wasting time," she said, coughing with each word. "And oxygen."

Jerem started for her, but her blaster came up and she fired a bolt right past his head.

He ran to the north, blinded by the horrid fog and his own tears. He had gone only a dozen strides when he heard the report of a blaster behind him.

On Jerem ran, desperately. He took some hope when he noted that the fumes about him were thinning somewhat, but at about the same time, he had to switch to the last oxygen pack. Soon after that, he came to a sheer wall, only about ten meters high, but one that he could not climb.

Nor could he afford the time searching for a way around it. On the very edge of desperation, Jerem pulled forward the controls of his flight pack. Before he fired it up, though, he hit upon an idea.

He pulled off his oxygen pack, tore the tube right from the side of his hood, and stuffed it into the intake valve on his flight pack.

He fired it up. It sputtered and coughed, but sure enough, he got into the air and up over the cliff, where he found the air even clearer, as if the stony barrier had somehow slowed the plague. But he took little hope when he climbed higher into the air and looked back, for there, in its full yellow-green glory, was the storm Danni had called about. Not a storm at all, but a huge cloud of noxious fumes, a cloud growing by the second, fanning out in all directions.

Flying on, Jerem glanced back several times to watch its progress. He figured it was spreading at about ten kilometers an hour.

ExGal-4 had less than two days before it hit.

Jerem pushed the flight pack full out and came out of the basin later that same day. He didn't land in the jungle and trudge through, but took his chances in the air, climbing above the treetops and soaring on. He did come down, and hard, when his pack ran out of fuel; he crashed through the branches and tumbled to the thick vegetation, losing his blaster in the process.

He was alone in the jungle, with no weapon, and with night falling.

He ran on.

It loomed before them as soon as they came out of hyperspace, the fourth planet of the Helska system, a gray ball of ice several thousand kilometers in diameter. No mist surrounded the planet, no clouds, no notable atmosphere. To the eye, it appeared quite dead.

Of course Danni Quee and the other two knew better than to trust simple appearances. Many systems boasted of living watery worlds beneath the seemingly dead facade of empty ice. Still, the surface of the planet, on this side at least, appeared perfectly smooth, with no sign of any recent, catastrophic impact.

"Maybe it missed," Bensin Tomri remarked.

"We travel halfway across the sector in this rattle-and-shake contraption, and maybe it missed?" Cho Badeleg sounded thoroughly disgusted.

Danni eyed Bensin hard, her look pointedly explaining that she didn't appreciate the man's sarcasm.

"I'm serious," Bensin retorted. "If the comet we saw hit that ball of ice, then why is it still here? It should have been blasted into a million pieces, with all of it hanging about in a floating maelstrom."

Danni looked back at the viewer. Bensin's words were true enough, she realized, and yet they knew from their observations on ExGal-4 that the incoming comet had indeed hit this planet.

"I am getting some strange signals from it," Cho Badeleg offered, working the controls of his sensors. He looked up at the other two, their expressions hopeful. "Energy."

"That could just be the reflection of the sun," Bensin pointed out.

Cho Badeleg shook his head. "No, it's different."

"How?" Danni asked, moving beside him.

"Different spectrum than I'd expect from reflected sunlight," the man explained, and he shifted aside so that Danni could get a look at his indicators. They showed nothing consistent, more of a pulsating emanation, but indeed, in wavelengths she would not expect from a frozen ball of water.

"Organic?" she asked, and Cho only shrugged.

"Maybe the comet was just a ball of gas," Bensin Tomri reasoned. "That would explain a lot."

"How do you figure?" Danni asked.

"Well, the planet would still be here, as it is," Bensin remarked. "And a combination of gases could give us almost any reading."

"But how did it stay together, crossing gravity fields?" Cho asked.

"All right, almost a ball of gas," Danni put in, seeing Bensin's reasoning. "A small solid mass at the center."

"With enough gravity to hold together a ball of gases that large?" Cho asked doubtfully.

"Spinning superfast?" Danni asked more than stated, her voice thick with excitement. They all caught on fast enough, and their eyes lit up.

"Call it in," Danni told Bensin.

"I haven't been able to reach them," the man replied. "The tower must still be down."

Danni considered that for a long while. "Broadcast it generally, then," she said. "We're going to need help with this."

Bensin looked at her hard.

"By the time anyone gets out here, we'll already have the primary investigation done," Danni explained. "It's our find now, no matter if the entire New Republic fleet comes swarming. You keep an eye on the readings," she told Cho Badeleg, "and I'll bring us around to the other side."

Bensin smiled at that notion and opened his communicator to all channels, issuing a broadcast concerning their position and potential findings.

"What was that?" Danni asked a few moments later, when the Spacecaster slipped around the side of the planet and a swarm of small meteors moved just ahead of them and out of sight around the far side.

"I got them, too," Cho confirmed, his expression curious. "Hundreds."

"What?" Bensin asked.

Danni throttled up. "Debris?" she asked, and she looked back at her companions, her face beaming. "I think we've got something here."

"Debris put into orbit from an impact," Cho Badeleg remarked, nodding.

Again, just ahead of them around the curving line of the planet, they spotted the meteor swarm, but it was fast lost in the suddenly blinding sunlight as they came out of the planet's shadow.

Danni squinted and groaned.

"I've still got them," Cho assured her. "Up ahead and moving fast." He paused and crinkled his brow. "Faster," he clarified, and that, of course, made no sense.

"And something else," Cho continued. "Down to the left. On the surface."

Following Cho's directions, Danni wheeled the not-so-agile Spacecaster about, angling the screen to show them again the surface of the planet, flat, except for one large mound, somewhat covered by a thin icy layer, but obviously something other than ice. It seemed to be a milky substance, covering a mound of rough-edged, many-colored stone, or bone.

"There's the source of the readings," Cho Badeleg said excitedly.

Danni brought them in slowly.

"Shouldn't we be going after those meteors first?" an obviously uncomfortable Bensin Tomri remarked, and his sudden sense of dread wasn't lost on the other two.

"If it's a creature, it's still alive," Cho Badeleg warned, staring at his sensors, not quite knowing what to make of the signals emanating from the mound.

"Let's go catch the meteors," Bensin remarked more firmly.

Danni looked to him, and then to Cho, and saw both mesmerized, one by the mound, one by his instruments. Then she looked back at the planet, and above the line of the planet.

"Oh, no," she muttered.

"Let's go catch the meteors," Bensin said again.

"The meteors caught us," Danni explained, and when the men looked up, they understood.

In soared the meteors, but they couldn't be meteors, given the formation, a classic attack wedge.

"Get us out of here!" Bensin screamed.

Danni worked furiously, bending the Spacecaster to the side and down. "Setting for the jump to lightspeed!" Danni called.

"That'll take too long!" Bensin cried, and his point was accentuated when the Spacecaster jolted from some impact.

"Just fire it!" Cho Badeleg agreed.

Danni angled up, looking for a clear vector where she could just launch into hyperspace and take their chances with colliding with some other body millions of kilometers away.

But the screen was full of the meteor-ships, buzzing about like starfighters. One drew very close, and the three looked on in surprise and fear as a small appendage sticking out its front, like a miniature volcano, erupted, spewing forth a burst of fire and a single glob of molten rock that hit the Spacecaster, jolting them hard.

"It's melting through!" Bensin Tomri cried.

"Engage the hyperdrive, Danni!" Cho pleaded.

"I did," she replied, her voice calm, almost subdued. She had engaged the hyperdrive engine—to no effect. She figured that the first jolts had been hits to that very drive, as if these attacking . . . things knew exactly where to shoot.

All three of the scientists jumped back reflexively as a glob of something hit their view shield. They looked on in helpless horror as it seemed to melt, or morph, right through the transparent shield, hanging like a ball of glue *inside* the window.

It pulsed and opened a single hole in its membranous form, and the two men cried out, and Danni dived for the weapons locker.

And then the ball inverted, seemed almost to swallow itself, and what came out of it, or rather, what it now appeared to be, was a humanoid head, disfigured and frightening, and fully tattooed.

"Good you have come, Danni Quee, Bensin Tomri, and

Cho Badeleg," the ball said—or not the ball itself, Danni realized, recognizing this thing, this creature, as some sort of a communicator and not the speaker himself. She didn't recognize his accent at all, and he seemed to be stuttering over every word. "I—Da'Gara," he went on. "Prefect and adviser to yammosk, war coordinator oo-oo-oof Praetorite Vong. Welcome my home."

The three, too stunned by this Da'Gara creature's recognition of them, of its knowledge of their names, couldn't begin to respond.

"You see my home, I be-bel-believe," Da'Gara went on politely. "You come me there. I show you splendor Yuuzhan Vong."

"What?" Bensin Tomri asked, looking to Danni.

"An invitation, I guess," Danni replied with a shrug.

"The see villip," Prefect Da'Gara explained. "Pet of Yuuzhan Vong."

The three deciphered his words enough to understand that he was speaking of the creature that had invaded their Spacecaster.

"To talk across long," Da'Gara went on.

"Living communicator," Cho Badeleg remarked, his scientist instincts somewhat overruling his fear.

"Where are you from?" Danni managed to ask.

"Place you no know."

"Why have you come?"

Da'Gara answered with a laugh.

"Get us out of here," Bensin Tomri pleaded with Danni. She looked at him, then snarled and turned back to her controls, determined to fly her way through.

But the meteors, the rocklike starfighters, were all about the Spacecaster, spewing molten globs at exact points to continually cripple the ship. Before Danni could begin to initiate any evasive maneuvers, they were down to one drive, and that at a minimal capacity; every other compartment in the craft had been breached, and the enviro-unit had taken several hits.

Danni straightened and looked helplessly at her companions.

"Choice none," the villip of Prefect Da'Gara remarked. "You fol-follow coralskippers in. Now! Or you melt and we take from you honor of gift to Yun-Yammka."

"Just run," Cho Badeleg pleaded, trembling so violently that he stuttered through the two words.

"Choice none!" Prefect Da'Gara warned.

Danni, full of frustration and anger, her scientific dreams shattered by some alien nightmare, tore open the weapons locker, pulled out a blaster, and splattered the villip all over the viewscreen. She scrambled to her feet, diving for the controls.

And then they got hit, again and again, and soon they were spinning, tumbling, out of control, and the planet seemed to rush up to swallow them.

And then . . . nothing.

Darkness fell, and still Jerem Cadmir ran on, stumbling in the blackness, and with exhaustion and fright, horrified with what he had seen and terrified of those dangers lurking all about him. The roars of the redcrested cougars traveled with him that night, and at one point he thought he saw one of the great animals eyeing him casually from a branch high above.

Whether imagination or reality, Jerem would never know, for he had just run on, for all his life, for all the lives of those at the compound. Aside from his locating device, he had only three things with him: the beetle, the plant, and a sample of the noxious fumes he had fortunately and unintentionally trapped within one of his sample bags.

He took little comfort when night turned back to day, for he could hardly think straight at that point. He thought he was traveling in the right direction and in-line, but his locating device was showing some signs of damage—probably from the fumes—and he couldn't be sure.

"Wonderful for all of us if I run right past the compound,"

he lamented. He thought he recognized one tangled tree, but in truth, they all looked alike.

How relieved he was, then, when he scrambled headlong over a thicket, cutting a hundred small scratches on his arm, and found another member of the ExGal team waiting for him.

"The compound?" Jerem gasped.

"Right over there," Yomin Carr answered, moving to help Jerem back to his feet. "Where are your companions?"

"Dead," Jerem said, puffing for breath. "All of them."

Yomin Carr pulled him up straight and stared at him hard.

"We found—we found—the storm, but it wasn't a storm," Jerem tried to explain. "Some kind of plague—a biological disaster. It overran us."

"But you escaped," Yomin Carr said.

"They gave me their oxygen," the man replied, and he began to tremble.

Yomin Carr shook him hard.

"One of us had to get back," Jerem went on. "To warn the rest of you. We have to fire up the Jolian freighter and get out of here."

"The Jolian freighter?" Yomin Carr echoed with a laugh. "That ship hasn't been up since the compound was first set up, and half of its components were scavenged for the station operating systems. We will never launch it."

"We have to!" Jerem cried, grabbing Yomin Carr by the shoulders. "No choice."

"A plague, you say?" Yomin Carr asked, and Jerem nodded excitedly. "Well, perhaps we will find a way to battle back against it. Or insulate ourselves from its effects."

"We can insulate," Jerem said, and he started past Yomin Carr, but to his surprise, the bigger man held him in place.

"But once it's upon us, we'll have no way to call out," Jerem tried to explain, and he tried to pull away. "The fumes . . ."

"Fumes?" Yomin Carr asked calmly.

"No time to explain," Jerem said. "We have to get out of here."

Yomin Carr yanked Jerem about and slammed him hard into a tree. Jerem, held there motionless, stared at the larger and suddenly imposing man in sheer disbelief.

"I could let you go to them," Yomin Carr said. "I could scramble into the compound beside you, yelling frantically that we must get the Jolian freighter up into the air."

"You don't understand," Jerem said. "The plague advances at a tremendous rate. It will be here in a matter of hours."

"Within three, to be more precise," Yomin Carr remarked.

Jerem started to respond, but then the weighty implications of Yomin Carr's last statement hit him fully and stole the words from his mouth.

"The gases will overwhelm the compound within three hours," Yomin Carr stated. "And all the planet in two days—sooner if favorable weather allows the atmospheric levels to hit critical mass."

"Favorable weather?" Jerem Cadmir echoed with confusion. "How do you know?"

Yomin Carr reached a finger up beside his nose and tapped the sensitive area of the ooglith masquer, signaling the creature to peel away.

Jerem Cadmir tried to retreat, tried to push himself right into the tree at his back when the masquer flaps receded and he saw the disfigured, tattooed face of Yomin Carr.

The Yuuzhan Vong warrior stood perfectly still, reveling in the exquisite tingles of agony as the masquer pulled away fully and slipped down beneath his loose-fitting clothing.

"I could take you back there and wait with you and the others for your doom to fall," Yomin Carr explained. "For of course, I've disabled the freighter beyond repair—not that you would have been able to get the rusted thing off the ground in any case. I could let you battle valiantly against the transformation, which you call a plague, and let you die dishonorably, at no warrior's hands, but simply from lack of oxygen."

Jerem was shaking his head, his lips moving as if he was trying to respond, though no words came out.

"But I feel that I owe you this, out of respect for your perseverance and resourcefulness in getting all the way back here," Yomin Carr went on.

Jerem exploded into movement, rushing off to the side, but Yomin Carr, his muscles toned by years of warrior training, caught him easily, one hand clamping under Jerem's chin, the other grabbing the hair at the back of the man's head. With frightening ease, Yomin Carr pushed Jerem low and tilted his head back so that he was looking up into that horrid, disfigured face.

"Do you understand the honor I offer you now?" Yomin Carr asked in all seriousness.

Jerem didn't respond.

"I offer you a warrior's death!" the Yuuzhan Vong cried. "Yun-Yammka!" He gave a sudden twist of his arms and shattered Jerem Cadmir's neck bone.

Yomin Carr let the limp man fall to the ground. He stood solemnly over Jerem for a long, long while, uttering prayer after prayer for the Slayer to accept this sacrifice. By Yomin Carr's reckoning, he had indeed granted Jerem Cadmir a tremendous amount of respect this day; he even went somewhat against orders by not allowing the scientists to battle the plague unimpeded.

But Yomin Carr could justify that. Jerem had seen too much of the plague and knew, and said as much, that they could not hope to battle it. Jerem would have prompted only a desperate flight attempt, and no real countering of the plague. The Yuuzhan Vong warrior nodded, agreeing with that reasoning, and reached down to inspect Jerem's body, finding the three valuable items.

He'd bring them back for inspection, allow the remaining six scientists to try to find some solution. That would satisfy his duties regarding the plague, for one of his goals here was to discern if the scientists could find some way to battle this powerful Yuuzhan Vong biological weapon.

Completing that duty would justify his showing respect to Jerem Cadmir.

Satisfied, the Yuuzhan Vong started back for the compound. All his rationales were in place, but he knew the truth in his heart.

He had killed Jerem Cadmir, not simply out of respect, not simply because the man had deserved a warrior's death, but also because he had wanted to, because he had enjoyed it. For too long, Yomin Carr had lived among the infidels, had spoken their language and accepted their strange and sacrilegious actions. Now the day of glory was almost upon him, the day of the Yuuzhan Vong, and he was eager, so eager.

At first Danni thought she was dead, but as her consciousness gradually returned, before she even opened her eyes, she not only knew that she was very much alive, though painfully wounded, but also sensed somehow where she was, and that thought—that she was within the living mound she had seen from the Spacecaster's viewscreen—filled her with dread.

Her right shoulder, dislocated, throbbed; both of her arms were held out straight. She could feel strong hands gripping her wrists, and the light touch of a poncho about her bare shoulders, and a wet stickiness about her feet as if she was standing in a gooey pool of mud.

She heard a gurgled cry, recognized the voice of Bensin Tomri, and forced open her eyes.

She saw the multicolored, rough-face walls, the hulking men—no, not men, she instinctively understood, but some other humanoids—disfigured and covered with tattoos, holding her arms out to either side, out straight, and so tightly that she could not move. She saw Bensin off to the side, standing, but with his head pulled back, another hulking humanoid beside him. That tattooed warrior lifted one hand up high, clawed it like a bird's talon, and drove it down into Bensin's throat. The warriors let go, and Bensin fell limp, too limp, and Danni knew that he was dead.

The hulking warrior, his hand still wet with Bensin's blood, came over toward her slowly, deliberately. Danni tried to struggle, but the two humanoids holding her gave sudden jerks, and waves of pain overwhelmed her, rolling out from her dislocated shoulder as the joint snapped back into place. She nearly swooned and rolled her head, and then he was before her and she saw him clearly, and she recognized him from the impersonating creature that had invaded the Spacecaster.

"Yomin Carr demand respect for Danni Quee," Prefect Da'Gara stated. "Do you und-under—" He paused and crinkled his face, struggling for the word.

"Understand," the woman said through clenched teeth.

Da'Gara nodded and smiled. "You understand the honor?"

Danni looked at him helplessly.

Then she felt the tingling pain, and the goo at her feet came alive and began to roll up her naked legs. Danni's eyes widened with horror and pain as the creature began its attachment, rolling higher and higher to cover all of her body beneath the poncho. She struggled and flailed.

Da'Gara slapped her across the face. "Do not dishonor Yomin Carr request," he growled in her face. "Show courage or I put you out to die in empty air of surface!"

That sobered Danni. She still squirmed—who could not as the creature attached itself, tendril by tendril into her pores?—but she bit down on her lip and stood firm, eyeing Da'Gara sternly.

The prefect nodded his approval. "Glad I that Danni not dead, as was Cho Badeleg, when we bring you down," Da'Gara said. "I expect to kill you myself and now, but honorably, this day."

Danni didn't blink.

"Reconsidered," Da'Gara explained. "Perhaps it better

you stand with me to see *zhaetor-zhae*—" He shook his head, recognizing that he was using the Yuuzhan Vong word. "To see glory of Praetorite Vong."

Danni shook her head, unable to comprehend what this was all about.

"You like see galaxy die?" Da'Gara asked bluntly. "That made long ago, for you see us enter, worldship. The begin of end."

Danni crinkled her face; she was getting the gist of Da'Gara's meaning, and the thought seemed absurd.

"Yes," the prefect said, and he brought his hand in and gently stroked Danni's cheek, which repulsed her more than if he had clenched his fist and punched her. "You see with me, and you see truth, the *zhaelor*, the glory of Yuuzhan Vong. Might you come to see and believe, and you join. Might you hold *viccae*—anger in pride—and you die. No matter. In thinking, I make Yun-Yammka more happy."

Danni wanted to ask what or who Yun-Yammka might be, but she just shook her head, too overwhelmed by it all.

Da'Gara turned away from the stunned woman and motioned to another warrior, who approached Danni holding a soft lump of star-shaped flesh. She recoiled instinctively, tried to fight with every ounce of her strength. But they were too strong, and the cry of her protest was muffled as the fleshy creature was put over her mouth. Her horror only intensified as its tendril snaked down her throat, gagging her at first, but then joining with her, becoming a part of her breathing system.

Eyes wide with shock and pain, Danni was hauled through the chambers of the worldship, to a large room with a circular hole in the floor. The actual opening was larger than that, Danni understood, seeing the ice all about that hole, and she couldn't understand why she wasn't colder, why they weren't all freezing.

That thought flew away, though, in an instant of sheer

terror, when Da'Gara walked up behind her and unceremoniously shoved her headlong into the hole and she fell down a long tubular worm to the watery depths below.

The prefect jumped in after her.

TEN

Running the Belt

"I wouldn't have expected anything less of Lando," Han remarked when the *Millennium Falcon* came out of hyperspace and into view of the planets Lando Calrissian had taken for home and office. All the region about the two planets looming before them was littered with spacecraft, everything from small starfighters to the huge freighters and even larger shieldships Lando had used to protect other vessels when he had been mining on Nkllon, a planet too close to its sun.

"More traffic than at the Core," Luke's voice piped in over the comm as the *Jade Sabre* came out of hyperspace right beside the *Falcon*.

That left only Jaina and the X-wing still to be counted, and Han glanced at his wife, noting her concern. The trip from Reecee had taken a week, and while that was no problem in the comfort of the *Millennium Falcon* or the *Jade Sabre*, such a journey could tax an X-wing pilot to her limits. To say nothing of supplies. Jedi going on long journeys usually slipped into a self-induced nearly comatose state, slowing their metabolism and, for all intents and purposes, sleeping through the journey. Jaina had learned the technique and had proven she could do it well, in her training with Mara.

But doing it in a training room was very different from doing it in an X-wing on a long and lonely journey.

Even Luke had questioned his wife repeatedly about whether Jaina was really ready for this or not. Mara had insisted that she was, and no one could doubt Jaina's piloting prowess. Since Mara was Jaina's official tutor, there could be no debate, not even from Leia and Han, neither of whom were especially thrilled about putting their daughter into any kind of danger.

So Jaina had flown out here in the X-wing, same course, same destination, same speed, as the other two ships.

Why wasn't she out of hyperspace yet?

That question hung palpably between Leia and Han, neither speaking it aloud, neither having to.

"Let me guess which planet is Lando's," came Luke's call, his tone dry and sarcastic. The answer was obvious. One of the planets before them was brown and appeared quite inhospitable, while the other was blue and green, with white clouds floating through its sky. The scene reminded both Leia and Mara of the two planets they had recently visited: hospitable Osarian and rugged Rhommamool.

"Luke, where is Jaina?" Leia called, doing well to keep the concern out of her voice. She heard laughter from the other ship—Mara's.

"Why isn't she out yet?" Leia pressed.

"Because Mara fed Artoo the wrong coordinates," Luke replied.

"A little test," Mara explained, coming on-line. "Jaina's nearby, but far enough out of the system so that she'll have few reference points to use in righting her course."

"She's probably panicking," Leia replied, and she could easily visualize the grin spreading on Mara's pretty face.

"For a while, no doubt," Mara answered. "But all she needs to do is look inside herself, to seek out the Force and its connection between her and us, and particularly to Jacen, and she'll fly in at any minute."

"And Artoo knows the real way in any case," Luke quickly added.

"You've got a mean streak in you," Leia remarked with a helpless sigh.

"Toward Jaina or toward you?" Luke asked, and again, Leia and Han could hear their sister-in-law laughing.

"Yes!" Mara answered.

Leia just sighed.

"If anything happens to Mistress Jaina, I shall personally scold Artoo-Detoo," a nervous C-3PO piped in. "Oh, he's the real troublemaker, you know. I am sure that he is quite enjoying this."

Leia glanced at the golden protocol droid. "Not like Mara," she muttered, and considering her present fears and feelings, she was only half kidding.

"Jaina's fine," Luke remarked. "If you reach out with the Force, dear sister, you'll feel her, very much alive and well."

Leia was about to do just that, but she didn't have to, for the sensors on the *Falcon*'s panel beeped, and sure enough, Jaina's X-wing streaked into view a moment later.

"Took you long enough," Mara called to her, and she left the channel open so that the folks on the *Falcon* could hear her, as well.

"A little problem with Artoo," Jaina remarked dryly, and they heard R2-D2 beep out his vehement protest.

Mara bade Jaina to take them in, and she did just that, but in a roundabout manner, circling wide of Lando's home planet of Dubrillion to take a look at the operations going on at the other planet, Destrillion. A stream of small ships flowed down to this planet, bringing raw minerals from the asteroids to the great processing plants Lando had set up. Another, smaller stream of larger ships flowed off world, heading for the huge freighters that were sitting in orbit.

All of the onlookers, even Han, who was so familiar with Lando's schemes, stared in disbelief. How could Lando have set up so complete and large an operation in so short an amount of time? He'd been out here for only a year, and yet it seemed as if his operations could supply half the galaxy!

Contact from the surface of the blue-and-green planet welcomed them—all the more enthusiastically after the controller heard the names of the ships and their occupants—and gave them coordinates for landing, and as they descended through Dubrillion's cloud cover, they saw that Lando's current home was no less impressive than his mining operation. The city was tightly clustered, with tall towers and high groupings of many starports. Luke noted that most of those open bays were empty, leading to the speculation that Lando entertained many guests who were quick in and quick out.

Like smugglers.

As the *Jade Sabre* swooped along to its appointed dock, Luke also noted a pair of X-wings on one platform, XJ class, like his own, the latest version of the starfighter. There weren't many of those advanced fighters flying about, and none at all outside the Star Destroyer and battle cruiser squadrons, with one notable exception. These fighters belonged to Jedi Knights.

The three ships set down on three circular bays, high above the surface, with low clouds drifting by. The landing zones were separated by narrow walkways, leading to a central hub, and a fourth walkway went out from that hub to the connected tower.

All of them disembarked and met at the central hub, with Jaina and R2-D2, who needed considerable help getting out of the X-wing, coming along last. The pair arrived just before Lando came sweeping out of the tower door, his huge welcoming smile, his eyes, as always, twinkling more than sparkling, giving the impression that there was something much more going on behind the man's every gesture and expression.

"Ha-ha!" he laughed, moving over to wrap Han in a great hug, and then put one over Leia—one that pointedly lasted a little bit longer, drawing a jealous scowl from Han. He went to Luke next, and then stood before Mara, shaking his head.

"You look wonderful!" he said sincerely, bringing a smile to the woman, and Lando crushed her in a huge hug.

"Not many people dare to hug me," Mara remarked.

"That leaves more of you for me, then!" Lando returned with a burst of laughter. He stopped abruptly and glanced over at Luke, but found the man nodding and smiling sincerely. Lando's greeting of Mara could not have been more perfect.

The man was much more reserved with Chewbacca, offered a salute to R2-D2 and C-3PO, and then turned his attention to the three kids.

"How much bigger are you gonna get?" he asked, holding his arms out wide in disbelief. "It's only been a year, but look at you! You're all grown up."

The smiles that came back at him were polite, and obviously embarrassed.

"What're you doing here?" Lando asked, turning to Han. "And why didn't you tell me you'd be coming? I could have prepared something."

"Somehow, I don't think we'll be bored," Han remarked dryly.

Lando chuckled, but stopped short, eyeing Han suspiciously, as if he didn't know whether to take that as a compliment or an insult. His bright smile returned almost immediately, though, and with a flourish and a skip in his step, the vibrant Lando led them into the tower. He gave them the complete tour then, from the posh rooms in his guest suites, to the control rooms of the robotic processing plants on the other planet, detailing with great pride the volume of various minerals making their way up to the freighters and off to the Core. They ended the tour in the huge monitoring chamber at the center of his city, an oval-shaped room, its perimeter mimicking the orbital path of the asteroid belt, Lando's Folly. The chamber walls were covered with one gigantic viewscreen, showing a real-time view of the asteroid belt. Lando led them to another large rectangular screen, set out from one wall, and the man at the control panel respect-fully moved aside.

Lando's ensuing demonstration did not disappoint. He se-lected a section of the asteroid belt and magnified it on the rectangular screen to the point where they could see the small droid mining ships testing, drilling, and extracting, then hop-ping onto another asteroid.

"How much can you get from them?" Han asked. "Really?"

"Most asteroids aren't profitable," Lando admitted. "But every now and then . . . ," he added slyly, rubbing his hands together, dark eyes twinkling.

He continued the demonstration a bit longer, answered questions about volume and costs of setup, then led them out of that tower to another, up, up, to an enclosed hangar that held several small craft, with single central pilot pods, wing pylons extending from either side, connecting solar array wings that featured a top third and bottom third angled at forty-five degrees back in toward the central pod.

Lando's guests, particularly the older ones, surely recog-nized the craft: TIE Advanced x1 fighters, the type favored by the elite of the old Empire, including Darth Vader. The sight of the distinctive fighters clearly affected both Luke and Leia, whose expressions drooped. Han looked at Lando and scowled.

"Best design for our purposes," Lando answered honestly.

"These are your belt runners?" Luke asked.

"It's the adjustable shock couch," Lando explained, leading the way to the nearest, and as they moved they noted similar, but larger, twin-pod craft, TIE bombers, farther back in the hangar. "Pilots in these things can take a real beating."

"Don't we know that?" Han asked dryly.

"So you fly these things through the asteroid belt?" Jaina asked, her expression and her tone showing that she was more than a little intrigued.

"Along Lando's Folly, not through," Lando corrected. "Against the flow of the asteroids. We've got a couple of particularly nasty sections mapped out." He stared at Jaina for a long moment, matching her eager expression. "You want to try?"

She looked at her parents first, for just a moment, and then at Mara, and it was obvious that she was pleading for permission.

The prep time seemed interminable to eager Jaina, but she paid attention as Lando's technicians explained the basic differences in flying one of their modified TIE fighters. While the foot yokes and hand controls were easy enough to pick up, the adjustable shock couch, a pivoting, bouncing contraption, was very different from the stable cockpit of an X-wing or landspeeder. And the most important difference of all, Lando's technician explained, concerned the inertial compensator. Unlike those on the X-wings and in most other craft, the ones on the modified TIE fighters could not be dialed down. The levels were preset, designed to give a pilot a good tactical feel of the craft, and often a wild ride, but would not allow the g's to exceed safe limits.

"Early on, pilots would strap in and dial it down to ninety-five," the technician explained to the three kids. "They'd bounce along until that inevitable collision, and then ricochet into a wild spin. We'd go get them, to find most unconscious. One almost died."

That last statement brought a concerned look from Leia, and Jaina knew that her mother was almost ready to cancel the runs then and there.

But then the technician assured her, and the others, that the problem had been fixed. "When you hit one now, you'll get the spin of your life," he explained. "But you'll live to brag about it."

As a final confidence booster, the technician then pointed out the repulsor shields, solid defensive arrays controlled not by the pilot and powered not by the ship's engines, but from a floating station, *Belt-Runner I.*

That news widened Luke's eyes. There were available technologies to make the TIE fighters able to withstand many asteroid hits, using combinations of shields and an enhanced repulsor system, but for many years, the militaries of both the Empire and the New Republic had been trying to perfect off-ship shielding, with greater power sources lending deflector shields to small starfighters, thus freeing the drives of the starfighters to the tasks of maneuvering, accelerating, and firing. Thus far, little progress had been made with the technique, and Luke understood that if Lando could perfect it out here, the value to the enterprising man would be many times greater than all the treasure he could leech off of all the asteroids of Lando's Folly. Maybe that was his real purpose.

"Also," the technician continued, moving over to pat a shining white metallic hump beside the shock couch, "these babies have been outfitted with hyperdrive."

Luke nodded admiringly; Lando and his technicians might be onto something truly impressive here.

"We'll keep them safe," Lando finished for the tech, and he offered a wink to Leia.

And then Jaina and the other two Solo youngsters got their test runs in the modified TIEs, including a half-speed crash into a mountainside, where they experienced their first real feel for the collision shields.

But even that exercise didn't sate eager Jaina. Lando showed them a posting board prominently displayed in the entry hall of the city's main tower, which listed the top pilots and their winning durations. She didn't know any of the names, except two: Miko Reglia, who was listed at seventh, and Kyp Durron, the current champion, with a time of eleven minutes, thirteen seconds.

Jedi Knights, the master Kyp, and his apprentice Miko.

Jaina had work to do.

She cruised within the prep coordinates in her TIE fighter now, within sight of the entry point to the asteroid belt. Jacen was in the run now, building a respectable time approaching the five-minute mark. Jaina couldn't see him, but she heard his calls—or at least, the calls out to him, for her twin brother was keeping fairly quiet, finding a sense of calm within the meditation of the Force, she knew.

He passed the five-and-a-half-minute mark—he'd be on the board.

"Keep going," Jaina whispered, but even as the words left her mouth, she heard her brother cry out, "Whoa!" and then just issue a long scream.

"He's out," came the call from *Belt-Runner I*. "Heck of a hit."

Jaina caught sight of him then, of the spinning running lights as the TIE fighter careened off into space. "Jacen?" she called out, and when no response came back, she reached out to her twin with the Force, feeling him securely through their tight bond and understanding that he was shaken up, but was very much alive and well.

She let it go at that, for Anakin was just starting his run. Jaina caught flashes of his ship weaving in and out of the rocks, and she heard his breathing and occasional shouts over her comm unit. He sounded more animated than had Jacen, more consciously attuned to his physical senses. Jaina understood the philosophical fight that had been waging between her brothers, each trying to find the correct balance between Force and physiology, and she wasn't surprised at all by the difference.

"We got him," came the call from one of Lando's tow ships, followed by assurances from Jacen that he was all right. Jaina could picture the look of relief on her fretting mother's face.

"I want to do it again," he added, and then Jaina imagined Leia's predictable scowl.

They crossed Jaina's line of sight then, TIE and tow ship. The modified fighter seemed perfectly fine, but still it was being towed. She took a deep breath, steadying her nerves.

Then she heard Anakin squeal with delight, and caught sight of his TIE, skimming the edge of one huge rock.

She clicked off the signal, preferring to turn her attention inward, to find the peace of the Force, the calm emptiness. Hardly conscious of the effort, she rocked the foot yokes back and forth, trying to get a better feel for the craft, and gave a quick push on the throttle, jerking her back in the shock couch.

The seconds slipped past as she fell deeper into the meditation.

She heard the call from the ground controller that Anakin had surpassed Jacen—wouldn't that make for fun conversation later on?—and focused back in to her surroundings, tuning the comm back to Anakin's signal in time to hear his boast.

"I got you, Jac—" he started to say.

Jaina saw the whole thing. Anakin stooped his TIE under a spinning rock, then pulled into a hard climb right before the face of another.

He couldn't avoid the third, didn't even see it until it was right in his face.

He hit head-on, the TIE fighter ricocheting straight up, spinning tail-over-front at a tremendous rate. Up, up, it went, and then it stopped spinning—Anakin must have fired a compensating blast—and just kept drifting, tilted and appearing quite dead.

"Anakin?" came the frantic call from the ground station, Leia's voice.

No answer.

Jaina gripped her controls as Leia cried out again, thinking that she could get to her brother quickest, though what good she might do, she didn't know. Before she fired away, though, Anakin's shaky voice replied.

"Amazing," he said, and he sounded sick, or as if he had just been.

"Are you all right?" came Leia's call and Lando's voice, at the same time.

"I think so."

"You beat Jacen," Jaina piped in.

"Who cares?" came the response.

Only then did Jaina understand how shaken her little brother truly was. Normally, the fact that he had beaten Jacen would be paramount in his thoughts, a sterling victory.

"That's enough," Leia said, apparently catching on to the same thing. "Bring it in, Jaina."

"Ready to fire!" Jaina called, clicking to a different channel and pretending she hadn't heard. She wasn't about to let Anakin's misfortune slow her down—she knew she should have gone first! "Am I cleared for entry?" she asked the air controller on *Belt-Runner I*.

"Fire away," he came back.

"Jaina!" Leia's voice came in, her mom-sense easily finding her daughter's new channel.

But Jaina throttled up quickly, speeding for the entry point of the belt. Most pilots went in at a virtual standstill, coming against the flow of the asteroids and using their drives only for dodging maneuvers. It wasn't a distance test, after all, but merely a duration challenge.

Jaina, though, fearing her mother would find a way to call it all off, hit the belt running . . . and fast.

She knew as soon as she entered that she had made a mistake. Before she could even really register any pattern to the incoming asteroids, she had to push hard on the stick, dropping the TIE into a straight stoop, then rolling out to the left desperately to avoid a long jag in the rock. Three-quarters of the way into that roll, Jaina pulled it to a halt and shot out diagonally, barely avoiding another asteroid and nearly clipping the back side of the first she had dodged. No time to take a deep steadying breath, for another pair came on, and Jaina put the TIE up on its side and somehow managed to slip between them, then rolled it over, top down, and pulled hard, dropping into another stoop. Before the warning alarm could begin to sound, indicating that she was nearing the boundary of the belt, Jaina brought the TIE about, shooting off to the side, making no headway into the asteroid course, but not losing any ground—which would have disqualified her—and buying herself a precious split second.

And in that second, she composed herself and recognized that she could not keep reacting. This was a game of anticipation, of preparing the move before you had to make it. That was why the four Jedi who had run, including two relatively green pilots, her brothers, had all climbed onto the board. Jaina ignored her blinking and beeping instruments and looked ahead at the incoming swarm, feeling their pattern as much as seeing it.

She turned "her nose into the wind," as the old water-sailing adage went, and plunged in headlong.

Han heard a low growl escape Leia's lips as Jaina soared into the asteroid belt. He draped his arm about his wife's shoulders.

"She heard me," Leia remarked quietly and coldly.

Han tightened his grip, pulling Leia closer. Of course Jaina had heard her, and of course Jaina had pretended differently, had gone after the run that had consumed her thoughts these last days. Leia would get over it, Han knew, but if Jaina had acceded to her mother's demand, had lost the challenge she had so desperately wanted, the chill between mother and daughter would have been lasting.

"She'll be all right," he remarked, but even he winced as Jaina's TIE, clearly visible on the great screens in the central control room, broke into its three-quarter roll and burst out at the very last instant. "She's the best flyer of the three."

Beside the pair, Mara's green eyes glowed with excitement. "Fall into it, Jaina," she whispered. "Let the Force be your guide."

Behind her, Luke kneaded her neck and shoulders and

smiled warmly, remembering similar advice from the spirit of Obi-Wan Kenobi, when old Ben had gone with him on his race down the channel of the Death Star. Don't try to register all the input from your eyes and other senses. Don't listen to your instruments at all—turn them off, if possible. Let the Force show you the patterns before you, the twists, the turns, the target.

Jaina was more into that flow now, they could all see, her turns coming hard, but less drastic, as if she was anticipating the next twist she would face.

Luke glanced at the timer clock hanging above them. Four minutes.

On she went, spinning and rolling, plunging suddenly, then swooping back up to a clearer region. But looking ahead of her, Luke recognized a seemingly insurmountable problem. Two thick clusters of asteroids were converging, the trailing group catching up to the other, and they seemed as if they would form a wall of stone the TIE simply couldn't slip through.

"Unbreachable pattern!" one of Lando's observing judges cried out, and those very words blinked off and on across his monitor, for the computer calculating Jaina's flight saw no way around the forming barrier without clearing the borderlines of the asteroid belt.

"Tough luck," Lando remarked. "Happens every once in a while."

"She'll get it," Mara insisted.

"Come on, Jaina," Leia whispered beside her.

Jaina recognized the convergence, like fingers interlocking to form a solid barrier, and immediately throttled down. Desperate, she glanced all about, looking for a seam.

There was none.

She looked to her instruments, all of them screaming and blinking, warning of impending collision. She punched her fist against her thigh in frustration, losing her composure, losing any chance.

But then she heard Mara's plea for her to fall into the Force, and then she heard her mother's voice, nothing distinct, but a general feeling of support and love from both of them.

Jaina steeled her gaze straight ahead and throttled up, attacking the mass. She had to buy time, nothing more, and the trailing group would surpass the first, and openings would reveal themselves.

She went in hard at the closest asteroid, spun over and down as she approached, and popped her repulsor coils, bouncing off harmlessly. Into another spin, she fired the repulsors again, ricocheting off the bottom of another asteroid. And then again, bouncing her backward—but not technically flying backward, which would have disqualified her.

And so it went, with Jaina playing like a bouncing ball, never impacting, but firing her repulsor coils at precisely the right moment to launch her sidelong, or up or down, or even backward, buying time and not distance as asteroids passed others, as some collided and went spinning at slightly new angles.

Jaina felt an opening, like a breeze finding an alley between tall buildings. She bounced away from yet another rock, barrel-rolled and dived, then reversed momentum, swooping up right before yet another asteroid, but coming around it, leveling off and shooting through the gap, waggling her wings to accommodate the angled exit.

Her eyes were half-closed as she felt the patterns; her TIE fighter swooped and turned, accelerating and throttling back before she was even conscious of the movements.

Nor was she conscious of the passing seconds, or of anything at all other than the clearest course before her.

Chewie's howl as Jaina broke through the seemingly impenetrable barrier, against the odds and against the computer calculations, very much reflected the mood of the onlookers, even Lando's crew. The Wookiee jumped up and down, grabbed the nearest technician and gave him a shake that set his teeth to rattling, and punched his huge hairy fist into the air.

"Was that good?" C-3PO asked in all seriousness, apparently missing the point of it all.

R2-D2 howled and screeched at him in response.

Leia reached over and squeezed Mara's hand.

"The kid can fly," Han remarked, his voice thick with something more than pride, with awe. He glanced up at the timer clock.

Five minutes, thirty-two seconds.

Jacen, still a bit unsteady from his collision, walked into the room then. He glanced up at the clock, then moved beside the others and took a measure of Jaina's progress. "She's found her inner peace," he remarked.

"Did you?" Luke asked.

Jacen nodded. "But I didn't have the flying skills to complement it," he admitted. "Jaina's got the whole package."

And so it seemed, as the screen showed her TIE flowing effortlessly through the maze of flying boulders.

The elapsed time broke the seven-minute mark, putting Jaina high on the board.

"She'll be no lower than third," Lando told them. "And no one's had a tougher course to fly." He turned to one of his techs. "Cut into all the broadcast screens," he instructed. "Put this out all over the planet."

"Let the betting begin," Han whispered into Leia's ear, and both smiled.

"I already had it piped into the other control rooms and the docking areas," the tech replied.

"I saw it on the way in," Jacen agreed. "Kyp Durron's out in the docks, watching every second."

The name reminded Luke that they had other business to attend to out here. But not now, he told himself. He studied

Jaina's flight pattern, then glanced back up at the timer clock. "Kyp's going to lose," he stated evenly.

The Force mounted within Jaina, a tangible pressure growing from second to second. It was all an incomprehensible blur, seemingly unguided movements that brought her within a hairbreadth of some asteroids, into wild turns and stoops, straight climbs and clever angles cutting the one open line between rocks.

On and on it went, though time seemed irrelevant, a concept lost in the deepest trance.

But the pressure built, surely, tangibly, and as Jaina became aware of it, that only stemmed her concentration further.

Her eyes popped open wide as she came around one spinning boulder to nick a tiny one, hardly a hit, but enough to push her out so that she clipped another, larger asteroid.

Around and around she careened, and she tensed coming out of one spin, to see a wall of stone looming before her.

Then she was spinning too fast to even register the movement, too fast to make any sense of the myriad images flashing before her. She collided with another asteroid—she felt that impact clearly—and then . . .

She was clear of the belt, and as her rattled senses settled, she worked the controls feverishly to stop the spin. She didn't know how much time had elapsed, hardly remembered her run at all.

In the control room, there was . . . silence.

Stunned silence. The timer clock had stopped the moment Jaina's TIE had exited the belt.

Twenty-seven minutes, twenty-seven seconds.

"The kid can fly," Han said again.

ELEVEN

Boom

Only six enemies remained, four men and two women, to oppose Yomin Carr. One of them was up on the tower now, wearing a full enviro-suit and trying to reattach the disconnected junction box.

It wouldn't matter, Yomin Carr knew. The molecular plague had swept by ExGal-4, had rolled over nearly all of Belkadan, and the toxic gases and swirling yellow and green clouds were too thick now, and too tumultuous, for them to get any message off planet. When the truth of the devastation had become evident, the remaining scientists had scrambled to ready the small freighter for liftoff. How easy it had been for Yomin Carr to sabotage the already dilapidated craft, rubbing wires together so that their rotted insulation disintegrated, causing shorts, or pulling connector plates right over rusted bolts.

The scientists had quickly abandoned any hope of fleeing, and instead focused on getting out a distress signal. But they were too late; the death of Garth Breise and their trust in Yomin Carr had sealed their fate.

Now the clouds and poisoned gases had caught them, and though the buttoned-up ExGal station could be self-sustaining in the oxygen-depleted air, they were trapped,

Mon Calamari juggerhead fish in a barrel, for Yomin Carr's harpoons.

The Yuuzhan Vong warrior casually walked out of the compound, wearing his starfish breathing adaptor, for he could not bring himself to trust the mechanical breathing apparatus of the enviro-suits. Quite comfortable in the devastation his beetle friends had wrought, he moved to the base of the tower and looked up, barely able to see the worker through the thick haze.

"How are the repairs going?" he yelled, his voice watery-sounding because of the mask.

"I got it!" came the cry from above, a woman's voice. "One more connection . . ."

Yomin Carr pulled the small ax from his belt and chopped down hard on the exposed piece of cable at the base of the tower, severing it cleanly. Then he replaced the ax and waited calmly, basking in the noxious haze of his glory.

A few minutes later, Lysire Donabelle, one of only two females left alive on Belkadan, came down the tower.

"It'll work now," she explained as she reached the bottom and began extracting herself from the safety harness and lengths of cord. "Just a connector," she started to explain, and then she turned about and froze, eyes wide behind her visor as she regarded Yomin Carr and his living aerator.

Yomin Carr held his hand out, motioning toward the new break in the line.

Lysire stared at it for a long moment; her visor fogged with her heavy breathing. She looked back at Yomin Carr, shaking her head in disbelief.

And then she bolted, rushing right past the alien.

He kicked her trailing foot behind her lead ankle as she passed, and in the same fluid movement, grabbed the air line at the back of her helmet and tore it free. Lysire sprawled facedown on the ground. Yomin Carr's foot stepped down on her back, holding her firmly in place.

Lysire wriggled frantically, gasping for breath as the yellow fumes slipped under her protective gear. Somehow in her desperation, she broke free, crawling, up to her knees, then regaining her footing. Yomin Carr could have caught her, and easily, but he did not, recognizing from her stagger that he had already won.

Lysire wobbled and swayed; her line to the compound door was far from straight. She staggered the last few steps and fell forward, crashing against the portal. Her hands moved, a feeble attempt to find the door's release, for her senses were almost completely gone by then.

Yomin Carr didn't make a move, didn't have to. He watched her slump against the door.

Then he stood beside her, off to the side, just looking out at the roiling clouds and thickening fumes.

A half hour slipped by. The seven scientists had buddied up for safety, two, two, and three, and while Yomin Carr's two partners thought he was sleeping in his private chambers, Lysire's partner knew that she had gone outside. It came as no surprise to Yomin Carr, then, when the compound door started to open.

Lysire Donabelle slipped down to the side.

"Lysire!" came her partner's cry, the woman falling to one knee beside her.

She glanced up then, apparently noting the movement, and her eyes went wide at the specter of Yomin Carr, at the horror of watching Yomin Carr's swiftly descending ax.

There was something symbolic about killing the last female on Belkadan, the Yuuzhan Vong warrior recognized. The seal of victory, the symbol that the humans and other intelligent species of this galaxy had lost their first encounter with the Yuuzhan Vong.

Yomin Carr tore the ax head out of the woman's chest, let her fall right over Lysire, then moved through the door, back into the compound.

Only four enemies remained, and two of them, Yomin Carr knew, were probably asleep.

Nom Anor wasn't comfortable at all, strapped in his seat and with tons of unstable liquid explosives burning bright behind him. The Yuuzhan Vong executor, who had come in from another galaxy, had never feared space flight—far from it— but this primitive two-stage rocket from Rhommamool made even the ion drives of the more conventional craft look superb, and those, Nom Anor considered far beneath the glory and sophistication of his own species's living worldships and coralskippers.

Beside him, Shok Tinoktin seemed only marginally more at ease, gritting his teeth against the g forces as the rocket zoomed into orbit.

Finally, though, they leveled off, the first burn completed, and Shok went to work piloting the large, ungainly craft toward the waiting *Mediator*.

"They're hailing us," Shok explained to his leader a moment later.

Nom Anor held his hand up and shook his head. "Finish the course setting," he explained. Any delay in responding he could brush away with the difficulties of aligning such a bulky and unwieldy ship as this. The discussion with the *Mediator* would come later, after he and Shok were safely tucked into their concealed A-wing.

"She'll fly right by them," Shok assured him a moment later.

Nom Anor unbuckled from his uncomfortable chair, Shok did likewise, and the two crouched and crept through the cramped capsule, Nom Anor pausing only to set the decoy in place in the pilot chair, utter a quick prayer to Yun-Harla, the Cloaked Goddess, the Trickster, and kiss one of his pet villips good-bye.

The Rhommamoolian rocket broke orbit, streaking out

toward the *Mediator*, and blasting its second-stage booster away. That booster rocket had never actually fired, though, for it wasn't needed, and wasn't really a rocket, but was, rather, an empty shell with an A-wing cleverly tucked inside.

From the enlarged cockpit of that A-wing, which had been modified to hold two pilots, Nom Anor and Shok Tinoktin watched the continuing plumes of the missile exchange between Osarian and Rhommamool. Starfighters from the *Mediator* buzzed the atmospheres of both planets, particularly Osarian, trying to knock down as many missiles as possible. Some of those bombs were getting through, the executor noted as the shell rolled about, giving him a view of Osarian and the large red bruises that were the thermonuclear blast clouds.

No wonder, then, that his offer to Commander Ackdool to come to the *Mediator* and negotiate fairly with the Osarians had been eagerly received.

The booster shell rotated some more and the great battle cruiser came into sight, dwarfing the Rhommamoolian capsule speeding for it, despite the fact that it was much farther away.

"Hold this line," Nom Anor ordered. Shok tapped his thrust-vector control jets, breaking the momentum of the roll and gently stabilizing the view on the *Mediator*.

"Open the channel."

Shok nodded and remotely opened the comm channel on the distant capsule. The relay couldn't send the picture, the image of Commander Ackdool, to the A-wing, for that would have given the pair away, but Nom Anor could picture the Mon Calamarian's face vividly, a phony smile of greeting stamped upon it as he issued all the expected diplomatic platitudes.

"My greetings, Commander Ackdool," Nom Anor said through his villip. The little creature, an exact likeness of Nom Anor, sat atop the decapitated body that had been placed in the capsule's pilot seat, and relayed Nom Anor's words with perfect inflection.

Ackdool had barely begun his insincerely warm greeting when a group of craft swooped out from dark space, closing fast on the capsule.

Ackdool cursed and ordered his fighters out, and Nom Anor and Shok Tinoktin heard a yelp of glee from somewhere in the commander's background.

"The Jedi Knight," Shok Tinoktin remarked.

Nom Anor nodded, thinking it perfectly ironic that the *Mediator*'s own starfighters would clear the way for the fake capsule.

Shok Tinoktin worked hard to keep both the *Mediator* and the capsule in sight so that they could enjoy the spectacle of the *Mediator*'s starfighters intercepting and chasing away the Osarian Z-95 Headhunters.

"Your friends from Osarian do not seem interested in talk, Commander Ackdool," Nom Anor said calmly.

"Osa-Prime is in flames," Ackdool came back, a slight crack showing in his cool diplomatic shell.

"We agreed to cease fire," Nom Anor said.

"You will be protected, all the way in to the *Mediator*, and escorted back to Rhommamool after our discussion," Commander Ackdool assured him, and from his formal tone alone, Nom Anor could guess that he had snapped to attention as he spoke. "On my word."

"As you will," Nom Anor said, cognizant of the fact that his villip couldn't nod. "Break up the screen," he quietly bade Shok Tinoktin, and the man complied, rolling the channel back and forth so that the communications' visual break seemed like a malfunction.

"Commander Ackdool?" Nom Anor's villip asked on cue, its tone full of trepidation.

"I hear you," Ackdool's crackling voice replied. "We've lost screen."

"The malfunction is here, I fear," Nom Anor said. "I see

nothing but Osarian ships. And I am without controls. I cannot evade them!"

"Be calm, Nom Anor," Ackdool replied. "My starfighters will protect you."

Indeed, watching from the shell, Nom Anor and Shok Tinoktin couldn't help but smile as the *Mediator*'s superior starfighters intercepted the Osarians and easily chased them away. One got a torpedo away, though, and only a brilliant maneuver by one X-wing, breaking from the pack and intercepting the torpedo with a line of laser fire, saved the undefended capsule from incineration. Still, the shock of the torpedo blast sent the capsule off course and into a continuing roll.

"I never doubted you," Nom Anor said calmly.

Ackdool's ensuing pause was telling, confirmation that his apparent cool in the face of death had just elevated the commander's respect for him. Nom Anor almost wished at that moment that he actually *was* in the capsule, that he would be meeting with Ackdool and the Osarians.

Almost.

"Without controls," Nom Anor growled, "I cannot even shut down my engines, and cannot change course. To the tar pits of Alurion with you, Ackdool. You promised sanctuary."

"We'll get you," Commander Ackdool assured him.

A moment later, the capsule abruptly halted its roll, and despite the fact that its engines were still firing and it was pointed at an angle that ought to have taken it far from the *Mediator*, it began drifting in toward the great ship.

"Tractor beam," Shok Tinoktin explained. "Those engines on the capsule will do nothing to hinder it. They'll pull her in and hold her until they can shut her down."

Nom Anor smiled and watched, not even bothering to answer Ackdool's continuing calls to him, as the capsule, flanked by starfighters, approached the *Mediator*.

The A-wing jolted, and the shell started to turn.

"We're bouncing along the atmosphere," Shok Tinoktin explained.

Nom Anor glanced at him, and poor Shok worked doubly hard to keep the *Mediator* in view, fearing the consequences if the executor did not witness this moment of glory.

The capsule disappeared into the *Mediator*'s lower docking bay. Shok Tinoktin reopened the visual channel.

"Boom," Nom Anor said, smiling at Shok.

"Boom," Nom Anor's villip echoed to Commander Ackdool.

The nuclear fission explosives packed into the shuttle detonated, vaporizing the entire section of docking bays, blowing out a huge section of the lower floor of the great battle cruiser, issuing a shock wave and a rain of white-glowing metal shards that folded many of the nearest buzzing starfighters in on themselves and lifted the tail of the battle cruiser, uprighting it ninety degrees before any stabilizing jets could halt the roll.

Nom Anor and Shok Tinoktin drifted away in their shell, caught by Rhommamool's gravity and pulled along the planet's rim. When they were far enough from the *Mediator* so that they wouldn't be detected, Shok blew the shell apart with laser cannons, and off they streaked in the modified A-wing, around the other side of the planet, confident that Commander Ackdool and his crew had too much to handle in just securing the rest of their ship to even notice their departure.

They made the jump to lightspeed soon after, leaving Rhommamool far behind. Nom Anor had pushed the conflict past the breaking point, beyond any hopes of peaceful resolution, and so his duty there was finished. Let them think he had died in the explosion on the *Mediator*, a martyr to the cause. Let the roused rabble he had left behind on Rhommamool die eagerly.

He was still considering the beauty of his plan and his faked ending when the A-wing came back to sublight hours later. Shok Tinoktin was fast asleep in the pilot chair in front of, and just below, Nom Anor, breathing rhythmically, contentedly. The coordinates had already been entered, and the A-wing was flying itself to the next destination, the next spot where Nom Anor could stir up the passions of the oppressed, could cause havoc to the New Republic and keep the fools so consumed by the civil wars and unrest among their own that they would not turn their eyes outward to the fringes of the galaxy, where far more dangerous trouble was beginning to stew.

The Osarian-Rhommamool conflict would explode fully now, he knew, and the New Republic Advisory Council would send in half the fleet to intervene and keep the warring planets at bay, while the councilors spent countless hours fretting over petty details, with half of them, no doubt, trying to find some way in which they might personally profit from the disaster.

Nom Anor worked hard to keep his personal disdain for the New Republic government from clouding his vision and allowing him to grow too optimistic. The Praetorite Vong, the Yuuzhan Vong war force that had come in to assist in the conquest of the galaxy, was not overwhelmingly large, by any means, and they couldn't afford to underestimate their opponents at any turn.

He looked to Shok for a moment, making sure that the man was asleep, then reached into a case at the side of his cramped seat and produced Da'Gara's sympathetic villip. In mere moments, the creature inverted to show the head of the prefect, complete with his starfish breather.

"How goes Yomin Carr's operation?" Nom Anor asked after the polite and formal greetings, and he was glad to be speaking again in the more comfortable Yuuzhan Vong tongue.

"Belkadan is dead to our enemies," Da'Gara assured him. "Yomin Carr remains there, my newest eyes in this region of the galaxy."

"He has turned the station's satellite scopes to our advantage then?" Nom Anor asked.

"Indeed, Executor," Da'Gara said. "Or he will, as soon as the storms pass. We are far from blind, though, for the war coordinator scans the nearby sectors."

"And are you pleased by what the war coordinator sees?" Nom Anor asked.

"This region is sparsely populated," Da'Gara answered, a twinge of regret in his voice. "The war coordinator's observations, along with the previous reports, prove that there will be little resistance while we gain a foothold."

Nom Anor nodded his approval—and relief. The Praetorite Vong would be vulnerable for a while, with only the one frozen planet as a true base. There was great advantage in using a war coordinator, a yammosk, for the attack. In addition to its own powerful energies, and true to its title as war coordinator, the creature could bring the forces of the three expeditionary worldships into tight focus and purpose, could allow the coralskippers to fly in perfect unison, thus making them many times more efficient. But there was a downside to such an endeavor, for if the New Republic somehow managed to bring all of their considerable firepower to bear on that frozen base planet and, impossible as it seemed, managed to destroy the yammosk, the resulting chaos among the Praetorite Vong could bring about complete disaster. The Praetorite Vong had to move slowly at first, allowing the yammosk to put all the base defenses in place, and to allow for the arrival of the next two fighter-packed worldships.

"Have you selected your next target?" he asked.

"Sernpidal," Da'Gara replied. "Third planet of the Julevian system and the most heavily populated planet of the entire sector."

"An ambitious step."

"But the largest threat to us," Da'Gara explained. "The yammosk has been watching them and is not secure in their too-common atmospheric breaches, nor in the multitude of communications transmissions emanating from the surface."

"If you are to be discovered, it will likely come from there," Nom Anor agreed.

"We will try to do it quietly," Da'Gara explained. "Perhaps through plague—perhaps similar to the molecular disaster Yomin Carr exacted upon Belkadan, though defeating outgoing communications from a planet as advanced as Sernpidal will prove no easy task, nor will the task of keeping our enemies on world for the course of the destruction. The war coordinator's own calculations put the former at seven-point-three to one against our success, and no better than one-to-one concerning the latter, even if we bring two full complements of coralskippers to bear."

Nom Anor spent a long while considering those odds, and as he grew uneasy about the chances—though still agreeing that Sernpidal had to be dealt with promptly—he turned his thoughts in a different direction.

"It must be something that does not directly connect an invasion, and certainly that does not reveal the scope of even our portion of the invading force," he said. He considered again the problems immediately facing the New Republic Advisory Council, and the firepower they would now have to employ close to the core of their galaxy to prevent complete catastrophe. "But not quiet," he explained. "No, let us destroy Sernpidal and kill as many enemies as possible, but let us use this disaster to lure some of our enemies' warships out to us. Taken in full, the New Republic fleet could possibly cause trouble for the Praetorite Vong, but if we can bring them out, little by little, they will prove of no consequence."

"Not quiet?" Prefect Da'Gara echoed skeptically.

"But not revealing," Nom Anor replied.

Another long pause ensued, both considering the problem at hand. Then the villip in front of Nom Anor correctly reflected the eager light that came into the prefect's eye.

"Yo'gand's Core?" Da'Gara asked.

The suggestion caught Nom Anor by surprise, and he almost dismissed it out of hand as preposterous. But he took the time to think about it, honestly considering the possibility. Yo'gand was a legendary general among the Yuuzhan Vong, the one most often given credit for turning the tide in the Cremlevian War and thus uniting the various Yuuzhan Vong tribes in generations long past. His "core" tactic had proven a decisive blow in that long-ago conflict, destroying Ygziir, the home planet of the most powerful tribe, and killing nearly all of the obstinate leaders in one fell swoop. Yo'gand had utilized the power of a strong dovin basal, the same gravity-focusing creature now used to propel worldships and other craft, by dropping it to the surface of Ygziir, where it focused one beam to latch on to the planet's core, the other to grab at the passing moon.

Since the destruction of Ygziir, Nom Anor's people had learned to easily counter the tactic, but these infidels, without understanding of the extragalactic creatures, and without the countering powers of other dovin basals, would have no way to determine the source of impending disaster—and they would not have the firepower to defeat it.

Nor would New Republic investigative teams figure out the true source, or the power behind it. Not until it was far too late.

"Make your noise, Prefect Da'Gara," Nom Anor said. "Destroy Sernpidal and plan your expansion. I will await your call."

"What?" a bleary-eyed Shok Tinoktin asked, coming awake groggily.

Nom Anor's villip inverted to its unremarkable state, and he replaced it in his bag.

"The call," Nom Anor replied. "The call of the oppressed, begging mercy from the uncaring councilors of the New Republic."

"Preparing your next speech?" Shok Tinoktin asked.

Nom Anor smiled. Indeed, he would soon be doing exactly that. His next speech to rouse the rabble, and then his next.

But soon, he knew, his speech would be one of conquest, an ultimatum to the New Republic to accede to the demands of their new masters or be utterly destroyed.

TWELVE

The Game, the Reality

"It was . . . strange," Jaina admitted to her brothers later on, as the three explored the wonders of Lando's newest home, such as the transparent pneumatic tubes that shot them from one tower to another, and the windbreak open-drop chutes that got them from the thirtieth floor to the first in a harrowing plummet. For the latter, they basically buckled on helmets and stepped into a hole, falling, falling, against the wind of a giant fan that slowed them gently and put them down on the lowest floor.

"You found your peace," Jacen replied.

"You practiced your piloting skills," Anakin put in quickly, and he and Jacen glared at each other. They had been at it again, arguing the inner gains of the Force against the practical skills to which it could be applied, ever since Anakin, soon after his abrupt departure from Lando's Folly, had found Jacen and the others in the control room, all of them standing quiet, stunned by Jaina's performance and waiting for the confirmation that she was okay.

Jaina shook her head and chuckled at the ridiculous debate.

"Were you conscious of your movements?" Jacen asked.

"In navigating the field?" Jaina said. "I don't even remember it."

"Because you let yourself go with the Force," Jacen reasoned, thinking that he had just scored a victory.

"Because she learned to apply the use of the Force *as an addition* to her physical piloting," the persistent Anakin declared. "Her actions were so automatic because she practices her flying. All the time."

"It's more than that," Jacen insisted.

"Then why didn't you do better?" Anakin asked.

"I never found the level of meditation."

"Because you don't practice enough," Anakin said. "That's why I beat you." He snapped his fingers in the air, as if tracking points. "I know how to apply the Force to practical tasks, not just sitting around in the dark, falling inward."

"Then why don't you ever win our sparring?" Jacen asked.

"I'll beat you right now," Anakin insisted, going for his lightsaber.

"You're acting pretty stupid for a couple of supposed Jedi Knights," Jaina said dryly.

"On the contrary," came another voice, and the three turned as one to see a man approaching, a noticeable swagger to his walk, a lightsaber dangling from his belt.

"Kyp," Anakin greeted.

Kyp Durron walked over, nodding to the boys and then dropping a long stare over Jaina. "Pretty good flying," he said at length.

"Pretty good?" Jacen asked with a chuckle.

Kyp glanced at him, holding a stern look for just a moment before a wide smile spread over his face. "Okay," he admitted. "Better than that. I knew I was in trouble as soon as I heard you were flying, Jaina. Now I'll have to go run the belt all over again, just to take back the lead."

"You going now?" Anakin asked, moving right before Kyp, obviously a bit in awe of the older Jedi.

"Not now," Kyp explained. "I'm heading off world, out of the system, actually. Got some work to do. My squadron's holding ready, waiting for me. But I wanted to find you guys and say hello."

"Your squadron?" Jacen and Anakin asked together, Jacen skeptically and Anakin hopefully.

"Some friends who fly with me," Kyp explained.

"Miko Reglia?" Jaina asked.

"And others."

"But no other Jedi," Jacen asked more than stated.

"Just some friends," Kyp explained. "If you three wanted to join in sometime—if your father and your uncle Luke would let you, I mean—you'd be more than welcome."

"Join in what?" Jacen had to ask.

"Work," Kyp said.

"Work?" Jacen's skepticism did not diminish.

"Stopping illegal trade, settling disputes," Kyp explained. There was no bravado in his tone, just a grim determination, the stern set of his eyes more intense than anything the three kids had ever seen from him.

"Is that the role of the Jedi now?" Jacen asked. "Chasing smugglers?" Both Jaina and Anakin stared at him incredulously, stunned that he would challenge the older and more experienced Jedi Knight.

"Is it not?" Kyp returned with a snort.

"There was a time when the smugglers were considered friends of the Jedi," Jacen dared to say.

"Like your father," Kyp reasoned.

"That was a different time," Jaina put in, physically moving between the two and trying to diffuse the tension. "A time when an illegitimate government ruled the galaxy."

Jacen shook his head, hardly seeming convinced.

"Do you think it beneath us?" Kyp asked, and he moved, politely but forcefully, past Jaina to stand right before Jacen. "When innocent people are robbed of all their wealth, or taken captive, perhaps, and tortured, is it not the province of the Jedi to come to their aid?" he asked, his voice rising with each word.

"It is," Anakin agreed.

"There is a difference between finding trouble in your path and going out of your way searching for it," Jacen said. "We are not galactic police."

"I've already heard all of this from your uncle," Kyp replied.

"And is there a better source for wisdom for any Jedi in all the galaxy?" Jacen asked.

"And yet, he didn't stop me from my self-appointed task," Kyp was quick to add, poking his finger Jacen's way to accentuate every word. "He asked me to temper my choices, but not to stop." He finished with a nod, then turned his gaze upon Jaina. "Magnificent flying, Jaina," he said. "I'll be back to give your record a run, and then I expect you to go after mine."

"You'll never catch me," Jaina said kiddingly.

Kyp patted her on the shoulder, his easy smile returning, and walked past. "Off we go," he explained, and he turned back, though he kept on walking. "My offer holds, for all three of you when you get away from your aunt and uncle. I could use more Jedi to round out the squadron."

He threw a wink their way and headed off toward the starport, where his X-wing waited. On Anakin's suggestion—and Jaina's insistence, for Jacen did not want to go—the three siblings climbed to the highest floor of the tower and moved out onto the skywalk balcony under the night sky to watch the departure. Somehow they knew that Kyp Durron wouldn't disappoint.

It started as music, Dembaline's *Shwock Dubllon*, or *Crested Wake*, the Mon Calamari composer's most rousing tune, piped across the loudspeakers of all the starport pads. The opening peak of the piece faded to a mill of somewhat discordant notes, gradually, gradually coming together, gathering as Kyp's squadron gathered in the air above, craft of all types, mostly older models: B-wings and A-wings, even a pair of Headhunters and a trio of older X-wings. A dozen starfighters wove red threads in the black sky with their plumes, a pilot's dance to the ever-building music.

Then the two XJ X-wings, Kyp and Miko, blasted through the montage, just as *Crested Wake* hit its roaring crescendo, and their dozen minions set off in rapid and disciplined order.

Jacen looked over at Anakin, who was clearly impressed, staring unblinking at the receding plumes. His little brother's thoughts were full of adventure and glory, Jacen knew, of hunting evil and furthering the cause of good.

Anakin didn't understand that things were rarely that black and white.

"Kyp's assembled quite a mix of fighters," Jaina remarked as the music died away. She looked at her brothers and shook her head. "He does know how to make an exit."

"And it's exactly hero shows like that which will confirm to Uncle Luke that he needs to reassemble the Jedi Council," Jacen replied.

"And a wise council will be pleased with shows just like that," Anakin put in.

"To show the galaxy the glory of the Jedi?" Jacen asked skeptically.

"To bring fear to those who would oppose the New Republic, and hope to those who want to live in peace under the rule of law," his brother answered.

"Enough!" Jaina pleaded with both of them.

And both heeded her request, and each shook his head and dutifully followed Jaina back into the tower, for neither was as certain of his viewpoint as he pretended.

"There they go," Leia remarked, as she and Han, Mara and Luke, Lando, Chewie, and the two droids watched Kyp's flashing departure from the balcony of Lando's private quarters.

"Count on Kyp to leave with style," Han said, and then, in a quieter voice, he added, "Probably still stinging from losing to Jaina."

"Took a Jedi to beat a Jedi," Lando observed, and he struck

a pensive pose, staring at Luke. "I know another Jedi who's a pretty fair pilot," he said at length, slyly. At his words, the others also turned to regard Luke.

Luke smiled and shrugged. He wasn't about to compete with the Solo kids. And Lando's attempted baiting, trying to play Jedi against Jedi in competition, simply served to strengthen his resolve to reestablish the Jedi Council. A Jedi should be more interested in competing against himself, to Luke's thinking. He could forgive the Solo kids their excitement and desire to compete for a spot on the board. Kyp, though, with more than ten years behind him, should understand better.

"We've got a completely different chart for the two-seaters," Lando explained. "No Jedi on that board."

Luke looked to Mara doubtfully. He had no desire to run the belt—he needed no challenge to prove his skills, as pilot or Jedi. But he understood that Mara might be seeing things differently. Perhaps she needed personal reassurance that she could still perform optimally despite her physical condition. Perhaps a run through the belt would give her the confidence that her decision to continue to play a vital role in their affairs, particularly those of Jaina, was in no way compromising the safety of any of those she loved.

"Do you want to give it a run?" Luke asked her, and Lando leaned in eagerly for the reply.

"I already did," Mara answered quietly, so that only Luke could hear, and he sensed that she was truly at peace, that she had garnered all the confidence she needed through Jaina's magnificent trial.

Luke marveled at how well she had read him, at how she had known that he didn't have any pressing need to go, but that he would have gone, willingly, if she had so desired. He stared at Mara for a long time, admiring her.

He always seemed to be doing that.

"I think we'll pass up the offer," Mara told Lando.

Lando started to protest, to spout the possibilities that the two of them might score the highest ever, a record no other pair of pilots would come close to touching. But then he glanced Han and Leia's way and saw them shaking their heads, ever so slightly, a signal for him to back off, a reminder of Mara's condition.

"Well, if you ever change your mind . . . ," he remarked with some regret.

It made sense to Luke when he considered it. Wouldn't Lando love to have the names Luke and Mara Jade Skywalker at the top of his dual-run board, as he now had the names of two Jedi Knights at the top of his single-run board! What fine advertising that would prove for the enterprising man, what notoriety for his reworked planet. And even more important, the gain in legitimacy for Lando's operation would be considerable indeed.

"What about you two?" Lando asked, turning to Han and Leia.

"I do enough steering through council meetings," Leia responded instantly, shaking her head, holding up her hand, and showing that she had no interest whatsoever in the challenge of the asteroid belt.

"Han and Chewie, then!" Lando said exuberantly. "They always bragged they were the best pilot pair in the galaxy. Let them prove it!"

"I'm too old and slow," Han replied, draping an arm across Leia's shoulders.

Chewie just gave a howl.

Jacen, Jaina, and Anakin entered the room.

"Did you see Kyp leave?" Anakin asked excitedly, moving quickly to Luke's side. "The music, the tight formation."

Luke nodded.

Jaina looked around curiously, focusing on Lando and her parents, then on Chewie, who seemed rather agitated, and then, finally, settling her gaze on her aunt.

"Lando wants Chewie and Han to take a run at the belt in

a two-seater," Mara explained. "It sounds like a good idea to me."

Leia pulled away from her husband, who gave her one of his typical plaintive smirks. In truth, she wasn't crazy about the idea of Han running into a such a game—even if Lando had guaranteed that there would be minimal danger. Her protective instincts couldn't stand up against that smirk, though. Han obviously didn't want to go, or didn't care enough to bother, and she was unable to resist the urge to prod him. "Me, too," she agreed.

Chewie issued a series of howls this time, telling them that he was intrigued by the idea.

"That's a kid's game," Han replied with a snort. "I'm too old and too slow and too sore."

"And too pocket hare," Anakin was quick to add, drawing a laugh from everyone—except, of course, Han.

"Moss Deevers and Twingo hold the current lead," Lando said, referring to a couple of two-bit smugglers, known for carrying bigger payloads in their drinking glasses than in their holds. It was often said of Moss, a Bothan, and Twingo, his Sullustan sidekick, that if they carried one-hundredth the cargo they had boasted about, they would be the richest rogues in the galaxy, and if they had dodged, shot down, or otherwise evaded one-hundredth the number of Imperial ships they had claimed, the Emperor would have been without a fleet long before the Rebel Alliance defeated him.

The two braggarts weren't especially well liked among the below-the-law folk Han and Chewie used to call friends, and Han had never had any use for the pair, particularly for Moss.

What good fortune for Lando, then, that these two happened at that time to be the leaders on his dual-run scoreboard.

"You won't even fit in a TIE bomber," Han remarked to the Wookiee. "Your legs'd stick out the bottom and we'd be kicking asteroids all over the place."

Chewie brought his fists up beside his head, mimicking the large ears of a Sullustan, and put a stupid look on his face.

Then he roared emphatically, reminding Han that Moss and Twingo would never let the two of them live down their cowardice. Both of the braggarts would use the news that Han and Chewie refused to try for the record as proof that the pair recognized and acknowledged Moss and Twingo's superior flying skills.

"Yeah, yeah," Han admitted. He looked around at the others, to see them all staring at him, all smiling. "What?" he asked innocently.

Those smiles were even wider when Lando's crew worked to squeeze Han and the giant Chewie into the twin shock couches of a TIE bomber. One unfortunate attendant twisted Chewie's leg the wrong way, and the Wookiee responded with a backhand slap—not a hard one, just enough to send the man tumbling a few meters. The crew finally managed to get the two into place; Chewie looked somewhat ridiculous, with his legs bent at such an angle that his knobby, hairy knees were nearly as high as his chin.

"Ready away?" came the call.

"How are we supposed to fly like this?" Han protested, looking doubtfully at Chewie.

The Wookiee howled.

"Well, you don't look fine!" Han retorted.

"It won't matter," Lando replied. "You won't get near to Moss and Twingo's mark of four forty-one anyway."

Chewie roared.

"Ready away!" Han cried.

"Always appeal to his pride," Lando whispered to Leia and the others with a wink, and as soon as Han and Chewie blasted out of the dock, they all headed back to the control room to watch the show. The three kids traded predictions on the way, agreeing that their father and Chewie would blast the previous record apart, but also coming to the conclusion that there was only so far the pair could go, for they weren't possessed of the needed sensitivity to the Force. In Jaina's eyes, they were practically flying blind, she explained, recounting the Force-given insight she had used to defeat the apparent wall of flying stone.

Both Jacen and Anakin, though they differed in their beliefs concerning priorities for the Force, agreed with Jaina's assessment.

Luke listened to it all with some amusement. None of them had come to truly understand the power and the limitations of the Force, and none of them, it seemed to him, truly understood the cleverness of their father. Luke would never underestimate the Force, but neither would he underestimate Han Solo.

Also, Luke knew that Han and Chewie had more than a little experience in navigating asteroid belts.

By the time the group arrived at the control room, the viewscreens wrapping all about them, Han and Chewie had put the TIE bomber through some practice maneuvers and were in position to enter the belt.

The controllers on *Belt-Runner I* called to the pair that their shields were up in full, and gave them the go-ahead.

"Great," Han responded dryly, drawing laughs from everyone in the control room.

The secondary, rectangular viewscreen zoomed in for a close-up of the TIE bomber as it slipped into the flow of the asteroid belt, a speck of light in the darkness, cruising effortlessly, it seemed, around the nearest obstacles, then navigating one cluster of spinning stones so seamlessly that it seemed like a ghost, ignoring the material.

"Beautiful," Jacen remarked.

Han wasn't exactly seeing things that way. In fact, from the moment he and Chewie had zipped into the asteroid belt, he had been letting out one long, terrified scream. What seemed from the ground to be a well-plotted, carefully calculated course of least resistance was, in fact, nothing more than a series of desperate reactions, and one lucky blow. For as the TIE bomber swerved on end around one asteroid, Chewie, elbows up high, slipped to the side and bopped Han off the side of the head.

Han was about to send the craft into a vertical stoop, a maneuver that would have slammed them headlong into another asteroid, one he hadn't noted, but the impact of Chewie's elbow knocked him away from the controls, and the TIE bomber continued its present course, somehow slipping between two asteroids that both Han and Chewie, and the observers on the ground, had assumed were too close together.

The maneuver appeared brilliant.

"Hairball!" Han yelled at Chewie.

The Wookiee turned so that his face was barely a centimeter from Han's and let out a howl. Then both looked back to the forward screen, saw an asteroid about to pancake them, and both let out a howl, throwing up their arms instinctively to cover their faces.

When they did, Chewie's too-high knee kicked the stick to the side, and the TIE bomber flipped into a sidelong roll and avoided the asteroid.

It appeared brilliant, at least.

Lando's voice came over the speaker. "You two got the kids standing here with their mouths hanging open."

Han clicked on his comm. "No problem," he said, and then he was fast to turn off the mike before he screamed, "You've got to be kidding me!" as a wall of asteroids rose up before them.

Han pulled left, Chewie right, and the TIE bomber . . . did nothing. Each saw the other's countering move, each reversed his angle, and the TIE bomber . . . did nothing.

"Go left, you stinking hairball!" Han shouted desperately, and then he errantly pulled right on his own stick, and since Chewie was correctly following orders, the TIE bomber . . . did nothing.

"Your left, not mine!" Han scolded, which was somewhat ridiculous considering that they were both facing the same way.

Chewie reached over, wrapping Han's hands and his stick with one big paw, and pulled both sticks together. The nimble TIE bomber rocketed off to the left, skimming across the facing of the huge wall. Han kicked the throttle up to full, and they barely slipped around the edge of the wall, then cut back to the right, into the flow once again—what should have been a simple maneuver made to look brilliant.

Into the flow they zoomed, going way too fast. Lando's voice crackled over the speaker, but they couldn't begin to pay attention to it as they tried to get back under control. One huge, spinning rock fast approached, and the two pilots, now finally in sync, dipped their nose below it, reversed throttle, and executed a perfect loop, barely skimming the asteroid's surface and using its gravity to bring some resistance to their flight.

They came out around the bottom at a much safer pace and fell into a smooth rhythm along a relatively clear stretch. Han glanced down at the timer, mostly to see if he and Chewie could get the heck out of there.

It wasn't running.

"What?" he asked, and he gave the instrument a bang.

Nothing.

Now Han did click on his comm. "Chrono's not running," he called. "What do we got for a time?"

His voice, somewhat breaking up, came over the speakers in the control room, and all glanced up at the wall chrono. Three minutes, thirty-three seconds, approaching a new record for two-seaters.

"Three thirty-three—you've almost beat them," Lando called, and he quickly added, "but all three of your kids are still way ahead of you," just to incite the pair to keep on flying, to keep the show going.

"What do we got for a time?" Han's voice came again, breaking up even more.

"He didn't hear you," Luke observed, and all the smiles

and nods of appreciation for the so-far fine run faded fast, picking up on the cue of Lando's suddenly grave expression. The technicians in the control pods bent low over their instruments, several opening channels to *Belt-Runner I*.

"Three forty-seven," Lando called loudly.

"Time?" Han asked again, obviously not hearing a word.

"Just a communication problem," Lando assured the others.

"More than that," came a call from one of the controllers. "*Belt-Runner I*'s lost all signal."

"All signal?" Lando asked.

"All," the man confirmed.

"What does it mean?" Leia asked, grabbing Lando's elbow.

"It means they're deaf," he answered soberly. "And it means that their shields are down."

All across the room, eyes opened wide in shock as the implications of that statement came clear. Luke left the control room at a run.

In the TIE bomber, Han and Chewie were settled now, cruising easily around the relatively clear area of asteroids, confident that they were in no danger, and even beginning to understand how they might use their systems to their advantage.

Had those systems been working.

"Skip off that one," Han instructed, pointing to a large and smooth-edged rock to the right. Then he brought his arm angling back to the left, predicting their flight course and pointing to the spot where they might slip through another approaching cluster.

Chewie did as ordered, bringing the TIE bomber swooping toward the asteroid on the right, meaning to just skim it and use the shields like some constant repulsorlift coil.

Skip they did, but by striking with their right solar array wing and no deflecting shields. The TIE bomber bounced away and into a spin, and the shocked Han and Chewie both looked out instinctively to see the damage: half the solar array torn away and the pylon bent.

They grabbed at the sticks and fought for control, pumping the foot yokes frantically. In the jostling, one of Han's belts popped open and he sprawled forward over his controls, launching the ship into a diagonal dive and roll.

Chewie reacted quickly, slapping the kill switch to Han's console, taking complete control of the craft, howling as Han yelled, working hard to correct the pitch.

"No shields, Chewie! No shields!" Han shrieked.

A lurking asteroid, a wall of stone, filled their viewport.

"Down! Down! Down!" Lando yelled, watching the spectacle, and so the TIE bomber started, diving in front of the stone, and then . . .

Nothing.

"The signal's gone!" one of the controllers yelled.

"*Belt-Runner I*'s got nothing, either," another added.

The rectangular screen switched views suddenly, showing a TIE fighter soaring out from a pad at full throttle.

"Find them," Leia whispered under her breath, aiming the words and the prayer at her brother, Luke, the pilot of that soon-to-be-belt-running TIE fighter.

THIRTEEN

Minus Thirteen

They cruised easily through the blackness, the piecemeal squadron Kyp Durron had titled the Dozen-and-Two Avengers, a name the Jedi expected would be often repeated throughout the galaxy before much longer. All of them had flown Lando's Folly several times in the modified TIE fighters, and all had done well, with several climbing onto the notable board. Even more important, through the extensive training the disciplined Kyp had forced upon them, they had learned to fly together, complementing each other's movements, anticipating rather than reacting. They wouldn't match up to the more notable starfighter squadrons, Kyp knew, like Rogue Squadron—not yet, but they were improving daily, and they were seeing more action than any of the others. Perhaps one day soon, the Dozen-and-Two would be spoken of in the same breathless manner as Rogue Squadron.

That was Kyp's hope.

Of course, if the three Solos, or any one of them, particularly Jaina, decided to join, the equation would change dramatically. The offspring of Han and Leia would bring immediate recognition and attention to the Dozen-and-Two—a name, Kyp realized, he would have to alter. Would that be a good thing? Were the fourteen members of his squadron ready for the attention, ready for the spotlight? Such notoriety would

aid them, no doubt, when battles were joined, for their enemies would likely be too afraid to properly coordinate their
movements and attack, but also, with the glory would come
greater enemies.

Were they ready? Was Kyp ready?

And what of the Avengers' leadership? Kyp had to wonder.
Jaina had surpassed him running the belt, and despite his
bravado, Kyp understood just how soundly he had been
beaten. He could fly the belt a hundred more times and never
come near Jaina's mark. The other pilots of the Dozen-and-
Two knew that, too. So if Jaina and her brothers joined the
group, who would lead? As it stood now, Kyp's only real rival
was Miko, the only other Jedi and easily the second-best pilot
of the bunch. And Miko, a quiet and unassuming type, who
spent most of his time practicing with his lightsaber or just
sitting alone under the starry canopy, held no apparent aspirations of leadership; he was, in fact, serving time as Kyp's apprentice, training under the more experienced Jedi.

All of those thoughts accompanied Kyp into the darkness
of space as he and his fellows departed Dubrillion. He wasn't
unsettled by the possibilities, though, but rather, contem-
plative, and in the end he simply decided that the gain would
outweigh any of the potential troubles. If the three Solos
joined the Avengers—the Dozen-and-Five, he supposed—
the squadron would soon be thought of in elite terms, and
their missions would become more important, more dangerous, and more profitable in terms of the gain to the cause
of law and the New Republic. The Dozen-and-Five—a dozen
regulars and five Jedi—could well become the greatest
squadron in the galaxy.

Of course, Kyp didn't really believe that the Solos would
join in, not all of them, at least. Luke Skywalker had been
typically diplomatic and respectful when he had met with
Kyp on Dubrillion, but he had also been somewhat stern and
disapproving. Kyp wasn't sure if Luke thought this smuggler
hunting a duty that was beneath Jedi Knights, or if he simply

objected to it on personal grounds—hadn't Han Solo been among the most notorious of smugglers at one time?—but in either case, Kyp had come away from the meeting with the definite feeling that Luke was not in favor of his present activities.

Yet neither had Luke demanded that those activities cease, and so Kyp led his squadron now to the Veragi sector, to a remote area bereft of star systems, an empty black space region except for an observation buoy Kyp and his friends had put in place at a hyperspace junction.

Following the signal on a secret and little-used channel, Kyp guided the squadron to the buoy. Miko Reglia put the others in a defensive ring about Kyp's XJ X-wing as Kyp docked with the buoy. His astromech droid, R5-L4—Kyp called him Elfour—quickly began downloading the information, passing it onto Kyp's viewscreen, fast-forwarding through days and days of emptiness.

Kyp sighed and relaxed back in his seat. Smugglers weren't easy to find anywhere in the galaxy, and were particularly rare out here in this region of the Outer Rim—except, of course, for those who went to Lando's planets for a little business and a little training. And Kyp couldn't go after any group that was anywhere near Lando Calrissian's operations, he knew, for the pragmatic profiteer would quickly exert his influence with people like Han and Luke to shut Kyp down.

The only movement showing on the viewscreen in front of him was that of the stars for a long, long while, and Kyp settled back for an uneventful hour. He perked up briefly as R5-L4 slowed the sequence to normal, recording the appearance of one suspicious freighter as it hypered into the region, but then sighed again as he watched that ship revector and hyper away, with R5-L4's computations showing that it was heading for Destrillion.

And so it went, hour after hour, with the records of the buoy showing nothing remarkable other than a couple of asteroids in areas previously unknown and a few freighters and even a couple of smaller, personal ships, but so far out and moving too fast to even warrant an inspection. But then, nearing the end of the records, a ship did show up where one didn't seem to belong, an outdated shuttle—*Spacecaster* class, according to R5-L4.

"Backtrack its course, Elfour," Kyp instructed. Its angle of approach into the buoy's field of scan seemed out of place, certainly nothing coming from the inner Core.

The word *Belkadan* flashed on the screen, along with its coordinates in the nearby Dalonbian sector.

"Vitals?" Kyp asked, and even as the word left his mouth, the history and present disposition of Belkadan scrolled before him, including the details of ExGal-4.

"Why would they be leaving?"

A question mark appeared on the screen, R5-L4 apparently not understanding the rhetorical nature of the question.

On Kyp's instruction, R5-L4 focused on the buoy records that followed the path of the departing Spacecaster, calculating its jump all the way to the borders of the Helska system, where it disappeared from scanners.

Then the droid went at the audio recordings, pieces of subspace chatter, mostly from Lando's operation. On Kyp's orders, the droid calculated the approximate departure time from Belkadan for the Spacecaster, then focused its inspection on that period and on those signals coming from the general direction of Belkadan.

Only one of the few clear words decipherable from the less-than-perfect detection jumped out at Kyp: storm.

Was Belkadan, and this station called ExGal-4, in trouble?

Kyp felt the adrenaline beginning to course through his veins, that tingle of excitement that always so charged him before adventure. He had a choice to make, for Belkadan was a long way from the Helska system, but as soon as he gave it any real thought, the answer seemed obvious. Whatever might have happened on Belkadan, some of the scientists had apparently escaped, though why they would make their way to the remote Helska system and not back toward the Core, or even toward Lando's operations or toward the not-so-distant Moddell sector, escaped him.

"Give me all the details of the Helska system," Kyp instructed his droid, and the scrolling began immediately and didn't last long.

There were no listed settlements in Helska, and no apparently inhabitable planets.

"Why?" Kyp asked quietly.

"Because you requested it," scrolled the oblivious droid's answer.

Kyp frowned and slid the screen away. "We're going to the Helska system," he called out to Miko and the others. "Plot it out."

And while they went to work, Kyp fashioned a report concerning Belkadan, a general call for someone to find out if the station there needed help.

Luke didn't even begin to slow as he plunged into the asteroid belt, didn't even hear the warning from *Belt-Runner I* that their shield generator was still acting up and they might not be able to offer him any protection.

He rolled the TIE fighter about one asteroid, then dived down through a pair of rocks that appeared suddenly around the back side of the first. No instruments for Luke; he didn't even have R2-D2 strapped in behind him, as was customary on the X-wing. He was flying by instinct and the Force, feeling the flow of asteroids and searching, searching, for the emanations of Han and Chewie.

He dodged another boulder, dived down under and around another, then shot up before a wall of the spinning rocks, leveling off and cutting deeper into the flow as soon as he noted a break in the array. He had come into the belt near where Han and Chewie had gone off the screens, but he couldn't recognize the asteroids he had been watching on the viewscreens.

Still, he knew that he was in the right vicinity.

"We've got the shields up and running," came the call from *Belt-Runner I*.

"Does that include the shields on the TIE bomber?" Luke asked, hoping for some confirmation that his friends were alive.

"If it's out there, and not too badly damaged, it should have shields," came the less-than-confident voice on the other end.

Luke continued to dodge and swerve, and was somewhat encouraged at first to find no debris.

But then a solar wing panel, smashed into a pulp, whipped by.

Luke took a deep, steadying breath. Leia was on the speaker now, pleading with him for some information. How could he begin to tell her?

He recognized then that his own grief would be no less than hers. His relationship with Han had started on rocky footing and had continued somewhat stormily for a long, long time. But despite the occasional arguments and philosophical disagreements, there was indeed a deep, deep bond between the two, as true a love as brothers might know.

How could Han be gone now?

Leia continued to plead; Luke shut off the communicator, deciding it would be better to tell her face-to-face.

He brought his TIE fighter into a barrel roll and flipped it head over heels halfway through, so that he came out in the flow of the belt instead of against it.

And then he saw them, perched on the back of an asteroid like a sand fly on the side of a moisture vaporator back on Tatooine. Somehow Han and Chewie had put the TIE bomber down on the large rock, and that feat seemed all the more impossible when Luke considered the damage the craft had sustained, with one wing torn away.

Luke came in slow, adjusting his thrusters so that he was barely inching in on the rock as he followed it along its course. Slowly, hindered as much by fear for his friends as by respect for the dangerous asteroid, Luke crawled up, up, past the TIE bomber to a point where he could get a look into its cockpit.

There sat Chewie and Han, arguing as usual, Han pointing one way, Chewie another, and both shaking their heads at the same time. Han had some blood on his forehead. Chewie noticed Luke in the TIE fighter then and gave a great Wookiee roar—Luke could tell because of the way Han grabbed at his ears.

"They're all right!" Luke called, clicking on the communicator.

"Where are they?" Leia cried.

"Why can't we see them?" Lando asked at the same time.

"Are they out of the belt?" Mara asked.

Luke started to answer Leia, then Lando, then Mara, then Leia again, and then just laughed at the futility of it all. It struck him then that Han and Chewie always seemed to be doing inexplicable things, that this was just another in a long series of amazing dodges against the claws of the grim specter of death.

"Han, can you hear me?" Luke called, rolling through the channels.

In response, to show that he could indeed hear but couldn't respond, Han held up his microphone, dangling at the end of a torn cord.

Luke nodded back, then inched his way around the downed craft, inspecting the damage. It wouldn't fly again, he knew, or at least not with any stability, and how Han and Chewie had ever put it down safely on the asteroid, Luke could only guess. Also, given that the ship's drives showed no signs of life, Luke doubted that the bomber had any kind of deflector shield working.

How, then, was he going to get Han and Chewie out of there?

"Lando," he called. "Are you guys reading my signals?"

"Got you loud and clear," Lando replied. "Hanging out behind that big asteroid. Is that where Han and Chewie are?"

"Hanging right on the back," Luke replied. "Any idea of how we can get them out of there?"

"Help's already on the way," Lando assured them. "We'll use a tow ship and suck them right out of there."

Luke, who was back in position above the downed TIE bomber's cockpit, saw Chewie howl again and saw Han's grimace, and knew that they, too, had heard. That brought another smile to his face, the thought of Han's disgrace at having Lando's machines come and pluck him out of danger. He'd never live this one down!

Luke stayed with the downed craft until Lando's tow ship arrived, bouncing through the asteroids. They did an impromptu check using a grabber arm to ensure that the shields were working well, then brought the shields down long enough to hook on a tow cable.

"It'll be bumpy on the way out," the pilot of the tow ship warned.

Luke stuck around just long enough to see Han's wry smile, then he turned his TIE fighter about and headed away, looking for an exit from the belt.

"We'll ignore the time spent baby-sitting Han and Chewie," came Lando's voice. "Just eleven more minutes riding upstream and you've got the new record."

Luke smiled, but he didn't even seriously consider the remark. He wasn't the least bit interested. He found his exit point and zipped away, cutting a smooth line through the belt and clear into the open space, heading back to Dubrillion, arriving on the planet long before the towing operation had even begun back at the belt.

He found Lando and the others still in the central control room, with Lando wearing a headset and bending over one panel, talking excitedly into a microphone.

"Always the hero," Mara said with a smile, and she wrapped Luke in a hug. Leia moved beside her and took her brother's hand.

"Give the credit to Han and Chewie," Luke explained. "I

still don't know how they got that broken piece of space junk onto the back of that asteroid."

"They always find a way," Leia said.

"The modified tractor transmitter," Lando explained, putting down the headset and moving to join the group. "The ion generators were still working on *Belt-Runner I*, but they couldn't get the power boost signal out to the other ships. You went in there naked, my friend."

Luke nodded and didn't seem either upset or concerned.

"Off-ship shielding is still a good concept," Lando pressed. "Planetary defenses will be all the stronger with fighters that can take battle cruiser-class hits."

"A limited, and limiting, concept," Luke replied calmly. "The backup systems needed to make sure all the shields don't blink out would be daunting. And if they did blink out, you'd have a bunch of ships running around in real trouble."

"They'd still have the shields from their own systems," Lando argued.

"But the safety net would be gone," Luke explained, concerned more with the psyche of the pilots. "They wouldn't appreciate how to fly it. It's the ability to operate on the very edge of disaster that makes a good pilot."

Lando shook his head and started to reply, but realized that, in light of Luke's rush into the belt shieldless, any rebuttal would prove difficult. Before he could even begin his argument, a shaken Han and Chewbacca walked into the room, Han with a towel wrapped around his cut forehead.

"That tin can you sent to get us hit every asteroid in sight on the way out," Han complained, but the others, too relieved to see the pair alive, merely smiled.

Chewie, though, wasn't finished with the complaining, and with a Wookiee, complaints usually took the form of action. He headed straight for Lando, arms outstretched as if he meant to choke the life out of the man. Luke and Mara, Leia and the three kids, all stepped in between, but all started sliding back as Chewie continued his stalk.

Finally, though, with Lando retreating to match the Wookiee's progress, Chewie backed off.

"Did we beat Moss and Twingo?" Han asked, breaking the tension.

Lando looked to his technicians. "We lost them at four forty-one," one replied ironically, the exact mark set by Moss and Twingo. Lando started to declare a tie, but took a glance at the still-fuming Wookiee, and abruptly decided, "Add five seconds for the time it took to hop on the back of the asteroid. Four forty-six, a new record."

"Who cares about the record?" Leia asked. "The flying alone to get you onto that asteroid was nothing short of remarkable, according to Luke."

"Best flying those two have ever done," Luke agreed.

The others added their platitudes, with words like *brilliant* and *amazing* thrown about.

Han was going to explain that Chewie deserved the credit, that the blow to his head had knocked him senseless for those few critical seconds, but the Wookiee interjected a long wail, a confirmation of their teamwork effort. They were a unit, comrades, the closest and most trusted of friends, and by definition of that bond, the credit for either one's exploits would be deservedly shared by the other.

Han took it all in with a wink to his Wookiee counterpart. "No problem," he assured them, his face twisting into a wry smile.

He did frown a bit when his gaze drifted to Lando, though, reflecting his honest feelings: fear and even a sickness deep in the pit of his stomach.

No problem indeed.

They came out of hyperspace and into the Helska system in a rolling, living formation, the Dozen-and-Two Avengers alternating their respective places in the wedge with coordinated barrel rolls and tight loops, brilliant precision flying that kept them on the edge of disaster—and also made their signal on any watching scanners much harder to decipher. Kyp Durron kept the lead at all times, though, with Miko Reglia on his right wing.

The system wasn't large, with only seven planets, and none of them too widely spaced. R5-L4 kept the data streaming across Kyp's viewscreen, detailing all the knowledge about the planets and the system, as the squadron cruised past the seventh planet, and then the sixth.

The fifth was a gas giant, an uninhabitable ball of roiling fury, so Kyp rolled past it with hardly a thought, focusing on the fourth planet, an intriguing ball of ice.

"I'm getting some readings from the fourth," Miko called in a moment later.

Following Kyp's lead, the squadron slowed. What had they stumbled upon? he wondered. A smuggler's den? Another scientific outpost—and if so, then why wasn't it on the charts, as required by New Republic law? It made no sense to him, and yet, he knew that the *Spacecaster*-class shuttle hadn't exited the system—if it had, the buoy would surely have detected it.

"Shields up and torpedoes ready," Kyp called on the open frequency to all the others. "Offset the wedge, two to my right."

The speedy A-wing on Kyp's left did a snap roll that put it right in line behind the trailing ship on the right-hand line of the wedge.

"Off-planet movement," came Miko's call, and Kyp's astromech confirmed it even as his wingman cried out. Indeed, he soon confirmed visually, there was movement, dozens and dozens of . . .

Of what? Asteroids?

Kyp's instruments revealed little at first, bringing in a jumble of signals that seemed to indicate some sort of life energy. "Hold back and cover my tail," he instructed the others, and he swooped away. His next impression was that these were indeed asteroids, albeit spectacular ones, showing many different colors. But as he drew even nearer, a chill ran up Kyp's spine.

R5-L4 issued a stream of protests, flashed signals on Kyp's screen that showed that there were some life-forms ahead, and then another, even more urgent signal brought Kyp's attention to his instruments. A tremendous energy bubble surrounded the frozen fourth planet.

Kyp looked back to the multicolored asteroids, noted the specific geometric shapes. Not one of the things looked exactly like another, but they all shared some features, the tapered nose, the aerodynamic sides.

These were craft, starfighters!

Kyp throttled up to full and yanked back, turning his nose up in a sharp loop. As he hit the top, he rolled about to upright and leveled off, shooting back the way he had come.

And on came the pursuit—"a swarm" was the only way Kyp could describe it.

"They're enemies!" he cried, and even as the words left his mouth, R5-L4 screeched and his X-wing lurched, slammed by something.

Kyp went through a series of evasive maneuvers, spinning down and out to the right, snap-rolling back to the left, and with full throttle the whole time. He took some comfort as he neared the rest of his squadron, screaming ahead in tight formation, laser cannons firing, torpedos flashing away.

"Meet me left, Miko," he cried, and he hook-turned to his right and continued the turn until he was facing back the other way, with Miko obediently on his wing.

Miko was firing, and so, too, was Kyp as he came out of the turn, blindly, desperately. He scored a solid hit on the nearest enemy, and that rocklike starfighter spun away, but the second zoomed past him, and in that close encounter, he saw that these were piloted ships. There was a canopy, resembling mica more than transparisteel, and behind it he saw the pilot, a barbaric-looking humanoid, its face a lump of pulsating flesh.

He shook off the disturbing sight and led Miko back to the right, back toward the rest of the squadron.

And they were into it thick, with enemy fighters swooping all about them, firing projectiles out of forward and side cannons that looked more like strange, miniature volcanoes. To their credit, the Dozen-and-Two were handing out most of the hits, many taking chunks off enemy vessels. But those vessels usually went into a spin and then came back out of it, leveling and heading fast to rejoin the battle.

"They can take a beating," Miko remarked.

"But they can't hand one out," Kyp noted, seeing several projectiles slam against a B-wing's shields, only to be repelled. "All right, Dozen-and-Two," he called. "Our shields'll beat them. Let's get organized and knock them off one at a time." He turned back to his droid. "Elfour, try to call them, all channels. Let's see if they'll surrender."

Even as he finished, a cry came back, from the B-wing. "My shields are down!"

Before Kyp could even respond, a host of enemy fighters soared into position and let fly swarms of volcano missiles, and that B-wing was halved again and again in rapid sequence, until a thousand little pieces littered the dark sky.

And then another cry of lost shields, and a Headhunter swiftly suffered the same fate.

Still, the remaining Avengers held their formations and hammered at the enemy fighters. Several were blasted into little pieces with concentrated laser fire, drilling chunk after chunk in the same spot until the whole of the ship cracked apart. But for every one lost, another dozen replaced it, and more and more were swarming up from the planet.

"No shield!" Miko cried.

Kyp looked at his wingman, perplexed. How was that possible? Miko hadn't even been hit, for he and Kyp weren't in the thick of it yet.

"Gravity well! I felt a tug, like a dozen g's pulling me out of my seat," Miko tried to quickly explain. "And then a hole in the shield, and then, nothing. My droid's babbling about magnetic fields, but I don't know!"

"Get out! Get out!" Kyp cried, to Miko and to all the others, and he pointed his own nose toward the main battle, thinking to cover the retreat. He came in spinning and firing, hitting one with a laser blast and then neatly tucking a torpedo into the cavity the laser had caused, blowing the enemy fighter to bits. He swerved between two more, taking a couple of inconsequential hits, then reversed throttle, with R5-L4 howling all the while, and flipped his X-wing about, a vicious maneuver that nearly stole his consciousness despite the fact that his inertial compensator was running at 97 percent. Kyp kept his cool and came out firing and had both the enemy fighters he had just passed spinning away, with pieces of them flying.

An A-wing flew past him, the pilot frantic, taking hits, with some of them thudding against the side and latching on, like molten goo.

"Oh, no," Kyp moaned, seeing those missiles melting right through the hull, one going right into the ion-drive connectors.

The A-wing blew apart.

Kyp spun about to meet the pursuing swarm, got a few shots off and took a few hits, but got past them.

He went in close enough to the bow of one enemy ship to spot another facet of it, or perhaps an added piece, for this looked more like a breathing, pulsing creature, a disembodied heart, and the readings coming from it were very different from anything Kyp had ever seen.

He felt a sudden tug and knew that his shields had dropped, and knew that this ship, or creature, or whatever it was, had just ripped them away with some type of magnetic or supergravity field. He focused his wrath on that notion, on this thing that had brought death so quickly to several of his friends.

Torpedoes away!

But they didn't get near the thing, seemed to stop in mid-flight, as if they were pressing their noses against an impenetrable barrier, and then just crushed in on themselves and blew apart.

"What?" Kyp cried, not daring to slow and inspect things further, for he was naked now, without shields, and with a host of enemy ships in pursuit.

"I'm hit!" Miko cried.

Kyp turned and turned, dived and spun, trying to find his friend, firing his laser cannons all the while, though he couldn't even slow enough to locate a target.

"My drives are down!" came Miko's voice. "No power! No power!"

Then silence.

Kyp saw another of his squadron, an older X-wing, disintegrate under a barrage of missiles, and he pointed his nose out of the system and took off at full throttle. He felt the pursuit at his back and worked hard to fix the coordinates so that he could make the jump to lightspeed. No time for heroics now; survival was the key, survival to return and report!

An A-wing appeared on his wing, the speedy craft pacing him.

"They're right behind!" the pilot cried.

"Keep it straight and fast!" Kyp called back, for these strange craft had not shown any ability to outrun them.

"But we're the only ones left!" the pilot cried.

"Steady and straight!"

And indeed, the enemy fighters couldn't catch them, but that surely did not end the pursuit, for another craft, a roughly oval-shaped rocky vessel, burst open a forward chamber, and a host of half-meter-long black winged creatures that somewhat resembled armored turfhoppers poured forth.

Kyp saw them and saw that they closed easily.

"Hyperdrive!" he cried to his new wingman.

"No coordinates!"

"Now!" Kyp ordered, and he engaged, and so did the

A-wing, but the A-wing had a trio of the vicious insectoids already on it, secreting a substance that melted through the hull, allowing the creatures to burrow in.

Kyp lost sight of the A-wing as the starlight elongated in that momentary freeze of reality that was initial hyperspace, but he understood, somewhere in his subconscious, that the other had not survived the jump, that the engagement of the powerful hyperdrive had blown the damaged A-wing to pieces.

Kyp came out of lightspeed almost immediately, fearing he would collide with a planet or zip through a sun. Before he could begin to try and calculate where he was, though, he saw that he, too, had not escaped unscathed, that he, too, carried a couple of unwanted passengers.

And one was coming through the canopy right at him, wicked pincers chopping excitedly.

"Sernpidal?" Han echoed incredulously. "You want me to go to Sernpidal?"

"A favor," Lando innocently replied. "Hey, I let you run the belt for free—" He stopped as Han frowned, reminding him that bringing up the belt incident might not be a wise thing to do when begging a favor.

"It'll take you two days," Lando said. "If I have to divert a freighter, I'll be spending more than the payload will bring in."

"Then don't sell them the ore," Han reasoned.

"Got to," Lando explained. "As long as I keep the outer colonies supplied, the New Republic looks the other way on some of my—how shall I put this?—under-the-table operations."

"Cost of doing business," Han said with finality, holding up his arms. He looked past Lando then, to Leia, who was standing in the hallway, arms crossed over her chest and frowning, a pose that poignantly reminded him that Lando could prove to be a very valuable ally at this time. Lando had

the network out here, the contacts they'd need if they wanted
to truly understand how the Advisory Council might be connected to the smugglers. Like it or not, Lando Calrissian was
a lever that both Luke and Leia desired in the turbulent political arena.

"Hey, even though your run didn't go well—and I'll give
you another try for free—Jaina got the record and so did you
and Chewie," Lando pleaded.

Han smirked, more at his wife than at Lando. "Sernpidal?"
he repeated, as if the very notion was preposterous, but in a
conciliatory tone.

Lando's smile nearly took in his ears, and he started
walking again toward the control room. "You'll be back before anyone realizes you're gone," he said.

One of the technicians came out of the control room then,
carrying a datapad. He spotted Lando and ran to the man, his
look somewhat nervous.

"Trouble?" Lando asked, taking the printout.

"From Kyp Durron," the technician explained.

Lando looked at the heading and chuckled. "The Dozen-
and-Two Avengers," he recited with a snort and a shake of
his head, for even Lando, known to be boastful and flashy,
recognized that Kyp was going a little over the line of pre-
tense here.

"What's the problem?" Leia asked, as she and Han moved
beside their friend.

"Outpost on Belkadan, in the Dalonbian sector," Lando explained. "Something going on over there." He looked to the
technician. "Did you try to raise them?"

"Nothing coming from that planet but static," the man
confirmed.

"Belkadan?" Leia asked.

"Small planet with a scientific outpost," Lando replied.
"Just a dozen or so scientists on planet."

"And what does this mean?" she asked, taking the printout.

"Probably means their transmitter is out," Lando replied. "Or maybe there's a solar flare wrecking communications. Probably nothing important." He looked to Han with a wry smile. "Since you're going out anyway . . . ," he began.

"Belkadan?" Han echoed, more incredulously than he had echoed *Sernpidal*.

"Just a few days out of the way," Lando said innocently.

"I haven't even agreed to go to Sernpidal yet," Han reminded him.

"Luke and Mara will go to Belkadan," Leia offered. "They've been wanting some time alone anyway."

Lando nodded, more than satisfied with the offer. His ships were all dedicated to business, and any diversions meant money lost.

They all met later on that day, and indeed, Luke and Mara were more than happy to take the excursion to Belkadan, while Han and Chewie would take the *Millennium Falcon* to Sernpidal with the payload for Lando. Leia begged off going, but suggested, strongly, that Han take Anakin along for the flight, and even suggested that Han might want to let Anakin take the helm again.

He just looked at her helplessly, his expression one of surrender. She was the ultimate mediator, and he had known all along, of course, that she would find a way to sort out the problems between father and son concerning Anakin's wild piloting near Coruscant.

The next morning, Han and Chewie went to the *Falcon*'s dock to find the hold thrown wide, with cart after cart being floated inside.

"And how much of this stuff is illegal?" Han asked Lando, who was supervising the loading.

"All above the table," Lando assured him with a less-than-confirming wink.

Chewie howled.

"Luke's going to want your help out here," Han said. "He's got some issues with Kyp Durron and his friends, and is going to need some information on some smuggling operations."

Lando dipped a low bow. "At your service," he said through a glittering smile.

Han knew what that meant, and he wasn't exactly sure it was a good thing.

They saw Luke across the way, then, offering a wave and moving with Mara into the *Jade Sabre*, R2-D2 rolling along behind them. A few minutes later, cleared by the tower, the green-hued ship blasted away, disappearing from sight in a matter of seconds.

"Quick ship," Lando remarked.

"You think Luke would give Mara anything less?" Han asked.

Lando looked up at the empty sky where the *Jade Sabre* had just departed, and nodded.

The *Millennium Falcon* took off an hour later, for a one-day trip that would prove to be the most harrowing journey of Han Solo's life.

FOURTEEN

Closer, Closer

R5-L4 screeched and wailed pitifully, sparks flying from its head as the insect creature's acid-secreting pincers slashed and tore, digging into metal as easily as if it was packed soil.

In front of the doomed droid, Kyp worked furiously to get his lifesuit secured before the final breach of his hull sucked all of his atmosphere away. He heard the cries of R5-L4, and they cut into his heart as deeply as if he was losing a dear friend, but he could do nothing until the suit was in place.

Sparks continued to fly, bouncing off the back of Kyp's canopy. A small burst of flame erupted from the droid, only to wash out instantly for lack of oxygen. But that was it for R5-L4; the screeching stopped.

Kyp was on his own.

He unstrapped and turned himself about, to see the insect-like creature feasting on the wires and boards that were the droid's guts, and to see another insect creature clinging to the lower wing on the right, gaining a foothold, it seemed, and intent on the ion drive.

Thinking quickly, Kyp shut down the drive and pulled the lever, closing the S-foils. The whole of the craft groaned as they came together, trapping the insect between them, but not crushing it. Kyp rocked the lever back and forth, opening and closing the foils, trying to dislodge the thing, or squish it flat.

It held its ground stubbornly, so Kyp just kept the foils as tight as they would get.

The insectoid monstrosity on the back of his fuselage was finished with its meal, and now those acid pincers came at the back of Kyp's canopy.

The Jedi waited, waited, hand on the button.

The pincers drove through; Kyp pressed and fell into his seat, grabbing a belt with all his strength. The canopy blew away with a tremendous shock that rocked the X-wing violently, knocking its nose down so that it was flying forward in a diagonal posture.

Kyp turned about, trying to figure out what to do with the one on the wings, but he stopped, stunned, for the creature on the back of his fuselage remained, back four legs clasping the X-wing, front two waving in the air. It was bent up at the back, head up, pincers stuck through the ejected canopy. Hardly thinking, reacting out of sheer horror, Kyp sprang to his knees, pulled the lightsaber off of his belt, and brought forth the glowing blade. A single clean swipe took the closest two grasping legs, and the backhand severed the last two, and the monstrous insect, and the canopy, flew away.

Anger welled in Kyp as he composed himself, as he thought about the losses this day, as he looked at the tattered remains of R5-L4. He knew the score, that none of his promising Dozen-and-Two Avengers had escaped beside him—and when a sudden explosion rocked the side of his X-wing, and that stubborn creature pinned between the wings somehow extended its pincers enough to breach the ion drive, he doubted that he would get away, either.

He crawled out of his cockpit, grasping tightly, understanding that he had no lifeline here, that one slip would send him floating helplessly in deep space. The X-wing was spinning now, over and over—Kyp couldn't really feel the movement in the zero gravity, but he could see the changing placement of the stars. He held on tightly, recognizing that the spin would likely soon exert centrifugal force and toss him away.

He had never known such desperation, a castaway on a life raft in the middle of the most vast ocean of all. But he was a Jedi, trained and proven. He dismissed his anger now, refused to give in to it, and approached logically, carefully.

The insect looked at him; the pincers snapped hungrily.

Kyp thrust his lightsaber right between them, the energy blade cutting deep into the creature's head. The insect went into a fury; the X-wing spun even faster, and looped head over tail, as well. For an instant, Kyp lost his grip, tumbling, tumbling, right off the back. His lightsaber fell from his grasp, but he reached out to it instinctively with the Force, needing the security of the crafted weapon though it would hardly help him in this situation.

Likewise, as soon as he had the lightsaber in hand, Kyp mentally grabbed at the spinning X-wing, putting a hold on it as secure as his strong arms ever could. Closer and closer he inched, until it was in his reach, spinning about, and he grabbed on to the tail and pulled himself to the fuselage.

Still trapped between the wings, the monstrous insect lay very still.

Kyp put his lightsaber away and used this vantage point to try and examine the damaged drive, to try to think of some way he might begin repairs. What could he do?

With a sigh, followed quickly by a determined grunt, he pulled himself over the edge of the fuselage back to his cockpit. He steadied the ship with attitude jets, then began a general inventory, trying to get a fix on where he was and on the extent of the damage. His hyperdrive seemed to be working, but with no canopy, he didn't dare engage it. He reached instinctively for his emergency kit, but stopped abruptly, recognizing that, with his entire canopy gone, there was nothing to patch.

What to do? Even if there was a habitable planet around, Kyp couldn't land without his canopy, and the lifesuit would serve him for only a few hours, or perhaps for a few days if he went into his Jedi trance.

But those thoughts were for later, he told himself determinedly. Next came the real test: he eased the ion drive back on-line. It fired, sputtered, and he found that only by rocking the throttle could he keep it going, and then only at low power.

He looked to the side, to the trapped and dead creature, and almost opened the wings. But then, keeping his cool, thinking ahead, Kyp understood that this alien life-form should be examined. Even if he didn't make it, those who later found his dead craft would need to see this creature.

Even if he didn't make it . . .

The disturbing notion echoed over and over in his thoughts. He sat back and forced himself to relax, relax, moving past a state of consciousness, into the flow of the Force. Envisioning his ship, he moved his thoughts beyond the mechanics of the vehicle, into the realm of the philosophical, the true purpose of the various components that comprised his X-wing. And then it hit him—not the perfect solution, but one that had a chance, at least.

Working on his own, with no astromech and only a basic engineering manual to guide him, Kyp altered the power grids of the ion drive, bringing them more completely to his shielding power. Then, holding his breath, he eased it back on-line. It offered no thrust this time, but, rather, created a bubblelike shield about him, one that he hoped might allow him to survive hyperspace. He laid in a course for Dubrillion. He kept searching the records as he went, though, and soon determined that there was another possibility, a remote planet named Sernpidal.

Torn, for he knew that he would find help at Lando's, Kyp finally decided, after yet another warning sputter and flutter of power from the wounded drive, to try for the closer Sernpidal. He altered the course accordingly and engaged the hyperdrive, focusing his consciousness on that tentative ion power-plant, attentive to its every sound and pulse.

He came out of hyperspace almost immediately, just an instant before the ion drive fluctuated, dropping his shielding canopy. It came up again almost immediately, and Kyp shook his head as he considered the daunting task ahead of him. He'd have to hop and skip in short hyperspace bursts all the way to Sernpidal. And all the time, he'd have to simply hope that the ion drive didn't die altogether.

He engaged the hyperdrive again, closing his eyes and feeling the vibrations behind him, easing as he needed to, not letting those sputtering jolts of the ion drive reach a critical level. His breathing slowed, his heart pumped even slower, preserving his oxygen, but he kept enough of his consciousness to feel those vibrations, to jump out of hyperspace and then, when the ion drive was ready, jump back in, playing the controls as one might rock a tired baby.

Danni Quee sat in an icy-walled dome-shaped chamber just above the frigid water and with hundreds of meters of solid ice above her. She wore only that loose-fitting poncho, for her other garments, the horrid, fleshy creature that had enwrapped her body, and the star-shaped creature that had violated her very insides, were gone now. Despite her lack of clothing, though, Danni was not cold. Strange lichen covered the floor of the place, emitting warmth and light, and probably oxygen, she figured, because she could breathe easily in here.

Her captors were horrible beyond anything she had ever seen, especially the huge tentacled brain that seemed to be guiding them, but in a strange sense they were also noble. Danni had not been tortured—yet—and had faced no intimate advances at all. She was a worthy enemy, the humanoid leader, Da'Gara, had proclaimed, on the word of Yomin Carr, and so she had been treated with a solid measure of respect.

Still, they meant to sacrifice her.

Now she was alone, hour after hour. Every once in a while,

the water would bubble and a pair of the tattooed barbarians would splash up, one keeping a weapon pointed her way, the other bringing food—squirming, eel-like creatures—and potable water. She wondered what was going on down there, in the lower depths, where the war coordinator's bulk rested, where the water was warmer because of volcanic activity. She wondered what was happening on the outside, beyond this frozen wasteland, in the galaxy that was her home. It would be conquered, Da'Gara had promised her, brought to its knees before the glory of the Yuuzhan Vong. And she would see it.

Danni got the distinct feeling that Da'Gara was hoping that she would stop being one of the infidels, as he called all the peoples of her galaxy, and see the light and truth of the Yuuzhan Vong way.

She didn't think that likely.

The water bubbled, signaling another approach. Danni looked toward it quizzically. She was expecting them—Da'Gara had told her that another worldship would dock soon, and that she could witness the glory of the arrival. Everything seemed to center on that word—*glory*—with the Yuuzhan Vong. She mentally prepared herself for the expected violation by the fleshy creatures, the suit and the horrid mask.

But then she saw something she could not have anticipated, and she drew in her breath harshly as a pair of tattooed barbarians burst out of the water, dragging a battered human man between them.

Da'Gara came in next, moving to Danni as the other two threw the new prisoner roughly to the floor, his fleshy, organic enviro-suit peeling back from his body.

"Some warriors came against us," the prefect explained through the watery gurgle caused by the star-shaped mask. "Some of your best, apparently." He paused and nodded toward the limp form on the floor. "They were destroyed with ease."

Danni looked at him curiously, more for the manner in which he was speaking than for the actual words. Before this, his inflection and pronunciation had been horrible, and he had scrambled the structure of nearly every sentence, but now that wording was noticeably smoother.

"You doubt our power?" Da'Gara asked, apparently cuing in on her expression.

"You've learned our language," she replied.

The prefect turned his head sideways and tapped a finger against his ear, and Danni saw something inside it, wriggling quickly like the back end of a worm. "We have our ways, Danni Quee. You will learn."

Danni didn't doubt that, and it made the Yuuzhan Vong all the more terrible.

The prefect steeled his gaze at Danni. "He is not worthy," he said, indicating her new companion, and then, with a sudden hand motion, he set the other two into action and they leapt into the water. Da'Gara continued to stare at Danni for a long while, then slipped into the dark water behind them.

Danni ran to the human. He wore no identification, wore nothing at all other than a tight pair of shorts. He carried many fresh scars, as though Da'Gara's warriors had wounded, and then healed, him. Given the prefect's last words to her, that this one was not worthy, Danni understood what that meant.

He would be sacrificed to the war coordinator.

Danni sucked in her breath and held herself steady. She, too, had faced the war coordinator, the horrid yammosk. Its two thin and sticky inner tendrils had entwined her, pulling her in, in, between the huge tentacles of the beast and toward those black eyes and that singular toothy maw.

But the war coordinator had not taken her, had deemed other purposes for her, which, Prefect Da'Gara had assured her, was an incredible honor—though Danni, her knees nearly buckling as she fought off a fit of fainting, had not appreciated it at all.

The war coordinator wouldn't do the same with this one, Danni believed. He would be wrapped in tentacles and brought in slowly to be devoured.

The man stirred, then blinked his eyes open slowly, in obvious pain.

"Where?" he stuttered.

"On the fourth planet," Danni replied.

"Starfighters . . . rocklike," the man stammered.

"Coralskippers," Danni clarified for him, for Da'Gara had told her the literal translation of the Yuuzhan Vong name. She eased the battered man's head down gently. "Rest easy. You're safe now."

An hour or so later—Danni really couldn't begin to keep track of the time—the man woke up, with a start and a cry. "Coming through the ship!" he yelled, but then he stopped himself as he became aware of his current surroundings. He looked at Danni curiously. "The fourth planet?" he asked.

Danni nodded.

"The Helska system?"

Danni nodded again and moved to help the man sit up. "I'm Danni Quee," she began. "I came out of the ExGal station on Belkadan—" The man's sudden look of recognition stopped her.

"*Spacecaster*-class shuttle," he said.

Danni looked at him incredulously.

"We tracked you," the man explained. "To Helska. We came to find you."

"We?"

The man forced a smile and held out his hand. "Miko Reglia of the Dozen-and-Two Avengers," he said.

Danni took his hand, but her expression revealed that she had no idea what he was talking about.

"A squadron of . . ." Miko had to pause—what, exactly, were they a squadron of ? "A squadron of starfighter pilots," he explained. "Led by Jedi Kyp Durron and myself."

"You're a Jedi Knight?" Danni asked, eyes widening, a flicker of hope flashing behind them.

Miko nodded and visibly settled down, as if the reminder that he was a Jedi Knight had put him in a completely different frame of mind. "Yes," he said solemnly. "I was trained at the academy, under Luke Skywalker himself, and though my training is not yet complete—I've been doing an apprenticeship under the tutelage of Kyp Durron—I am indeed a Jedi Knight."

Danni glanced back at the water. She believed Miko's claim, and in light of that, she wondered if she had found a weakness in her enemies. Prefect Da'Gara had called this one unworthy, but how could a Jedi Knight be unworthy in the eyes of any fellow warrior? Perhaps Da'Gara and his fellows had underestimated this man, and perhaps Danni could find some way to exploit that error.

She looked back to Miko, to see him sitting calmly, eyes closed in a meditative pose.

"What are you doing?" she asked.

Miko blinked his eyes open. "Calling out," he explained. "Projecting my own thoughts and trying to sense those of any other Jedi Knight who might be in the area."

"Will it work?" Danni asked eagerly, moving closer.

Miko shrugged. "Jedi have a connection, a common understanding of the Force that brings us together."

"But will it work?" the pragmatic Danni pressed.

Again the shrug. "I don't know," he admitted. "I don't know if Kyp escaped, and I don't know how far away he, or any other Jedi, might be."

That was all the answer Danni needed. She came to the conclusion then that they couldn't depend on this mystical thought-projection. They needed their own plan.

"Who are these people?" Miko asked after a pause. "Smugglers?"

Danni burst into laughter, despite herself. Smugglers? If only it was that simple, and explainable. "Maybe they, the

Yuuzhan Vong, were smugglers," she replied, "in their own galaxy."

Miko started to respond, but stopped short and stared hard at her, the implications of her words obviously hitting him.

"They're not from our galaxy," Danni explained.

"Impossible," Miko replied. "A lie they told you to keep you afraid."

"We tracked them inbound," Danni went on. "Right through the galactic rim. We thought it was an asteroid or a comet, and when we figured out where it was headed, three of us came out to investigate."

"The other two?" Miko asked, but Danni was shaking her head before he ever finished.

She thought of Bensin Tomri and Cho Badeleg then, of Bensin's horrible ending, and saw it in light of Da'Gara's words concerning this man, Miko. She didn't want to witness that scene repeated.

"What are they doing here?"

"The Yuuzhan Vong want it all," Danni explained.

Miko looked at her skeptically. "Conquest?"

"The whole galaxy."

Miko snorted. "They're in for a surprise."

"Or we are," Danni said gravely.

"How many?" Miko asked. "How many planets? How many comets, or asteroids, or whatever they might be, came in?"

"Just one," Danni answered, and she added, "so far," before Miko could respond. "Others will follow, I'm sure."

"They'll need ten thousand times this number," Miko declared.

"It's not just about numbers," Danni pointed out. "They've got ways, and weapons, we don't understand. It all seems to be based on living organisms, creatures they've trained, or bred, to serve their needs."

"Like the suits they put us in," Miko observed, and both he and Danni shivered at the memory.

Danni nodded. "They've got their ways," she said.

Miko waved his hand dismissively. "We were taking them out three to one," he explained. "And we were just flying starfighters, and most of them outdated. The alien fighters wouldn't stand up against a Star Destroyer or a battle cruiser."

"You were winning, but you did not," Danni reminded.

"Only because they found some way to get our shields down," Miko started to say, but he stopped, his words hanging ominously in the air.

"Don't underestimate them," Danni scolded, and she wondered then if she might have found the reason that Da'Gara apparently held little respect for Miko. "They've got tools and weapons and technology foreign to our sensibilities. Weapons we might not easily be able to counter. They're confident, and they seem to know us better than we know them."

Miko started to climb to his feet, unsteadily, and Danni moved to support him. A moment later, he gently pushed her away, then went into a dancelike routine of slow and deliberate balancing motions. When he finished a few moments later, he seemed to have found his center. "We have to get off planet," he said, glancing all around and, finally, up at the encasing ice.

"It's hundreds of meters thick," Danni remarked.

"We have to find a way," Miko said, his tone full of determination. "I don't know if any of the others got away, but someone has to get back to inform the New Republic. Let's see what these aliens—what'd you call them, the Yuuzhan Vong?—can do against some real firepower."

Danni nodded resolutely, bolstered by the offered strength of the Jedi Knight, and hoping, hoping, that Prefect Da'Gara had indeed underestimated him.

"We lost more than a dozen," Da'Gara admitted, and the eyes on Nom Anor's villip narrowed dangerously. "But when we discovered their weaknesses and used the dovin basals to counter their blocking energy shields, the battle turned our way," he quickly added. "We can beat them now, one to one, one to ten."

"How many?" the executor asked.

"Eleven enemies were destroyed," Da'Gara reported. "A twelfth was forced down, and though two escaped, the grutchins were in swift pursuit. We believe those last two enemies were destroyed."

"You believe?" Nom Anor echoed skeptically.

"They jumped past lightspeed, what they call hyperdrive," Da'Gara explained. "Still, at last sighting, several grutchins were attached before the jump, and many more went in pursuit. They could not have survived."

Nom Anor gave a long pause that Da'Gara didn't dare interrupt. The prefect understood the problems here. Even releasing the grutchins had been taking a huge chance, for unlike many of the Yuuzhan Vong's bred creatures, grutchins were not rational, thinking, or even trained beasts. They were instruments of destruction, living weapons, and once released, they could not be controlled or recalled. Those that had not made the jump piggybacked on the enemy starfighters or in immediate pursuit, but had stayed in the region with the coralskippers, had been destroyed—it was too risky to try and capture a mature grutchin. That loss was not significant, for the insectoids bred and matured quickly, and those lost would soon enough be replaced. Of more concern were the many that got away. Likely they had destroyed the starfighters and were now running free in the galaxy. They couldn't reproduce, for they had no queens, but grutchins were aggressive creatures and would continue to seek out and attack other ships in the region. Soon enough they might draw the attention of the New Republic, turn the eyes of the enemy to this sector of the galaxy's Outer Rim, and that could bode ill for the Praetorite Vong.

That's what had Nom Anor concerned, and rightly so, Da'Gara knew, but still, what other choice had his warriors? They could not chase the enemy through a lightspeed jump, after all, for the dovin basals fronting the coral-skippers, sensitive as they were, could not hold any lock on enemy ships through such a ride.

"Your new prisoner," Nom Anor prompted. "You believe him to be Jedi."

Now Da'Gara fully relaxed, pleased to relay this grand information. "He is, Executor."

"Take care with that one," Nom Anor warned.

"He is with the woman," Da'Gara replied. "There is no escape."

"You have begun the breaking?"

"We use the woman against him," Da'Gara confirmed. "We have told her that he is unworthy, as we have told him. We will execute him a thousand times in his mind, if that is what we must do. And when he is within the grasp of the war coordinator, pulled toward the great maw and expecting death, his willpower will ebb."

Nom Anor's villip echoed his chuckle. Da'Gara knew exactly how the executor felt. The breaking was a common procedure used against captured enemies of the Yuuzhan Vong, mental torture over physical torment, a shaving away of the sensibilities and determination until the unfortunate prisoner was left broken on the floor, sobbing like a baby, his mind snapped from a succession of expected horrors, of promised, terrible deaths.

"We will measure his willpower carefully, Executor," Da'Gara assured him. "Then we will know the limits of the Jedi, and know how to exceed those limits."

The villip's look was purely contented now, and Da'Gara knew the expression to be an accurate reflection. What luck that they had, so early on, been able to capture a Jedi! Now, while Nom Anor continued his test of the Jedi's physical abilities with the disease he had inflicted upon Mara, Da'Gara and the yammosk could learn so much more about the mental prowess of these supposed supercreatures.

"Above all else, denigrate him," Nom Anor suggested. "He is not worthy—that is your litany, that is the message we will use to infiltrate his willpower and crack the barriers apart. And all the better that you still have the woman Yomin Carr told you about to use as a measuring rod against him. She is worthy, he is not. That should effect some weakening."

"Then we are in agreement," Da'Gara assured Nom Anor.

"Our secrecy nears its end," Nom Anor replied. "With the escape of the two craft—"

"They did not escape," Da'Gara dared to interrupt, something he would normally never do to a peer. In this case, though, the prefect understood the necessity of setting the premise. Still, he breathed a sigh of relief when Nom Anor granted him that conclusion.

"They may have loosed a warning beacon," Nom Anor explained. "Even if not, the inevitable actions of the vicious grutchins may turn some attention in your general direction. Also, what brought the starfighter squadron out to you in the first place?"

Da'Gara had no practical answer. He had hoped it was just a twist of fate.

"You are a long way from the Core," Nom Anor continued. "And the New Republic has much to contend with close to home: the Osarian-Rhommamool conflict is full-scale now, and several other minor wars have begun, both interplanetary and within planetary governments loyal to the New Republic. They would not have sent a squadron out there without cause, if that squadron went out under any specific orders. See what you might learn from the captured Jedi."

"My intention exactly."

"And beware, Prefect Da'Gara," Nom Anor said ominously. "When is the rest of the Praetorite Vong to arrive?"

"The second worldship will dock this day," Da'Gara answered. "The third within the week."

"Prepare your defenses properly, and do not let down your guard," Nom Anor warned. "If the New Republic knows of you, or if either of those fleeing starfighters did escape, you can expect much more formidable opponents within the week."

"We will be ready."

"See that you are."

The villip abruptly inverted, the connection broken, and Prefect Da'Gara relaxed and rubbed the kink out of his neck, made sore by his standing at perfect attention throughout his discussion with the great executor. He had already communed with the war coordinator, and the yammosk had assured him that the humans and their pitiful energy weapons were not to be feared. The planet was a fortress now, with the yammosk emitting its own energy fields and using dovin basals to focus them instantly. Once the second and third worldships, each carrying full payloads of coralskippers, were in, let the humans come.

Da'Gara grinned wickedly as he considered his other order of business, the breaking of the Jedi. He had assisted with other breakings during his prefect training, of course, but this was his first time ever overseeing one.

To the warrior, always looking for weakness in his enemies, it was indeed a pleasurable experience.

Danni and Miko climbed to their feet when the water started to churn, and looked to each other, each trying to confirm that this was the time for action. A slight nod, one and then the other, and the pair moved to opposite sides of the small chamber and waited, with Miko going down into a squat and pressing his palms together before him.

Danni, too, went into a crouch, watching the churning water. But then she looked higher, to Miko, and marveled at his posture and preparedness. She could see the taut muscles of his arms straining under the isometric press, building pressure as if to literally explode into action.

A Yuuzhan Vong head, black hair chopped erratically, fleshy star-shape over the face, appeared, and then the arms, one hand holding a short staff, came over the rim, grabbing hold and propelling the powerful humanoid out of the water and onto the lichen-covered floor.

Danni circled, and turned and clawed at the wall, as if trying to run, demanding the creature's attention.

Another Yuuzhan Vong warrior came up, and then a third.

Miko exploded into motion, launching himself sidelong against the three, knocking one back into the water, the other two to the floor.

Danni dived atop one, grabbing his weapon with both hands and pressing her forearm into the warrior's throat as she did. She drove down with all of her considerable strength, but this was a Yuuzhan Vong warrior, hugely strong, and within a split second, he had Danni up high enough so that her press on his throat was not choking him.

Desperation drove her, though, and so she clung to the staff with one hand, keeping it at bay, and she freed up her other hand enough to get a grip on the warrior's face, working frantically to avoid his snapping jaws as she wedged her fingers under his star-shaped mask.

Miko and the other alien scrambled to their feet and squared off, and then the third practically leapt out of the water, staff at the ready.

"Unworthy," they kept saying, circling, circling, waving their weapons, but shortening the blows, more to measure the Jedi's reaction than to initiate any real attack routines.

Miko kept his cool and his balance, taking care not to over-react. He saw Danni struggling with the remaining soldier, the warrior rolling over atop her and gaining the upper hand.

He dismissed the image, reminding himself that he couldn't begin to help Danni until he had first helped himself. The Yuuzhan Vong behind him thrust his weapon like a spear, and Miko jumped ahead and to the side, and when the warrior before him took that as an opportunity to come in hard, the skilled Jedi dropped one foot back and turned sidelong to the blow, deflecting it harmlessly aside with his open palm. Like a snake, he struck, with that same blocking arm, elbow flying up high, arm snapping straight, the side of his hand knifing into the Yuuzhan Vong warrior's throat.

Even as that opponent staggered backward, though, Miko felt the pressure from behind and could not finish the attack, forced instead to turn his attention to the newest foe, scrambling and slapping, barely deflecting the thrusting staff, and not enough to avoid a stinging clip on the side of his chest.

Danni heard the rush of Miko's blowing breath and found herself in a tight corner, with the heavy Yuuzhan Vong warrior, staff horizontal above her, pressing down hard, overpowering her, bringing the weapon shaft across her throat. With strength born of desperation, Danni wriggled and drove her knee straight up between the alien's legs, and when his breath came out in a rush and he froze—whether startled or in pain Danni couldn't tell—she yanked the staff away from him. Hardly slowing, she punched out, left hand, right hand, left hand, swiveling the staff, smacking it against her opponent's head on alternating sides.

The Yuuzhan Vong brought a hand up to block, and Danni slipped in one last hit and kept pushing, turning the warrior's head aside and wriggling out from underneath. She planted the bottom of the staff on the ground as she turned sidelong and pushed up to her knees; then, not daring to break the movement, she scrambled up to her feet and turned in a spin, letting her hands slide down the smooth weapon to the end, then coming around with a mighty swing that caught the warrior on the shoulder, then bounced up to the side of his head, launching him into a sidelong flip that left him dazed on the floor.

Miko, meanwhile, worked frantically, one hand slapping after another, to parry the barrage of attacks from the staff-thrusting Yuuzhan Vong, using the same always-balanced twists and maneuvers he would with his lightsaber when battling a remote. He fell into his meditation, anticipating instead of reacting, trying to follow the telling movements, disturbances, of the Force as an aquatic creature might sense the shifting currents displaced by another.

He tried another tactic, as well: to use the Force to get a better feel of his opponent, an understanding of the alien's tactics and intentions.

He might as well have been trying to read the intentions of empty deep space.

But still, even without that intuitive advantage, Miko found that he could anticipate the movements enough to keep up with the attacks, blocking, slapping, occasionally trying to grab or twist. He kept his foot movements minimal at first, trying to conserve energy, trying to lure his opponent into a state of advantaged complacency.

But the warrior he had chopped was regaining his footing, and Miko was out of time.

In came the staff, a straight thrust for his belly, an attack Miko had slapped out and dodged with a subtle hip twist three times already. This time, though, he knifed his hand down under the weapon and backhanded it up over his shoulder as he stepped forward and to the side of his enemy, leaving him an open punch for the Yuuzhan Vong's masked face.

He chose instead to insinuate his free hand between the warrior's arms, rolling over and grabbing onto the staff, while his other hand, up high from the parry, rolled over the staff the other way and grabbed on. Miko pulled down with that upper hand, yanked up with the lower, but at exactly the moment his opponent tried to apply counterpressure, the Jedi suddenly and viciously reversed his momentum, shoving down with his low hand and rolling his upper hand back under the staff and forcing it up and over, to slam hard against the alien's forehead.

A sudden and vicious yank tore the staff free of the warrior's grasp, and Miko quickly thrust its butt end into the Yuuzhan Vong's face, closing one eye and sending him staggering backward.

Up came Danni, right behind the stubborn warrior, and

even as Miko turned his attention to the remaining enemy, the one still clutching its chopped throat, Danni brought her staff down hard on the back of that one's head. The warrior dropped like a stone.

The remaining Yuuzhan Vong broke for the hole in the floor, thinking to dive into the water, but Miko came alongside in a rush and kicked out the warrior's trailing foot, tripping him headlong.

Danni caught him in midfall, looping her staff about his throat and turning brutally, bending his head to the side and putting him in a helpless choke. He grabbed at the staff and tried to punch at her, but his air supply was gone and he went limp in a matter of a few seconds.

"Get their cloaking creatures," she instructed, but Miko was already trying to find some way to extract the creature from its host.

The first Yuuzhan Vong Danni had clobbered started to get back up. She walked over and slammed him in the back of the head, dropping him to the floor.

Finally finding the pressure point beside the nose, they managed to strip two of the aliens of their ooglith cloakers, but it took them a long while—and several more smacks to the heads of waking warriors—to figure out how to lure the creatures onto their own bodies. When they did, they shivered with the intense pain, the little flickers of exquisite agony, as the creatures enwrapped them.

Then they turned their attention to the star-shaped breathers, but it took time to muster the courage to actually put the things on. Danni gagged repeatedly, fighting revulsion, as the creature sent its joining tendril down her throat and to her lungs.

When she was done, she saw that Miko was already wearing his.

"Are you all right?" Miko asked, his voice watery.

Danni nodded. "They won't recognize us easily with these on," she replied. "We've got to find some pattern to this place."

"Where they keep their ships," Miko agreed. He didn't finish the obvious thought—once they found the ships, how would they possibly fly them?—but he didn't have to.

Danni knew the score, and she led the way, diving head-long into the frigid water. As soon as they got under, the two could see the distant lighting of the core area of the main Yuuzhan Vong base. Within that glow resided the main bulbous portion of the long-tentacled yammosk, they knew, and so, neither wanting to be anywhere near the horrid thing, they gave the lights a wide berth, picking their way to a point above it along the ice, walking their hands on the rough surface rather than swimming, until they came in sight of the tubular creature holding open the pathway to the surface ship.

Surprisingly, the bottom end of that tube did not appear guarded, and so they worked their way down its side. They paused at the lip and stared at each other, sharing their trepidation. Danni started to go under, but Miko grabbed her shoulder and held up his hand. He closed his eyes, finding his center, then rushed down and around the bottom, into the tube, leading with the staff he had taken from one of the soldiers.

Danni held her breath, and just as she started to follow, Miko poked his head around and motioned that the way was clear.

They inched their way up perhaps twenty meters before they cleared the water. Then they climbed, appreciating how well the tubular creature was designed, with riblike bones, easy stairs, encircling it. And the path was clear, all the way up; both thought this, too, remarkable, but neither voiced the fear openly.

Up they climbed; and then above, Miko, who was still leading, noted the wider opening and the multicolored hues of the alien worldship. Again the Jedi led the way, but this time without hesitation, for Danni was right behind, pressing on. They came into a large chamber and spent a long moment letting their vision adjust to the change in light. At first, they thought they were alone, but then Danni's eyes widened and she pointed to a small alcove to the left, where a single, tattooed figure stood quietly.

"You need not your gnullith here," Prefect Da'Gara told them, turning about. He was not wearing one of the star-shaped creatures—and his lips curled into a smile. "The worldship produces its own atmosphere."

Danni glanced at Miko, and then all around, looking for other guards.

"It took you longer than I had anticipated," Da'Gara calmly stated.

Miko broke into motion, leaping forward, staff twirling above his head.

But Da'Gara, too, moved quickly, extending both his arms, throwing with one hand a pie of goo that hit the floor before Miko, and merely opening his other hand, from which flew a small, ball-like creature, its wings humming fiercely.

Miko skipped aside, dived into a roll to recover his balance, and came up to his feet in a rush, thinking to close the last few steps to Da'Gara. But the goo had moved with him, had somehow expanded, widening like a stream-fed puddle, its surface rippling with waves. The Jedi moved again, a step back, then skittered back the other way, and then, the gooey substance pacing, even gaining on him, he took a step forward and leapt into a somersault, trying to clear it.

No such luck. The goo reared up and caught Miko's feet as he came around, and though the Jedi moved with such agility that he was able to land standing, he was caught. He retracted his arm to throw the staff like a spear, but the goo reacted with frightening suddenness, a portion of it flowing right up Miko's legs and torso, enveloping his arm, even reaching out to catch and hold the missile as it left his grasp.

Danni cried out for him, but her call was cut short, a gasp of air blasted from lungs, as for the third time she tried to dodge the ball-like creature that had flown from the prefect's hand. The buzzing thing had come back at her each time. This time, the living missile seemed to anticipate her movement, altering its course accordingly and slamming her right in the chest with such force that she was knocked back onto the floor. For a long moment, she lay stunned and very still, staring at the multicolored chamber ceiling. Then she heard Da'Gara's mocking laughter.

She knew she had to get up now, to help Miko, and she rolled to the side, pushing up on one elbow.

And then she was standing, suddenly, hoisted to her feet by two other Yuuzhan Vong barbarians. Before she could begin to try to fight back, she felt something wet and sticky on her wrist, and then that arm was wrenched back behind her and slammed into her back, sticking fast. A similar movement from the other warrior had her other arm pinned, as well, and they jerked her about to face Da'Gara, and to see Miko stuck firmly in place.

"Did you believe that you had a chance?" Da'Gara calmly asked Miko. He advanced to stand right before the trapped Jedi. "I told you honestly that you were not worthy. You cannot begin to resist us."

A growl escaped Miko's lips, and he struggled futilely against the goo's hold. Da'Gara, his smile wider than ever, leaned closer, pulling free Miko's gnullith with one hand and using the other to flick a finger up under the Jedi's nose, hitting the exact spot to send a wave of pain through the man. "Too easy," Da'Gara whispered into Miko's ear.

He motioned to his warriors then, and they hauled Danni behind him as he moved back toward the alcove on the left. "It is good that you have come," he explained to her as they turned the corner. Around that bend, the wall was translucent, offering a superb view of the frozen surface and the multitude of stars beyond.

And one of those "stars" was approaching, growing larger and larger.

Danni's eyes widened as she realized what she was seeing:

the huge coral ship extending its membranous parachute, the ice below it beginning to vaporize and fog and fly away.

"Oh, there will be more, Danni Quee," Da'Gara whispered into her ear. "Do you see the truth now? Do you understand the futility?"

Danni didn't respond, didn't blink.

"There are ways for you to join with us," Da'Gara remarked.

Again, she stubbornly held her ground.

"You will learn," Da'Gara promised. "You will learn the glory of the Praetorite Vong. You will learn your place." He turned to the two warrior escorts. "Bid Prefect Ma'Shraid to join us. She will enjoy watching the yammosk devour the unworthy one."

Danni fought hard to hold steady her breathing, to not betray her horror. She said nothing and offered no resistance—how could she?—as she was dragged back through the main chamber, where other warriors had come in and were working on Miko and the gooey chains.

It all came as a rush to Danni, a blurring of reality and what she could only think of as a dreamscape. She was tossed back into the tube, went sliding and bouncing and falling back into the water, its iciness biting at her in those few places where the ooglith cloaker was not properly shielding her. Down they went, and her bonds were removed, and weights were applied. Down they went, deeper into the sea, toward the glow that marked the main base. Once again Danni came to appreciate the marvel of the ooglith cloaker, for she did not feel much of a pressure buildup as they descended, as if the living suit was somehow warding the weight of the depths.

The immense tentacles of the yammosk, the coordinator and central brain of the Praetorite Vong, hung in the water all about her, like banners strewn to mark the spot of celebration. Rocky reefs, covered with brightly glowing simple creatures, served as bleachers, and upon these, Da'Gara's warriors stood in force, at quiet attention, the intensity of their steeled gazes diminished not at all by the gnullith, which almost hid the variety of scarring and tattoos on their faces. Danni was brought to a place at the rear of the line, far from the core of the yammosk.

But through the crystalline clear water, she could see that horrid face, the two bulbous black eyes, the puckered maw, and the great central tooth.

No one seemed concerned with her; the warriors all stood quietly, eyes locked ahead, though the two flanking Danni kept a firm grip on her arms.

The great yammosk belched forth a huge bubble then, which rolled out, expanding, expanding, to encompass Danni and all the gathered Yuuzhan Vong, and to her amazement, that air pocket stayed in place about the grounds, holding back the waters. She saw the gathered aliens remove their gnullith, and then one of the guards holding her pulled the breather from her face, as well.

Prefect Da'Gara appeared sometime later, in ceremonial red robes that Danni had not seen before. He ascended a platform before the yammosk and held his hands out to his people.

No sound came from him, and yet Danni knew that he was communicating with his minions, and as she let herself fall deeper into that thought, and as she closed her eyes and concentrated, she, too, could begin to comprehend the prefect's thoughts. The call wasn't coming directly from Da'Gara, she came to realize, but was being relayed from him and to his people through the mental power of the gigantic yammosk. The creature was a telepath, obviously, its power great enough to facilitate communication throughout the gathering.

The title Da'Gara had given to the yammosk, war coordinator, suddenly resonated more deeply to Danni.

With the telepathic call for order, the communal bonding facilitated by the yammosk, completed, Da'Gara walked to the front of the platform and began speaking aloud. Danni didn't understand the language, of course, but by concentrating on the continuing waves of energy from the yammosk, she found that she could comprehend the basics of his speech. He was talking about glory, about the Praetorite Vong and this grand conquest they had been assigned. He spoke enthusiastically about Prefect Ma'Shraid and the second worldship, and about a third that would soon land. He talked about the skirmish with the starfighters, and the ultimate victory.

Then he went back to exalting Ma'Shraid, and Danni understood the purpose of that focus a moment later when a low humming reverberated through her body and all heads snapped to the side, looking back, away from Da'Gara and the yammosk. A great tube, like the one that led from the first worldship under the ice pack, slid down toward the yammosk's air bubble and then breached the shield at the rear of the gathering.

In came the warriors of the second worldship, rank upon rank, hundreds upon hundreds, a force larger than that Da'Gara had assembled. In they marched, male and female, all tattooed and mutilated, with athletic builds and finely toned muscles, and all with that same intense, fanatical gaze. A woman wearing red robes akin to Da'Gara's came last, borne on a litter by four strong warriors. While their comrades formed ranks intertwined with Da'Gara's soldiers, a show of common purpose and obedience that was not lost on Danni, the litter moved to the front platform, and the woman, Ma'Shraid, took her place beside Da'Gara.

He offered her the floor, and she immediately offered prayers to many gods. Then she fell into a similar discourse of glory and duty, speaking of the honor to have been chosen to serve with the Praetorite Vong, and of the glory they would all soon know, particularly those who would die in the conquest.

It went on for hours and hours, and Danni saw not one head nod with boredom. The level of energy alone nearly overwhelmed her, a devotion so rare among her own people.

Finally the speeches ended, with Da'Gara's call to the

yammosk, and then Danni felt a vibration ripple through her body, a power so intense that she feared she would simply explode.

As if in response to that wave of energy, a second litter appeared, not from the tunnel, but from around the bleachers. This one was curtained above so that Danni could not see the one being borne.

She knew, though.

Four warriors marched to the point at the end of the twin ranks of warriors, the farthest point from the yammosk's bulk, perhaps a hundred meters from Da'Gara and Ma'Shraid.

The curtains came down; there stood Miko Reglia, stuck fast to a post.

Again came the vibration, rippling through Danni. She could just sense the despair and helplessness that emanated from the yammosk; but those emotions were created for and aimed at Miko, she could tell, for his expression fell and his shoulders drooped. She could only watch in horror as two thin tendrils snaked out from either side of the yammosk's puckered maw, soaring out before the lines of warriors and to the litter. They grasped Miko and, with frightening power, yanked him free of his bonds and began dragging him in.

At first the Jedi struggled, but he apparently recognized the futility of that attempt and so he closed his eyes—he was again finding his point of meditation, Danni knew.

But again came the waves of the yammosk's thought-energy, rippling through them, pulling at Miko's heart and chipping at his willpower.

Danni understood. The creature wanted him to show his fear, wanted him to break into a tirade of despair and hopelessness.

"Fight it, Miko," she whispered, and she wished that she, too, was a Jedi, so that she could somehow communicate to the man, lend him her strength that he might die honorably.

Miko tried to look away, or down, tried to close his eyes and muster his internal strength. He was determined to meet his doom with courage and calm, but he could not keep his eyes closed. The yammosk would not let him. He knew then that this was the end, a horrible, painful death. He saw the maw, growing larger and larger, saw the rows and rows of smaller teeth behind that dominant fang, then saw, as he inched even closer, the fleshy interior of the creature's mouth.

He had never been afraid of death—he was a Jedi Knight—but something was different here than he had ever foreseen, some darker sense of dread and emptiness that questioned his very faith. Logically he knew the source to be the yammosk, a trick of the telepathic creature, but logic could not hold against the waves of despair and horror, against the certain knowledge that this was the very end of existence!

Closer, closer. The mouth opened and closed, chewing before the meal had arrived.

Closer, closer.

FIFTEEN

Awaiting the Goddess's Arrival

"Anybody here care to lend a hand?" Han asked sarcastically, ending with a frustrated sigh. Anakin had just put the *Millennium Falcon* down on Sernpidal—no easy feat, as the planet did not boast much in the way of landing docks. Basically they had come down within a walled field, on the ground, in the middle of the low, sprawling city. While there was plenty of activity around them, people of various species rushing to and fro, there seemed to be little or no organization to it all, and certainly not a one had made any movements to help with the unloading of the *Falcon*.

Finally, Han rushed out the door of the walled bay, into the path of two locals, white-skinned men with red eyes, wearing the traditional Sernpidal dress: red-striped white robes with huge hoods.

"Who runs the dock?" Han asked.

"Tosi-karu!" one of the men screamed frantically, and both started to run away.

"Well, where do I find this Tosi-karu?" Han demanded of the speaker, moving swiftly to intercept.

"Tosi-karu!" the albino yelled again, pointing to the sky, and when Han tried to hinder the man's progress, he slapped Han's hands away and did a nifty spin move, sprinting away to the side.

"Tosi-karu!" Han yelled after him. "Where?"

"Oh, you would have to look up to see that one, I fear," came another voice, calm and controlled.

Han turned to see an older man, not an albino Sernpidalian, leaning on a staff.

"He flies?" Han asked skeptically.

"Orbits would be a better word," the old man replied. "Although she could fly, I believe, if the local legends concerning the goddess are true."

"Goddess?" Han echoed, shaking his head. "Wonderful. So we put down during some kind of holy day."

"Not really."

Han looked around at the continuing bustle, particularly of the locals, rushing, averting their eyes. "I'd hate to see it during the holy days, then," he muttered. He turned back to the old man. "Are you the dockmaster?"

"Me?" the man asked with an incredulous chuckle. "Why, I'm just an old man, come out to spend my last days in peace."

"Then where is the dockmaster?"

"Don't know that there is one," the old man answered. "We don't get much traffic out here."

"Wonderful," Han muttered. "I've got a hold full of goods—"

"Oh, I suspect you'll find little trouble in getting them unloaded," the old man said with a chuckle.

"You *should* stop and help us," Anakin said to a group of Sernpidalians at the doors on the other side of the walled bay. He put tremendous Force emphasis on the suggestion, weighting the word *should* heavily.

The Sernpidalians slowed and turned to regard the boy and the Wookiee, and for a moment, it seemed as if they meant to stop and help. But then one yelled "Tosi-karu!" and the group hustled away.

Chewie howled.

"What do you mean, Luke could do it better?" Anakin asked. "They're obviously preoccupied."

Chewie let out a series of growls and roars.

"Yes, it does matter!" Anakin insisted.

It wasn't often that Anakin heard the Wookie chuckle, and the sound cut deeply when aimed at him. "I'll get this fellow," he said, moving toward another Sernpidalian who was hustling by.

Chewie's huge arm draped in front of Anakin's chest, easily holding him back. Then the Wookiee stepped right in front of the Sernpidalian and, when the albino tried to move around him, froze the man in place with a great Wookiee roar.

Only for a second, though, and then the Sernpidalian turned on his heel and ran screaming away.

"Oh, you're right," Anakin said dryly. "That's much more effective."

Chewie, eyes narrowed dangerously, turned to regard him.

Han looked at the old man skeptically.

"He's a big one," the old man noted, eyes wide, and Han heard Chewie moving behind him. He turned to see the Wookiee and Anakin, with Chewie grumbling about something and Anakin shaking his head.

"They won't even stop to listen," Anakin complained. "I can't even begin to tell if there's any organization to this place. Chewie scared a few, but they just yelled some things I didn't understand and ran off."

Han considered the words for a moment, then glanced at the old man, and back at Anakin. "What are you sensing?" he asked.

Anakin's eyes opened wide; he was obviously surprised that his father was asking him anything about the Force. Han was as Force-blind as Anakin was sensitive to it, after all, and rarely had he ever asked for any Force-related insights to any events, usually trusting his own instincts and luck instead.

Anakin closed his eyes for a long while. "Fear," he said at length.

"Oh, there's a lot of that," the old man said. "Why wouldn't there be?"

"But something else," Anakin started. He looked hard at his father. "It's more than fear," he decided. "Especially with the ones like that." He pointed to a group of locals rushing past on the opposite side of the avenue, their red-striped white robes flapping behind them in the dusty breeze. "It's almost . . ."

"Religious?" the old man asked, again with a wheezing chuckle.

"Yes," Anakin answered even as Han scowled at the old man. "Spiritual. They're afraid and full of hope all at once."

"Tosi-karu," the old man said, and he started walking away.

"Tosi-karu?" Anakin asked. "That's what one of the people at the other door yelled."

"Hey!" Han called, but the old man continued away, chuckling and shaking his head with every step.

"Tosi-karu?" Anakin asked again.

"Some goddess," Han explained. "There's something weird going on down here. I don't know what Lando's got us into, but I've got a—"

"Bad feeling about it?" Anakin finished, managing a sheepish grin at stealing his father's trademark line.

"Lot to do," Han corrected. "I want those holds emptied, and us out of here as soon as possible."

Chewie growled a protest—it was a lot of work, after all.

"We're going to empty them by ourselves?" Anakin asked doubtfully.

"No," Han replied with his unrelenting sarcasm. "We're going to find some help."

Before Anakin could even finish his sigh, a great cry came rolling down the street, a hundred voices, at least, joined as one. "Tosi-karu!"

"The goddess is here," Anakin remarked.

"Well, let's go and see if she's in charge," Han remarked, and he led them down the street. Around the next corner, they found the old man, sitting comfortably on a doorstep, hands crossed over the top of his walking stick.

"We thought we'd go meet the goddess," Han remarked dryly.

"No need to go any further, then," the old man replied.

That stopped them in their tracks, and Han eyed the old man suspiciously. "You?" he asked.

In answer, the old man laughed and pointed toward the sky, out to the east, and the three turned to see the moon rising in the still-blue sky.

And what a moon! It seemed huge, as if it was a second planet the size of Sernpidal. Han spent a moment remembering the information he had garnered about the place when schooling Anakin on their flight and descent plan. Sernpidal did have a moon—two of them, in fact. One was substantial, nearly a fifth the size of Sernpidal, but the other was much smaller, perhaps only twenty kilometers or so in diameter.

Han, Anakin, and Chewbacca watched in amazement as the moon broke the horizon, lifting up in the eastern sky, higher and higher, soon to crest overhead.

"Moving pretty fast," Han remarked.

"Faster every hour," the old man replied, drawing curious stares from the three.

"Which moon is that?" Anakin asked curiously, and he turned to Han and the old man, his expression fraught with fear. "That's Dobido, isn't it?"

"Dobido's the tiny one," Han replied.

"Indeed it is Dobido," the old man said.

Han and Anakin stared hard at each other, the old man's words—*faster every hour*—reverberating in their thoughts. Chewie put his hands over his ears and roared.

"Are you saying that Dobido is coming down?" Han asked, echoing Chewie's words.

"That would be my guess," the old man replied calmly. "I

think the locals' explanation that Tosi-karu has arrived is a bit more far-fetched."

The three looked up at the moon, now passing its crest above them, speeding for the western horizon.

"How long?" Anakin asked breathlessly.

Han started to attempt some calculations, but without any points of reference, soon gave up that exercise. Another thought interrupted anyway, a more pressing one. "Get back to the *Falcon*," he cried, and he sprinted back toward the dock, Anakin and Chewie following quickly.

"It may already be unloaded," the unflappable old man called after them, ending with a wheezing chuckle edged with profound sadness. Anakin paused and stared at the old man intently.

"I was elected the mayor," the old man explained with a sigh. "I was supposed to protect them."

"Hurry up!" Han called back to Anakin, his tone almost desperate.

Indeed, when the three returned to the *Millennium Falcon*, they found the unloading process well under way. Scores of people of many different species crowded around the ship, most throwing out cargo, but a few opportunistic others taking the time to go through the goods.

"Hey!" Han yelled, rushing the mob and waving his arms frantically.

They ignored him, even when he grabbed a couple of people and pushed them aside.

"Get away from my ship!" he demanded repeatedly, running all about, always seeming to be a step behind, as one or another of the mob broke open a cargo carton and ran off with the contents.

Chewbacca took a more direct route, running to the landing ramp and moving up high, then cutting loose one of his patented thunderous roars. That caught the attention of more than a few, and even those who did not outright flee took care to keep far from the Wookiee.

And Anakin's method was different still, the boy walking calmly among the looters, "suggesting" to them casually that they would be better off leaving. The inflection of his words, his use of the Force, made him many friends that day, friends who were glad to take his advice.

It took the three more than half an hour to clear the area, and another half an hour, with Anakin and his sensitivities guiding them, to clear the hidden stowaways out of the *Falcon*.

Han then wasted no time, didn't even bother to call in to the ground controllers for permission. He put the *Falcon* up, straight up, a lightning run to orbit, and put in a course to chase the rushing moon.

"There it is," he said to his son as they came over the horizon, moving to close pursuit. "Ten trillion tons of danger."

"Torpedoes?" Anakin asked.

Han looked at him incredulously. "That'd be like shooting a bantha with a tickle stick," he replied. "It'd take a Star Destroyer to blast that moon, and even if it did, the falling pieces would devastate Sernpidal."

"Then what?" Anakin asked.

"Never seem to have a Death Star lying around when you need one," Han muttered. He glanced over his shoulder at Chewie, who was busy checking readings and working some calculations.

The Wookiee stared intently at the screen, scratched his hairy head a couple of times, then issued a wail, poking the screen.

"Look at what?" Han protested, swiveling his chair about.

Chewie roared emphatically.

"Seven hours?" Han echoed, stunned. "Let me see that." He slapped the Wookiee's hand away, but his scolding ended abruptly as he read the line Chewie had been indicating.

"Our day just got better," Han said, looking back to Anakin. "Sernpidal's got seven hours."

Anakin's jaw dropped open.

"Only chance is that the moon skips along the atmosphere for a while before crashing through," Han explained.

Even as the words left his mouth, the ridiculousness of the whole situation struck him profoundly, left him shaking his head. "This moon's been in orbit for a million years," he commented. "How is this happening, and why now?" A look of suspicion crossed his face, a look that made clear that he wanted to discuss this further with a certain shady operator who had sent him out here.

"You think Lando knew?" Anakin asked, his tone skeptical.

Han offered no response to that theory, but he did wonder if one of those characters with whom Lando dealt might have something to do with all of this—if one of them, perhaps, wasn't pleased that Lando was delivering cargo to a rival. But still, who knew how to bring down a moon? The whole notion seemed utterly preposterous.

To Han, who had spent the better part of the last thirty years fighting against, and utilizing, utterly preposterous plans and equipment, nothing seemed impossible.

The scope on the console to Anakin's side beeped.

"What do you got?" Han asked.

Anakin bent over the scope. "Weather satellite."

Han looked at the moon, rolling along before them. "Get us to it," he instructed his son. "Download its banks," he told Chewie. "Let's see if we can find any clues, or a pattern."

A few moments later, Anakin brought them right up beside the weather satellite, an older Thunderstorm 63 model, and Chewie wasted no time in tying the *Millennium Falcon*'s computers into the satellite's banks.

Han took the helm back from Anakin and, as soon as Chewie was finished, used some nifty flying to bring the *Falcon* in close to the moon, even circumnavigating the thing a few times to try and see if there were any added features—a few well-placed ion drives, perhaps. The close inspection offered not a clue, though.

"Keep your eyes open," he instructed Chewie, as the

Wookiee swapped places with Anakin, moving back to his customary seat at Han's side.

Chewie growled his assent and worked in perfect sync with Han to keep the *Falcon* moving slowly and deliberately, as close to the moon as possible.

"Seven hours," Han muttered. "How are we going to get all those people off the planet in seven hours?" Even as he finished the rhetorical question, he put out a general distress call, signaling any and all ships in the region to proceed with all haste to Sernpidal.

That was a call few, if any, would hear in time, he knew.

"You see anything?" he asked Chewie.

The Wookiee growled and shook his head.

"It's coming from the planet!" Anakin cried behind them, and they both instinctively looked down toward Sernpidal and then, when nothing seemed apparent, glanced back at Anakin.

The boy rushed forward, bearing a printout from Chewie's download from the weather satellite. "Look," he said, pointing to a diagram he had generated with the data to show the plotting of Dobido's last two weeks of movement.

The circles showed the smooth ellipse of the orbit until only a couple of days before, when the moon had taken a sudden dip in trajectory with regard to the planet.

"Look at the descent," Anakin explained. "Every time it crosses this part of the planet, it comes down steeper. Something's pulling it down."

Han and Chewie studied the diagram, and sure enough, they could see that every time Dobido crossed over the region of the planet near Sernpidal City, it did indeed dip.

"Maybe they're calling it home with their prayers," Han muttered.

"Something's doing it," Anakin replied, too enthused to catch the joke. He poked his finger against the printout. "Something in the exact middle of this arc." He traced his finger to his estimate of that point, a spot not too far to the east of the city.

Han looked at Chewie, and the Wookiee turned to Anakin, calling for the printouts.

"It's got to be there," Anakin said to Chewie as the Wookiee pored over the data.

Chewie looked up at the boy, then at Han, and howled his agreement.

Now they had a clue, and perhaps a solution would follow.

Han laid in a course for that region, the *Falcon* swooping under Dobido and breaking right back through the atmosphere. He and Chewie studied the region east of the city, looking for some clues, or for a ship, perhaps, like an Interdictor cruiser, known for its gravity-well projectors that could simulate the tremendous effects of a stellar body in hyperspace and prevent fleeing ships from making the jump to lightspeed.

Meanwhile, Anakin studied the movement of Dobido, which was again crossing the area of greatest descent. Sure enough, the moon dipped noticeably in its trajectory, and Anakin updated Chewie's calculations with the new data.

Han heard his groan. "What do you got?"

"No way will the moon skip off the atmosphere," Anakin explained. "Not if that pull remains. And I'm guessing under six hours, not seven, because the descent increases with every pass. One more thing . . ." He paused, waiting for them to turn around. "Not that it really matters, but I think the moon will hit Sernpidal City."

"What a coincidence," Han said dryly.

Chewie growled his accord, and it was the first time Han had ever heard such an obvious display of sarcasm from the Wookiee.

Sernpidal City came in sight again a moment later, the *Falcon* turning about in its patrol. "There's fifty thousand people in that city alone," Han remarked.

"And probably no more than a hundred ships," Anakin added.

A long silence, a long moment of dread. "We've got to find the source," Han demanded.

They took the *Falcon* right in for the dock. Han prepared himself to argue with the controller, to succinctly tell the man to back off, but no call came out to them at all, and as they neared the place, moving to a lower position, they understood why. A huge quake rocked the city, with waves of moving ground rolling under buildings and down streets, toppling walls and throwing pedestrians wildly.

"Good thing it's not a coastal city," Anakin remarked.

At the reminder, Han brought the *Falcon* out of its descent and zipped away to the south, toward the nearest seacoast. Nestled in a valley on the back side of the mountain range south of Sernpidal City was a large village, a settlement of several thousand.

Anakin groaned as the *Falcon* climbed past the initial peaks. Han didn't even have to ask why. The boy was extremely sensitive to disturbances in the Force—he had just felt the death of the mountain village.

Sure enough, as the *Falcon* crested the last peaks, they saw the disaster, the rushing sea swarming into the valley, washing away homes, trees, everything, with such sudden, violent force that before they even dipped lower they knew that everyone in the valley was already dead.

Han swooped back to the north, accelerating, and brought the *Falcon* in at a straight run to the docking bay. A crowd swarmed about the gates as the ship arrived—people suddenly realizing the fact of their impending doom and desperate to find an escape.

Han looked to Chewie. "You load the ship," he instructed. "Pack them in as tight as you can."

"We've got to mobilize all the other ships," Anakin said. "We can't let any take off unless they're full."

Han nodded. "Still not enough," he reminded. "We've got to find that source and take it out."

"I can find it," Anakin volunteered.

Han froze and looked at him hard.

"I can," Anakin insisted. "Then you and Chewie come in with the *Falcon* and blast it."

Han spent a long moment studying his younger son. He understood that he'd be better suited than Anakin to do the necessary evacuation work here at the docks—it would take someone of Han's age and experience, someone who could maintain respect, and, in the absence of that, control the crowd with cunning. Anakin would be able to do much, particularly with any use of the Force, but this situation might become politically charged soon enough, especially if Sernpidal's authorities—and where were they, anyway?—showed up to investigate, bringing with them all those layers of intrigue that always accompanied such situations. Given that, Han's experience would prove invaluable.

Still, the thought of sending Anakin to find this unknown source, this instrument powerful enough to bring down a moon, terrified him.

But he had to trust in his son.

"We'll get you a landspeeder," he said. "You get out there and find the source, and call in the coordinates right away. Don't play around with it, just call it in."

Anakin nodded and moved to the weapons locker, strapping a blaster onto his belt opposite the lightsaber.

"Don't you try to do it yourself," Han demanded. "You find it, and call it in, and get the hell out of the way."

Anakin stared long and hard at Han, the two locking gazes, and a moment of trust passed between them.

Sernpidal City was even more chaotic than Han could imagine. Many locals were out in the streets, on their knees, crying and praying for Tosi-karu to make her arrival.

The irony of those prayers was not lost on Han.

Many more people swarmed the docking gates, and every now and then the sound of a blaster echoed through the buzzing air. Han had figured that if they loaded every available ship to capacity, they might be able to get the bulk of the city's residents out of there, but when he came down the landing ramp and saw the magnitude of the chaos and panic, he doubted they would ever come close to accomplishing that.

From a bay not far away, a small shuttle blasted off, and watching it streak into the sky, the three were horrified to see people hanging on to its landing legs. One after another, they fell, shrieking, plummeting to their deaths.

Another quake ripple rocked the city, buckling one of the walls right into the *Falcon*, though the tough old ship appeared to sustain no damage.

"Clear that!" Han yelled to Chewie. The Wookiee rushed back inside, and a moment later, the forward laser cannons fired, three short bursts, and the rubble was blasted to pieces.

"You'll never get there," Han said to Anakin.

"I've got to try."

Han looked at his son. He didn't want to send the boy out into this maelstrom, with quakes and riots and general panic, but neither could he deny the necessity. If they didn't find the source, and soon, tens of thousands, perhaps hundreds of thousands, would die.

He grabbed Anakin by the arm and ran down the ramp with him, drawing his blaster and waving it about to keep the scrambling mob at bay. Outside, they did indeed find a landspeeder, with a familiar old man, the mayor, sitting calmly on a bench beside it.

"Hey, that's mine!" another man protested, seeing Han help Anakin over the side and into the cockpit.

"Go with him, then, if you want," Han shot back. "Or help me get some of these people onto my ship."

After a split second's thought, the choice seemed more than obvious, and the man ran past Han and back toward the waiting *Falcon*.

"What are you doing?" Han asked the mayor, who had come waddling over, a large pack on his back.

He shrugged. "Waiting for the goddess to arrive, I guess," he answered with a chuckle. "I knew you'd come back."

Han looked at him curiously.

"Hero type," the old man said calmly. "Can you stop the moon from falling?"

"I haven't got that kind of weaponry," Han answered.

"Is it being pulled down here by something?" the surprising old man asked. "By a gravity well, an Interdictor cruiser, perhaps?"

Han's look became even more skeptical.

"I haven't always lived here," the old man explained. "And I'm no stranger to the more advanced ships." He gave another, self-deprecating chuckle. "Maybe that's why the Sernpidalians elected me mayor."

Han motioned for him to come on. "Go with my son," he instructed.

"Where shall we run?"

"Just go," Han growled. "He'll explain the plan on the way."

The old man climbed in, and Anakin handed him the charts, then put the landspeeder into full throttle, zooming down the street.

A roar from Chewie told Han that there was trouble brewing back inside the *Falcon*. He reminded himself to thank Lando profusely when he got back, then ran for his ship.

SIXTEEN

Worthy Opponent

They didn't, couldn't, say a word as the *Jade Sabre* approached the now-yellow-and-green planet known as Belkadan. Luke and Mara had done their homework on the way to the planet, and they held no doubts, with visual inspection looming before them, that something on the planet had gone terribly, terribly wrong.

It wasn't the lack of response, other than the incredible amounts of static, whenever they tried to hail the scientific outpost, ExGal-4. In truth, any response would have surprised them, for merely in observing the planet, they knew.

Belkadan was, to their way of looking at things, dead.

"What were they doing at that station?" Mara asked.

"Observations," Luke replied. "Just staring out at the galactic rim."

"That's what ExGal tells the public," Mara said skeptically.

Luke turned to regard her. "You think this is an experiment gone wrong?"

"Can you think of anything else that might have done this?" Mara asked. "You've read the reports on Belkadan— full of huge trees and small seas, and with clear air and blue skies. The only thing that kept the place from being more appealing was the rather difficult animals that called it home."

"The reports from the station indicated that they lived behind protected walls," Luke agreed.

"So if animals had found their way in and destroyed the station, it wouldn't be so surprising," Mara reasoned. "Do you know any animals that could cause this?" She waved her hand at the viewport and the curving line of Belkadan's horizon, and the roiling, noxious-looking clouds.

"The reports from their headquarters on Coruscant and from this particular station give no hints that anything more than observation was going on here," Luke said, but his tone wasn't so firm. How could it be, with such devastating evidence as the view before them? Something had gone very wrong down there, something brutal, and Luke understood that such catastrophes were usually the work of reasoning beings.

Mara glanced down at her console's smaller viewscreen, scrolling the information of the composition of the clouds. "Carbon dioxide and methane, mostly," she explained, and that came as no surprise to either her or Luke. "In tremendous concentrations. Even if there is a layer of breathable air below, it would be too hot down there to support much life."

Luke nodded. "We've got to go down and see."

Mara didn't disagree, but her concerned look was not lost on Luke. Neither was her color; Luke had noted that Mara's complexion had paled as they had approached Belkadan, and he could sense a bit of her internal weakening. The flight from Dubrillion had been easy enough, but Luke now feared that all of this, the trip to the Outer Rim, the tour of Lando's incredible city, and now the journey out here to Belkadan, might be proving too taxing for his wife.

"We can call back and do a few more readings," Luke offered instead. "ExGal will muster the right ships to come out and see what happened here."

"We're here now," Mara pointedly reminded.

Luke shook his head. "We haven't got the right equipment," he explained. "We can do the preliminary scan, and relay that information, but the *Jade Sabre* isn't really built for flying into that mess."

Mara's expression shifted from surprised to angry as she came to the obvious conclusion that Luke was trying to protect her. "The *Jade Sabre* can fly through a firestorm," she replied. "She can blow a starfighter out of the sky and run circles around Star Destroyers. She's as good a shuttle as anyone will find, and better than anything ExGal will put together."

"Neither of us are trained in—" Luke started to say.

"There might be people still down there," Mara harshly interrupted. "They might even be hearing our call, but unable to respond. So we should just fly away? Back to the safety of Lando's planet?"

"Nothing with Lando is ever safe," Luke replied with a halfhearted smile, a feeble attempt to lighten the mood.

"But he does have doctors, right?" Mara said sarcastically. "Because we need doctors."

"Doctors?" Luke echoed, but the word died on his lips, for he knew Mara had seen right through him and his attempts to protect her, and that this, above anything else in all the galaxy, brought up the fires in the independent woman. Luke could yell at her, even insult her, during their occasional arguments, and she'd give it back to him tenfold, but never, ever, would Mara Jade Skywalker accept condescension. She was ill, true, but she would not be treated as if she was incapacitated. Their course now seemed obvious; their duty compelled them down to the planet, to the outpost to rescue survivors or, perhaps, to retrieve bodies, and to retrieve, as well, any information that might tell them what had happened to Belkadan.

Luke buckled his harness tight about him. "It'll be a rough ride down," he remarked. But he understood that, for him, the ride down to Belkadan wouldn't be half as bad as the ride back to Lando's might have been had he insisted on it.

As soon as the *Jade Sabre* broke the rim of Belkadan's atmosphere, Luke understood just how much his last words had been an understatement. Violent winds buffeted the shuttle, and some unforeseen electromagnetic imbalance sent the sensors and other instruments screaming out error messages and alarm bells. Systems failed and then came back on-line; at one point, there was a sudden drop to the right, and both Luke and Mara thought their harness belts would cut right through them. Behind them, secured in a pod much like his seat on Luke's X-wing, R2-D2 screeched and chattered.

A few seconds—which seemed like hours—later, they broke through the roiling clouds and hit an air pocket that put them into a straight drop for nearly a thousand meters before they slammed back to a stable ride.

Then they saw the devastation, the reddish brown forest streaming lines of noxious vapors skyward. Mara hit Luke with a succession of questions concerning air quality and wind speed and altitude, but her copilot could only shake his head, having no answers, for none of the instruments were giving him plausible readings. He looked back to R2-D2 and asked the droid to try to make sense of it, and R2-D2's answer scrolled across the screen, a jumble of incoherent letters and symbols.

"Are you all right?" Luke asked the droid pointedly.

R2-D2 whistled like a drunken pirate.

"Do you see that?" Mara interrupted, indicating the data screens.

Luke moved in close and read carefully. "Sulfur," he said, and looked up. "A volcano?"

"If we're going out, we're going to need breath masks," Mara remarked.

They were flying manually now, by sight and by gut. Mara shut off all heads-up displays, leaving the screen open for normal viewing, and brought them lower, the swift shuttle skimming the treetops. "Any idea of where we'll find that station?" she asked.

Luke, his eyes closed as he delved into emanations from

the Force, replied, "We have coordinates, but that won't do us much good without instruments."

"Are you *feeling* anything?"

"Belkadan's not dead," Luke replied. "It's just . . . different."

That much seemed evident to Mara as she stared out the window at the living trees emanating the fumes. She thought for a moment to fall into the insight of the Force, as well, but seeing the perplexed look on her husband's face, changed her mind and concentrated on her flying instead.

She turned the shuttle north and brought it up, just under the cloud level, accelerating to a swift flight.

"We won't spot anything from here," Luke reasoned. "Not even a distress signal." He stopped his complaining a moment later, though, when he came to understand Mara's thinking, when the thick air gradually began to thin as they approached Belkadan's northern pole, an ice cap that seemed far less substantial than the documents about Belkadan had indicated it would be. It seemed as if the increased heat on the planet was already making a difference.

"Oh, smart woman," Luke said with a smile.

The ride smoothed out and the cloud cover thinned even more, and the instruments came back on-line, a little bit, and enough for the two to get some fix on the exact polar coordinates. Using these as their base, they turned in-line for the coordinates of the ExGal station, eyeing landmarks along their way, even downloading an image of the mountains along that general line. Off they went, up high again and straight toward target. R2-D2 kept the calculations going, measuring speed and, thus, distance, and within minutes, the droid could calculate their coordinates closely enough to know that they were in the vicinity of the ExGal station.

Mara executed a few long-banking turns, trying to spot the station amidst the jungle canopy, while Luke alternated between looking and *feeling*. It was in one of those Force-sensitive transitions that the Jedi found their answer. "Left," he told Mara. "About thirty degrees."

She didn't ask, just turned.

"Hold it steady," Luke told her, feeling the sensation growing. Warmer, warmer. "Over that rise," he announced, opening his eyes, and sure enough, as soon as the *Jade Sabre* crested the ridge, a thin tower came into sight, and a walled compound behind it.

"ExGal-4," Mara announced.

Patiently awaiting his retrieval to a position of more immediate value, Yomin Carr heard the whine of the *Jade Sabre's* powerful drives as the shuttle made its first pass overhead. He got to a window in time to see the ship's second pass, and though he, like his people, was no supporter of anything purely technological, he had to admit that this ship, with its sleek fish-head design and swept-back tail fin and its flared side pods protecting the twin ion drives, was among the most beautiful he had seen. It cut the vapor trails with hardly a wake and with movements swift and sure.

Smiling with satisfaction, the previously bored warrior strapped on his vonduun crab shell–plated armor and his bandolier of flying thud bugs, did a quick check of his pouch of sentient and binding blorash jelly, and took up his amphistaff, another living creature, a vicious serpent that could harden all or part of its body to the consistency of stone, including narrowing its neck and tail so that they would cut like a razor, or could become supple and whiplike for its Yuuzhan Vong master. In the hands of a true warrior like Yomin Carr, the amphistaff could become a deadly missile weapon, as well, a spear to hurl, or it could spit forth a stream of venom twenty meters with stunning accuracy, blinding opponents instantly and killing them slowly, over many agonizing hours, as the poison seeped in through pores and wounds.

Back at the window, Yomin Carr watched the sleek shuttle put down just outside the compound walls.

The Yuuzhan Vong warrior's smile was genuine; he was going to enjoy this.

They came out of the security of the *Jade Sabre* tentatively, and none more so than R2-D2, who was so concerned with the eerie and dangerous surroundings that he failed to pay enough attention to his companions and kept bumping into Luke. They couldn't stay on planet for long, they knew, even with their breath masks, for it was too hot, and every step would literally suck the moisture right out of them.

Mara started for the compound door, but Luke noted something off to the side by the tower, and pulled her by the arm that way. As they approached, they noticed that all the ground in the area was covered by strange-looking little reddish brown beetles.

"They're all dead," Luke noted, stepping gingerly over the crunchy insects, and R2-D2 blew whistles of protest and flat out refused to follow—until, of course, something hidden deep in the jungle canopy roared and then the little droid zoomed through the beetle cluster, crunching them up with his wheels, spraying the tiny carcasses up into the air in his wake.

"But it's not the air, apparently," Mara noted, turning a glance toward the jungle canopy. "Some of the creatures have survived."

"Well, if some of the creatures have survived, then so should the people inside the station, some of them, at least."

"Unless what we're hearing are new creatures, adapted to the atmosphere," Mara noted, and she checked a gauge at the side of her collar and shook her head. She and Luke might be able to breathe without help from their equipment, but the air was certainly of terrible quality.

The three moved to the wall, toward the gate showing on this side of the compound, a stained metal door.

"Blood," Mara noted.

Luke pulled open the casing of the security lock to the side. "Tap into the codes," he ordered R2-D2. The droid started for the box, but Mara whipped out her blaster and put a shot right into the contraption, frying it. The metal door resounded with the click of lock tumblers disengaging.

"Direct," Luke noted sarcastically.

"What's it going to hurt?" Mara asked.

Luke conceded the point with a shrug and kicked the door open, leading the way in. The compound was deserted, a sight made even more eerie by the sharp contrast caused by the vivid light filtering through the cloud cover. "Empty dock," he noted, pointing to the space vacated by the departure of the Spacecaster.

"Could be just for landing supply ships," Mara reasoned.

R2-D2 put in a series of clicks and whirs.

"True enough," Luke agreed. "They'd have to have some way to get up to their satellite's telescopes, and to get off planet, if necessary."

"It doesn't get any more necessary than this," Mara noted dryly.

"Whether they left or not, there are data banks inside," Luke remarked, leading the way toward the main building. "We'll get some answers."

R2-D2 zipped right behind him, and Mara was fast to follow, though she paused a few steps later and bent down, finding yet another of the strange beetles. This one, unlike all the others, was still alive, though undeniably groggy and slow. She carefully picked it up and brought it close before her eyes, noting a clear liquid oozing from the end of its tiny mandibles.

"What is it?" Luke asked, turning back to see his wife with the beetle in her hand and an intense look upon her face.

Mara shook her head slowly, her gaze locked on the little creature and its wriggling legs and clapping mandibles.

"You think that these bugs are somehow related to this

disaster?" Luke asked. To his distress, Mara, instead of answering, wiped her finger across the mandibles, collecting some of the oozing liquid, then brought the finger right before her eyes.

"There's something about this . . . ," she said slowly.

"Probably poison," Luke reasoned.

Again Mara slowly shook her head. "Something different," she tried to explain, and her voice seemed to falter. "I don't know . . ."

Luke noted how hollow her eyes seemed, as if the beetle, or this planet, was somehow draining her. He wanted to ask if she was all right, but wisely held the question, reminding himself that his capable wife didn't need his worry.

Inside, the station was quiet and dim and cooler, and with air that was much more breathable. Also, many lights, mostly panel indicators, were still on, and those quiet, usually indiscernible background sounds, the hum of computer drives and glow lamps, permeated the air.

"It's like a tomb," Mara said, and both she and Luke instinctively recoiled from the mere volume of her voice, the sudden breaking of constant, low-level hum.

"Let's find the main computers so that Artoo can tap in," Luke suggested.

"Everything still seems to be functioning," Mara remarked as they started on their way, padding down the darkened corridors with all speed, for none of them wanted to stay in this place any longer than absolutely necessary. They turned corner after corner, opening every door they passed. Both Luke and Mara had their lightsabers in hand, though when they noticed each other poised as if expecting an attack, they both put on curious expressions. Logically, there should be no danger here.

But something about the atmosphere of the place, the panel lights glowing in darkened rooms . . .

"Here it is," Luke called, pushing open one door to reveal a large circular room.

"Great setup," Mara remarked when she entered, seeing the array of the seven control pods.

"And the place is still alive," Luke added. "So where is everybody?"

R2-D2 rolled into the room, down the ramp from the refreshment dais, and onto the main floor. He went to the nearest pod and extended his computer interface, linking up.

"Download everything they've got," Luke instructed, and the droid beeped and clicked his agreement.

Luke replaced his lightsaber on his belt, then moved to the pod next to R2-D2. Mara did likewise and moved to the central command pod, and both of them went to work, trying to determine the condition of the equipment. It was all working, they soon understood, but no clear signals were coming through from the orbiting satellites, or from anything else, it seemed.

"It's the cloud cover," Luke remarked. "Nothing's getting through."

"And maybe no distress signal could get out," Mara added.

Luke nodded. "That'll take a few minutes," he said to her, drawing her gaze to the droid. "Let's go and see if we can find anybody."

The two had grown more comfortable with the place by then, and so they thought nothing of leaving R2-D2 alone in the big room, or of splitting up once outside the room, so that they could cover more ground. R2-D2, though, didn't share that level of comfort. He began whistling a tune more nervous than singsongy while he continued his work on the download, trying every trick he knew to extract the information more quickly.

Maybe the whistling would help.

There was no one about, and given the blood on the entry gate, Mara thought nothing of walking into formerly private quarters. She checked lockers and closets, even coat pockets and private desks. In one room she found some scribbled notes in an old-fashioned flimsiplast journal, dated just over a week earlier, describing the increasingly foul air and the inability of the station to raise any communications off planet, or even to find the feeds from the satellites.

The writer went on to detail the investigation to this point, how someone named Yomin Carr kept saying that this was all a passing weather oddity. The page ended ominously: *Perhaps it is natural, but I believe it is linked to*

"To what?" Mara asked aloud in frustration. She ruffled the flimsiplast but found no further writing, then opened the desk drawer, to see more unused flimsiplast, some metal clips, writing utensils, a couple of data cards, and some small bottles.

She reached for the data cards, thinking there might be more information there, but paused as one of the bottles caught her eye. She turned it about so that she could better see its contents.

A beetle.

Mara took the beetle she had collected outside out of her pouch, comparing the two. They were the same species, obviously, and that made her wonder even more if these creatures were somehow connected to the disaster. Had this scientist suspected the same thing? Did he believe the disaster linked to the beetles?

She took the journal and the bottle and headed back into the hallway, turning to follow in the direction Luke had gone.

A screech from behind, from R2-D2 in the control room, turned her fast the other way.

The droid wasn't trying to interpret the information as he absorbed it, was merely trying to make the transfer as fast as possible. He was well on his way, figuring the download to be about 70 percent complete, when he swiveled his domed head about and saw the dark, caped figure rise up from behind a low railing at the side of the room. He knew at once that it wasn't Luke or Mara, and hoped that it was just one of the missing scientists.

No such luck, as the droid discovered when the figure came out of the shadows, leaping atop one of the pods in the front row, clad in some dark plated armor unlike anything R2-D2 had ever seen, and holding a snake-headed staff.

He roared at R2-D2, a stream of curses and snarls—"Infidel! Perversion! Sacrilege!"—and stomped his foot down on the console, sending up a spray of sparks.

R2-D2 tried desperately to flee, but he did so before he disengaged his interface connection, and so when he then tried to pull free, his bulk was twisted at the wrong angle. The droid whistled and beeped, trying to call for help.

The caped menace pulled something from the bandolier about his chest and threw it, or rather, simply let it go.

R2-D2 wheeled back the other way, his interface connection disengaging even as it tugged back, and the resulting abrupt shift toppled the droid onto his side. And just in time, for the flying thing zoomed past, smashing into the pod, driving right into it, and R2-D2 screeched. His dome swiveled about, to look up, and there was the warrior, standing above him, staff poised for a destroying blow.

"Eeeooowww!" the droid squealed, and rolled to the side.

The door at the back of the room banged open and Mara rushed in. "Stop!" she cried. "We are not your enemies!" Her words trailed away as the figure leapt away from the pod, closer to her, to stand in all his warrior glory, dark armor gleaming, his disfigured face staring coldly at the woman.

And what unnerved Mara most of all was the feeling inside her gut that this warrior, this monster, somehow knew her.

The two stood and stared for a long while, neither blinking, the test of wills before the inevitable battle. Off to the side, R2-D2 managed to manipulate his torso, pushing against the console while extending his arm, to upright himself. He skittered right off, but the noise alerted the caped warrior, and

he launched another missile—was it some kind of bug?—
the droid's way, this one clipping the console right behind the
fleeing R2-D2, showering him with sparks and bringing forth
another frantic "Eeeooowww!"

Mara reached for her lightsaber but, recalling her weakened state, drew her blaster instead and had it leveled the warrior's way before he turned back to face her.

"It is an abomination," he growled.

"It's a droid," she corrected.

"Exactly my point," the warrior replied with a wicked grin.
"An abomination. A sign of the weakness that pervades your
people."

"My people?" Mara asked. "Who are you?"

"I am Yomin Carr, the harbinger of doom," he said with a
sinister laugh. "I am the beginning of the end for your
people!"

Mara's face screwed up with incredulity.

"Do not mock me!" Yomin Carr roared, and he pulled another thud bug from his bandolier and let it fly at Mara.

She took a shot at it, but it dodged, and then she had to dive
aside, once and then again as it swooped around. It started to
loop for a third pass, but this time, she got her aim and blew it
out of the air.

Yomin Carr continued to laugh.

Mara turned her blaster on him. "I think you'll be coming
with me," she said.

He laughed louder and started to reach for his bandolier.

"Don't make me," she warned raising the blaster threat-
eningly.

He just laughed and continued, and she shot him. But the
magnificent, plated armor turned the blast aside.

Eyes wide with disbelief, Mara had to move again, and
quickly, as Yomin Carr tossed out another thud bug, and another, and another. She wisely abandoned her blaster, tossing
it aside and drawing out her lightsaber. Then she went into a

frantic dance, twisting and parrying, lightsaber intercepting the darting thud bugs as they came at her in rapid succession.

Yomin Carr's laugh turned into a growl as he nearly emptied his bandolier, a dozen thud bugs darting and spinning at Mara.

Her glowing blade worked in a furious, humming blur, whipping up high and to the side, down low—and when she couldn't catch up to that low-flying missile, she deftly hopped it—and then back up, connecting with one zooming creature barely a centimeter from her face. She turned about and sliced across, picking two out of the air, then dropped into a squat, the lightsaber flashing up above her head to take out a diving bug, then swishing down to the side, forcing another to alter its course. It tried to turn about, but had too much momentum and smashed into the back wall, crashing in deep.

Mara spun about to face Yomin Carr, dived into a forward roll to regain her balance and to avoid any forthcoming attacks. Her lightsaber was at the ready as she came up, but the next missile plopped down—harmlessly, Mara believed—a couple of meters in front of her.

The armored warrior leapt forward, landing perched on the railing in front of the woman. She started forward to meet his charge, lightsaber working against the movements of his staff.

The gooey pie on the floor before her expanded suddenly and grabbed at her feet. Quick as any felinoid, sensing the movement, Mara launched herself into a back flip, and then another.

But the goo spread to pace her and caught her by the feet, rushing to encompass her ankles and hold her fast. Yomin Carr howled in apparent victory.

Mara's lightsaber swished down, cutting through the goo easily, separating it into two parts, but each of those parts continued to move, grabbing stubbornly.

"You'll not defeat it," Yomin Carr promised, and indeed,

each passing moment and each passing movement brought both the jellies up higher on her legs, trapping her even more.

R2-D2 wheeled out into the hall, aware of what was happening with Mara and knowing well that there was nothing he could do to help her directly.

But Luke could, the droid understood, and so he wheeled down the corridor, squealing and clicking. A security holocam mounted high on the wall gave him an idea, and he rushed to the wall, knocking clear the security console and whirring through the codes, tapping into cam after cam until he spotted Luke, scrolling through some screens on a computer in a private room.

Accessing a complete diagram of the station, R2-D2 soon isolated the room, and off he went, still screeching and beeping.

The goo grabbed at Mara, but despair surely did not. She kept her head and her cool, and moved her lightsaber through a wild blur of motion, slashing, cutting, the tip even brushing against her pants leg as she sliced the gel from her body. On and on she went, seemingly wild but actually precise—so much so that she soon had the goo chopped up into little pieces—and she still kept the presence of mind to arch her blade back out in front to intercept yet another thud bug zooming for her.

The warrior came on, staff sweeping down, and Mara ducked at the last moment, came up tall, and sent her lightsaber up high with a rolling motion that kept the staff out wide.

Yomin Carr dropped to one knee and brought his staff horizontally above him, hands out wide, to intercept.

Mara fully expected that her powerful lightsaber would shear through the staff and end the fight abruptly, but amazingly, the tattooed warrior's weapon caught the lightsaber, accepting the brunt of the hit without apparent damage, and

Yomin Carr twisted his hands to the side as he came up fast, throwing Mara's blade off aim.

She should have stepped back to regroup, but the jelly, the many tiny jellies, still held one of her feet firmly, and she could only twist back so far, and not far enough for her to bring her lightsaber in to parry.

Yomin Carr stabbed with the snake-head end of his weapon, and to Mara's horror, that head opened wide its maw, fangs dripping venom. She slapped her hand inside the angle of the blow, against the shaft just below the head, and was quick enough to retract it as the snake head turned in to bite at it.

The lightsaber's glowing blade swooped in an up-turning circular parry between the two, forcing Yomin Carr back, and with that moment of pause, Mara slashed it down beside her foot again, cutting in half the last piece of jelly large enough to hold her. Then she leapt back, though not far—it was as if she had wads of gum stuck to the bottoms of her feet.

"You are worthy," Yomin Carr congratulated, and started to nod and used the ruse to swing about quickly, his staff elongating and becoming supple suddenly, more a whip than a bludgeoning weapon.

Mara tried to leap back, but the jelly, still grabbing at her, slowed her down. She pivoted to the side, bringing her weapon out to intercept.

The whip snapped around the lightsaber, a strike so perfectly aimed that the head still came in across the woman's arm, fangs cutting deep scratches.

Yomin Carr howled in victory, but Mara took the burning hit, focused her energies suddenly on that part of her body, and forced a blood rush out of the wound, washing away the poison before it could begin to take hold. She accepted then that this opponent possessed weapons that she could not anticipate, and so she went on the offensive immediately, charging ahead and launching a series of thrusts and slices that had

Yomin Carr backing, and all the while, he tried to retract his weapon to staff form, to give him something with which to parry.

But his retreat was short-lived. He flicked one hand in a reverse movement, sending the remaining length of whip, ending in that wicked snake head, back out at her.

She dropped her left knee down and back, pivoting away from the warrior, and brought her lightsaber in a rolling motion down and then stabbing back over her dipping left shoulder, a perfect angle to intercept the rushing snake head, the tip of her blade diving into its opening mouth. She came up in a rush, arm pumping and slashing, tearing the snake head apart, and then she bore on, right up to the large warrior.

His backhand got inside her movement, though, the other, hard end of his weapon smacking her across the shoulder and knocking her to the side. She rolled with it, accepting the blow, and spun down low, swiping across at his knees.

He leapt above the cut, and then again as Mara came across with a backhand, and then brought his weapon, now fully a staff again, down at her seemingly exposed head. Mara turned and brought her elbows flying up, her lightsaber coming across horizontally to intercept and hold the weapon at bay.

Yomin Carr did not relent, pushing down with all his strength—frightening strength to Mara for, indeed, she, even with all of her inner power and determination, could not hold him up. She reached into the Force then, trying another tactic on the man, and then she nearly buckled, for there was . . . nothing.

That was the only way she could describe it. Nothing. It was as if the Force was not a part of this warrior, as if he refused to acknowledge its existence in such a profound manner that it did not exist for him.

Mara had to rely strictly on her fighting skills, pitting her speed and precision against this opponent's brute force. With a sudden, desperate twist, rolling her left hand over her right, she snapped the descending staff harmlessly down to the side and in front of her, and then she started up, thinking to come in at the warrior up high.

But she had jelly on one knee, goo that halted her progress abruptly and nearly sent her sprawling to the floor. That proved fortunate for Mara, though, for Yomin Carr reacted more quickly than she believed possible, straightening and slashing his staff across viciously, a blow that would have taken her across the head or neck if she had continued upward.

Quick to improvise, she stabbed the warrior, who was as surprised as she by the fact that she was still down low, in the knee. Then, as he howled in pain, she slashed her lightsaber across, taking him out at the knees and dropping him hard on his back. He started to roll toward her, bringing his staff across for her head, but she had the tip of her weapon out in time, pointed at his breast, and his own momentum drove him into it, the lightsaber finding a crease in that magnificent plated armor where the blaster had not, puncturing the coat and Yomin Carr's chest, poking into his heart.

He froze in place, staring hard at Mara. "You are worthy," he said once more, and then he just stared at her, and it seemed again as if he somehow knew her. "Jedi," he whispered.

That flicker of recognition went away, all light in Yomin Carr's eyes faded, and he lay very still.

The door burst open and Luke came rushing in, a squawking R2-D2 hot on his heels.

It all hit Mara then, the exertion, the wounds, and something about the very nature of this poisoned planet that tugged at her insides, as if this disease within her fed off the perversion that was Belkadan. "Get me out of here," she whispered to Luke, trying to rise.

She needed his help, especially in cutting away the last of the stubborn jelly.

"Finish the download," he instructed R2-D2 as he helped

Mara into a chair. "Do you know who that was?" he asked her, and he moved to the dead warrior, inspecting the tattoos, the disfiguring wounds, the strange plated armor and weapon.

"His name is Yomin Carr." Mara shook her head. "I think he knew me," she said, and Luke gave her a curious stare, one she could not in any way answer.

Luke went back to his inspection. "Artoo, bring up images of all the scientists," he instructed. "Let's see if this was one of them."

The droid whistled and did as instructed, but none of the records showing those stationed on Belkadan bore any resemblance to this barbaric warrior.

Luke looked back to the body and shook his head. "There must have been another species living on this planet," he reasoned. "Or they invaded."

The droid was finished soon after and the three left the control room, with Luke carrying the heavy warrior over his shoulder, and Mara, unsteady on her feet, carrying his staff and using it for support. They got to the *Jade Sabre* without incident, and Luke settled the exhausted Mara into place.

"Will you two be all right for a few minutes?" he asked.

Mara looked at him, surprised, but then nodded.

"We've got to find out," Luke explained.

"He had weapons we don't know of," Mara told him. "Living missiles, and the stubborn jelly. And that staff," she said, indicating the snakelike creature. "There may be other enemies."

Luke nodded and started away.

"And, Luke," she finished, "I could not use the Force to gain any insights on him. It might be some kind of training against Jedi tactics. If he has allies similarly trained, they'll be upon you before you expect it if you try to sense them."

Luke paused, considering the information. "Get the ship into the air," he decided. "Run a guard for me over the compound and be ready to blast open holes in the walls if I call to you."

"Will the communicators even work?" Mara asked.

"Let's see," Luke said, and he exited the *Jade Sabre*. Once outside, he called through his comlink, and though the signal was weak and full of static, Mara and R2-D2 could indeed hear him.

Luke went back into the station cautiously, while R2-D2, with help from the exhausted Mara, put the *Jade Sabre* into a sentry pattern just above the compound.

Luke returned a short time later, having completed his search, bearing a sack bulging as if it had two Taikawaka kicking balls inside.

Mara looked at him curiously. "I found them in room B7," Luke explained, looking to R2-D2, who ran a quick check on his downloaded schematics and brought the name *Yomin Carr* up across the viewscreen.

Luke reached into the bag and pulled out a brown leathery item that looked like a ridged ball.

"A helmet?" Mara asked.

Luke shrugged. "I found just these two, on a shelf in the closet," he explained, and then he looked at his wife hard. "I think they're alive."

Mara, having witnessed a living staff and apparently living jelly, was not overly surprised. "Put them in a safe place," she replied. "They're probably bombs."

Luke started to chuckle, but realized almost immediately that she wasn't kidding. He took the bag and its contents to a strong locker at the back of the *Jade Sabre*'s bridge and closed it up tight.

The departure from Belkadan was no easier or smoother than the entry, and it quickly became apparent to Luke that his wife was not faring well. Even after they had cleared the clouds and broken out of Belkadan's turbulent atmosphere, Mara's face remained blanched, and her head lolled about weakly.

"Did he hurt you?" Luke asked.

"No."

Luke stared at her, his concern clear on his face.

"It was just being there," Mara tried to explain. "I started feeling worse as soon as we neared Belkadan. Down there . . ." She paused and shook her head helplessly. "It was as if this disease within me was somehow bolstered by the plague affecting the planet."

"And the beetles?" Luke prompted, nodding toward the two specimen jars Mara had put on a shelf at the side of the control console.

His wife picked up the one containing the living beetle, bringing it right before her eyes.

"You believe they somehow caused the damage to Belkadan," Luke remarked.

Mara looked at him, having no practical response, no real evidence.

It was just a feeling, a slight sensation that these creatures were simply too foreign, and it was a feeling that Luke surely shared.

But could it all—Belkadan, the beetles, the barbaric warrior, Mara's illness—be somehow connected? And what about Mara's insistence that this warrior was somehow devoid of, or rather, unconnected to, the Force? Hadn't she just had a similar experience with another, a troublemaker in a civil war?

"The man I fought—Yomin Carr," she began, again shaking her head, at a loss. "I don't know if it's me, if this illness has caused some holes in my sensitivity to the Force, or if . . ."

"Just like you said about the Rhommamoolian rebel, Nom Anor," Luke prompted, and Mara nodded.

"I couldn't sense a thing, with either of them."

"But didn't you say that Jaina and Leia shared your perceptions of Nom Anor?"

"Or maybe they were just reading my own failings," Mara

reasoned. "Maybe I was projecting something, some kind of a Force shield over the Rhommamoolian even as I was trying to read him."

Luke let it go at that, but he didn't believe the explanation at all, and neither, he could tell, did Mara. Something very strange was going on here, something bigger than Belkadan or than the Rhommamoolian rebel, something that might even have implications for Mara's illness.

He could feel it.

They turned as one, hearing a voice behind them. At first, they thought it was R2-D2, but the droid was in place, still running his analysis on the multitude of downloaded files.

The voice came again, from the closed locker, and while the first part of the speech was too garbled to decipher, both Luke and Mara thought they heard the name *Carr* clearly.

Luke ran to the locker and pulled it open, then brought forth the bag and dumped it onto the floor.

And then he jumped, and Mara cried out in surprise and horror at the disembodied head that seemed to have replaced one of the leathery balls.

"*Torug bouke*, Yomin Carr," the head said. Neither Luke nor Mara recognized the language. "*Dowin tu gu.*"

"It's not real," Mara observed, moving over, even nudging the thing a bit to upright it. While the specific features of the head did not resemble the warrior she had recently battled, the scarring and the tattooing looked similar.

The head said something else they could not comprehend, lips and eyes moving as if it was indeed the actual speaker. One phrase jumped out at them, the voice inflection seeming to give it great importance: *Praetorite Vong*.

As it finished speaking, the leathery bag inverted suddenly, rolling back in on itself and appearing again exactly like the other one.

"A hologram recording," Mara remarked, daring to prod the seemingly lifeless thing again.

"For Yomin Carr," Luke agreed. "From his superior, is my guess."

"These are communication devices, then," Mara reasoned. "But for whom?"

"Did you get all of that, Artoo?" Luke asked, and the droid beeped affirmative.

"Can you translate?" Mara asked.

"Ooo," R2-D2 replied sadly.

"Threepio will figure it out," Luke insisted. "Once Artoo can transfer the information to him."

Mara nodded.

"The Praetorite Vong?" Luke mused.

"What's going on?"

Luke didn't have any answers for that one.

"Artoo, have you got anything on space activity near Belkadan yet?" he asked the droid.

R2-D2 whistled and clicked something in response.

"Check the charts of the last few days, for incoming or out-going ships," Luke suggested.

R2-D2 whistled and clicked the same pattern again, and this time Luke understood that the droid was trying to show him something. He and Mara moved over beside R2-D2, and immediately an image came up on the small viewscreen atop the droid's work pod, a replay of ExGal-4's tracking of the superspeeding comet streaking in from outside the galaxy.

Luke blew a sigh and wondered then if they should go back to Belkadan to see if there might be other evidence they had missed.

"Fast forward it to conclusion," he instructed R2-D2, and they followed the course of the comet, across the sectors until it was lost from view. R2-D2 brought up ExGal's determinations about its course: the fourth planet of the Helska system.

Luke and Mara watched it all in disbelief, with too much to digest, too many possibilities, and none of them adding up in a good way.

Luke directed R2-D2 on what to search for, then went back to the pilot chairs with Mara and laid in a course for the fourth planet of the Helska system.

The ice of that fourth planet seemed a tomb to his heart, a cold-encasing eternal torment for the Jedi Knight. Miko sat curled in the lichen-lighted and -heated chamber, head down in his arms, an attempt at meditation that would not come, the road to freeing emptiness blocked by the barrier of horrible recollections.

He saw that maw, the chewing, pointy teeth, and felt the great power of the yammosk overwhelming him, mocking him and all of his Jedi training.

Nothing he had ever known in all his life could have prepared Miko for the tactics and devious techniques of the Yuuzhan Vong mind-breaking. In his training, he had faced the dark side of the Force, the specter of his innermost horrors, but even that paled beside the reality of the yammosk.

How many times had the horrid creature feigned his execution? How many times had he been drawn in to within a hairbreadth of those chewing teeth? And each time, no matter what logic might yell at him, he could not believe other than that this would be the moment of his death.

That reality did not get any easier with repetition.

And worse: Each feigned execution replayed in his mind a thousand times, and each of those recollections seemed nearly as vivid as the actual experience. He could not sleep, could barely force down enough food to keep himself alive.

Across the chamber, Danni watched it all helplessly, knowing that her companion was near to breaking. She had tried everything to comfort him, had held him while he thrashed in his dreams, had offered him her words of comfort and her shoulder to cry on.

But it didn't matter, she knew. These Yuuzhan Vong warriors, whoever they were, had clearly decided, for some reason that escaped Danni Quee, that Miko, the Jedi Knight, was not worthy, and so they were going to destroy him utterly, his heart first, then his mind, and finally his body.

And she could only watch.

SEVENTEEN

The Last Pose of Defiance

The ground rumbled and rolled, and a great wave of splintering rock reared up at them, toppling a building into the street. Anakin banked the landspeeder and throttled up, weaving in and out of falling and bouncing chunks of stone, sweeping past people screaming in terror and pain. A couple of soldiers, Sernpidal City guards, stood by the northern checkpoint exit, waving for Anakin to slow.

He didn't.

Outside the city, the quakes were even more violent. A strong wind was blowing now, and Anakin feared that the atmosphere itself might be compressing under the disturbance of the descending moon. He knew the calculations, knew that they still had a couple of hours before the moon came crashing down, but he had to wonder if the planet would hold together that long, or if the residual disasters, the quakes, the brewing violent winds, the rushing seas, would destroy the place so that by the time the moon arrived, there would be nothing left to kill.

He pressed the landspeeder on, redlining the drives, and almost felt as if he was in the asteroid belt again, moving on instinct, on anticipation instead of reaction. Beside him, the old mayor sat quietly, apparently comfortable, hardly jumping even on those occasions when a bouncing stone or rolling wave of dirt nearly buried them. Anakin gave him hardly a thought, other than a quick survey, visually and with the Force, an inspection that showed him the old man was truly calm, that it was not a facade, that he had come to accept his doom without despair.

Somehow Anakin used that calm to keep his own cool head. He checked his coordinates to ensure that he was in the right area.

But what was he looking for?

A gigantic machine? An Interdictor cruiser, with its gravity-well projectors? There were none about. A rift in the planet's surface? Again, nothing, other than the cracks from the tremors.

He slowed the landspeeder and closed his eyes, feeling the sensations about him, feeling the calm of the old man, the unrest of the planet as it was pulled and twisted by the swiftly passing low moon, the fear of the creatures, reasoning and animal, a palpable terror that the young Jedi could almost taste in his mouth.

Anakin looked deeper, deeper. Anything exerting the kind of power necessary to grab on to a moon could not be invisible to the Force.

The moon, now enormous, crested the horizon, rolling up into the sky. The wind roared; the ground swelled and rolled.

And Anakin felt the tug, not on him, not on anything except for that moon. He opened his eyes, though he kept his mind in that other sensibility, and there before him, he clearly "saw" the tractor beam.

He throttled up the landspeeder, swerving through a ravine between two unstable peaks, a move that almost cost him dearly as one huge boulder smashed down right behind the small craft as it passed. Speed was their ally, for the rocks on both cliff walls were crumbling fast, but as they neared the end of the narrow valley, they were hit by tremendous head winds, as if all the air was being squeezed. Anakin glanced up at the moon and saw a tail of fire trailing it, the first contact with the atmosphere.

"We're barely moving," the mayor commented calmly.

Anakin banked to the side, climbing along one narrow trail, trying to get behind a jag in the stone, and nearly getting smashed against the wall by one particularly furious gust. He made it, though, skimming into a narrow channel and running the length of it, and when he came out, he found the wind diminished enough so that he could again make forward progress.

Exiting the pass, they came to a wide and empty field, a barren stretch of stone and dirt, a bowl within the low mountain range. Anakin immediately spotted the crater in the middle of that field and didn't have to fall back into the Force to know that this was the source. He approached swiftly but cautiously to within a dozen meters, then shut the landspeeder down and hopped out, running low to the ground, not knowing what to expect.

The crater was not large, barely a couple dozen meters across, nor was it deep, perhaps ten meters, and there in the bottom sat something that resembled a huge, pulsating, dark red heart, with deep blue spikes all about it. Anakin studied it, looking for some controls, or some connection to a power source.

"What is it?" the old man asked when he joined the boy at the rim of the crater.

Anakin looked more deeply, using the Force, seeing the thing more distinctly and coming to the unnerving conclusion that not only was this definitely the source of their troubles but that it was a living creature. Gasping for breath, he drew his blaster.

"That thing's bringing down Dobido?" the old man asked incredulously.

"Get back," Anakin instructed, taking aim. The old man didn't move, but Anakin, so entranced by this completely alien and undeniably powerful life-form, didn't notice. He leveled the blaster and fired.

The energy bolt ripped down into the crater and then . . . disappeared. Just flickered out, like a candle in a strong wind. He fired again and again, but the bolts seemed to have no effect.

"What is it?" the old man asked again, more emphatically.

"Get in the landspeeder and go back for my father," Anakin instructed, pulling the lightsaber from his belt.

"The ugly one or the big hairy one?" the old man asked.

Anakin ignored him and moved one foot to the very edge of the crater.

And then he and the old man went flying away, jolted by a sudden and violent thrust of the ground. The young Jedi scrambled about, to see dirt and stones flying from the crater, a volcanic eruption, it seemed, without the lava.

It ended abruptly, and Anakin rushed back, only to see a deep, deep hole where the creature had been. He understood: the creature had recognized the attacks and had reversed its gravity pull, probably latching on to the core of Sernpidal, and was now far, far below.

What was he to do now?

A familiar roar turned his eyes skyward, and he saw the *Millennium Falcon* swooping down from the mountains. It landed fast on the gravel plain to the side, and the landing ramp dropped almost immediately, Han running down to his son, and many other people, refugees, poking their heads out of the *Falcon* to see what might be going on.

"We've got to get back!" Han cried. "Chewie's organizing the retreat from the planet, but we've barely got enough ships!"

"The creature's down there," Anakin replied, pointing to the crater. "It's a living thing!"

Han shook his head. "Doesn't matter anymore," he replied with a wry twist of his lips, and Anakin understood. For Sernpidal, it was too late. Even if they somehow managed to kill this creature or stop its tractor beam, Dobido's orbit was lost, and the moon would come crashing down.

"Every second means someone else dies," Han remarked, and Anakin sprinted for the ramp. The old man, though, didn't follow; instead, he walked back up to the crater rim.

"I must at least ensure that this devil doesn't escape to destroy another world," he explained, smiling, and he opened his cloak and produced a meter-long tube.

"Thermal detonator," he said. "You should be leaving."

"You're crazy," Han started to say, but the old man, the mayor of Sernpidal City, just went over the edge of the crater and calmly leapt into the hole.

The *Falcon* had barely lifted away when the detonator blew, lifting tons and tons of dirt into a gigantic mushroom cloud over the gravel plain.

"Strange old man," the stunned Han muttered.

Anakin stared out the window, back toward the area of the original crater. He felt no more pull from the alien creature. "He got it," he informed his father.

Han nodded. The old man hadn't bought them a minute of time, hadn't saved Sernpidal at all, but still, they both understood, he had done something truly valuable and heroic.

For Prefect Da'Gara, it was the moment of highest glory, honor, and spirituality, the epitome of his purpose, the reward for his efforts, the most welcomed task.

He stood alone on a pedestal before the yammosk, the creature's massive eyes boring into him. Chanting the appropriate prayers to Yun-Yammka, he lifted his hand to gently touch the creature between those eyes, along a huge blue pulsating vein, the point of transference.

Then they were joined as one, the yammosk's consciousness overwhelming Da'Gara's. The prefect felt the binding power of the war coordinator, the purpose of its being, and through its sensitive energies, he felt the commune that was his task force, the Praetorite Vong.

Da'Gara fell deeper into the yammosk, gave it his feelings as it recited its own to him, and they knew they were of like mind. It was time to expand, to reach out and begin consuming vast reaches of the galaxy.

But first, they had to lure a portion of their enemies in, destroy the New Republic's warships on a Yuuzhan Vong battleground, where the yammosk's control and coordination were complete.

The prefect left the meeting both exhilarated and exhausted, physically drained but emotionally charged. He went right to his private quarters, to Yomin Carr's villip, but then changed his mind and opened contact to Nom Anor instead.

The executor responded immediately.

"We reach out this day," Da'Gara explained.

"Go with glory and victory," came Nom Anor's proper response. "Die as a warrior."

Da'Gara snapped to attention. "We shall not dishonor the Yuuzhan Vong," he answered, again the proper response. "Sernpidal dies this day."

"And her people?"

"Many attempt flight, and there, our warriors will find their next challenge," Da'Gara replied. "The war coordinator has dispatched four full battle groups to intercept and to give chase. They will allow the refugee convoy to lead them to the next planet in line, and there they will begin the open warfare."

"Do-ro'ik vong pratte," Nom Anor pronounced.

Da'Gara sucked in his breath at the bold proclamation. *Do-ro'ik vong pratte* was the war cry of the Yuuzhan Vong, the call for ferocity unbridled, the absolute releasing of the basest of warrior emotions. Under such a command, Yuuzhan Vong warriors became the hunter in the closing strides of the stalk, the purest killers.

"Do-ro'ik vong pratte," Da'Gara agreed. "And woe to our enemies."

By the time Han got the *Falcon* back to Sernpidal City, the docking area was gone, broken apart by the tremendous upheavals, with all its walls flattened. A few people ran about, screaming, a few others remained prostrated on the streets, praying to Tosi-karu.

But most had been packed away, and dozens of ships, everything from single-seaters, inevitably with two people crammed in, to freighters, were up in the air, preparing to fly away.

Han spotted Chewie almost immediately, the Wookiee waving one long arm and holding a pair of children under the other. "Help him," he instructed his son, and Anakin rushed away, pushing through the mob that packed the *Falcon*, to the lower landing ramp. Han brought the ship in low and slow, compensating for the roaring winds. "Hurry, hurry," he muttered to himself. Debris was flying everywhere, and only luck alone had kept Chewie and those kids from being washed away in it.

He edged the *Falcon* down lower, to within a few meters of the ground, and moved over Chewbacca's position.

"The kids are in," Anakin called over the intercom. "I'm getting Chewie in now."

An explosion rocked the city, a few blocks to the side of the *Falcon*, and a small shuttle started to rise above the remnants of one wall, but quickly shut down and disappeared from view.

Han banged a fist on his console. "You got him, kid?" he called to his son.

"Chewie's going for the shuttle," Anakin called back. "I'm going, too. Meet us there." Even as Anakin finished, Han saw Chewie go running out from under the *Falcon*, drawing his bowcaster as he went.

Anakin came close behind, gaining ground as Chewie slowed to blow a hole in the wall between them and the downed shuttle.

"We've got to clear it," Anakin shouted as he came through that wall, to find the tail end of the shuttle buried under a pile of debris too thick about the lone ion drive for the ship to dare risk a takeoff.

Chewie charged right in, bowcaster firing, cutting up the bigger chunks. He grabbed pieces with one strong arm and sent them flying aside.

"Hurry up!" came a cry from the open port on the shuttle's side, a woman standing inside. "I've got a packed ship. We'll all die."

Anakin studied the pile and the Wookiee's progress. He heard the *Falcon*'s engines humming as the ship hovered over the wall behind him, and for a moment, he thought of instructing his father to vaporize that rubble pile with the laser cannons, as Chewie was trying to do with his bowcaster.

He shook the improbable plan away and utilized a different power source, an inner source, instead, reaching out mentally to the rubble, using the Force to lift it away, huge piece by huge piece. Another quake rocked the city, the falling moon making its appearance on the eastern horizon, seeming much larger than even on its last pass, and this time with a huge fire trail spewing out about it. Immediately the wind increased to deafening proportions.

But Anakin held his calm and worked the pile methodically. The Wookiee roared his approval and helped as much as he could with his conventional methods, and soon enough, Chewie fell back, hailing the woman inside with great and urgent howls.

"Take her out!" Anakin cried to the woman, translating the Wookiee's words. "Take her out fast!" He and Chewie fell back as the shuttle blasted away.

It rose only a dozen meters before being blown aside by a huge gust of wind that pummeled the area and sent Anakin and Chewie scrambling.

The more powerful *Millennium Falcon* held its ground, though, and the lower landing ramp was down, with Han perched on it, extending his hand to his son and his partner. "Come on!" he cried. "It's ending fast!"

Chewie fought powerfully against the wind, making some progress, and then Anakin was beside him, practically floating off the ground, pulling him along with the strength of the Force.

A tiny, pitiful cry rang in their ears. Both glanced all around, discerning the source, spotting large eyes peering out at them from under a half-buried bulkhead.

Abruptly, Anakin let go of Chewie and changed course, and the Wookiee, with only a quick glance to Han, followed.

"Go back to the ship," Anakin instructed, yelling at the top of his lungs. Even so, his voice was barely audible in the howling wind.

Chewie growled and shook his hairy head.

"I'll use the Force to get us both back, then," Anakin said. Another pitiful cry came out at them. "And whoever's under there!"

They went to work wildly on the bulkhead, tossing aside debris with muscle, physical and mental, and then Chewie reached in and pulled out a small boy, barely a toddler. Together, the three turned for the *Falcon*, struggling on as the storm increased, as the ground heaved and broke apart, as the thunderous wind roared on, the *Falcon*'s powerful engines straining to hold the ship's position.

They were near, so close that Han could almost grab Anakin's extended hand, when a barrage of debris swept past. Chewie held his ground and turned his powerful body to protect the toddler, but a piece of stone clipped Anakin's head, costing him his concentration and launching him far in a rolling, bouncing tumble.

Han's eyes widened with horror; Chewie thrust the toddler into Han's arms before he could begin to move, and then the Wookiee turned about and half ran, half rode the wind to catch up to the fallen Anakin.

Han handed off the toddler and rushed back for the

cockpit, knowing the two could never get back to the *Falcon* against this mounting storm. He brought the *Falcon* in fast but steady, moving to the spot even as Chewie lifted Anakin in his arms.

Han locked her in place and rushed back to the landing ramp, pushing aside those who had moved into position to help. But the *Falcon* couldn't hold position now, and she drifted up and to the side—or maybe it was the ground dipping down and to the side—her engines roaring in protest.

"Chewie!" he cried, hanging right off the ramp now. Several others crowded about Han, holding him in place by the legs. He reached desperately for the Wookiee, but the *Falcon* was up too high.

Chewbacca gave his friend a resigned, contented look, then threw Anakin up into Han's waiting arms.

The ground rolled and bucked, and suddenly, Chewie was far, far away.

Han cradled Anakin to the floor just inside, and the boy was conscious again, struggling to his feet as his father rushed back to the cockpit.

Han worked furiously over the controls, bringing the *Falcon* around, swerving about buildings. The communicators crackled with the frantic cries from other ships, some blasting away, others unsure of where to go.

Han ignored it all, focused entirely on finding his lost Wookiee friend.

Anakin came up beside him, falling into Chewie's chair.

"Where is he?" Han cried.

Anakin took a deep, steadying breath. He knew Chewie so well—surely he could find his friend with the Force.

And he did.

"To the left," he cried. Han brought her about. "Around that corner!" Anakin cried.

"Take it!" Han told him, and he ran back to the landing ramp. "Get me to him!"

Anakin worked furiously over the controls, the ship vibrating so violently that he thought it might just shake apart. He turned her up on her side to get down one alley, and swooped around another teetering building.

"Oh, no," he breathed, for there stood Chewie, his back to the *Falcon*, and in front of the Wookiee, a fiery Dobido was streaking down.

"Closer!" came Han's voice.

Chewie turned about and took one step toward Han and the *Falcon*, and then a burst of tremendous, hot wind blasted through, tossing him to the ground, toppling buildings. One pile of rubble crashed atop the *Falcon*—her shields groaned in protest—and sent the nose of the ship up, up.

Anakin fought her back to level, started to turn her about to find the Wookiee, but saw instead, in all her devastating glory, the last descent of Dobido, the arrival, to those faithful natives still praying in the ruined streets, of Tosi-karu.

They were out of time. Anakin knew it immediately. If he turned for Chewie, if he did anything other than take her straight up and out, the explosion of the crashing moon would tear the *Falcon* apart.

He heard his father's pleading cry to get him back to Chewie.

He pointed the *Millennium Falcon* skyward and punched the throttle.

Han saw.

A battered and bloody Chewie regained his footing, stood up high on one pile of rubble, and faced the descending moon with arms upraised and a defiant roar.

The scene receded quickly, but Han kept his eyes locked on the spot, burning that image of the very last moments of his friend's life indelibly into his consciousness. And then he saw the beginning to the final cataclysm as Dobido plowed into the city.

The landing ramp rose suddenly, locking into place—Han

knew it to be the doings of his son—and then the *Falcon* went spinning away as the shock wave hit her.

Han didn't even consider the danger to him and the others, not even to his son at that critical moment. He just thought of Chewie, of that last tragic image, the Wookiee shaking his fist at the great, unbeatable enemy.

A fitting last pose of defiance, but one that did nothing to mend the tear ripping through Han's heart.

EIGHTEEN

Storm Brewing

"Keep a high orbit," Luke said to Mara as he sat in the cockpit of his X-wing, the small starfighter at rest in the rear compartment of the *Jade Sabre*. "If I get in trouble, I'm going to jump to lightspeed to get out of there, and I expect you to do the same."

"Right behind you," Mara assured him, her voice still showing some of the strain from their ordeal on Belkadan.

"Right in front of me," Luke corrected. He could visualize his wife's wry grin as she heard that command for about the tenth time in the last hour. The two had come into the Helska system quietly, using the sun as a visual and tracking barrier in their approach toward the fourth planet. They had no idea of what might be going on here, of whether the warrior Mara had slain on Belkadan might be related to whatever it was that streaked through the galactic barrier to collide with the fourth planet, of whether the plague that had all but destroyed Belkadan had emanated from this place. Perhaps it was all coincidence, the sighting followed by the destruction of Belkadan. Perhaps Yomin Carr had become deranged by the same metamorphosis that had apparently afflicted the trees of the doomed planet.

Luke didn't think so. He sensed something here, something deep and dangerous, like a resonation in the fabric of the Force itself. As a strange and dangerous disease had come into Mara, he feared that one had come into the galaxy, and there was only one way to find out. Furthering that line of thought were the leathery balls they had brought from Belkadan. Someone, something, had tried to communicate with Yomin Carr, using a language that neither Luke nor Mara had ever heard before, and one that R2-D2 couldn't even begin to translate.

C-3PO would get it, though, Luke believed, for the protocol droid was programmed with every known language, even archaic and unused, in the galaxy. That thought brought a shiver to Luke, for, given the information they had garnered on Belkadan, could they even be sure that this language was from the galaxy?

Even if it was not, Luke was confident that dependable C-3PO would figure it out.

"Break it open, Artoo," he instructed the astromech behind him. R2-D2 punched the appropriate codes into the X-wing, which were relayed to the *Jade Sabre*, and the tail fin of the shuttle opened like a scissors' blade. A moment later, the X-wing slid out easily into empty space, floating behind the *Jade Sabre*, and as soon as there was enough room between them, Luke swooped down about the shuttle and throttled past her, giving a salute to Mara. They had decided that he would go to the fourth planet in the more nimble X-wing, while Mara played a role as a wider-range reconnaissance and provided cover fire, should that be needed.

The X-wing's layered S-foils were closed now, giving it the appearance of a two-winged starfighter. Luke did a quick check of all systems, then called back to Mara, offering the coordinates for his run.

Then he put it straight for the Helskan sun, as they had agreed.

"You got that planet tracked?" he asked R2-D2.

The droid's replying whistles seemed as much annoyed as affirmative, and Luke, despite his fears, managed a grin.

"Let me know when you're getting too hot," he said, and he opened up the throttle a bit more, his speed mounting, as well, from the gravitational tug of the flaring sun.

Luke felt the press on his chest and dialed up the inertial compensator to 99 percent. In his screen, the sun grew and grew, but he knew what he was doing, and held complete faith in R2-D2's navigational abilities.

As they neared, the hull temperature and R2-D2's complaints both beginning to rise dramatically, Luke veered to the right and cut around the sun in close orbit, then vectored out at tremendous speed along R2-D2's designated coordinates, a nearly straight line toward the fourth planet, and one that would keep the sun right at the X-wing's back all the way. If there were any enemies on the fourth planet, they might not detect his approach right away—and that approach, given the tremendous boost in speed afforded them by the sun's gravity, would be fast.

In just a few moments, Luke spotted the planet, growing from a speck, to fist-sized, to fill his viewscreen. He scissored the wings and broke right again, whipping into orbit, dropping down, down, to where he could visually examine the icy planet's surface.

He felt it all around him: an energy field. He could feel the tingles in the roots of his hair, could hear them in the crackles over his comm system, and could see them in the fuzzy lines breaking across all of his instrumentation panels.

R2-D2 whistled something out at him, but that sound, too, broke up among the energy interference.

Luke shut down most of his instruments, flying on eyes and instinct, and went down even more. He had already completed his first full orbit, but his speed was decreasing fast, and so this second round promised to reveal more to him.

"Luke," came a crackle, Mara's voice. She continued to talk, but only a few words came through. "There's . . . back side . . . dots."

"Play it back internally," he instructed R2-D2. "Filter out the static and try to figure out what she's saying."

He brought the X-wing down even lower, skimming the surface, using his eyes and his mind to try and figure out what might be going on here. Something was definitely amiss, he knew, he sensed. Some nagging feeling of danger.

And then it hit him, a sudden jolt that dipped the nose of his X-wing and dragged the ship as if he had suddenly entered water.

Behind him, R2-D2 shrieked, and all the rest of Luke's instruments, particularly his navigational assist controls, just shut down.

And the icy, barren surface seemed to be rising up to meet him.

They limped away from Sernpidal, a line of freighters and shuttles and every other type of ship as could be found on the Outer Rim, a line of bedraggled, horrified refugees, of men and women who had just seen their homes destroyed, of men and women who had just lost family and friends to a tragedy so inexplicable and devastating that they simply could not even begin to make any sense out of it.

Behind them, Sernpidal, a spinning dead sphere, its atmosphere torn away, continued its orbit, an altered course now for the power of the impact and the huge cloud on one side of the planet, a clear bruise.

Sernpidal was a dead thing, oblivious to the pain and the destruction. It would go on through the eons, devoid of life.

Han Solo stared at the wobbling planet for a long, long time, his eyes registering the truth that his heart could not.

"We've got a hundred and eleven ships in the convoy," Anakin said, coming up behind his father nervously, not really knowing what to say or do, whether to hug Han or run away from him.

Han turned to face his young son, his face blank as if he had not heard.

"A hundred and ele—" Anakin started to reiterate.

"You left him," Han said quietly, calmly. The accusation hit Anakin as hard as any punch ever could.

Anakin stuttered over several replies; he wanted to shout out at his father for even saying such a thing. He had saved the *Millennium Falcon* and the scores of people crammed aboard her. "We had to get out of there," he finally managed to reply. "The moon was coming down—"

"You left him," Han said again, more sharply.

Anakin swallowed hard in the face of that glare. He had been given no choice on Sernpidal, he reminded himself, and surely his father had to know that logically. They were too far from Chewie, with the moon too close and falling fast. They could not possibly have reached Chewie and gotten him aboard. Anakin wanted to say all of that, wanted to rush back and get the logs of the incident, certain that they would back up his reasoning.

But he couldn't. He couldn't give any answer at all, other than to stare helplessly against the reality of the most despairing, empty expression he had ever seen on the face of his father. Always his father had been his hero, the great Han Solo. Always his father had been his strength and his answer.

And now . . .

Now the great Han Solo seemed a pitiful, broken thing, an empty shell.

"You left him," Han said again, and though his tone had gone back to quiet and calm, this third time he uttered the accusation, with the element of surprise gone, it cut Anakin even more deeply. "You turned and ran away while Chewie stood his ground and died."

"I couldn't—" Anakin started to reply, and he was biting his lip now and blinking back the tears.

"Chewie, who had just done everything to save you," Han said with a growl, poking his finger into Anakin's chest. "You left him!"

Anakin turned and ran off.

Han looked all around, as if conscious only then of the fact that a dozen sets of eyes had been on him and his son the whole time. Offering nothing more than a scowl in explanation, he stormed back to the *Falcon*'s bridge and took his seat.

How alone he felt when he turned and saw the empty seat beside him.

"Artoo, what is it?" Luke cried, his X-wing spiraling down. But the droid had no answers. Luke flipped the sensors back on, but neither a tractor beam nor a possible power source registered.

Luke found a level of calm and clearheadedness, calculating the time he had left. Mara's frantic voice came over the communicator, but it was too broken up and Luke just shut the thing down. He noted a lump on the planet's otherwise smooth surface, but he had no time to investigate further.

He turned the X-wing up and put out full throttle, going head-on against the pull, more to try and determine the strength of the beam than with any hopes of breaking away from it. To his surprise, he did make some progress.

"Put the shields up full," Luke ordered R2-D2 as soon as he understood that he could not hope to break free with pure power.

The shields went up and were almost instantly torn away— but in that moment, as if the beam had suddenly focused just on the shields and not on the X-wing, Luke's ship shot up. But not out—the beam was back on it in a moment, grabbing hard, and the energy cost of bringing up those shields had been taxing on the drives, so much so that Luke quickly deduced that he dared try that tactic only one more time.

But now he had a plan.

With R2-D2 shrieking in protest, Luke turned the X-wing about, nose down, and kept the throttle hot. The planet rushed up to swallow them.

"Ready the shields," Luke instructed the droid.

R2-D2 beeped and whined in protest.

"Just do it," Luke said. He searched for the source, but could see nothing, could read nothing on his instruments. He could tell where it was, though, for it was obviously pulling him straight in. He backed off the throttle suddenly, reversing engines, hoping the abrupt change would buy him enough time, and he emptied his three banks of three proton torpedoes. Nine missiles swooped down ahead of him.

They hit the ice pack hard, one after another, and with the X-wing rushing right behind.

"Shields now!" Luke cried, and he pulled hard, leveling out of the stoop and punching his throttle out full.

The X-wing shuddered from the concussions of the torpedo blasts, from the tractor beam ripping the shields away yet again, but Luke was betting that the beam was concentrated, and he was right, for the ship rushed out of the pull, breaking clear and running away, barely twenty meters above the icy surface.

"Check the damage," Luke ordered. He banked around, giving the area of devastation a wide berth in case the source of that devilish beam remained, and headed for the mound he had spotted.

He knew instinctively that this was no normal mountain, and when he looked deeper with his insight, he hit a wall, an empty space in the Force.

Luke clicked on the communicator in the hopes that Mara, from her high vantage point, might give him some insight, but then he saw the planetary rim beyond the structure come alive with buzzing specks that could only be ships.

He zoomed in at the mound and turned to go about it, firing his repulsors to get a jump away from it. He turned, turned, the g's pressing his face to the side, 180 about and then up, and at full throttle. That's when he first understood the toll his evasive maneuver from the tractor beam had taken. His right drive sputtered and died, and when he tried to close his wings again for deep space flight, he found them locked into position.

And the specks appeared larger now, closing fast, and Luke was out of torpedoes.

I'm going back, Han told himself. Chewie found a way to get off planet.

Logically, it seemed impossible. Han had seen the Wookiee standing resolute, the moon descending, and there was no doubt that Sernpidal itself had died only a moment later.

But logic could not play here, in Han's emotional turmoil. Chewie *had* escaped, somehow, he told himself repeatedly, and so he believed.

He called to the next ship in the long line, a freighter, and offered the coordinates for Dubrillion, then he brought the *Falcon* about hard, turning back for Sernpidal, turning back for Chewie.

". . . need help!" came a distress call, screaming across all channels from one of the convoy ships before Han had gone halfway through the maneuver. "Now!" the ship's pilot called out. "They're coming through! Giant bugs!"

Han grumbled and muttered a stream of curses, but he could not ignore that call, and so he brought up the coordinates of the call and put the *Falcon* on course for the hailing ship, a shuttle far back in the line and off to the side.

"Insects," he muttered sarcastically, but even as he said the word, his skepticism faded in the face of what his eyes were plainly showing him.

Insects. Large ones, huge turfhopper creatures, boring through the titanium-alloy hull of the shuttle as easily as if it was soft dirt.

"Breach! Breach!" came the desperate cry from the ship.

Han brought the *Falcon* in fast, and brought his shields up to full, and even cranked off a shot with his forward laser cannon, blasting one hovering insect into a million pieces. But there was little he could do for the doomed shuttle. He saw a pair of insects boring into the ion drives, and tried to call out a warning to evacuate.

All that came back were sounds and cries of battle joined within the shuttle's hull.

And then . . . the shuttle exploded, disappearing in a blaze of sparks and a puff of flame.

Han flew the *Falcon* all about the area, seeking any remaining enemies. He called to the convoy and set up an open line of communication, a calling tree, so that every ship remained in constant contact with at least two others. He ordered them to close ranks, and moved them along with all speed, as fast as the slowest ship in the line could go.

Then he had to decide. His heart longed for Sernpidal, for Chewbacca, but how could he abandon these helpless people now, with some strange enemy apparently in the region?

Han's instruments noted another ship a long way off and not moving very quickly. It was too far for him to get any identification, type, or call signal. Figuring that if he could see it, then it certainly could see the convoy, he opened a channel to it, calling out.

No response.

Han called again, then put his communicator through a search of all frequencies.

"Kyp . . . damage . . . aid," came the call back.

Han answered, guessing from the familiar ring of the voice that it had come from Kyp Durron, and the same message played back to him again, and again. It had been recorded and put on automatic send, he understood, and he feared that Kyp Durron might be already dead.

Han called to the lead ship in the convoy. "You got that ship on your instruments?"

"That's affirmative," came the reply. "And we're picking up a distress call, probably automated."

"Yeah, I got it, too," Han said. "You keep your line and your course. Get some of the quicker ships running a watch line along both flanks. Bug things."

"Is that what got the *Juliupper*?" came the reply, referring to the shuttle that had just exploded.

"Bug things," Han said again. "I'm going out to that other ship—I think it's a friend of mine. You hold the line and I'll be back soon enough."

He clicked off the external communicator, then, after a moment's pause, turned on the ship's internal intercom. He sat staring at it for a long, long while, then blew a sigh. "Anakin," he called. "I could use a copilot up here."

A few moments later, his son walked tentatively into the control room and quietly slipped into the seat beside him.

"We've got a distress call," Han explained, his tone cold and calm, offering no clue if any forgiveness was being extended, or if the interaction was just pragmatism. "I think it's Kyp. Got himself into some kind of trouble. Maybe with the bug things."

Anakin looked at him quizzically.

"If you'd been up here, you'd have seen them," Han replied, his words as much as his tone reminding his son that his childish tantrum had cost the *Falcon* a copilot for the last hour.

Anakin wanted to yell back, to tell his father again that he had flown off Sernpidal to save the *Falcon*, that they had run out of time, that there was nothing they could have done to save Chewbacca. Even to determined Anakin, those words seemed hollow indeed in light of the reality, in light of the fact that Chewie was gone, was dead, and that the Wookiee had died saving him.

The burden of that awful truth bowed the boy's head.

It didn't take Luke very long to determine that the approaching flight of these strange-looking starfighters were enemies. They came at him hot and angry, firing small, molten projectiles.

Luke didn't have any shields.

He dived and rolled, went into a loop, but broke out of it before he had gone halfway through it, recognizing that any predictable course would get him blown to pieces.

Sure enough, as he barrel-rolled out of the loop, a swarm of projectiles flashed past, intercepting his previous course.

Luke leveled out, R2-D2 screaming behind him, all four of his laser cannons firing away. He didn't score a hit on any enemy ship, but his volley took out a line of projectiles flying his way. Still, a couple got through, and Luke had to put the X-wing into a snap turn to the right, and then another immediately after it. He wasn't sure the ship could even take this beating, and R2-D2's cries indicated that the droid might not survive the jostling, either.

He executed a third snap turn and broke out of it back to the left, locking fast on two enemy ships along the same line and firing away, blowing the first into bits and then pounding through to take a huge chunk off the second, sending it spinning away.

Luke sensed the danger from the side and behind, and went through the only open avenue, back to the right yet again, punching the X-wing to full throttle.

The remaining ion drive screeched in protest and could not deliver the full desired thrust.

Luke was running, but the enemies were catching him, closing in from all sides.

"It is Kyp," Han noted as the familiar, and obviously wounded, XJ X-wing came into clearer view. "Oh, no," he added, for the instruments were screaming at them, and a glance to the side told him why.

A swarm of insects, zooming in for the X-wing and for the *Falcon*.

"They baited us," Han insisted. "They used Kyp to lure us in."

"You think they're intelligent?" Anakin asked skeptically.

"I think it worked," was all that Han replied. "Get ready for some hot flying, kid!"

Anakin set to work with his instruments.

"Get to the top guns," Han instructed, referring to the pod

of quad laser cannons atop the *Millennium Falcon*. The old ship had two such pods, one above and one below, along with a single gun on the front that could be controlled from the cockpit.

As he started to rise, Anakin heard his father quietly add, "Be alive, Kyp."

Anakin rushed out into the hall, around the corner. He had to push several people out of the way to get to the gunnery seat—he thought of asking if anyone else knew how to operate cannons, so he could send them to the second pod down below. But he quickly reversed his thinking. If his father wanted someone else on the other guns, his father would make the request.

He scrambled up the ladder and squeezed in, settling and strapping into the swiveling chair, feeling the trigger and stick in each hand. Anakin loved this place, considering the fast swiveling chair and the thumping guns as a test of his reaction and skill, and even more than that, given the speed of targets, a test of his intuition, his bond with the Force. Now he had a chance to use the guns in a real setting, and despite the very real danger, he could not deny his excitement.

That feeling didn't last long, though, not with the events of Sernpidal so pressing on his thoughts.

"Don't let these things get anywhere near us," Han warned gravely, his tone bringing Anakin back to the situation at hand, making him rub his sweaty palms across the ridged sticks. He looked at the situation unfolding in front of him, and at the wounded X-wing, hoping, as had Han, that Kyp was somehow still alive.

"And don't blow Kyp out of the universe!" Han added suddenly, and Anakin winced, as if that had been a direct reference to his other recent failure. He heard his father mumbling then, and perked up his ears.

"Dammit, Chewie," Han was saying quietly. "How am I gonna get that thing in tow without you?"

Anakin pulled back, feeling as if he had intruded in a place where he did not belong, and tried to regain his focus on the situation at hand, though Han's plea to his dead friend stung the boy profoundly. He took a deep breath, his wounded expression solidifying into a determined scowl. He swung the rotating cockpit around, sighted a group of incoming insect-like creatures, and locked on. Then he waited, waited, holding his shot, keeping his calm.

"Trying to hit them as they pass?" his father cried out to him.

Anakin ignored the sarcasm and kept his cool, waiting, waiting. They were almost on the *Falcon* now—Anakin could see their bulbous eyes and the absolute ferocity reflected in them.

He let them fire, all four laser cannons, the long barrels retracting as each burst blazed out. Insect parts and flashes of light filled his screen, a wave of devastation, and the young Jedi quickly rocked the cannons about, triggers held down and barrels blasting, sweeping the insect parts away.

But more were coming, many more, and fast! Anakin swiveled and let fly a volley, then spun back and powered off another, and then another, and when one insect zipped out of harm's way, he followed it down and to the side, catching up and just ahead, and—*whump!*—blew it to little pieces.

It wasn't enough.

"They're on the hull!" Han cried.

Anakin dropped back down the ladder into the main deck and rushed out, pushing through the crowd, then diving into the lower storage area and readying the tow cable. He heard his father call out for him, repeatedly, heard something about the shields hardly slowing them down, but he kept his calm, and as the *Falcon* came over the drifting X-wing, he fired the grapnel out, hooking it about one of the wings.

Then he ran, hearing his father's cry that the *Falcon* was about to be breached. Anakin didn't go right to the bridge, though, but to the main power transfer alcove. He had

been working in here after his disastrous descent to Coruscant, working with . . . Chewbacca, and he knew the layout
pretty well.

He flipped the main, shutting down all but the *Falcon*'s es-
sential life-support systems. He heard the cries of fear from
the many passengers, but put them away, locked them out of
his thoughts. The insects were on the hull, his father had said,
and so he pulled free the main cable and juiced the power
back on, then climbed with the sparking thing in hand, up, up,
to the top hatch. Gently, so gently, Anakin fed it through the
tool release, more and more until it looped back down. And
then he held his breath.

The main cable touched the outer hull and sent a burst of
electricity across it, firing up the *Falcon* like a holiday candle.

"What're you doing?" came Han's cry from below. "We
got no power!"

"Just washing off the hull," Anakin replied, and he slid
back down into the alcove. "Go and see if it's clear."

Han looked at him sternly, but then did go back to the
bridge, and sure enough, all of his readings indicated that the
insectoids had been zapped from the hull. Many floated by,
not charred or blasted, but stunned at the least.

The lights flickered; all the power came back on-line.

"Nice move, kid," Han whispered under his breath.

A moment later, the laser cannons roared to life above the
bridge, plucking the floating monsters out of the sky.

Han smiled in spite of himself, checked the tow line to
make sure they had Kyp's X-wing firmly in their grasp, then
headed back for the convoy, for a freighter where they could
bring the X-wing aboard and see if the Jedi was alive or dead.

Luke flew purely on instinct, on anticipation and reaction
combined, a dazzling, dipping, dodging display that had the
horde of enemy fighters wildly trying to keep up—and even
brought a pair of them crashing together at one point—and
had R2-D2 howling the whole time. For Luke was too fast for

the astromech, his course changes too abrupt for the navigation instrumentation to calculate and correct.

Luke came out of one sweeping arc with a pair of enemies on his tail. He gently twisted and turned, and avoided the firing projectiles—just barely, with one grazing the underside of his upped right wing. "Please give me this," he asked his ship, and he throttled up as fast as she would go.

The enemy fighters paced him, closing.

Luke reversed the throttle, the wounded ion drive roaring in protest. He sensed a collision and dived down to the side at the last possible second, and both enemy fighters flashed past.

The X-wing's four laser cannons let loose, scattering the two rocklike fighters all across the sector.

But there was no time to stop and cheer, for more were on him fast, from every conceivable angle. Luke growled and went through every twist and turn, cannons blasting away, reacting with lightning precision.

It wouldn't be enough, he knew, not this time, not against this many opponents.

An explosion to the left caught his eye, and then another, and then the *Jade Sabre* appeared, blasting through the enemy line.

"Flying catch!" came Mara's cry.

Luke swerved that way, and the *Jade Sabre* swished past him, and he could see her tail compartment opened wide. He took the X-wing straight in, as fast as he dared, screeching in and firing his repulsors as he entered the hold, then the instant his momentum broke, shutting down everything so that the X-wing literally dropped to the floor with a resounding thud.

"I'm in! I'm in!" he cried, and he looked back to see the fishtail sliding closed.

He felt the rocking as the *Jade Sabre* took a few hits, but she was built to take them, Luke realized. He scrambled out of his starfighter and ran along the corridors, getting tossed with every evasive turn. By the time he got to the bridge, Mara had things in hand, rocketing around the system's fifth planet just enough to get a boost from the gravitational pull, and then tearing off into deep space, the enemy fighters quickly losing ground.

"Something bad's happening here," Mara remarked.

"Something connected to Belkadan and that warrior," Luke agreed. "I feel sure of it."

"And there were a thousand ships coming up to get you," Mara explained.

Luke considered the situation carefully for a long moment. "Back to Lando's," he said at last. But Mara was already feeding in that course, acting on the same thought: If there were this many of the strange fighter craft around this planet, how many others might be out wandering the sector? How many might have been at Belkadan, and how many were now at Sernpidal?

Or Dubrillion?

Kyp Durron walked into the cockpit of the *Millennium Falcon* a couple of hours later, having come across on a walking dock, a tube extending from the freighter that had collected his X-wing to hard-dock with the *Falcon*'s upper hatch.

"Elfour's gone," he said quietly, obviously wounded deeply by the loss.

Anakin could sympathize with his grief, understanding that his own grief at losing either R2-D2 or C-3PO would be considerable indeed, perhaps rivaling the pain he felt for Chewie's loss. Han, though, shrugged, and even snorted a bit, as if the loss of a droid was hardly comparable to that which he was now feeling.

"What were those things?" Han asked a moment later.

Kyp shrugged. "We followed a ship from Belkadan to the fourth planet of the Helska system," he explained. "And there we got—" He paused and swallowed hard several times, and both Han and Anakin looked back at him curiously.

"All thirteen of the others?" Han asked, catching on, and now his visage did soften to an expression of sincere sympathy.

Kyp nodded grimly.

"By those bug things?" Han asked.

"They came after," Kyp explained, and he went on to detail the rocky starfighters, telling how his buddies had their shields torn away one by one. "The bug things chased me and one of my pilots out when we jumped to lightspeed."

"They can go to hyperspace?" Anakin asked incredulously.

Kyp shrugged, for the answer seemed self-evident.

Han started to reply, but he paused, staring intently at his console screen.

"What?" both Anakin and Kyp said together, Anakin leaning over and Kyp moving closer to see. Scores of signals were appearing, and then more and more and more. Large signals, stronger than any the insectoid creatures might show.

"Tell me about these starfighter things again," Han insisted.

They put the call out immediately to the convoy, to break ranks and head for Lando's place with all possible speed. Many ships reported that they could make the jump to lightspeed, but many others, too much fallen into disrepair, simply couldn't. They'd have to be towed with tractor beams, which would slow the convoy considerably. Han instructed several smaller, faster ships to fly on ahead, to get to Lando and tell him to get his defenses up and ready, and then the *Falcon* swerved in and out of the remaining fleet ships, organizing the tow, coaxing the beleaguered refugees on. The pilots of all the towing ships agreed on an acceptable speed, and they laid in their course and jumped to hyperspace.

Anakin checked the instruments the whole time, plotting the course and speed of the enemy starfighters—if that's what they were—and calculating the time until they were overrun.

They all breathed a little easier a short while later, when the young Jedi announced that they would indeed make Lando's planet ahead of the enemies.

But not by much.

NINETEEN

The Perfection of Teamwork

"We've got more cannons than people to operate them," Lando said with that wry grin of his. "From salvage operations, mostly. Taken from the burned-out hulks of Imperial Star Destroyers."

Han wasn't surprised. Lando was among the most capable men he had ever known, and Lando was most capable of all at taking care of Lando and Lando's interests.

"We got your cargo unloaded," he snapped.

Lando stared at him, confused.

"On Sernpidal, I mean," Han went on. "We got your cargo off right before the moon fell. You think your business connection will be satisfied with that?"

"Hey, buddy, it wasn't my fault," Lando said, patting his hands in the air.

"It was your fault that we were there!" Han growled at him.

"And twenty thousand people are glad that you were!" Lando retorted, pointedly reminding his friend that, though the loss of Chewbacca was a bitter price to pay, the efforts of Han, Anakin, and the Wookiee had saved thousands and thousands of people.

Han chewed his lip, his fists clenching and opening at his sides, unsure of whether he should let this inevitable battle with Lando explode now, or put his pain and anger aside until the danger had passed.

"We can't look back at any one decision that brought us to this place," Lando said quietly, shaking his head. "If I hadn't asked you to go to Sernpidal, you wouldn't have, and Chewie would still be here. But a lot of other people would be dead right now, probably including Kyp, and we'd have no idea of what was coming against us. In that case, all of us, Chewie included, would be in serious trouble."

The logic was sound, Han had to admit privately, but still, it did little to hold his broken heart together. "They'll be coming at us in swarms," he said. "How many fighters can you put up?"

Lando's expression was not so cocky at that question. "We've got the fighters—it's the pilots we're lacking."

"Even with your belt-running game?"

"You know who that attracts," Lando remarked. "You think any of them will stick around when they hear there's an armada moving against us?"

Han paused and considered the reasoning, and found that he could not disagree. He had dealt with smugglers all of his life, and he knew that most of them, above all else, saw to their own needs and safety first. And maybe, he mused, in this situation, that policy was right. Maybe they'd all be better off fleeing Dubrillion and running to the Core, where they could get some real firepower to back them up. He was still playing out that debate in his mind when one of Lando's men called them over to a data screen. Lando spent a long minute reading it, his expression turning fast to a frown.

"We might have more pilots than I expected," he said, turning the console toward Han.

Han hardly glanced at it, focusing on Lando instead.

"Our enemies are already buzzing about the sector," Lando explained. "We just got a call back from a couple of pilots who flew off planet before you arrived. They were under attack, against some kind of multicolored starfighters—they claim the things looked like flying lumps of rock."

"Like the ones Kyp described," Han said somberly.

"We might do better just sitting tight on the planet," Lando remarked. "Give them the sky, while we bury ourselves in bunkers. I've got mining tools that can burrow us underground too deep for their weapons."

Han didn't completely disagree, but he knew what had just happened to Sernpidal, and he deeply believed that all of these sudden catastrophes were connected. If they buried themselves behind defensive barriers, those enemy starfighters might not be able to get at them, but Dubrillion had a moon, a big one.

"Get patrols out across the planet right away," he said. "Look for craters, look for energy fields and beams."

Lando, who had just heard the story of Sernpidal's brutal end, didn't have to be told twice.

"Han!" came a shout from down the corridor, and Leia came rushing out a door, C-3PO right behind her. "Oh, I heard!" she cried, running up and wrapping her husband in a tight hug. "Anakin told me."

Han buried his face in Leia's dark hair, buried his expressions and let his inner turmoil remain a private thing. His frustration with Anakin and the evacuation of Sernpidal had not abated, not completely, even with his son's quick-thinking heroics against the insect creatures. Nor had he even begun to come to terms with the loss of his closest friend, his trusted companion and copilot for decades. And he couldn't begin to talk about it now, without the weight of it defeating him, rendering him useless for that which was to come. His family was here, Leia's hug pointedly reminded him, his wife and his three children. If he wasn't sharp now, if he wasn't at his very best, they might all be killed.

Leia broke the hug and pushed her husband back to arm's length. "He died saving Anakin," she remarked quietly.

Han nodded, his expression stern.

"Anakin's feeling horrible about it," she said with concern.

Han started to respond, sharply, that the boy deserved to feel horrible, but he bit it back. Still, that edge found its way onto his face momentarily, long enough, apparently, for perceptive Leia to catch it. "What is it?" she prodded.

Han looked away from her, to Lando. "Hurry up with that search," he instructed, and Lando took the cue, gave a curt bow and a wink, and rushed away.

"What is it?" Leia prompted again, staring hard at Han, even reaching up to gently push his chin so that he was looking at her directly.

"Just some search to secure the planet," Han answered.

"With Anakin, I mean," Leia clarified. "What is it?"

Han blew a long sigh and stared at her hard. "A disagreement over our retreat," he explained.

"What does that mean?"

"He left him," Han blurted, ending with a sputtering growl. He shook his head and gently but firmly moved Leia aside. "We've got to get ready for the attack," he said.

Leia held on to his arm, forced him to turn back.

"He left him?" she echoed suspiciously.

"Anakin left him, left Chewie," Han spat.

Leia, too shocked to respond, just let go, and Han stormed away, leaving her full of questions and fears.

"There was nothing else I could do."

Jacen paused at the door, hearing his little brother's words. He had learned of the disaster at Sernpidal, had caught his mother crying over Chewie's demise, and he had suspected, though he had no proof other than one of his father's glances at Anakin, that his brother had somehow been involved.

"You're sure of that?" came another voice inside the room, Jaina's voice.

"The moon was dropping fast," Anakin replied. "All the air was lighting up with fire."

"From the compression," Jaina reasoned.

"We didn't even know where the wind had taken Chewie, or if he was even still alive."

"But Dad said he saw him," Jaina replied, and Jacen winced at hearing that, fearing that Anakin was lying to cover something.

"That was too late," Anakin admitted. "That was even as we started blasting out of there. We had, maybe, four seconds before impact. How could we get to him and get out of there in four seconds?"

The door opened and Jacen walked in. He stared hard at his little brother, more out of sympathy than accusation, though that didn't appear to be obvious to Jaina and Anakin, given their fearful expressions.

"You couldn't," Jacen said, and Anakin looked surprised indeed to find his older brother apparently backing him up. "If the air itself was starting to burst, the *Falcon* wouldn't have been able to reverse course against the rush. You'd have probably crashed right on top of Chewie, or right beside him, and then you'd all be dead."

Anakin blinked repeatedly, blinking back tears, Jacen knew. He could appreciate what his brother was going through. His own grief was intense and overwhelming—Chewbacca had been like an older brother, or a playful uncle, to all of them, and even closer to his father than Luke was. But he realized that Anakin's grief, mixed as it was with such obvious guilt, likely dwarfed his own.

"Dad doesn't see it that way," Jaina offered, and she looked back to Anakin with sincere pity. "He's pretty mad."

"He's outraged," Jacen agreed, and Jaina sucked in her breath and gave him a look.

"He's out of his mind with anger," Jacen pressed, "about losing his best friend. It's not really about anything you did or didn't do," he told Anakin. "It's about losing Chewie."

"But I—" Anakin started to reply.

Jacen walked right up to him, dropped his hands on his brother's shoulders, and stared him in the eye hard. "Could you have gotten to him and pulled him to safety?" he asked, his voice dripping with the intensity of the Force, forcing both Anakin and Jaina to hear and register every word, every syllable, with crystalline clarity.

Anakin seemed as if he would topple as the weight of that question, the point central to his emotional existence at that time, fell over him, as he replayed those last terrible moments on Sernpidal.

"No," he answered honestly.

Jacen patted his shoulders and turned away. "Then you did exactly the right thing," he said. "You saved the rest of them."

"But Dad—" Anakin started.

"Dad's not half as devastated and angry as Chewie would have been if he knew that all the rest of you were going to die trying to save him," Jacen snapped back before Anakin's reasoning could even begin to take form. "Can you imagine trying to face the fears of your own death knowing that your best friends were going to die because of you? How would Obi-Wan Kenobi have felt if Uncle Luke had rushed back in to help him in his last fight with Darth Vader? He'd have been horrified, because Uncle Luke would have thrown his own life away and destroyed the only chance the Rebel Alliance had against the Empire. Chewie's the same way. He saved you, saved the son of his dearest friend, and the act cost him his life. He died content in that knowledge."

He turned away from Anakin then, looking back at Jaina, who stood open-mouthed, obviously stunned by his eloquence. Behind him, he heard Anakin sniffle, and knew the flood of tears, held back thus far because of that terrible guilt, was about to pour forth.

And he felt like crying, too, something he didn't want to do in front of his little brother, and surely not in front of his sister.

With a nod to Jaina, Jacen rushed out of the room.

Jaina went to Anakin then, wrapping him in a big hug—and he didn't even try to pull back from it. He buried his face in her thick hair, his shoulders bobbing.

"The *Rejuvenator* is at Ord Mantell," Leia explained, looking up from the console and the communicator. "She can be here in three days."

Lando looked over at Han, neither of them thrilled by the news. Leia had been calling out all morning, trying to locate some real firepower within the region, but Dubrillion was far from the Core and far from any current New Republic activities, leaving the *Rejuvenator* as the closest major warship. Unfortunately, the swarm of enemy ships would likely arrive within two days, if they kept their present course and speed.

And that was a big if, Han knew. Those tracking the incoming ships had indicated that they were accelerating, which left a bad taste in his mouth. If those ships were accelerating now, why hadn't they done so earlier, and thus caught up to the defenseless refugees? Han knew when he had been baited, and he had to wonder now if he and the other refugees had inadvertently led their enemies right to Dubrillion.

"Put out the call for the Star Destroyer," Lando said to Leia. Then he turned to Han. "We'll hold them off until the *Rejuvenator* gets here."

"Anything from your brother?" Han asked Leia, who just shook her head. They believed that Luke and Mara would have made Belkadan by that time, were perhaps even on their way back, but they had heard nothing to confirm that belief.

"We might still be able to get out of here," Leia offered. "We pack the fastest ships and head out for Ord Mantell, and put a call ahead to the *Rejuvenator* to have them meet us halfway."

"That warship doesn't pack half as much firepower as Dubrillion," Lando argued. "If we're going to fight them anyway, I'd rather it be right here."

Leia looked to Han, who nodded that Lando had a point.

"We'll hold them off and let the *Rejuvenator* come in here to help," Lando went on, his tone showing more confidence, as if the plan was fully unfolding even as he spoke. "And if we can get the call relayed down the line, we can have half the fleet here in a matter of a week."

"If they listen," Leia reminded him. "The New Republic has got its own problems, and closer to home. I don't think they'll send out half the fleet to worry about some minor problem at the Outer Rim."

"Minor?" Lando echoed incredulously, and Han winced as if he had just been slapped. After all, Han had just seen an entire planet destroyed. But the councilors wouldn't view things in the same way as Han, or anyone else out here at the Outer Rim, Leia knew without a doubt. They had cities with more people in them than every planet in the closest three sectors combined, and stories of complete catastrophe rolled in to Coruscant every day. They'd send some help, of course, likely in the form of a single explorer ship, or a squadron of X-wings, if Dubrillion was lucky.

"The *Rejuvenator* has got a task force with her—a few smaller cruisers, gunships, cargo support, and even a crew transport," she explained. "We'll put out the call for them to come in with all speed."

"And we'll have the way clear for them to link up with our own forces," Lando said confidently. He looked to Han. "What do you plan to do with the *Falcon*?"

"I'll be up there fighting," Han promised, and there was indeed the promise of death in his eyes, a cold, hard stare, as chilling a look as Leia had ever seen on his face. He was transferring his grief into anger, she knew. He was intending to make every enemy pay for the loss of his closest friend.

A shudder coursed down her spine.

Jacen, Jaina, and Anakin walked into the control room then, their expressions equally solid and determined. "We'll be up, too," Jaina declared.

"Oh, no," Han started to argue.

"We're Jedi Knights," Jacen interrupted. "You can't keep us out of the fight."

"I don't need three copilots," Han shot back.

"And you've already got one, because I'm coming with you," Leia declared. Everyone in the room turned to regard her curiously. Leia had long ago traded in her warrior garb for one of diplomacy. But she steeled her gaze, an expression that offered no room for compromise.

"There you have it," Han agreed. "Your mother's flying beside me."

All three of the kids were shaking their heads, telling Leia clearly that Han was missing their intention.

"I'm not your copilot," Jaina agreed. "I fly better in a starfighter."

"Oh, no," Han said again, shaking his head emphatically.

"You've got plenty of ships," Anakin protested to Lando.

"And there aren't any better pilots on Dubrillion than us," Jacen added. "And if we lose the battle up there, the fighting will come down here in a hurry."

"I'd rather be up there fighting, where I have the advantage," Jaina agreed, and Leia knew that it was confidence, not bravado, carrying those words, a confidence well-placed, given Jaina's top score among the belt-runners. Once again, Leia was reminded of the splendid job Mara was doing with her talented daughter, emotionally as well as physically.

"All three of us can fight," Jacen added. "You know that, and you need pilots."

Han started to reply, stopped, and took a deep and steadying breath, then looked to Lando. "Can you give them shields from on planet?" he asked. "Like the ones they had in the asteroid belt?"

"I'm bringing *Belt-Runner I* back in," Lando replied. "For all her power, the ship's got no offensive arrays, so she'd be a sitting target up there. I'm going to put her in high dock but keep her powered up, so she'll be able to lend some shielding power to the equipped starfighters as long as they stay close to home."

"How many starfighters can we equip?" Han asked, and he narrowed his eyes, obviously plotting.

But Lando shook his head, throwing those visions far away. "Not an easy thing to do and takes up too much room," he explained. "And too much time. I couldn't even get the *Falcon* wired to take the power-shield boost within a week, and I'd have to take away half of your systems just to make your power grid accessible to the signal."

"So you've got a few TIE fighters and a couple of TIE bombers," Han remarked.

"Enough for the kids," Lando replied with a shrug.

"Those TIE fighters don't carry any weapons," Jaina protested. None of the three kids liked where this conversation was going.

"They do now," Lando assured her with a cocky grin.

Jaina eyed him skeptically.

"Not much," he admitted. "Just a single laser cannon and one bank of torpedoes. It'll take some pretty amazing flying for you guys to hand out any real damage to the enemy fleet . . ."

He paused there and let the words hang in the air, and Leia saw the intrigue mounting on the faces of her three children. She looked back to Lando and wasn't sure if she should be grateful or angry with him for the sly way he had just played on the egos of her three children. For Leia, despite her recognition of their skills, judgment, and training, and despite her understanding that the situation here was purely desperate, wasn't thrilled at all about the prospect of having the three kids up there in the middle of the fighting. She looked to Han, but she found no answers in his perplexed expression, and indeed, there seemed few options. They had seen the tracking data on the incoming force, and it was huge.

"You stay close to the planet," Leia said.

"All three of you!" Han added, loudly and firmly, poking his finger at the kids.

"Within reach of *Belt-Runner I*'s help, and the planet's turbolasers," Leia finished.

Jaina and Jacen beamed at the news that they wouldn't be left out of it this time.

There was no smile on the face of young Anakin, though. He stared at his father, looking for some hint of forgiveness.

He found none.

Jaina and Jacen started out of the room then, sweeping Anakin up in their wake.

"You think Mom will be able to help Dad up there?" Jacen asked Jaina, honestly concerned. "She hasn't done much flying lately. Maybe one of us should go with him."

Jaina considered the words for a few moments, then shook her head, reminding herself that her mother was no novice to action. Sure, Leia and Han were older now, but both still had plenty of fight in them. "They'll hand it out to the enemy," she assured her brother. "What's Lando got that can match the *Millennium Falcon*?"

Jacen returned his sister's smile and turned the conversation toward their own strategy for the upcoming battle. They looked to Anakin to join in, but he was obviously paying no attention to them at all, lost somewhere deep inside himself.

Indeed, Anakin's thoughts were locked in the past, replaying those last terrible moments of Sernpidal, again and again, trying to determine if he had indeed done something wrong, if there might have been something, anything, he could do to change events, to save Chewbacca.

Logically, there seemed no answers. Logically, Anakin had to believe that he had done the right thing, taken the only option available to save the *Falcon* and the many people aboard her. But logic couldn't hold in the young boy's heart, not against his father's judgmental look, not against the reality that Chewie was gone, was really gone, and there was nothing anyone could do about that.

"They're in the system," Leia announced. She sat in the *Falcon*'s second seat, beside Han, with a nervous C-3PO standing behind them, chattering away about everything and nothing all at once.

"Possibly you could intercept their transmissions," the droid remarked. "I would be most happy to translate if they are in a language unintelligible to you." He went on, offering his skills, and Han turned to Leia and scowled.

"Couldn't we have just left him behind?" he asked.

With a smile, Leia glanced briefly back to C-3PO—a friend, and one she usually considered fine company—then turned her attention forward again.

"Or I could translate our own communications into code," the droid rambled on, despite the fact that neither Han nor Leia was listening to him.

Han nodded to Leia. He could hear the first sounds of battle, from the starfighters Lando had put on patrol along the orbits of the outer planets. Pilots called in descriptions of the incoming enemy fleet—which matched exactly the descriptions Kyp Durron had offered of the enemy starfighters.

"You hear that, kid?" Han asked, clicking on the comm to the top gunnery pod.

"It's going to be a rough ride," Kyp replied. He was seated comfortably in the gunnery pod atop the *Falcon*, having offered to sit in as gunner. He hadn't quite recovered from his escape ordeal yet, not enough for him to take a ship of his own into the fight—and Lando didn't have a ship he wanted to fly anyway.

Leia opened up the communications to all channels, scanning and listening, and the reports came in fast and furious, cries for help, cries of victories scored, warnings that the enemy force was rolling in closer to the inner planets, closer to Dubrillion and Destrillion.

"Getting hot out there," Han muttered.

Leia understood his tone, recognizing the nervous edge that went beyond his fears of battle. Like Leia, Han wasn't afraid for himself, but for his three kids, each flying a TIE fighter down there, below, in close orbit to Dubrillion.

The *Falcon*'s console warning signals chirped in, and glancing down at the small viewer, Han and Leia caught the approach of the first retreating friendly starfighters, just a few greenish blips on the screen.

And then, abruptly, that screen practically turned red for the sheer number of ships tracking in behind them.

"Too many!" came a cry over the comm from one of the starfighters, and Han and Leia could certainly appreciate the sentiment.

Han took a deep and steadying breath. He expected Leia to tell him to go to the lower gun pod, that she could take the helm, but he knew that his place was up here, flying the *Falcon*. "Just feed me the data as it comes in," he said to pre-empt any requests. To his surprise, though, Leia stood up. He looked at her curiously.

"I'll be in the lower gun pod," she explained, and Han's expression turned even more incredulous.

"I feel like shooting something," Leia said, and though it was obviously a joke, a statement made to alleviate the tension, neither Han nor Leia even cracked a smile.

Han stared at his wife for a moment, at her grim expression. Then he nodded and Leia kissed him on the cheek and headed for the lower gunnery pod. Han, too, could do some shooting from up here, just the small front lasers, but his real job was to keep the enemy fighters in line for the bigger guns.

"Can you hear me?" came Leia's call over the comm.

"I got you," Han assured her. "Make sure you hold the left flank, and, Kyp, you've got the right."

"Ready to start these monsters singing," Kyp called back.

Han shook his head at the man's unending cockiness. He,

too, had that in him, but strangely, he didn't feel overly confident at all at the moment. He looked down at his tracking instruments, the screen glowing red from the sheer number of blips.

Not confident at all.

They heard the reports, as well, and the first cries of battle joined and the first losses to their comrades cut deep into the hearts of the three younger Solos as they swept past Lando's tallest towers in their shield-enhanced TIE fighters. *Belt-Runner I* was working perfectly on them, they knew, but their first runs since coming up from Dubrillion had shown them that the shield effect grew minimal as soon as any of the TIE fighters broke out of the planet's atmosphere.

Their father's subsequent orders had been unyielding and thoroughly predictable: they were to run out the duration of the battle as surface patrol for Dubrillion. The three weren't pleased, but in truth, their only advantage over ordinary starfighters was the shield enhancement, and without it, they weren't even fractionally as good as normally equipped TIEs.

"Watch your wing!" came one cry over the comm.

"On my tail! On my tail!" came another.

"Kruuny, get out of there!" came a third.

"Keep your calm, kid," came a familiar voice, Han's voice. "And hold your course. I got you."

"I can't shake him!" the troubled pilot, Kruuny, cried.

The kids heard the *whump!* of the *Millennium Falcon's* quad laser cannons.

"Thanks," an obviously relieved Kruuny said.

"On your tail now, *Falcon*!" came another frantic voice.

"We got him," the unshakable Han replied.

Jaina grasped her stick so hard with frustration that her knuckles whitened; she gritted her teeth so tightly that her jaw hurt. "Going up to black space," she called to her brothers.

"You know Dad's orders," Jacen protested, but Jaina had already put her nose up, with Anakin right behind her.

"We'll stay atmospheric, but just within," Jaina explained. "I want to see what's going on."

The three TIE fighters came into black space a moment later, that thin area between atmospheric and space flight. Outside the reflective light of the planet's atmosphere, they could see the streaks of the raging battle now, lending a visual to the constant stream of cries and tactical calls on the comm. Focusing on Han's call, and on the rushing lights above, Jaina thought she had spotted the *Falcon*.

"A dozen breaking for Dubrillion!" came Jacen's sudden call, and Jaina turned to regard her brother in the fighter beside her, then followed his look to the horizon, where a squadron of enemy ships were firing through the atmosphere.

"They'll come above the city from the southeast," Jaina explained. "Let's go!"

And down the three went, bursting back into the daytime blue sky of Lando's planet.

"Shields strengthening," Anakin reported.

The TIE fighters roared over the city, swerving in and out of the tall towers. Jacen called out first, spotting the flight of enemy fighters coming in hot, their volcanolike cannons firing repeatedly.

The three TIEs soared out of the southeastern corner of the city, charging to meet the challenge.

But then the surface cannons roared to life, a blazing, thunderous volley of blue-streaking energy bolts filling the sky.

"Back!" Jaina called, pulling into a loop that turned her back for the city, and her brothers followed suit. As they came back around for a visual, Jaina's eyes confirmed what her sensors were already telling her: the strafing enemy fighters had all been destroyed.

Far from satisfied, though, the battle-hungry trio went right back up to black space.

"Widen the formation," Jaina ordered. "And keep your eyes open. Let's get the next group before they get in range of Lando's cannons."

Even as she finished, a smaller group of enemy fighters soared down at Dubrillion. The three TIE fighters rushed off to meet them, Jaina in the middle, with her brothers moving out wide at her flanks. As they approached the incoming five enemies, the boys rolled back in, wingtip to wingtip with Jaina. They worked in unison, seeming more like one starfighter than three, each with its single laser cannon roaring to life.

A pair of enemy fighters disappeared under the sudden barrage, but the remaining three reacted fast, leveling to meet this new threat. Their cannons blared, and the three Solos didn't try to evade, but took hit after hit.

The shields held; the ships came together.

A trio of torpedoes, a burst of laser fire, and the threat was gone.

That particular threat at least, for now calls from Dubrillion's surface mingled with the cries from the swerving and dodging fighters above. More enemies had come in at the city, from every angle, and the three Solo kids knew that Lando's gunners were hard-pressed.

"This is Gauch in TB-1," came a call from one of the TIE bombers. "We've got them."

Jaina led her brothers back into blue space and saw the TIE bomber rolling out from the city, trading hits with several enemy fighters, but taking all they could hand out with its enhanced shields.

The city, though, was starting to take a beating, with fires burning in several buildings. The surface turbolasers continued to thunder away, scoring hit after hit, but for every enemy fighter that went down, a dozen more seemed to take its place.

"Let's go!" Jaina cried.

"*Belt-Runner I* here!" came a cry. "We're hit! We're hit! Taking shield energy back!"

"We're stripped!" Anakin confirmed, and Jacen and Jaina, too, glanced at their instruments to confirm that *Belt-Runner I* had taken back the shielding power. "What do we do?"

"Don't get hit," a grim Jaina returned, and she led the way down, soaring in between the buildings, dodging the volcanic missiles and tremendous surface-cannon blasts, her lasers blaring away.

"I'm hit!" came pilot Gauch's voice. "Can't hold it! Can't—"

A huge fireball rolled up from the eastern side of the city, a poignant reminder to the three young Jedi that this time was for real.

Jacen got the first kill, firing off a shot as he rounded a tower, scoring a hit blindly on an enemy fighter and luckily avoiding the return shot.

Another enemy had him in line, though, and he started to cry out.

Jaina blew past him, firing her second torpedo, and that enemy, too, went away.

"Thanks, Sis," Jacen remarked, and he followed Jaina's bank down to the left. They found Anakin pursuing one enemy, but with a trio pursuing him. He shot through a gap between towers, then pulled up fast as the fighter he was chasing crossed through the crosshairs of one of those mighty surface cannons and seemed to simply disintegrate. And as Anakin rose, he found his siblings diving down on either side of him, lasers blasting away.

Anakin cut sharp to the right and reversed throttle, breaking his momentum. He hung motionless for a moment, then, just as he started to drop, kicked the throttle in full and double-kicked his foot yokes, right and then left again hard, dropping his nose so that he looped right under and about, slashing down. A subtle shift in his angle of descent put him on the tail of a fleeing enemy fighter, which he took out with a trio of laser blasts, left, right, and dead center.

Anakin went up as Jaina and Jacen went up, the three, each with another kill, rejoining above Lando's main center. They heard cheers coming over the comm, followed by a "Keep 'em running!" declaration by Lando, but it seemed as if the city was secured for the time being, for many of the enemy fighters were gone and the cannons continued to pump away at those remaining.

"Dad told us to stay low because of the shields," Jaina called to her brothers, and before they could answer, she turned her nose to the sky. "Shields are gone anyway," she explained. "Let's go and join the bigger fight."

"We can't . . . ," Jacen started to protest, but his voice trailed away.

Jaina smiled. She knew that her father wouldn't quite see things the way she had put them to her brothers.

But that was a fight for another day.

The three TIE fighters soared into black space, out of Dubrillion's atmosphere altogether. They saw the streaks of light of the continuing battle; their instruments told them that many other craft were all about them.

Multicolored coral blew to sparkling bits before them as one enemy fighter, and then another, fell victim to the thundering quad lasers.

Han focused on that sight, the opening escape route for the *Falcon*, while Leia worked the bottom guns, taking out another stubborn enemy. Their right flank got hit several times, until Kyp had the forward path cleared enough so that he could swivel the big guns around and begin popping away.

"Oh, dear," C-3PO wailed as the *Falcon* took another shuddering hit. "I do believe there are too ma . . . aa . . . aa . . . ny!" he added, flying away under the jolt of another hit, waving his golden arms frantically, and though his eyes couldn't really widen with horror, to Leia, turning about to regard him, they surely seemed to. "We'll all be killed!"

"Shut him up, or I'll toss him out," Han warned.

Han put the *Falcon* up on edge, ignoring Kyp's protests to "keep it steady," and ran the gauntlet between several enemy fighters. He saw an X-wing cut down from the left, four lasers blasting away, but with a swarm of pursuers on its tail.

"Too hot!" the X-wing pilot called. "Breaking for Dubrillion!"

"Go!" Han muttered under his breath. On the other side, an A-wing tried to streak away, but got pummeled by volleys of rocky missiles, heated stone that latched on and bored through the hull, pocking the ship. The pilot cried out for help, but Han couldn't get to her in time, and then, as she tried one last evasive maneuver, she cut back too fast and slammed headlong into one of the pursuing enemy fighters, both ships exploding in a shower of tiny bits.

"We're running out of ships," Leia warned.

"Shields gone!" came a cry from the X-wing pilot, a call they had heard repeatedly over the last few minutes, and one that echoed ominously Kyp's description of his first encounter with the enemy fighters.

Han banked that way. "Clear them out!" he called to Kyp, as the pursuers of the diving X-wing came into view.

"Got 'em!" Kyp assured him, and the quad lasers blasted away, clearing off a line of those pursuing ships. Still, Kyp and the *Falcon* couldn't get them all, and the X-wing seemed doomed, but then, suddenly, came a burst from the other side, rising from Dubrillion as it grew larger and larger in the *Falcon*'s viewscreen, a trio of laser-cannon pulses taking out the pursuit and allowing the X-wing to break free toward the planet.

Han and Leia's elation at the rescue lasted only the few seconds it took them to discern the source of the reinforcements: three modified TIE fighters.

"Break back to the planet!" Han cried to his children. "Use Lando's shields!"

"*Belt-Runner I*'s down," Jaina replied. "No shields there, either."

"Break back!" Han screamed.

"Too many up here," Leia added. "We're all heading home. Let the surface guns take them!" Even as she finished, the three TIEs zoomed past the *Falcon*.

"Go ahead," came Jaina's voice. "We'll fight the retreat."

"Break back!" Han screamed again, trembling with a fit of rage.

Leia called out to him over the comm, sensing, and sharing in, his distress. She knew it was worse for Han, though, understood that he was on the very edge of control here, his grief and horror for Chewbacca wrapping itself around his fears for his children, elevating his sense of loss and dread to the breaking point. He put the *Falcon* into a tight turn—Leia wasn't surprised—bringing her around to follow the TIE fighters, and already the two parents could hear the banter of their children as the three intercepted a host of enemy fighters.

Mostly it was coordinating banter, the you-break-left-I've-got-the-right sort of calls that pilots always shared, but there was something else, something that unnerved and bolstered Leia all at once.

It was their tone.

For the kids were into it with all the passion of seasoned warriors, flying heart and soul, full of energy, full of spirit. Han and Leia heard the whoops of delight as enemy fighter after fighter went away in a burst of sparkling pieces.

But both parents held their grim countenance, for both had seen enough battles to understand that those whoops of delight would become cries of despair in an instant if one of the three got blown apart. And now, by their instruments and the visible streaking lines before them, it seemed as if the element of surprise had flown, as if the enemy fighters were converging in an orderly and devastating fashion on the three hotshots.

"Get there, get there," Han muttered repeatedly through gritted teeth, pushing the *Falcon* to her limits.

Something jolted them hard then. Not a missile, but a grabbing beam, and a moment later, indicator lights began flashing that the *Falcon*'s shields were faltering.

Up above, Kyp blazed away with the cannons, but those hits that Han had been ignoring, the glancing blows to the side, began to take on more profound implications.

And both Han and Leia heard their three children calling out that there were too many to fight.

"Break back to Dubrillion," Jaina cried, the most welcome call Han and Leia had ever heard.

But then Anakin's voice, cold and calm, chimed in. "No," he said. "Follow me."

"Too many!" Jacen complained.

"We've run the belt, they haven't," Anakin said grimly.

Leia's eyes popped open wide. "They've got no shields," she whispered, more to herself than anyone else. But she heard Han's groan and realized that he had heard her.

A series of whumps from the top laser cannons reminded them that their children were beyond their reach, that they, too, had no shields and there were simply too many enemy fighters between them and the kids, between them and the belt, for them to get anywhere near the three TIEs.

Han pulled the microphone from the console and roared into it, "Break back!"

No response, just static—the kids had already entered Lando's Folly.

Jacen was the third in, and nearly the first out, for almost as soon as he entered the asteroid belt, he had to dive into an evasive turn and roll to avoid one spinning rock. He cut around the bottom of the asteroid, but couldn't begin to breathe easier, for he found an enemy fighter coming in hard from his left, firing away, and there was no way he could dodge that missile.

An asteroid rushed past his left, taking the hit, and then

came a second, larger explosion, as another asteroid swept past, colliding with the enemy fighter and its distracted pilot.

The reprieve proved short-lived, though, for a horde of enemies had come in right behind the three young Jedi, braving the asteroids with fanatical single-mindedness.

Anakin, in between his brother and sister, saw Jacen's near miss, then near takeout by the volcanic missile, and though his own path had been somewhat clearer thus far, he could certainly understand Jacen's call that they had to get right out, that it was simply too noisy and wild in here.

The three swooped and dived, Anakin nearly colliding with Jaina; only her deft flying kept the two TIE fighters apart. And all the while the enemies came in fast pursuit. Another smashed into an asteroid, but that hardly deterred the horde.

"Take us out, Jaina," Jacen implored his sister.

Anakin ignored the call and fell into a sense of calmness. Something had guided him in here; something had beckoned to him, promising him a better battlefield against the overwhelming odds.

The Force.

He knew it was the Force. In here, the three young Jedi could use their insights where the pilots of the enemy fighters, whatever they might be, could not. He knew that, instinctively, but now that he was in the midst of this insanity, asteroids, missiles, and enemy ships buzzing all about him, doubts began to fester and grow. He saw Jaina cut up ahead of him; then, using a brilliant barrel-roll-and-swerve maneuver to cut between a pair of asteroids, she rolled off the face of a third and came around firing, her single laser striking three rapid hits on an enemy fighter.

She was in the mode, Anakin realized without doubt. If only he could tap into it . . .

Hear me, came the youngest Solo's telepathic call to his siblings. *Join with me.*

"Anakin?" came Jacen's conventional reply. Jaina didn't reply, and Anakin sensed that she had already accepted his call.

Three as one, the young Jedi telepathically imparted. *Let go. Lend me your eyes.*

It all happened in a matter of seconds, the three young Solos finding communion, a telepathic joining and bond. Now each flew with the added perspectives offered by the other two flanking craft, giving each extra eyes, extra perceptions. No reactions now, just the purest of anticipation, as all three gave in to the Force.

They wove with perfect precision, replacing each other in the line, bringing cannons to bear from slightly different angles, ones their enemy-fighter counterparts couldn't anticipate or react to in time.

They came around asteroids with ease, beginning their firing before they ever could logically know that an enemy was around the back side, but shooting with perfect accuracy, blowing fighter after fighter out of the sky, or taking those in close pursuit through such a maze of asteroids that the enemy ships inevitably slammed into one or were forced to break off the chase.

Their symbiosis mounted, and Anakin, as the focal point, felt they were working together and with the Force as he had only dreamed was possible. The perfect squadron, joined in thought and purpose, communicating with each other as quickly as the internal workings of his own brain.

The enemy fighters couldn't come close to pacing the trio; any that got near were just blasted out of the sky or run into asteroids.

Anakin led his siblings in a turn, rushing hard back into the bulk of the enemy forces, dodging asteroids and missiles, scoring hit after hit.

He fell deeper into the Force, his hands moving as a blur, his mind whirling. Under one asteroid, over another, around a third and then a fourth, firing at those precise moments to score hits, spinning snap turns at those precise moments to dodge enemy missiles.

Faster and faster it went, all a blur, Anakin trembling under the strain, feeling the pressure from his siblings as they, too, fell deeper and deeper. It was perfect fighting, perfect teamwork, the three slicing the enemy ranks apart, thinning them with every pass and forcing more and more to abandon, if they could, the insanity of Lando's Folly.

Too much information coursed through Anakin. He was trembling violently, he knew, though he hardly felt it. Missile after asteroid after missile zipped across his line of sight—or was it Jacen's line of sight? Too much, he knew, too insane.

He trembled; he telepathically called to his siblings. He desperately tried to hold the bond together.

"Anakin!" he heard Jaina's call over the comm, and he realized then that he had passed the breaking point, that the bond was gone.

"Can't—hold—it—" he called back through gritted teeth as he descended into a trembling fit of the purest intensity, fighting hard to hold his consciousness.

"Vector out!" Jaina cried, and one thought accompanied those words: Jacen's telepathic instructions to turn and burst into hyperspace.

The course angle indicated by those instructions continued to change as Anakin went on, Jacen keeping pace with the movements of the TIE fighter and the relative asteroids.

Anakin clipped one, just a bit, causing little or no damage to his ship but sending him into a disastrous spin.

Go! came Jacen's command, followed by the almost-magical weight of persuasion of the Force.

Anakin pumped his yokes desperately, trying to level off, trying to hold his focus as the stars whirled about him, as the asteroids and enemies cruised past him. He couldn't straighten at all; it was only a matter of seconds before he was splattered, and then . . .

He was gone, shot out of Lando's Folly in the blink of an eye.

He heard Jaina's calls for him for just an instant, and then he heard no more as blackness rushed up to engulf him.

Jaina and Jacen managed somehow to extricate themselves from the belt, with some fancy flying and a good share of dumb luck.

Han and Leia, returning from the gunnery pod, watched it all from the cockpit of the *Falcon*, sitting in stunned silence. They could hardly believe what they had just witnessed, the beauty and the precision, and the loss of their youngest child.

The fighting was over, for the time being, at least, for the remaining enemies were fleeing, headed for the outer planets, and then beyond.

"Where is he?" Han cried at Jaina and Jacen.

"He jumped to hyperspace," Jacen tried to explain. "He was in a spin. He had to get out—"

"Did you get a course setting?" Han interrupted.

There came a long pause, and Han and Leia understood the truth of it. Anakin had just blasted out of there haphazardly, had leapt into hyperspace without any understanding of where it might take him, or if other solid bodies might be in the way.

He could be anywhere by this time; his atoms could already be scattered all over the sector.

"You two get back to Dubrillion," Han instructed. "We're going after Anakin."

"We'll go with you," Jaina started to offer.

"Back to Dubrillion!" Han roared at her, as angry, as on the verge of losing control as Leia had ever seen him, as his kids had ever heard him.

Han shut down the channel then, bringing the *Falcon* under Lando's Folly, staring out at the vastness of empty space beyond. He had no idea if the TIE fighter had survived the leap, or if Anakin had.

He didn't voice that fear to Leia; he didn't have to.

She knew.

TWENTY

Point of View

The reception was triumphant indeed for Jaina and Jacen when they put their TIE fighters back down to dock on Dubrillion. Dozens swarmed about them, cheering wildly, for it was widely understood that, had the young Jedi not taken a sizable group of enemy fighters into Lando's Folly, thus disrupting the entire attack formation, Dubrillion might have fallen, and certainly would have taken much more damage than had been sustained.

The brilliant flying of the three Solo children had been viewed on the screens throughout the city, the brightest light to shine through the dark day.

So here they were, climbing out of their cockpits on the low docking bays they had been assigned, with technicians rushing out to them and a horde of cheering people on the ground below, lifting their arms in gratitude. But neither Jacen nor Jaina felt much like celebrating at that time, for they had no idea of where their brother might be, or if he had survived. And even if he had, the battle up there had been painful, with many losses sustained, and they both had seen the damage to the city on their way back in, with several buildings burning, many ground cannons flattened, and *Belt-Runner I* aflame. At that particular moment, the cost of battle didn't seem worth the victory to the twins.

"He's all right," Jaina said to Jacen, walking over to join her brother. "I can feel it."

Jacen nodded his agreement, but the sentiment did little to bolster his spirits, for the young man now waged a personal battle. He had been caught completely off guard by such use of the Force as Anakin had shown to him up there in the asteroid belt, when the three had joined so symbiotically to act practically as a single fighting unit, the perfect squadron. He and Jaina had similarly joined on previous occasions, using the Force to heighten their twin bonding, but never had Jacen understood the level of joining, of perfect teamwork, that Anakin had so stubbornly pressed upon him during their many hours of philosophical argument. In light of that display, Jacen had to question his own philosophy concerning the Force as a tool for improvement of the self, this strictly inner usage designed to allow a Jedi to discern his or her place in the universe. No, Anakin had proven to him, vividly, the limitations of his philosophy, had shown him that perhaps the potential of the Force as a tool for perfect teamwork was too great for them to ignore.

If the Force could be used as such a binding tool for complementing fighters, then how could the Jedi not use its power to maintain order in the galaxy?

He looked at Jaina, and she studied his stern expression carefully. "Perhaps I was wrong to always train alone," he admitted.

Jaina continued to stare, and then a smile and a nod came over her as she caught on to his present thinking. "Anakin has been thinking about a link like that for a long time," she explained. "He's often told me his plans to form a Jedi squadron, acting so much in harmony that nothing could stand against them."

Jacen looked past her, to the viewscreen on one wall showing a continuing picture of Lando's Folly. "It's a good plan," Jacen decided.

"And not one that goes against your beliefs," Jaina remarked.

Jacen shrugged, not so sure.

"For more than a year now, I've watched both of you limit yourselves," she said with a warm smile, and she punched Jacen in the shoulder.

The crowd closed in around them then, cutting short the private discussion.

"You're doubting because you're afraid for Anakin," she offered as they were swept away. "Mom and Dad will find him."

Jacen nodded and strained a smile for the benefit of those around him. Inside, though, he continued to debate the philosophies. He told himself repeatedly that the *Millennium Falcon* would soon return with Anakin in tow. Perhaps then he and his little brother could have some serious discussions, could figure out a bit more balance between their seemingly conflicting viewpoints.

Out of any real power and truly battered, Anakin entertained doubts not unlike those of his older brother. For, from the beaten young Jedi's point of view, his philosophy concerning the Force as an outward-projecting tool also seemed deficient. If he had been stronger emotionally, as was Jacen, if he had trained himself to deeper levels of meditation instead of concentrating on the outward battle skills, the mentally joined run through the belt would not have so overloaded his sensibilities.

Now, drifting in empty space, Anakin had to wonder if his sudden breakdown had proven disastrous to everyone. He did not know how badly his error had cost him, personally—for would he simply die out here, alone?—or his siblings. Had they managed to run out of the belt without him? Had they maintained a joining between them—he knew that they had bonded similarly in the past—or had the shock of Anakin suddenly breaking free and blasting out of there cost them everything? And what of the enemy fighters? Had the path to Dubrillion been left wide open for them?

It was for Jaina and Jacen that the young Jedi now worried the most. He could accept his own death, if that was to come, but why should his brother and sister pay for his personal weakness?

He took a deep breath, nearly overwhelmed as that truth hit him soundly: If his brother and sister were all right, if their flight through Lando's Folly had indeed saved the day at Dubrillion, then Anakin could accept his fate.

As Chewbacca had accepted his fate on Sernpidal.

Anakin leaned back in his seat and closed his eyes. He sent his thoughts out, seeking some connection with Jaina and Jacen, trying to defeat the thousands of kilometers between them, to feel them, to know that they were still alive and okay.

There was only the emptiness of space.

Anakin feared that he would die alone. More than that, though, he feared that his brother and sister were already dead.

"They refuel and rearm," Da'Gara said to Prefects Ma'Shraid and Dooje Brolo, who commanded the third worldship, last of the Praetorite Vong, which had landed on the ice planet earlier that same day.

"But the planet—Dubrillion, they call it—remains," Ma'Shraid dared to voice.

"As we knew it would," Da'Gara assured her. "This was but a probe, the war coordinator testing the defenses of the next planet in line. We learned of their smaller starfighters from the encounter with the unworthy one and his comrades. Now we have learned of the larger defense structures, and have seen the most brilliant level of flying our enemies can present against us."

"And were those larger defenses formidable?" Dooje Brolo asked. "And was that level of flying impressive?"

Da'Gara snorted. "The power ship, which provided the strongest shields to a certain type of starfighter, was destroyed," he informed them. "As were more than half the surface batteries. And now, rest assured, Dubrillion's starfighter fleet has been reduced to a handful."

"Does the war coordinator wish for my coralskippers to join in the battle?" Prefect Dooje Brolo asked eagerly, the warrior gleam in his dark eyes.

Da'Gara shook his head. "The coralskippers return to inflict damage upon the sister planet of Destrillion," he explained. "They will not remain in the system for long, just long enough to bait our enemies. We do not wish them to know our true strength." He stood up tall before his fellow prefects, staring at them hard. "The war coordinator has shown to me that more powerful ships are on the way to protect the planets. We wish to bring them here."

The other two nodded and smiled. The planetary defenses already in place on the ice planet were formidable indeed, and growing stronger by the moment. Now, with Dooje Brolo's added contingent of nearly a thousand coralskippers, along with larger yorik coral battle craft, they had no doubt that the force assembled, unified by the willpower of the great yammosk, would overwhelm whatever came in at them.

In the back of his mind a tiny voice of concern reminded Da'Gara that he had not heard from Yomin Carr, not even a response to the villip message he had sent his agent on Belkadan. But as quickly as he recognized that concern, he dismissed it. Events were unfolding that required his complete attention.

"It will be a glorious day," Ma'Shraid remarked.

"And then we will turn our attention fully to the two planets of Dubrillion and Destrillion," Dooje Brolo said.

"And then we will reach further to the core of the galaxy," Da'Gara assured them. "The yammosk and I have foreseen it. As for those two planets, we will use them for our resource needs, and perhaps create our second base upon one."

Ma'Shraid sucked in her breath, and Dooje Brolo's eyes widened when he caught on to her suspicions.

"The war coordinator will spawn?" Ma'Shraid asked.

"Sooner than we believed possible," Da'Gara informed her. "And the second yammosk will be trained immediately through its mental joining with the parent. We will establish our second base as soon as the immediate threat is eliminated, and that second base will allow our great war coordinator to focus on yet another spawning. Also, though I have not had contact with my agent, I believe that the metamorphosis of the planet of Belkadan is nearly complete, and we may soon plant yorik coral there, to grow rapidly."

The other two prefects looked to each other and smiled. The Praetorite Vong would soon reach the second level of conquest—perpetuation—and once that had begun, the pitiful, disassembled peoples of this galaxy could not possibly resist.

"It will be done," the two recited in unison.

The *Millennium Falcon* zoomed away from Lando's twin planets, then out of the system altogether, past many of the straggler enemy fighters moving to join their fleeing comrades. A few even turned as if to engage the *Falcon*, but the ship was too fast for them, had already built up a speed that the smaller ships simply couldn't pace.

From the *Falcon*'s top gunnery pod, Kyp Durron called out eagerly, "I've got them!" as the *Falcon* approached one group, and then added a disappointed "Hey!" as the ship roared right past the enemies.

"How could he take a chance like that?" Han scolded, aiming his ire at Leia and ignoring Kyp completely. "How could any of them? I thought we had raised our kids with more sense than to dive into an asteroid belt with a bunch of fighters chasing them!"

"The odds of such an adventure actually succeeding—" C-3PO began, but Han cut him off with a scowl.

Despite the grim situation, the very real possibility that their son was in serious jeopardy, Leia couldn't help but smile, even chuckle, and shake her head incredulously. "I wonder where they get that from," she remarked.

Han looked at her curiously.

"I know another couple of reckless pilots who took unbelievable chances," Leia reminded. "I know of one who once flew into an asteroid belt with a host of Imperial fighters on his tail."

Han couldn't miss the reference: he had indeed done exactly that. "That was different," he insisted.

Leia shook her head again at the absurdity of it all, but Han just scowled at her profoundly. Leia let it go at that, understanding the deeper emotions at work on her husband, his fears for his children and not his own safety, and an even deeper feeling of guilt concerning Anakin, considering the last few confrontations between the two, the entire dialogue between father and son since Chewbacca's demise.

"We're going to have to go to lightspeed soon," Han muttered, his frustration evident in his tone. Where were they to go? What direction and how far? They had not been able to track Anakin's sudden departure, and the possibilities as to where he might have flown off to seemed endless.

"If he used the sixth planet as a guiding beacon out of the belt, he'd have headed in the general direction of Dantooine." He was talking to himself more than to Leia as he tried to sort out the course. As he spoke, he moved his hand along the top of his navigational panel, as if he was trying to feel out the right choice as well as reason it out.

Leia grabbed that hand suddenly, lifting it from the controls before Han could lock anything in. He looked over at her, at the vacant expression on her still-beautiful face.

"What?" he asked.

"I hear him," she replied, and as she finished, as the truth of her own words came clear to her, her lips curled up into an inevitable smile.

TWENTY-ONE

False Serenity

"I'd be lying if I told you that we weren't surprised," Lando assured Luke soon after the *Jade Sabre* put down on Dubrillion later the same day as the battle. Mara had gone off with Jaina and Jacen, to hear the stories of the fight, but Lando had insisted that Luke come with him right away. "We found it on the outskirts of the city," Lando explained. "The pilot was already dead, but we still found it with our sensors tuned to detect life-forms."

Luke, walking fast to keep pace with the obviously excited Lando, looked at him curiously.

"The ship," Lando explained. "It's a living organism, not a machine. And it's beautiful—to look at *and* in pragmatic design."

Luke's skeptical expression remained, but he didn't question Lando further until a few moments later, when they turned a bend in the hallway and came before a huge window, beyond which lay the interior dock that now held the captured alien fighter.

"That's a living organism?" he asked, somewhat surprised to see how much the captured ship resembled the craft that he and Mara had just battled about the fourth planet of the Helska system. He couldn't deny Lando's claim of the beauty of the thing, though, now that he had the chance to see one up close and not buzzing about him in battle. This one was roughly triangular in shape, resembling a miniature version of an Imperial Star Destroyer. In his fight with such fighters, Luke had thought their sides smooth, save the many volcanic cannons, but now he understood that the whole of the ship was even more integrated than that, like one piece of what looked like living coral.

Lando nodded. "And as beautiful a starfighter design as my scientists have seen," he explained. "Fast, and can snap-turn with an A-wing, and with more firepower than almost anything that size we can put up."

Luke looked at the multicolored craft carefully. There were many tubelike projections growing on it, protruding from various places and bending in various angles. They looked like no gun turrets he had ever seen, but he remembered well the volcanic missiles launched from the craft.

"The pilot wore a mask," Lando went on. "No, more than that. It was a connection to her . . . companion."

"Her companion?"

"More that than a ship," Lando tried to explain, grasping for the proper words. Indeed, neither he nor his many skilled scientists had ever seen anything quite like this, at least not on a starfighter. "The pilot was connected to her ship," he said. "It's like she was riding it more than flying it, like the Sand People on Tatooine and their bantha mounts."

Luke glanced at him somewhat accusingly—this was too important a matter for Lando and his friends to be making guesses about.

"We can't know for sure yet," Lando admitted. "We're testing the thing, but no one's about to put that mask on . . . yet."

"Sure I am," Luke answered, staring hard at the strange starfighter, and he started for the door.

Lando looked at him quizzically, eyes widening as he caught on to Luke's intent. He finally caught up to the Jedi, just as Luke was beginning to climb the side of the small craft—and with Lando's scientists looking on with complete amazement. Lando grabbed Luke by the arm, turning him about. "We don't know enough about it," he claimed. "Like this thing at the nose," he added, pointing to the front of the starfighter, where some of the multicolored coral-like substance had been chipped away, revealing a thumb-sized, dark red, membranous ball.

Luke climbed down and moved for a closer inspection.

"It's alive," Lando explained. "Or at least it was, we think."

That brought a curious look from Luke.

"And it's not a part of the bigger ship, any more than the pilot was," Lando went on. "You should see her—the pilot, I mean—full of muscles and full of tattoos, and with her face all scarred and her nose broken, probably a dozen times."

The description only further confirmed Luke's suspicions that all that was happening—on Belkadan, in the Helska system, and this attack here at Dubrillion—was closely related. He remembered vividly the appearance of Yomin Carr; it could not be coincidence that both he and the pilot of this ship bore such a resemblance of—could it be?—uniform.

"Have you seen the body Mara and I brought back?"

"Not yet," Lando admitted, and then he caught on. "Same thing?"

Luke nodded, then stared hard at the membranous ball mounted in the starfighter's nose; it was clearly dead, showing no more life energy than would a rock. He nodded to Lando, then moved right back to the side and started up the starfighter, despite Lando's protests. With no hesitation at all, he climbed into the cockpit, a snug fit. He saw the mask to which Lando had referred sitting before him, and tentatively reached for it. It was alive, he knew before he touched it, and was indeed a part of the larger organism and not some separate creature. This was a living ship, a mount, as Lando had described it.

Without further hesitation, Luke pulled the mask and helmet over his head, and immediately he felt the joining.

And he heard . . . a voice, a distant murmuring, in what sounded like the same language he had heard the membranous ball on the *Jade Sabre* use.

Luke fought hard to focus all of his instincts and thoughts, for while he couldn't make out the particular words, he could discern a pattern to them.

He pulled off the mask and climbed out of the cockpit.

"You're crazy," Lando remarked.

"We need Threepio," Luke replied, and he looked back at the amazing starfighter, hoping that the droid would be able to decipher the language, wanting—needing—desperately to learn all that he could about this ship, and about the people who flew it.

But even as Lando and Luke stepped into the hallway, Luke's train of thought, his mounting excitement about the possibilities of discovery here, abruptly halted, for he saw his wife not so far away, staring at him, the look on her face telling him that something was terribly, terribly wrong.

Luke looked to Lando and understood then that the man knew, had known. "I had to show you this stuff," Lando remarked, somewhat an apology. "I . . . I thought this was important. I thought that maybe you already knew, that you had picked it up on communications on your way in."

"What is it?" Luke demanded, his anxiety escalating with each word.

"She'll tell you," Lando said, patting his friend on the shoulder.

It was a moment of tears and memories, a time for Luke and Mara to feel the weight of the loss of Chewbacca and to remember all their times with the Wookiee, and all the times the Wookiee had saved them and those they loved.

It was that unreal moment that inevitably followed the death of a loved one, the same impact and feeling of helplessness, of smallness, that Luke had experienced when he had watched Obi-Wan Kenobi fall to the swishing lightsaber of Darth Vader. That dreamlike moment every being experienced of loss of control, of insignificance, of sudden and stark realization of vulnerability and mortality. Both Luke and Mara called upon their understanding of the Force then, of the binding truth of life, and found comfort there. As Ben Kenobi had remained with Luke, as Yoda remained with Luke, so, too, would Chewbacca remain an integral, living being within the hearts and minds of those who so loved him.

It was a moment of grief, and one, both Luke and Mara understood, that could not last the appropriate time. And it was a moment of terror, of fears for Anakin, out there alone in the vastness of space, yet those concerns, too, could not supercede the urgency of the moment.

Something very big and very bad was going on.

They had to get to work.

"The key is that planet," Luke explained to Lando, after the man had shown Luke two other surprises they had pulled from the downed enemy starfighter: a suit, more like a second skin, and a star-shaped creature with a sixth appendage, similar to the mask within the starfighter. Both were alive, and Luke had dared to experiment with them, even going so far as to let the suit creature slide up his body and join with him, and to put the mask-thing onto his face, resisting the urge to gag and the ultimate revulsion. Now he understood the truth of the fourth planet of the Helska system; now he knew that their enemies were living not on the frozen planet, but beneath the icy crust, in the cold watery depths.

"The ice ball?" Lando replied skeptically when Luke revealed his suspicions.

Luke nodded. "That's the base, and I've got to get there."

"You already were there," came the reminder.

"No," Luke said. "I've got to get down onto it, down *into* it."

The skeptical look on Lando's face only increased.

"They're not on the planet, but it's the base for all of this,"

Luke explained. "I'm sure of it. And if they're not on the planet, they've got to be underneath the crust."

Lando nodded and rubbed his chin. "There is a way," he admitted.

"You've mined ice planets before," Luke reasoned.

"I've mined every type of planet," came the response. "And there are ships used to get through the crust of icy planets, both for individuals and for larger expeditions."

"Where can we find them?"

Lando nearly laughed aloud. If there was a vessel used for mining any type of planet, it was here, at Dubrillion's sister planet, Destrillion, part of what Lando called his prototype fleet. Just to make sure that technology wouldn't be lost or hard to locate, Lando always procured a single version, at least, of every new innovation, to keep it safe for study and, if need be, replication.

"I can have one here before the morning," he told Luke. "I don't know what kind of condition it'll be in."

"But you can fix it," Luke prodded.

Lando shrugged. "Should be able to."

Satisfied with that, and exhausted from the trials of the last few days, both physical and emotional, Luke took his leave. He went back to his quarters, where he found Mara peacefully asleep, a sight that surely bolstered him. She needed this rest, Luke knew profoundly. Her mind and body had taken a step back in her battle with the disease that raged within her, the good fight weakened by the physical and emotional demands of their recent escapades. And now, her grief over Chewie and her fears for the missing Anakin could only be suppressing her ability to battle that disease.

Not wanting to disturb her, Luke left the room, left the building altogether, walking outside under Dubrillion's starry night sky. He saw Destrillion rising in the east and was struck by the serenity of the sight, contrasting so greatly with the heightening tumult beneath the softness.

Luke stood calmly and stared long and hard, becoming one

with the galaxy about him, feeling its rhythms, its timeless-ness, its seeming indifference to the events of transient mortal beings.

And in that joining, Luke heard a call, and that call, he knew, came from his nephew, from Anakin, alive and alone and reaching out.

Luke's first instinct was to run for the *Jade Sabre* and blast off after Anakin, to follow the call and bring the missing young Jedi to safety.

He smiled and resisted the urge. He had heard the call, and thus, so had Leia, as she had heard his call when he hung, wounded and desperate, under Lando's Cloud City. She would bring Anakin home.

Indeed, at that very moment, the *Millennium Falcon* was speeding for the drifting TIE fighter. Leia had heard the call, loud and clear, and had actually viewed the star formations through Anakin's eyes. Using that visual image, she'd had little trouble scrolling the navigational computer and locating the sector.

Now the only fear was that they would not arrive before Anakin's wounded TIE fighter gave out, or before some of the enemy starfighters happened upon him. So Han and Leia's relief was palpable when they came out of hyperspace in the region and located the TIE fighter with conventional sensors, and when Leia heard the continuing telepathic call to tell her that her son was indeed alive and well.

They docked soon after, and once Anakin had boarded the *Falcon* and run into his mother's waiting arms, Han put the TIE in tow and turned back for Dubrillion.

Somewhat more tentatively than he had rushed to his mother, Anakin, with Leia hovering behind, walked onto the *Falcon*'s bridge, where his father was waiting.

Han turned and stared hard at his son, and then his stern edge melted away and he bolted from his seat, wrapping Anakin in a bear hug. He jumped back almost at once, though, and slugged his son in the shoulder. "You ever do that to me again, kid, and I'll kick you from here to Coruscant!"

The scolding hit Anakin's ears like the sweetest music ever played.

They were back on Dubrillion the next morning, landing soon after the curious mining craft that Lando had spoken to Luke about was towed in. It was called an iceborer, also known as a stylus ship, Lando told Luke, because of its shape: long and narrow, with a tapered front end. The pilot would lie down along the length of this translucent cylinder, head forward.

It didn't look promising to Luke.

"It's not for long-distance flight," Lando explained. "It'll have to be towed to the Helska system."

"How does it get down and through the ice?"

Lando led him around to the front. "Pretty simple," he said. "We've got a shaped, vaporizing heat charge up here. You fire it off just before you hit, it drills a hole in the ice before you, and you dive in before it freezes up again."

Luke snorted. "You're kidding, right?"

"You've got to be good," Lando remarked with a sly grin. "Coming out is the same thing—you do plan to come back out, don't you?" he asked, only half-kiddingly. "Except that the process getting off planet takes a bit longer, a slow burn and crawl until the sensors indicate the ice is thin enough for a second, less violent charge."

They were interrupted by Jacen's call, "They're back," as the young man ran into the room and to Luke's side. "Mom and Dad, and they've got Anakin!"

Luke nodded, not surprised. "And Threepio," he said eagerly to Lando. "Let's get some more answers."

"It's not a difficult language at all, Master Luke," C-3PO announced a short while later to Han and Luke, as they sat discussing plans. Off to the side in the small room, R2-D2 beeped and clicked, adding his own interpretations to that which C-3PO had just heard. "Somewhat like the Janguine tongue of the jungle barbarians of—"

"What'd it say?" an obviously impatient Han interrupted.

C-3PO turned to regard him.

"The message to Yomin Carr," Luke pressed.

"It was indeed," C-3PO said to Luke. "And might I comment on your sharp hearing in catching that name amidst the fast-talking jumble of—"

"What'd it say?" Han pressed again, his tone even more forceful.

"The movement of the Praetorite Vong is under way. Your part, for now, is done. Good work," C-3PO obediently recited.

"Praetorite Vong?" both Han and Luke said together.

"I heard that before," Luke added.

"Some sort of mercenary band?" Han asked him.

"A big one, if that's what it is."

"From Janguine?" Han asked skeptically, looking to the droid.

"Oh, I'd hardly think that likely," the droid responded. "The jungle barbarians have not been around for more than three hundred years. Their language was long ago absorbed by the mountain Mooloolian tribes—"

"Then from where?" Han demanded. "Where in the galaxy do they speak such language?"

"Maybe nowhere," Luke answered ominously, turning all eyes to him. "Come on, Threepio," he bade the droid. "I'm not done with you yet."

The four went out then, moving along the corridors to Lando's research chambers. They came to the side of the enemy starfighter unhindered by Lando's technicians—one even offered a polite bow to Luke and Han and skittered away from the ship as they approached.

"Up you go," Luke said to C-3PO.

"What? In there, Master Luke?" C-3PO started to protest, but the droid was already rising, the emanations of Luke's projected Force power moving him as surely as any tractor beam. "Master Luke!" he cried several times, and then he was gently put down in the cockpit.

Luke climbed up beside him, reached in, and brought forth the mask. "Put it over your head," he bade the droid.

"Master Luke!"

"It doesn't hurt," Luke promised, flashing that still-boyish smile, and he helped C-3PO to get the thing on. "Now listen to it," he explained. "Hear it carefully and remember every word."

"They call it a coralskipper," C-3PO, fidgeting in the cockpit, soon informed them. "They breed it to serve as starships, both fighter and larger."

"What powers it?" Luke asked, and the droid relayed the question through the mask, and in the strange language.

C-3PO found, and reported, two answers, one conventional, the other far beyond their comprehension—which gave both Luke and Han pause. First, the coralskipper could move along much as it fired its guns, using the opposing force of that "spitting." And it could refuel and rearm by eating rocks. The simplicity and the efficiency stunned Luke.

"How do you know that?" Han interjected.

"Because it is telling me that it is hungry," the droid replied, his tone rising dramatically at the end of his statement, becoming little more than a wail.

"It can't eat you," Luke promised the droid, patting his shoulder. "Come on, Threepio. We really need you here."

C-3PO conversed with the ship a while longer, then explained that the second propulsion system was tied back to that thumb-sized creature in the nose and had something to do with focusing gravity fields.

Luke thought back to his fight in the Helska system, to the loss of his shields. Might it be that this same creature was able to so accurately focus its gravitational grasp that it could tear the shields off a starfighter?

He leaned hard against the side of the coralskipper, taking many deep breaths. This whole thing was mounting ominously; it was apparent to him now that this was indeed an extragalactic intelligence at work, an obviously hostile one, employing methods and organic technology far different from, and perhaps superior to, anything the New Republic could use to counter.

Belkadan, the Helska system, Dubrillion, and Sernpidal were not unrelated events.

Soon after, the four rejoined their companions and Lando in the central control room with their grim information.

The one piece of good news was the arrival of the *Rejuvenator*, an *Imperial II*–class Star Destroyer, along with a sizable and impressive task force, including a half dozen of the new *Ranger*-class gunships.

TWENTY-TWO

Turning It Back

"It won't work," Mara remarked, standing with Luke and staring at the little iceborer, the stylus ship, which seemed terribly frail for the mission Luke had assigned to it.

"Lando's used this technology before," he replied.

"Going into a planet full of enemies?" came his wife's curt response. She turned up her hand, extending her fingers one at a time as she counted off the drawbacks. "You'll have no weapons, none from the ship, at least; no shields, other than the forward heat and impact protection; and not enough speed to outrun a Headhunter, never mind one of those coralskippers."

Luke stared at her long and hard, a smile widening on his face. Ever since the return from Belkadan, Mara had been in her room, recuperating, a poignant reminder that she was very ill, and yet here she was, concerned about him.

"I should be the one to take the iceborer in," she said.

Luke's smile evaporated. He knew the source of that remark, knew that she was, in fact, saying that her life was more expendable because she was ill—by all other examples, terminally ill.

"No way," he replied.

Mara looked at him hard.

"If you suffer a relapse down there, you'll jeopardize the

whole mission," Luke stated flatly, elevating the discussion to the good of the mission and not to a condescending level that showed his concern for his wife.

"And if I have a relapse flying your carry ship?" she asked with thick sarcasm.

"You won't," Luke replied with all confidence, and he chuckled and started past her.

Mara just shook her head and watched him walk away for a few moments, then turned back to regard the seemingly fragile stylus ship and just sighed.

"They're almost done with it," Jaina told her brothers as the three watched the repairs on the strange little ship.

"Uncle Luke's really going to take that thing in?" Anakin asked. "And he's really going to wear that living suit and mask they found with the pilot?"

Jacen and Jaina exchanged concerned looks.

"He's trying out the suit right now," Jaina explained. "Why don't you go and check it out?"

Not catching on to the pointed dismissal and anxious to get a glimpse of the alien artifacts, the ever curious Anakin took his leave in a hurry.

"Uncle Luke's the wrong one to go," Jacen said to Jaina as soon as they were alone.

"I'm more concerned about Aunt Mara," Jaina replied. "She slept most of the day and was still exhausted when she got up to eat dinner. Did you see the dark circles under her eyes? Her disease is getting the best of her right now, mostly because she's too preoccupied with all of this."

They stared at each other long and hard, knowing that they were of like mind, though neither was brave enough to put the thoughts to words at that moment.

"We can't let Mara go," Jaina remarked.

"We can't stop her if Uncle Luke goes," Jacen replied.

"You think they'll wait for the *Rejuvenator* and her escorts to come in before they leave?" Jaina asked.

"I think they'll go first," Jacen replied. "I heard Uncle Luke say as much to Dad. He doesn't want to wait for anything, but his plan is to get the iceborer off planet just in time to meet up with the incoming fleet."

Jaina merely nodded; she had gleaned similar information from C-3PO.

"What's that?" Jacen asked, motioning toward a crane bringing another craft in to a scaffolding beside and above the iceborer.

"Carry ship," Jaina explained, who had interviewed Lando's technicians extensively on this subject. "You can't dock the iceborer, or put it in a hold, because it's not maneuverable enough to break away safely. They'll load it onto the missile pod of the carry ship, and that ship will just point it in the right direction and shoot it off."

"And the iceborer pilot has to stay in the stylus ship the whole time?" Jacen asked. "For the duration of the entire flight?"

"The whole time," Jaina replied. "They use an air tube and a power transfer line from the carry ship to conserve all the power possible on the little iceborer, but whoever flies in that thing is going to be lying flat out and cramped the whole way to the Helska system."

Jacen looked at her, smiled, and nodded.

Jaina spent a long while dissecting that look, making certain that Jacen was entertaining similar ideas to her own. "I can fly the iceborer," she offered.

"Seems to me that your skills would be better suited for the carry ship."

Jaina thought about it and didn't disagree. If they had to pull a quick retreat from the Helska system, she'd be a better choice at piloting the main craft.

"Where's Artoo?" Jacen asked. "We should leave a message."

Luke paced the room, while Han, Leia, and Lando sat at the small round table, arguing about whether they should go ahead and attack with the assembled fleet or wait for more firepower to come in. On the table sat a viewscreen, the imposing image of Commander Warshack Rojo of the Star Destroyer *Rejuvenator*, with his shaved head, furrowed brow, and a single, glittering diamond earring.

"We should go straight to Helska," Commander Rojo insisted. "The Ranger gunships will handle any of the smaller—what did you call them? Coralskippers?—while *Rejuvenator* takes out whatever base those barbarians have set up. It will be a clean sweep, I assure you, and then we can get on with the more important issues facing the New Republic. You may join us in-system, if you desire."

Han and Leia exchanged concerned smiles, not sure at all that Commander Rojo was getting the message that this likely *was* the most important issue facing the New Republic. Leia was hardly surprised by the apparent underestimation.

"Six days," she argued. "We'll have three battle cruisers, an Interdictor ship, another Star Destroyer, and their accompanying task forces in by then."

"We need not wait," the commander, a hardheaded Corellian, said. "I've enough firepower to level the enemy base, and the planet it's on, if need be."

Leia gave a helpless sigh—she knew well enough how stubborn a Corellian could be—and turned to her brother as he paced by the window. Luke had told her that she would never convince the commander to wait until the other ships arrived, and since she had resigned her post on the council, she had no authority to order him to wait. They had put out a call to Coruscant, but it would be a while before they received any response—Leia's estimation of six days was a hopeful one, at best—and by that time, Rojo hoped to have this whole mess cleared up. Rojo's confidence did not bode well for Leia's hopes of assembling a larger fleet, she knew, for the commander had likely been, or soon would be, in contact with the more skeptical members of the council, assuring them that he could handle this and they need not divert any more of their military assets.

"We're going," Rojo said firmly. "And if we have to go alone, then so be it."

Leia sighed.

Luke started to turn to say something to the stubborn man, but a flash beyond the window caught his eye. He moved closer, staring into the dark night, and saw a ship soar out of dock, into the sky. He knew at once which ship it was: the carry ship, *Merry Miner,* and its iceborer companion.

"Mara?" he asked quietly, wondering for a second if his wife had decided to take on this dangerous mission by herself.

But his words made little logical sense; Mara couldn't have gone alone, for it would take two pilots to accomplish the task, and he didn't believe that she would have taken Jaina on such a dangerous trek without consulting Leia. A sickly feeling came over Luke then, inspired by the thought of Mara's potential copilot, as he guessed who might be flying the *Merry Miner* and who might be accompanying her.

He turned to the others, his expression speaking volumes.

"What is it?" Leia asked.

He ran past her, to the door, and out into the hall.

"Good evening, sir," C-3PO said as Luke barreled into him, knocking him back against the opposite wall.

"Not now," Luke said, rolling away from the droid, side-stepping R2-D2, and sprinting down the corridor.

"But Artoo, sir."

"Not now!" Luke cried.

"A message from Master Jacen," the now-frantic C-3PO yelled. Luke skidded to a stop and came running back, just as Leia bent to R2-D2 and activated his hologram recorder.

"Uncle Luke," came the greeting, as a tiny image of Jacen appeared in the hallway. "Forgive us our presumption, but it seemed obvious to me and to Jaina that you're needed with the fleet in the main attack force. We know what you intended within the fourth planet: to explore and determine the strength and purpose of our enemies. I—we—can do that, Uncle Luke."

Han gave something akin to a growl, and Leia joined in.

"Keep Aunt Mara at rest—she needs it," Jacen's hologram went on. "Jaina and I will be fine, and will carry out the mission perfectly. We promise."

The image went away.

"I'm gonna kick his—" Han started to say.

"Jacen's right," Luke interrupted, and both Han and Leia, and Lando, as well, stared at him in disbelief. "I wish they had come to me first," Luke went on. "I wish they had better coordinated their intentions."

"But you think that sending Jacen down into the planet is the right choice," Leia finished for him.

"As good a choice as any," Luke replied without hesitation. He grabbed Han by the arm, as the man started away—and from the look on Han's face, it was obvious that he was heading straight off for the *Millennium Falcon*.

"You're raising Jedi Knights," Luke said to him in all seriousness. "Warriors, explorers. They can't turn away from the duty that is before them just for our peace of mind."

"They're just kids," Han argued.

"And so were we when the Empire unveiled the Death Star," Luke reminded.

"Speak for yourself," Han growled. He narrowed his eyes as he stared hard at his friend. "I just went halfway across the galaxy pulling one of them back, and now I've got the other two running off in another direction," he muttered through gritted teeth.

Luke looked to Leia and managed, with his expression, to coax a smile onto her face. "Get used to it," he said to Han. "And enjoy it while you can. You won't be able to keep up with them much longer."

Han pulled roughly away and muttered a stream of curses, and only then did Luke begin to understand the depth of his anger and frustration. He had just lost Chewbacca, and he wasn't about to lose anyone else!

"It is settled then," came the voice of Commander Rojo behind them. "It has begun."

"Just because they went out doesn't mean that we have to send the whole fleet in pursuit," Leia replied. "Han, Luke, and I can go after them in the *Falcon*."

"Their leaving actually hurts your intentions, Commander," Luke added. "If our enemies detect the carry ship, they'll be waiting for the larger fleet behind them."

"A band of smugglers," Commander Rojo said derisively. "Or some puny liberation group. They've found a new technology, and they believe that with it, they can challenge the New Republic. But they have nothing that will stand before *Rejuvenator*. I go."

And he did just that, dipping a curt bow and abruptly breaking the comm link.

Han and Luke looked at each other for a long moment. "Why'd you have to make them Jedi?" Han asked, and it was obvious from his tone, from the fact that he finished with that typical Han Solo snicker, that Luke's argument had gotten through to him.

"You coming with us?" Han asked Lando.

"I thought I'd stay here and make sure the planetary defenses are in place," a flustered Lando replied as soon as the surprise of the question wore off a bit.

"Glad to have you," Han said, ignoring the answer and turning to Leia. "Go get Anakin. He's handling the gun pod."

"You, Leia, Anakin, and Kyp," Lando reasoned. "Four's plenty for the *Falcon*."

"Me, Anakin, Leia, and you," Han corrected. "Kyp's going to lead a starfighter squadron off *Rejuvenator*. Already arranged it with Rojo."

"My fighting days—" Lando started to insist.

"Have only just begun," Han interrupted.

Lando threw up his hands in defeat, and the group moved

away, Luke to go and rouse Mara, for he thought this too important a moment to keep her out of it, despite her exhaustion, and the others to find Anakin and to ready the *Millennium Falcon*. A short time later, the *Falcon* and the *Jade Sabre* blasted away from Dubrillion, along with every worthy warship Lando could muster. Off planet, they rendezvoused with Rojo's contingent, and after one last attempt by Leia to talk the proud commander out of going at that time, they all blasted away, full speed for the Helska system.

Jaina brought them in perfectly, the sun between them and the fourth planet, just as Luke and Mara had done on their trip in.

"Uncle Luke fed all the coordinates into the *Merry Miner*'s navigation computer," Jaina called down to Jacen, who was lying flat out on his stomach in the narrow iceborer attached to the carry ship. "Might get warm down there—we're in for a close pass."

"I'm going to sunburn every inch of my body," Jacen remarked, a not-so-subtle reminder that he had climbed into the iceborer practically naked, wearing just a loose-fitting skirt, purloined from the dead pilot of the captured coralskipper. Even worse for him, because the entry hatch was so tiny, Jaina had to kneel behind him and very indelicately push him in, and all the while with him conscious of the fact that he was wearing only a skirt. A skirt! It'd be a long time before Jaina let him live that indignity down.

"I can come around and let you fly free before we ever get out of the Helskan sun's sensor shield," Jaina offered.

"That's a long way for this thing to run," Jacen observed.

"You'll be running on my power, not yours."

"Sure, but without any guns," Jacen came back, and his tone was sarcastic, even lighthearted, as if he was just blowing off a bit of his nervousness.

"Just let them get close to you and blast that heat charge

into them," Jaina returned with a laugh. Her tone grew serious immediately as she continued, "You ready?"

"Don't miss," came the reply.

Jaina banked the carry ship around the sun, flying completely by instruments—which she never liked to do—for she was trusting the guidance of the coordinates Luke had put into the nav computer. She saw the screen before her focus in on a point of light, the fourth planet, and watched it grow and grow as the magnification increased. "I got it, Jacen," she informed her brother. "Everything's lining up. If you fire any correcting jets, they might see them, so sit tight and trust my aim."

"Let her go," Jacen replied.

"And don't stay down there more than a few minutes," Jaina added. "I'm sitting pretty helpless up here."

"If they find you, turn it back to Dubrillion," Jacen said in all seriousness.

Those words—ridiculous words, by Jaina's estimation, for she would never, ever leave her brother behind—echoed ominously in her thoughts as she watched the coordinates align perfectly and gently squeezed the trigger.

The stylus ship, Jacen belly down and head forward, rocketed away.

It was a smooth and quiet ride for Jacen, absent the hum of any drives. A good portion of the iceborer was translucent, giving him the feeling that he was almost free-flying in empty space, a sense of serenity he had not expected in the face of the looming danger. He had to shake it away quickly. Jaina's orders that he not stay down there more than a few minutes were more than just words, he knew; were necessity if he and his sister were to have any chance of slipping away.

Now came the task that Jacen had feared since they had left Dubrillion. He brought his bare toe down and prodded the alien suit—the ooglith cloaker—according to C-3PO's best translation—then held his breath as the obedient creature began its joining on his feet, then rolled up his legs, just as Anakin, after watching Luke's trial with the thing, had described.

Jacen squirmed and tried in vain to fall into some meditation, to leave the tingling stings of the inserting appendages far away. But it was too personal, and he felt them, every one, and so very keenly. At last, it was complete, and as horrible as that experience had been, Jacen knew the next would be even worse. Slowly, his hand faltering several times, he brought the star-shaped mask, the gnullith, up to his face and fought aside his gagging as the tube snaked down his throat.

By the time he had finished, he looked ahead to see the fourth planet looming large before him. He knew that his uncle Luke had set the coordinates to bring the iceborer down right near the mound he had perceived as the home base, and knew that was where he should go.

But then Jacen heard a call in his mind, a cry of distress, a cry for help, that he could not ignore.

He focused his thoughts on that cry, closed his eyes, and let the Force be his guide. Hardly thinking of the action, he gently touched the guidance jets, igniting a short burn that turned his nose to the side—and, he feared, likely alerted his enemies to his presence.

Down, down, he went, and he noted sparks of light—coralskippers—rising over the horizon on the far side of the planet. "Come on, come on," Jacen muttered, urging the ship on but not daring to fire another jet.

Down, down, until all his screen filled with the grayish white pall of the frozen planet. He glanced to the side, to see the horde of coralskippers closing, looked back as he descended across the last few hundred meters.

He almost forgot to fire the charge. But he did squeeze the trigger, and the shaped bomb leapt ahead of him, burrowing into the ice and then exploding with a tremendous flash, the shock of it jolting Jacen and the iceborer violently. He couldn't see a thing beyond the ice and vapor, couldn't tell if the charge had cut through to the water below.

But he couldn't stop and wait, either, and down he plunged, bouncing through the remains of the crust, careening left and right and nearly getting knocked unconscious.

And then . . . it was quiet. So serene, as the iceborer dived into the calm and cold waters below the crust. Behind him, the hole fast froze, and he could only hope that the pilots of the approaching coralskippers believed him dead in a fiery crash or that his vessel approaching their planet was not a ship at all, but a missile launched at the planetary base.

Either way, it didn't matter to Jacen. All that he knew as his senses returned was the solitude and the welcome gloom.

And that call—and it wasn't far away.

"Uh-oh," Jaina whispered. Her instruments had picked up Jacen's unexpected rocket firing and the subsequent approach by enemy coralskippers. She had seen the explosion on the surface of the fourth planet and could only hope it was the proper and planned explosion, that Jacen had blasted through the ice crust. She had to put those hopes aside, though, for now she had her own problems. Those coralskippers had turned her way, speeding off planet. They couldn't see her, she knew, visually or with instruments, not with the Helskan sun right behind her.

They were backtracking Jacen's path, a trail that would lead to her, and the protection of that shielding sun wouldn't hold for long.

The *Merry Miner* carried no weapons and, even with the improvements Lando's crew had made to her, wasn't particularly fast.

Jaina turned back, closing her forward viewscreen as the glare of the Helskan sun exploded into view. She had to be perfect now, had to run so close to the sun that the coralskippers wouldn't see her, and couldn't follow her if they did. This was her one advantage: the *Merry Miner* was solid, built to explode whatever worlds might provide valuable ore. She could get in close, very close, to a sun—certainly much closer than a typical starfighter.

Jaina kept her attention glued to her navigational readings, bringing the ship in, in. She tried to ignore the other instruments screaming at her about the rising hull temperature, tried to ignore her own sensibilities that it was indeed becoming rather warm, even inside the ship.

Her ion drives groaned in their fight against the sudden increase of gravity; even with the bulkhead closed over her viewscreen, Jaina could see the brilliant glow shining through the supposedly tight seams.

She turned aside, leveling off into a tight orbit and using the gravity as a whip, as Luke and Mara had done, fast moving around the back side of the sun. She fought through every second, manipulating instruments to compensate against the pull, tugging hard to keep the *Merry Miner* from plunging into the Helskan sun.

Ion drives groaned, instruments screamed in protest, and Jaina, feeling the g's and the violent vibrations, groaned, too, and gave a yell, executing a vicious turn as she whipped around the back side. Then she had to hold on for all her life as the ship struggled through the tremendous gravity pull and tore free with a jolt that sent the young woman sprawling. She scrambled back to the console and retracted the bulkhead, beginning a quick assessment of the damage.

"Uh-oh," she said again, for though the *Merry Miner* had performed admirably and had come through the ordeal fairly unscathed, the swift coralskippers had not broken pursuit, had flown at a faster and higher orbit about the sun.

They saw her now, she knew, and she was out of tricks.

Jacen truly appreciated the simple, yet brilliant, design of the iceborer. He brought the little ship up against the planetary crust and extended small grabber arms to secure her in place. Then he took a deep breath, hoping it wouldn't be his last, hoping his uncle Luke's information concerning this gnullith and the insulation of the ooglith cloaker he was wearing was accurate. He punched the three-key sequence for underwater ejection, then brought his hand back as a locking panel slid over the instrument board. Other panels fell into place, encasing the man in a watertight compartment, its forward wall the outer hatch, and then, through a series of locks protecting him from any pounding pressures, water was brought in to him, filling the compartment.

At first, Jacen held his breath as the water came over his face, but then, his hand securely on the abort button, he dared to take a breath.

It felt watery and bubbly and somewhat uncomfortable, but he was okay, drawing air through the symbiotic appendage of the star-shaped creature. And he was not cold, and he paused a moment to consider how magnificent this living bodysuit truly was.

The outer compartment slid open, and Jacen crawled out into the open water. He spent just a moment checking his equipment, his lightsaber and the small sensor key that would guide him back into his ship, and then he turned his attention to the watery world about him. He saw the lights in the distance, far away and far below. At first, he thought them to be some natural phenomenon, volcanic activity, perhaps, and wondered if he was giving the ooglith cloaker too much credit. Maybe the water here wasn't really all that cold. As he crawled forward, walking his hands along the crust, to get a better angle of the glow, he recognized the lights for what they were: some sort of organized base!

A host of worries crossed through Jacen's mind at that moment. He felt that he looked enough like one of the coral-skipper pilots, with his mask and the second-skin clothing, even the skirt that the alien pilot had worn—he prayed that the male pilots wore the same uniform as the females—but how would he communicate with them? How would he slip by any sentries?

He took another deep and steadying breath, reminding

himself that he was a Jedi, and that Jedi, above all else, could improvise through tight situations. And there was one other thing aiding him, for that mysterious call had not abated, and seemed even stronger now, and very close.

To Jacen's surprise and relief, it didn't appear to be coming from the distant, lighted base, but from up here, near the crust.

He moved swiftly, reminding himself that time was of the essence, crawling along the underside of the great ice crust, letting the call guide him. Then he came to an abrupt halt, for not far away before and below him came a procession of lights, a half dozen, rising through the water, toward him.

Jaina bit her lip and throttled the *Merry Miner* out to full, though the speed of the closing coralskippers mocked her attempted run. She thought to turn about, to plunge again into the shielding vicinity of the Helskan sun, but then realized that even that option had closed to her, for some of the coralskippers had fanned out to block her way back.

"They've got me," she muttered, and for the first time since she had begun training with Mara, Jaina felt truly helpless, as if all her work becoming a Jedi could do nothing now to save her.

She started to put out a telepathic call, a farewell, but then, sensing something, she opened her eyes . . . and nearly toppled with relief.

The *Rejuvenator* came out of hyperspace right before her. Other ships—cruisers and gunships—appeared, and before Jaina could even open a channel and warn the approaching fleet, the great Star Destroyer dropped into attack mode. X-wings and other starfighters zoomed out of her bays; her great forward laser cannons opened up, streaks of light sizzling past Jaina.

"Hey there, *Merry Miner*," came a familiar voice, and Jaina had never imagined that she would ever be this happy to hear Kyp Durron. "You need a little help?"

A squadron of X-wings roared past, the lead ship waggling its wings at her.

"You're going to need more help when I get you back home," came another voice, her father's voice, and the *Millennium Falcon*, and then the *Jade Sabre*, came into view.

"Get behind us," Luke added. "We'll take care of these guys."

Jaina gladly did as told, letting the *Falcon* and the *Jade Sabre*, and the whole fleet, soar past her, between her and the coralskipper group. The quickly diminishing coralskipper group, she realized as she brought the *Merry Miner* about and took a quick survey of the battle. The enemy had been taken by surprise, it seemed, and coralskipper after coralskipper went up in a blaze of sparkling pieces. Others did manage to turn for home, but then came yet another voice, across all channels.

"This is Rojo," it said. "Let's take it right to their home."

Jaina throttled up to full. She had to keep up. She would be of no help in the fighting, of course, but she couldn't forget that her brother was on that planet.

Jacen didn't know whether to flee or fight, but found the point to be moot, for the nearest masked alien waved him into line.

They think I'm one of them, Jacen told himself, bolstering his confidence, and he nodded and started forward.

He was met by the scowling eyes of all six, and he understood then the dynamics at work here. He might be one of them, but something in either his uniform or demeanor indicated that he was of lesser rank. He paused a moment to study the group, their order and any differences he might find to distinguish each.

The eyes, he realized. The apparent leader, the one who had motioned to him, had only one eye. In place of the other was some kind of strange node, looking grafted on. The skin around both of his sockets, the only part of his true skin that was visible because of the ooglith cloaker and the star-shaped breather, was heavily tattooed. Jacen noted that each succeeding warrior carried fewer scars or tattoos on that one exposed region.

He remembered the dead alien pilot back at Dubrillion and the warrior his uncle had brought back from Belkadan, both bodies maimed and tattooed, scars crisscrossing scars. If his guess was right, both of those humanoids at Lando's base must have been high-ranking members of this strange people.

Following that intuition, Jacen moved deferentially back down the line, taking the last position and following the group up to the ice cap, then along the surface to a hole that led into an airy, roughly dome-shaped chamber. Jacen knew at once that this small room held the unknown caller. He went in slowly, at the end of the line, poking his head out of the water tentatively. He had to fight hard to keep his eyes from widening in horror, for there in the corner curled a man, a Jedi Knight, and one that Jacen knew! The lead warriors of his procession had already moved next to Miko Reglia, had already begun punching him and grabbing at his arms, trying to hoist him up.

Jacen glanced to the other side, to see a woman—a beautiful woman, her fighting spirit obviously still intact—standing agitated but helpless between a pair of enemies.

To Jacen's surprise, he recognized the woman, and not Miko Reglia, as the source of the telepathic call.

He climbed up into the chamber and moved beside the last warrior that had come in, the lowest-ranking besides himself, he believed.

That warrior scowled at him and pointed back to the hole.

"Yuth ugh!" he growled, and Jacen understood that the warrior wanted him to get back into the water.

The last, the least, was meant to take a post as a sentry, he guessed, and now he was the last.

Jacen turned back to the cold water.

"Come, Miko," he heard the leader of the group say, and he

was surprised that these disfigured barbarians spoke his language. "It is time to die."

Jacen stopped, despite himself.

"Leave him alone," the woman across the way pleaded. "You're just going to fake it again. They don't mean it, Miko!"

She ended her speech abruptly, with a gasp, as the warrior beside her doubled her over with a heavy punch to her gut.

"Yuth ugh!" the other warrior screamed at Jacen again. Jacen looked up and noted that the warrior's eyes had widened in surprise.

"Bos sos si?" the warrior asked him, pointing to his belt, where his lightsaber hung.

Jacen glanced right, to see the two leaders hoisting Miko up brutally, then glanced back to the left, to see two of the four over there coming toward him, demanding to know what it was that he carried on his belt.

He pulled the lightsaber free and extended the glowing blade, cutting a sweep that slashed through the nearest warrior's knee, severing the leg and dropping him with an agonized howl.

"Go, Miko!" Jacen prompted his fellow Jedi, but he knew before he even looked that way that Miko didn't have much, if any, fight left in him, that he was a broken shell of a man.

This was Jacen's fight.

TWENTY-THREE

Into the Web

Through the eyes of the war coordinator, Prefect Da'Gara watched another coralskipper explode into a shower of flashing bits. "All glory to you, warrior," he mumbled reverently, the appropriate farewell to one killed gloriously in battle.

He was not distressed at the sight of one of his warriors dying in the battle on the far side of the Helskan sun, though. To die in battle was among the highest honors a Yuuzhan Vong warrior could achieve.

Nor was Prefect Da'Gara distressed that the battle was apparently going against the small coralskipper force the war coordinator had dispatched to meet the incoming enemy force. This group was supposed to lose, was supposed to retreat and, in doing so, bait the enemy in closer, closer, to the true power of the Praetorite Vong, to the thousands of waiting coralskippers, both small single-pilot craft and larger ships with a multitude of gunners, to the great ground-fire capabilities, both missile and gravity well, to the powered energy of the yammosk itself, an energy that bound the Yuuzhan Vong together and that would undoubtedly disrupt and even destroy any enemy ships wandering too close to the mighty war coordinator.

In came the remaining coralskippers of the pursuit group, soaring around the Helskan sun, flat out for the home base.

And in came the pursuing fleet, more than a dozen large ships, including one huge and impressive vessel, and scores and scores of smaller craft.

A wry smile spread across the eager prefect's face. The victory this day would be major, greater by far than the death of Belkadan or of Sernpidal.

They are joined? the prefect communicated to his war coordinator.

The creature's confidence brought an even wider smile to the prefect's face. He felt it then, the common bond sent out by the yammosk to all the Yuuzhan Vong warriors, the coralskippers returning and the thousands more even now in hiding on the back side of the planet. This was the true glory of the war coordinator, a perfect communication and coordination tool. And Da'Gara felt the yammosk's confidence in the planetary defenses, comprised mostly of an energy field brought up by the great creature's personal powers, along with the many volcano guns of the three worldships, leeching their energy from the planet itself; and the many strategically placed dovin basals with their devastating tractor beams that could bring down a moon, never mind a starfighter; and more general gravity wells that would disrupt technologically based communications and systems.

In they came, and Prefect Da'Gara waited eagerly.

Han kept the *Falcon* back as the bulk of the fleet soared in, as did Luke with the *Jade Sabre*, both of them keeping a protective watch about Jaina and her defenseless carry ship. Given the beginning of the battle, the rout on the far side of the sun, it seemed as if Commander Rojo had been correct in his estimation of the enemy forces.

Now, with the brief respite, Han had to find out about his oldest son.

"Where's your brother?" he called to Jaina, and her pause told him all that he needed to know.

"Luke, I need you," Han called.

"I heard," came the response. "We'll get to the planet as soon as the *Rejuvenator* and her escorts clear . . ." Luke's voice trailed off, and as soon as Han looked ahead, to the mounting battle, he understood why.

Thousands of coralskippers had come out at the approaching fleet, zipping and zooming in and around the many starfighters. What had been a rout and chase was suddenly a scene of absolute chaos, of battle joined—heavily.

"Stay back here!" Han ordered Jaina, and he throttled up the *Falcon*, rushing to join the fight, the *Jade Sabre* pacing him all the way. "Get those guns singing, kid," he called up to Anakin.

"Don't call me kid," came Lando's dry response from the bottom gun turret. He finished with a startled cry as a pair of coralskippers soared past the *Falcon*.

Up front, Han and Leia ignored them, more intent upon the sudden barrage of ships that had come out to challenge the fleet. Ahead and to the side, a pair of Ranger gunships opened up, dozens of batteries on each sending lines of laser fire streaking out in a myriad of directions, forcing all the nearby coralskippers into wild and desperate, and often unsuccessful, evasive maneuvers.

"Impressive," Han remarked.

"Newest and best," Leia started to reply, but she stopped short and flinched when a cruiser off to the side of the *Falcon* went up in a huge explosion.

And then a larger coralskipper rushed in at the nearest Ranger gunship. They heard the banter between the two gunships, one commander saying that he had the coralskipper, all guns trained forward, and calling for the other to cover his attack.

And so the gunship cut loose, a tremendous barrage of flashing lasers that streaked at the coralskipper . . .

And disappeared.

"Gravity well," Han muttered breathlessly. "Just like that thing on Sernpidal."

Then Leia cried out, and Han lurched to the side as she cut the *Falcon* sharply and turned her up on edge, then dived down before a pair of approaching coralskippers.

"They've got a gravity well," Han tried to explain. "A big one."

Even as he finished, Leia brought the *Falcon* up and around, the gunship spectacle coming back into view. The coralskipper continued to somehow absorb the laser blasts, bending them into a field of such tremendous gravity that they seemed to simply disappear. The coralskipper soared past the firing gunship, moved in between it and its companion, which also opened up all guns.

And then the strange enemy craft began to spin. Faster and faster, bending the laser streaks.

Han and Leia heard other nearby pilots screaming for the gunship commanders to get out of there, and so they seemed to be trying, breaking off their attacks and turning tail to the coralskipper. But they couldn't break free and began inadvertently circling the coralskipper.

Faster and faster they went, tighter and tighter the orbit.

They came crashing together, all three, and at that precise moment, the coralskipper gravity well dissipated and they all went up in a tremendous flash of brilliant energy.

Han glanced nervously at Leia. The Ranger gunships were the second-best thing they had brought out here, and they had just lost a third of the group.

And now they heard the calls from Kyp and the starfighter pilots, waging a blistering, weaving battle against a swarm of the enemy ships, and those calls were not of victory, but of surprise.

"They're better than we thought," Leia remarked, watching and listening to the distant spectacle of that battle, for the X-wings—top-of-the-line starfighters—were barely holding their own.

"Give us support, *Rejuvenator*!" came Kyp's plea.

But the *Rejuvenator* had her hands full, coralskippers

buzzing her from all angles and somehow avoiding her devastating cannon arrays.

"Going in for the planet," Commander Rojo's call came across all channels, and the great Star Destroyer throttled up and soared fast for the frozen planet, her forward batteries beginning the barrage against the surface.

Han winced at that sight, and so did Leia: Jacen was still down there.

The *Jade Sabre* cut across their viewscreen, lasers firing, coralskippers on her tail.

"Got you, kid," Han called to Luke, but he had hardly started after his friend when he had to pull back, cutting hard the other way to avoid the coralskippers cutting across the *Jade Sabre*'s wake to open fire on the *Falcon*.

The quad laser cannons above Han began thumping away.

"They're coming in hot!" Anakin cried from the pod above.

"Keep it steady," Lando piped in. "We'll take them."

Lando ended with a startled shriek, and the *Falcon* was jolted several times from hits on the left flank.

"Where did they come from?" Lando called.

Han and Leia put the *Falcon* through all her moves, dipping and spinning, cutting fast, even pulling snap turns as if it was a tiny starfighter, usually to C-3PO's accompanying cries.

But the coralskippers were good, amazingly so, pacing the larger ship's movements and keeping their attacks wonderfully coordinated.

Suddenly, the thumping stopped from above, and no blue-white streaks shot out from above the *Falcon*'s bridge.

"Anakin?" Han cried, thinking the worst. "Anakin!"

Commander Rojo soon came to recognize that he was in trouble. The coordination of the coralskipper attack against his prized ship was nothing short of brilliant, and those starfighter squadrons sent out to run guard for *Rejuvenator* had all they could handle in running guard for themselves.

Even worse, while the gravity wells coming at the Star Destroyer didn't seem anywhere near strong enough to tear her shields away, the stunning focus of targets by the coralskippers, coming in at different angles but attacking the very same spots, was drastically weakening areas of the Star Destroyer's defensive arrays.

Rojo narrowed his gaze, staring hard at the planet growing larger on the viewscreen, *Rejuvenator*'s forward batteries pounding away at the icy surface.

They had to find a weak spot, Rojo knew.

Damage reports chimed in from all about him, relating mounting problems on the *Rejuvenator* and relating the growing losses throughout the fleet. And then came the general alarms as an unknown planetary energy field gripped the great Star Destroyer. All of those alarms that were not local to the bridge washed out in a flood of static.

Commander Rojo knew that he was running out of time.

Anakin wasn't hurt, but neither did he begin to respond. He sat in his pod, watching the coralskippers, their coordinated, too-synchronous movements. They couldn't be improvising in such a pattern, with all of their movements so amazingly complementary. There was no way they could possibly communicate and react so fast.

It seemed eerily familiar to Anakin.

"They've joined," he called down to his mother and father. "Just like me and Jaina and Jacen in the asteroid belt."

"It's just good flying," Leia returned.

"I've seen better," Han added.

Anakin shook his head throughout the responses, not buying them for a moment. He watched the dance about the *Falcon*, and about the *Jade Sabre*, watched the larger dance of coralskippers going on all about him, and he knew, and he was afraid.

For not only had those small groups attacking the *Falcon* and the *Jade Sabre* apparently found a level of symbiosis above the norm, but the entire enemy fleet had! Anakin sucked in his breath. He remembered how effective he and his siblings had been in such a state, and there were only three of them.

The coralskippers numbered in the hundreds, if not the thousands.

And they were acting as one, he sensed, he knew, joined by something that was like the Force, but that was not the Force.

He tuned in to the fact that his father and Lando were both screaming at him then, and so he went back to his guns.

The battle continued to deteriorate for the New Republic forces, and the primary target of the enemy, obviously, was *Rejuvenator*, with a swarm of coralskippers buzzing her, nipping at her shields, and stinging her hull beneath.

"We've got to get to Rojo," Luke called in to Han. "We've got to get those fighters off him and buy him some time."

"Great," Han muttered sarcastically. "Now I'm running bodyguard for a Star Destroyer." He turned a sly eye on Leia. "You see anything crazy about that?"

Jacen almost got a second Yuuzhan Vong right through the chest with his lightsaber, but the warrior was faster than he had anticipated and arched back enough so that the weapon barely nicked. And then the others circled the young Jedi, two producing thud bugs, the others pulling clublike melee weapons from their bandoliers.

Jacen sent out his blade in a wide-sweeping arc, forcing those closest back; seeing the opening, he leapt across the hole in the floor, forcing the Yuuzhan Vong to follow. Two loosed their thud bugs, the little, living missiles whipping out for Jacen.

His lightsaber flashed right, then down and left, picking them both off.

Four of the Yuuzhan Vong came rushing around the hole; the fifth reached for another living missile, but as he did,

Danni leapt onto his back, clawing at his face. The alien warrior growled and drove his elbow hard into her gut, but she clenched her teeth against the pain and clawed on, her fingers working under the gnullith. But then the powerful warrior had her by the arm, stopping her progress in removing the mask.

Danni improvised, pressing her finger against the side of the warrior's nose, the release point for the ooglith cloaker. As the peeling began, he released Danni, and she fell back, just a step, then lowered her shoulder and slammed him toward the hole.

In he went, head first, and though his breather remained somewhat in place, a rush of water slipped down his throat and into his lungs, and even worse for the warrior, his protective suit did not hold, the ooglith cloaker continuing its retraction. The freezing water sucked the heat out of the thrashing Yuuzhan Vong's exposed body. He tried to turn about for the chamber, and did manage it, finally.

Too late. His arms wouldn't respond properly; he remained disoriented, with one appendage of the gnullith out of place and obscuring his vision.

He clawed and scraped, and gained no ground back up toward the chamber, and the cold, cold water closed in.

Danni didn't see it; another Yuuzhan Vong let fly a thud bug for her, and she couldn't get away from it, and she couldn't begin to block it. It caught her in the center of her chest, blowing away her breath and her consciousness, throwing her back and to the floor.

The *Falcon*'s cannons, top and bottom, thundered away. Most of all, it was Anakin in the top pod keeping the increasing number of coralskippers off of the *Falcon*. His work with the guns, spinning side to side, tracking and leading perfectly, proved nothing less than spectacular.

Beside the ship, the *Jade Sabre*, with better gun controls on the bridge, and those controls worked by the skilled Luke and

Mara, and with newer, faster, and more maneuverable thrusters, had an even easier time of it, but still, the ship made little real progress in getting close to the swarmed *Rejuvenator*. And now Commander Rojo was calling out desperately for assistance through the almost-opaque shield of static, and one side of the Star Destroyer sparkled with hit after hit, inflicted by a continuing line of coralskippers.

Then a barrage of larger missiles roared up from volcano-like cones lifting up from the planet's surface.

Rojo cried out one last time.

Then he was gone, his ship flaming and angling down past the fourth planet, a rush of internal explosions coming up to outdo even the continuing barrage by the deadly coralskippers.

It was purely overkill, for *Rejuvenator* was already dead.

Jacen blocked the swing of a club, spun about to bring his lightsaber in line to block a strike from the other side, and in the middle of the turn, snapped the lightsaber back, quickly and briefly, to intercept yet another thud bug.

Then he did make the block, and countered with a roll-and-thrust maneuver that sent the alien attacker leaping backward.

But another moved in to block, and Jacen couldn't finish the move. And he had to turn back anyway, spinning fast to pick off two attacks, one up high, one down low, coming at him in superb coordination. He ducked, purely on instinct, and the next thud bug shot over his head—or almost over, for Jacen's weapon tip shot up, skewering the thing even as it passed.

A series of several sharp twists and cuts picked off three more attacks from three different opponents.

A brilliant defense, but Jacen was working wildly and was making little ground against his enemies. These warriors were skilled; Jacen might be able to beat any of them one against one. Maybe, and maybe, with luck, he could defeat two.

But not four. No way.

He continued to spin and to slice, to fight completely defensively because to do otherwise, even within the grasp of the Force, would be to die. He chopped one club aside hard, then spun, expecting an attack from the other side.

And indeed, he did see the two aliens over there coming at him, and hard, and it took him a moment to register the truth of the attack, to see the human hand covering each face, tearing at the mask.

Miko Reglia drove on, accepting the punishment in exchange for getting his fingers into that all-important ooglith cloaker release point. And as he had the living suits beginning their retraction, the battered young Jedi dug in his heels and pushed on even more powerfully, bearing his surprised enemies into the hole and going in right behind them.

He felt the freezing water drawing out his life force, felt the thrashing, the punches, the kicks, but Miko Reglia, in this final act of defiance against the Yuuzhan Vong breaking, held on stubbornly, preventing the two warriors from scrambling back out of the hole, determined that he would not die before them.

Back in the chamber, one of the remaining Yuuzhan Vong made the mistake of lurching toward the hole in an attempt to catch his falling kin.

Jacen wasted no time, leaping ahead, lightsaber flashing, going for the off-balance alien and then, when that warrior's companion came in to defend, turning the attack fast upon him, scoring a quick kill with a thrust to the chest.

His lightsaber cut through easily, coming out swift and sure, then swept behind the staff of the remaining warrior as he tried to get back to defensive posture and took the alien's hand off at the wrist. A halt of momentum, a turn of the wrist, and Jacen poked his energy blade deep into that warrior's chest, as well.

"Miko!" he only then heard Danni cry, and he turned to see her crawling for the hole. "Miko!"

Jacen glanced around, looking for solutions. "They brought an extra suit and mask for him," he said to Danni. "Get into them!" And then he dived into the hole.

Danni, suited, went in a few moments later, bearing one of the lichen torches the Yuuzhan Vong had carried into the chamber. She nearly jumped right out of her ooglith cloaker when Jacen appeared suddenly before her, shaking his head gravely, indicating to her that Miko Reglia was dead.

He took her hand and pulled her along the underside of the ice crust, back to the waiting stylus ship, and somehow they managed to squeeze in side by side.

Stunned and horrified calls jumbled through the open channels on the bridges of both the *Millennium Falcon* and the *Jade Sabre* after the destruction of *Rejuvenator*, most prominent among them, Kyp Durron's cry for a general retreat.

"Jump to hyperspace!" Kyp instructed. "All the way back to Dubrillion!"

"Do it," Luke seconded across all channels. "All haste!"

"Jaina on *Merry Miner*," came the call. "Uncle Luke, Jacen's still down there!"

Luke winced, not at her proclamation, but at the sight of another Ranger gunship blowing apart.

"We'll take you in, Jaina," he called back. "Get close between the *Falcon* and the *Jade Sabre*. We'll take you in."

The battle was disintegrating before them, New Republic starfighters, cruisers, gunships vectoring away from the ice planet, each with a host of coralskippers in hot pursuit. The other way, toward the planet, went the tight formation of three ships, laser cannons firing from the lead two. They dived down, holding their relative positions, into the atmosphere of the planet, an atmosphere thick with mist from the barrage of *Rejuvenator* before she went down.

They felt a tingling energy all about them, permeating their craft and their very bodies, felt the turbulence, the energy, and the gravity wells reaching up to grab at them, and even Luke and Mara Jade Skywalker, reputably as fine a pilot team as could be found in all the galaxy, had all that they could handle in keeping the *Jade Sabre* steady and on track. Luke knew the coordinates he had fed into the iceborer's nav computer, so he led the way. Jaina tried to call in, saying something as her voice broke apart about Jacen altering course near the planet.

It didn't matter, Luke knew. He tried to reach out for Jacen with the Force, and at first nearly toppled with fear at hearing no response. But then he realized that it was this energy field interfering, extending even into that personal level of communication. He closed his eyes and reached in deeper, past the physical energy barriers, and he heard.

Coralskippers came down at them, or rose up to meet them, and the laser cannons thundered on. They kept their run straight and true, and all of them knew that they couldn't keep this up for very long at all. The planet rolled below them; they drew closer.

"Lock in coordinates for hyperspace!" Luke called repeatedly.

". . . not leaving him!" came a portion of Han's reply.

Luke reiterated his instructions, in no uncertain terms. "We'll jump as soon as Jacen blasts free," he explained, but again, Han came back with a determined, "We're not leaving him!"

Jaina's screech followed. "I'm hit!" she explained.

"Jaina!" Leia cried.

"I can hold it," she determinedly replied.

An explosion tore through the ice pack up ahead, and a narrow shape lifted into the air. Before either Han or Luke, Leia or Mara, could call out instructions, the *Merry Miner* swooped between the lead ships, rushing straight out to literally catch the leaping stylus ship with perfect timing, and before any of the four adults could offer any cry of congratulations, the *Merry Miner* disappeared, leaping to lightspeed with perfect precision.

On the bridge of the *Jade Sabre*, Mara glowed with pride and with awe.

Both pilots on the bridge of the *Millennium Falcon* were struck all but dumb, until Han finally managed to whisper, "The kid can fly."

An explosion shook the *Falcon*, and then the ship dipped suddenly as a tractor beam from the surface nearly caught it, poignant reminders that it was past time to leave.

Coralskippers came at the two ships from every conceivable angle, missiles firing, and the surface batteries opened up, and the dovin basal gravity wells grabbed at them. But this was old news to the four pilots, particularly to Han Solo, and the ships went out past the reach of the Yuuzhan Vong and to hyperspace, *Falcon* first and *Jade Sabre* right behind.

They had escaped, barely, and so, apparently, had Jacen. Still, none of them were ready to call this day anything close to a victory.

TWENTY-FOUR

One Trick to Play

As soon as the *Merry Miner* left the region, and then Jaina confirmed that the *Jade Sabre* and the *Millennium Falcon* had gotten out, as well, Jacen breathed considerably easier. He pulled off his breather, trying not to spit all over his close-quartered companion, then pressed the pressure point, releasing the invasive cloaker. Despite all the seriousness of the situation around him, all the grief and all the loss, he couldn't help but be self-conscious as that skinlike covering peeled away from him, rolling down past his belly, sliding under his loose-fitting skirt, then lower, down his bare legs and feet.

Leaving him feeling quite naked, and leaving him, as Danni likewise released her mask and cloaker, conscious of the fact that she was in a similar state, wearing no more than a tiny loose-fitting shift.

Above that level of tension, Jacen noted that his companion's shoulders bobbed with quiet sobs.

"We're out now," he said to her softly, and then he looked at her, really looked at her, and nearly lost his breath at the beauty he saw there. In truth, Danni was a mess, with bruises on her face and her curly blond hair matted and ragged. But Jacen didn't see any of that as he looked hard and for the first time into her green eyes, into the pain he saw there, both the vulnerability and the inner strength, as he stared into her mind and her spirit, remembering that she, and not Miko Reglia, had been the one to put out the telepathic call, though she was not a Jedi Knight.

She could be, Jacen realized then and there, and a great one, at that.

He was conscious, too, of the press of their scantily clothed bodies together within the confines of the small stylus ship.

"You're safe now," he said, his voice barely a whisper, and he worked his hand up from his side, taking care as to where it brushed, then brought his fingers gently against Danni's cheek.

"Miko," the woman said quietly.

Jacen nodded that he understood—about Miko and about the ordeal this woman had apparently suffered on that cold planet. He dared to bring his hand around to the back of her head, his fingers sliding into her thick shock of hair, and he pulled her close.

Danni didn't resist. She buried her face in Jacen's strong shoulder and allowed the tears to flow.

As soon as the three ships came out of hyperspace, and still far from Dubrillion, Luke opened channels to the other two. Jaina piped it down to Jacen and Danni in the stylus ship, and Han moved to open it up to the rest of his ship—until he noted that Anakin and Lando were already entering the bridge.

And so it began, the analysis of what had just happened, the expressions of shock that this still-unknown enemy had so thoroughly routed such a formidable New Republic fleet.

Still unknown?

A hush engulfed the other eight when an unfamiliar voice piped in, Danni Quee beginning a long and thorough explanation of this enemy they now faced, the Praetorite Vong, from the time they had breached the galactic rim, to their journey to Belkadan, to her experiences under their control.

Only Luke interrupted her compelling story, just enough to explain to Danni the ultimate fate of Belkadan.

The woman swallowed hard, and seemed to swallow it away, going on with a determination that they could all hear in her voice, and that Jacen could see clearly in her eyes.

He joined in when she got to the end of her tale, the escape, the rescue by Jacen, the death of Miko Reglia. When the pair finished, there was near silence for a while, except that the people on the *Falcon* and the *Merry Miner* could hear Luke and Mara speaking quietly about something.

"Care to let us in on the secret?" Leia asked.

"We were talking about the creature Danni spoke of," Luke replied. "The yammosk." Then, his voice lowered and thick with meaning, he added, "The war coordinator."

"Yeah, that's what she called it," Han said dismissively, missing any understanding of the gravity of Luke's tone.

"That's why they fought so well," Anakin blurted.

"You think that yammosk creature was somehow binding our enemies together?" Leia asked.

"I know that they fought too synchronously," Luke replied. "Too *coordinated*, and without any communication that we could hear, or even sense."

"The Yuuzhan Vong were always talking about being joined together by the war coordinator," Danni put in.

"You felt the power when we went down into the atmosphere," Luke added, and Mara, beside him, agreed.

"Absolutely," Leia replied.

"I didn't," Han said. "I just know that my instruments were a bit whacky."

"I felt it," Jaina put in. "I felt it a long way out from the planet. But down near the surface, it was incredible, overwhelming."

"So that creature is what turned our enemies into such a tremendous force," Leia followed the reasoning. "That creature brought them together into a singular fighting unit."

"Like me, Jacen, and Jaina in the belt," Anakin put in.

"Then we have to destroy that creature," Luke reasoned.

"You won't get near it without an army of soldiers," Danni said without hesitation. "Even if you can get back down under the ice crust, you'd be battling hundreds of Yuuzhan Vong warriors."

In fact, Luke was entertaining that very thought. If he could take the iceborer stylus ship back down and somehow work his way to the great yammosk . . .

"And the yammosk itself would stop you," Danni added. "It's huge, and that energy you felt about the planet pales in comparison to what it can do up close."

"Uncle Luke is Jedi," Anakin came back, somewhat indignantly.

"So was Miko Reglia," Danni replied. "And the yammosk overwhelmed him, repeatedly."

"Jedi Master," Anakin retorted defiantly, but then Luke cut in, diffusing the tension and changing the subject.

"Can we rally enough firepower in here to take out the whole planet?" he asked, and the hesitation in his voice was an accurate reflection of the trepidation in his thoughts. How many ships would they need? And how many would be destroyed before they ever came close to accomplishing the task?

"That'd take half the fleet," Han reminded.

"Or more," Leia added grimly. "We hardly hurt them today, and what will we be left with for defense at the Core if we bring the fleet out here and lose?"

"The Praetorite Vong will walk across the galaxy, one system at a time," Danni added, and as she was the expert among them on their enemies, those words rang ominously indeed.

"How else can we beat it?" Luke asked in all seriousness. "What can we do, here and now, to defeat the yammosk?"

"I've got some heat charges that would do some damage to that ice crust," Lando offered.

"If we could even get them to the right places on the surface past those gravity wells," Han said.

"I don't think they'd do much good anyway," Danni put in. "The yammosk is down deep, where the water is warmer from the volcanoes."

"Too bad we couldn't just shut the volcanoes off and freeze the thing," Jacen added.

Then came a short pause, and Luke started to break it by asking how much damage *Rejuvenator* had been able to inflict with her laser batteries, taking that line of questioning to the point with Danni and Jacen to learn if they, since they were under that ice crust, had even felt the pounding. He was cut short, though, by a surprisingly animated Anakin.

"We can," he said, and when his father returned with a "huh?" he added, "We can shut the volcanoes off. Or at least we can freeze the water around them."

"How're we going to do that?" Han asked. "It's already about as cold around that planet as it can be."

"Almost," Anakin said slyly. "But not quite."

"Absolute zero?" Luke asked. "How are we going to do that?"

"Evaporation," Anakin replied.

"Huh?" Han said again.

"Nothing steals energy faster," Jacen agreed, remembering the science lessons Anakin was recalling, lessons that he and Jaina, too, had been taught at the Jedi academy.

"If we can speed up the evaporation around the planet, we'll cool it down," Anakin said.

"And how do we do that?" Han asked skeptically.

"You infuse the process with energy," Jaina explained. "Like the energy of sunlight drying up puddles."

Han snorted. "If we can get that amount of energy out here, we can just use it to destroy the planet," he reasoned.

"Unless we turn the yammosk's energy back in on the planet," Danni said suddenly, and except for Han's increasingly predictable "huh?" there came a few moments of dead silence, as the others all considered the logic of the notion.

"Lando?" Luke called.

"Why're you asking me?" the man came back.

"When you were on Nkllon, you did some serious energy reflection," Luke replied, a sly note edging his voice, showing that he thought he might be on to something.

"You mean the sunlight?" Lando asked. "We did more hiding from it than turning it back. Running behind the panels of the shieldships, and—" He paused, and those on the *Falcon*'s bridge with him saw his face brighten.

"Shieldships," he said evenly.

"I thought they were all destroyed," Danni said. She had heard the tales and had not seen the great ships in close orbit to Destrillion.

"Well, I had to build a few more," Lando replied, and his tone gave Luke the image of the man's always wry grin. "Couldn't lose the technology, after all."

"Get them out here as quickly as you can," Luke ordered. "There's mountains of mist around the planet already, from the pounding *Rejuvenator* gave to the place. And if we turn right back after being so routed, we might catch our enemies by surprise, perhaps even with many of their fighters away from home, heading out to find the remnants of our fleet.

"You'd better bring back Kyp and all the starfighters and gunships we can manage, too," he added. "Just to help protect the shieldships while they move in close and do their work."

"Already making the call," Lando assured him.

They set up a rendezvous at a nearby planet, one where Jaina, Jacen, and Danni could get out of the *Merry Miner* and go aboard the other ships, with Jacen taking Lando's place in the *Falcon*'s bottom gun pod, Danni going to the *Jade Sabre* with Jaina and Mara, and Luke going back in the *Jade Sabre*'s hold, prepping his X-wing for the coming fight.

It took a while for the lumbering shieldships to get there from their docks at Destrillion. The fleet that had come out to run guard for the ships was nowhere near as large as Luke and the others had hoped. Although Kyp Durron had returned with a large squadron of starfighters, none of the Ranger gunships had joined his force, their commanders opting to wait for more New Republic firepower to arrive.

Those commanders were in error, Luke knew, for as he considered the level of the rout at the Helska system, the coordination of the enemy force, and the sheer power of the energy field protecting the planet itself, he understood that the New Republic would never rally enough of an armada to win out there. And likely, those Ranger gunships and the others who opted to remain at Destrillion would see more fighting from the Yuuzhan Vong gone on the offensive than those with Luke trying to surprise the planetary base.

Still, he considered retreating back to Dubrillion with his makeshift fleet, digging in their heels there, and trying to hold out long enough for battle cruisers and Star Destroyers to arrive—though if they came in scattershot, he realized, they would run the risk of being picked off one by one by the Yuuzhan Vong force. Perhaps they should try their cooling plan with the entire fleet, or as much of the fleet as the councilors would send, assembled. But there was the rub, for Luke understood, above all else, that paralyzing, bureaucratic, self-serving council and could hardly count on them acting prudently and correctly.

Even with the disappointments, then, Luke knew that they had to press on, and quickly. The aliens had not been caught by surprise with the first assault, and without any element of surprise this time, the plan had little chance of working.

They came in hot, on the very edge of disaster, plotting coordinates and speeds that brought them out of hyperspace practically as a singular unit, and right near the fourth planet of the Helska system. So close, in fact, that a pair of ships, the one cruiser that had joined the fleet and a starfighter, slammed right into that planet, so close together that another pair of starfighters clipped wings and went spinning and exploding away, one of them taking out a third in the process.

Luke, who had ordered the dangerous jump, could only wince at the losses, and at the notion that they were acceptable losses, for this ragtag fleet could not have done it any other way.

For now, suddenly, and before any Yuuzhan Vong had risen against them, they were already moving into place, the six great, umbrella-shaped shieldships falling into orbit around the ice planet and decreasing that orbit with each rotation.

At first, the pilots of those shieldships reported little energy, but then, suddenly, as if the war coordinator had simply flipped a switch, each of the pilots cried out that the energy readings on their honeycombed hulls had suddenly soared. The yammosk had awoken to the threat.

And the coralskipper swarm rose up, not nearly as large as the one that had previously countered the fleet, for Luke's hope that many would be out on the hunt proved well founded.

"Cover for the shieldships," Luke called through all channels. "Give them the time they need." He left it at that, not adding that neither he, nor Anakin who had originally suggested this, nor any of Lando's scientists who had signed on to the idea, had any notion at all of how long that might be.

Luke's X-wing led the *Falcon* and the *Jade Sabre* into position, protecting one of the shieldships as it worked to deflect the energy back at the planet, while the other fighters similarly went to their positions, some holding defensive arrays while others, using decoy as defense, charged the coralskippers, then vectored away, bringing pursuit after them and thus away from the shieldships.

That would be Luke's tactic, as well, as soon as he had the other two ships in place, only he intended to take it to a higher level, intended to dive right down into that atmosphere, turbulence, energy, and all, bringing as many coralskippers as possible to the defense of their immediate home.

Prefect Da'Gara rushed to join with the yammosk when word sounded of a second attack. At first, the prefect feared that the first attack might have been a ruse, and that this second fleet would prove much larger and stronger, despite all the indications and reports that there were no mighty enemy ships remaining in this region of the galaxy.

When the yammosk communicated to him the truth of the attackers, though, that this force was minuscule compared to the previous one, and that the only notable additions were the giant shieldships, vessels the fleet attacking Destrillion had inspected and, after determining that they were not military, had ignored, Da'Gara was at a loss.

Why would they come back?

The only logical answer seemed to be tied to the escape of the prisoner, Danni Quee. Was this a rescue mission? Was Danni Quee, then, still on the planet?

Was this entire attack merely a ruse to allow the young woman some cover as she tried to get off planet?

And why the giant shieldships?

The yammosk held a theory about that: The enemy was going to try to use these ships to defeat the energy field about the planet, perhaps to turn the energy back on the planet in the hopes of defeating the dovin basal gravity wells or the tracking of the surface cannons. The war coordinator was not worried, for despite the proximity of the great umbrellalike ships and the fact that they were reflecting energy back at the planet, it could still feel the consciousness of the coralskippers, could still guide the battle.

Prefect Da'Gara's fears went away in the face of the confidence of the war coordinator. In addition, the yammosk sent out the call to the nearest of those coralskipper squadrons that had already departed the system, out hunting.

Even without their return, the war coordinator estimated that the enemy fleet would be repulsed in short order, or utterly destroyed if they stayed in the region even briefly. The biggest danger, then, seemed to be that Danni Quee might find some way to get off planet. That would be unfortunate, Prefect Da'Gara felt, for he had an affinity for the woman and wanted to study her further.

But it really made very little difference. The enemy, in desperation, apparently refusing to admit the truth of their previous routing, had returned, and the outcome this time seemed even more assured.

Thus, when reports that a lone starfighter, an X-wing class, had broken into atmosphere and was running fast and strong low to the planet, Prefect Da'Gara ordered a huge portion of his coralskippers to take it out and, in the process, to conduct a search of the surface for the escaped prisoner.

Maybe they could win again and he could keep Danni.

Luke's hull sensors, and R2-D2 in back, indicated that the temperature had begun to drop. Not dramatically, but noticeably. The thin air around him was tingling, alive with energy, the yammosk's own assault combined with the reflective power of the ever lower shieldships. A tremendous fog was coming up from the icy surface of the planet as the energy altered the state of the matter—and, to the heightening of Luke's optimism, that fog was dissipating almost as fast as it was rising, a mounting cycle of evaporation.

Also, the fog gave him some cover, which he needed. For all of his flying skills, Luke was into it thickly already with a host of coralskippers, the craft spinning and attacking from many angles all at once, acting as a singular opponent.

He didn't even worry about his laser cannons or his torpedoes. His tactics here were purely evasive, ducking and then rising suddenly in a tight loop, then plunging down the back side of that loop into the fog. Most of his instruments were useless now, caught in the web of pure energy, and so he was flying purely on sight and on instinct, falling to the Force, the one great sensor the energy power of the yammosk couldn't seem to fully intercept.

Flying in the opaque fog, feeling the mounting cold, and hearing R2-D2 chattering out a host of undecipherable beeps and whistles, Luke cut fast to the side, narrowly avoiding a collision with one coralskipper, then dived down halfway through that snap turn.

Then, knowing the planet was rushing up to squash him, Luke Skywalker pulled for all his life, tightening the turn, hoping he could level off and come around before plunging full speed into the ice.

Jaina felt the adrenaline pumping as the *Jade Sabre* got into it hot and heavy with the coralskippers. She was piloting, with Mara handling the main guns and Danni Quee trying to help out wherever she could.

Jaina had to use conventional methods rather than the Force to coordinate her flying with that of her escort ship, the *Millennium Falcon*, for her father was piloting that one. But Han was a great pilot, and Jaina had never before appreciated just how great. He and the *Falcon* took the point position, with the *Jade Sabre* running cover for him, and it seemed to Jaina that every turn, every dip, and every rise Han executed put yet another coralskipper into the gun sights of either Jacen at the bottom gun pod, or Anakin thundering away up top.

Even with all of that wondrous flying, though, the *Falcon* was overmatched, with too many coralskippers buzzing about. Now Han had to use his speed—and trust that Jaina would keep up with the even faster *Jade Sabre*—to stay ahead of the coralskippers, to keep them chasing him around and leaving the shieldship alone.

And they seemed to be doing that, Jaina noted, with this

one and with all the shieldships, as if they didn't understand the potential danger. Given that level of detachment, she went through a brief moment of doubt, wondering if the plan had any chance at all, if the energy would be enough, if the evaporation would be enough, and if it would even matter to the volcano-warmed water, in any case.

No time to ponder, though, for as the *Falcon* broke off, the *Jade Sabre* found herself fully engaged. Now it was Jaina's turn to show her stuff, and the young pilot went at the task full ahead. She cut a barrel roll, coming out right in the path of a coralskipper, and Mara let the guns fly, blasting the thing apart.

Jaina cut a turn inside the explosion, bringing her about thirty degrees and into another exchange. This time, the coralskipper got off a couple of shots, but the *Jade Sabre*'s shields handled the hits, and the return fire overwhelmed the smaller craft.

Another turn, another shot. A dive and sudden climb, another shot.

A snap roll, putting them right in line with another approaching craft, and . . .

Nothing.

Jaina took the missile hits, snap-turning to the side, cutting back onto the course of the *Millennium Falcon*, which had sped around the far side of the shieldship.

"Why didn't you take him?" she asked Mara, and when there came no response, Jaina glanced to the side.

Mara was slumped in her seat, her head lolling to the side.

The shock stunned Jaina. She dived over the woman, screaming, "Aunt Mara!" But the situation was too hot for such inattention to the controls.

And so they got hit, again and again, and by the time Jaina could get back to the controls and try to straighten the *Jade Sabre* out, her shields were nearly gone, and one drive was sputtering, and one bank of attitude jets was shut down.

And the planet was coming up fast.

Jaina fought with all her strength; behind her, Danni rushed onto the bridge, asking what she could do to help.

The *Jade Sabre* tumbled down, out of control.

Luke pulled with all his strength and cried out for R2-D2 to help him. The droid's response came back sluggish and undecipherable, though, for R2-D2, outside of the protective canopy, was too cold.

Luke closed his eyes, continuing to pull but expecting to slam into the planet at any second.

The nose came around, slowly, slowly, and back to horizontal, and the X-wing shot along, skimming the surface. But with the deadly ice only a couple of feet below him, Luke could not yet breathe easier.

He fired his repulsor coils just to get some lift, then angled up, zooming out of the fog, back into the swarm of coralskippers. Again he didn't bother to fire off his lasers, just wriggled and spun, weaving his way through the tangle.

Then he was out of the group, though many had turned on his tail to give chase.

Luke sensed that it was growing colder, that the temperature was dropping faster and faster, though without his sensors, he couldn't begin to measure the actual rate, or begin to guess the bottom end of that drop or the final effect.

He could only hope.

And then he saw the *Jade Sabre* spinning down, breaching the atmosphere and dropping out of control, and his heart sank.

Han and Leia brought the *Falcon* screaming around the edge of the shieldship, guns blazing—and blazing, too, was the converse side of that shieldship, facing the planet, glowing with radiated energy.

Before they could begin to comment on that, though, another sight caught their attention and held it fast, dropping their hearts and their hopes: the *Jade Sabre* tumbling, disappearing into the atmosphere.

And there was nothing, nothing at all, that they could do for her, for Mara and Danni, for their daughter.

Luke throttled her up to full, estimating an intercept course for the falling ship. He saw her try to straighten, saw one engine straining against the fall, and knew that someone, at least, was still at the controls.

But he knew, too, that whoever that was, the effort would be in vain, for that one drive didn't have the power to break this momentum in time.

Unless . . .

Luke pushed his X-wing out to full, angling at an intercept course right below the falling ship. Then he flipped his X-wing over, coming through in a rush, and just as he passed under the *Jade Sabre*, just before the two ships collided, he fired off every one of his repulsor coils, sending a jolt of propulsion at the underside of that falling ship.

With great satisfaction, Luke spun his ship back over and saw the *Jade Sabre* climbing again, back off planet. But the maneuver had cost him altitude and had put his momentum, once again, downward. He was confident that he could level off and break the dive, but the situation had changed suddenly, for the atmosphere about him had changed.

The fog was burning away, some evaporating, some just coagulating into ice crystals, hanging in the air like flak. And while Luke did clip some of those icicles, crunching through the maze, many others shrank—so fast that they seemed to be just withering away to nothingness.

They had reached critical point; the evaporation had taken on a life of its own, and at a frightening speed.

More and more coralskippers appeared on the scene, some climbing up from the planet, others, many others, vectoring in, returning to the call of the yammosk. Han, Leia, and Lando's relief at seeing the *Jade Sabre* climbing off planet again went away in the blink of an eye as a gigantic shieldship exploded.

All the frequencies jammed with cries from the escorting starfighters and cruisers, screams that shields were gone, calls for help.

Another glittering explosion filled the *Falcon*'s viewscreen, a cruiser blasted apart. And then another, smaller, as a starfighter got cut to pieces.

"What's taking them so long?" Han growled, aiming his frustration at Lando.

Lando held up his hands helplessly. "I don't even know what we're trying to do," he insisted.

"Threepio, you got any answers?" Leia started to ask, but she ended with a scream, and Han yelled, "Left!" as a group of coralskippers rose up before them suddenly, firing away.

The top cannons thundered a response, and Jacen, in the lower pod, got one and then another. But there were too many, and they were flying too well, crossing each others' trails with such precision and coordination that the *Falcon*'s gunners couldn't find many open shots.

Han winced as the *Falcon* jolted from hit after hit. "Come on!" he growled at his console when the shields went away, momentarily, and the lights blinked.

Another shieldship, this one on the back side of the planet from the *Falcon*, exploded.

"We should break off," Lando remarked.

"We can't," Leia retorted sharply. "This is our chance."

A third shieldship went away, and that chance seemed a longer shot by far at that moment.

But then a pair of coralskippers, in opposing spins before the *Falcon*, came together with a devastating explosion.

"Nice shot," Han called.

"I didn't," Anakin replied.

"Me, neither," Jacen said.

Han and Leia looked at each other, then at Lando.

Another pair of coralskippers nicked in a close cross, both spinning off wildly. To one side, Anakin blasted apart one enemy fighter, and then another, and then another, and Jacen got one on the other flank.

The calls from the other ships filling the channels seemed to reflect similar, sudden successes.

"It's working," Leia breathed.

"We're still outnumbered," Han reminded, and as a poignant exclamation point to his remark, a fourth shieldship blew apart.

Han put the *Falcon* up on end, cannons blazing as it zoomed through a host of coralskippers.

"Turn her back!" Anakin called. "We can get every one of them before they get near our shieldship."

But none of the three in the cockpit were even listening, nor was Jacen, who had stopped shooting. They all just stared ahead, at the planet.

The fog around the planet lifted, the view of the icy world becoming more and more clear, until within a span of seconds, there was not a wisp of vapor in its atmosphere.

Han's breath came back to him, and Leia gasped in delight as a familiar form grew before them, the *Jade Sabre* breaking out.

Before they could even begin to call out to Jaina, though, the planet seemed to grow fuzzy and distorted, as if they were looking at it through a glass globe.

"The Mezzicanley Wave!" Anakin squealed. "The fourth state of matter! It's got to be freezing below it. The water's got to be solidifying, at least!"

"That's why these guys can't coordinate their attack anymore," Jacen added. "Their war coordinator's in a deep freeze."

Indeed, many of the coralskippers, confused perhaps, had broken from the battle and were zooming back toward the planet, presumably to protect their base. And as Han and the others watched, the planet's rotation slowed, and slowed even more.

"Unbelievable," Han muttered.

"It won't last for long," Jacen explained. "The energy's gone, so the evaporation's done."

"And what happens when the planet starts up again?" Han asked ominously.

"Well, with the expansion created by the ice . . . ," Jacen began, and that was enough for Han, who got a typically bad feeling about this.

"Luke," Leia whispered breathlessly.

"Get out of here! Get out of here!" Han cried through all channels. "Full retreat!" And despite Leia's continuing plea for her missing brother, Han brought the *Falcon* screaming around, pointed her nose away from the fourth planet— which was beginning to rotate faster again—and punched the throttle, slowing only long enough for the *Jade Sabre* to come zooming by.

It hit Han then, and hard. The reality of what he was doing, of his retreat, so much like the retreat Anakin had pulled on Sernpidal, leaving Chewie behind. He almost turned the *Falcon* back around, plunging toward the planet in a desperate search for Luke.

Almost.

But he could not. If he had been alone, then there would have been no hesitation, but he was not alone, was responsible for more lives than his own.

As Anakin had been.

All the rest of the fleet broke off, too, turning tail and running, with the shieldship tug pilots releasing their lumbering shields and running off for all their lives.

Great quakes rocked the surface of the planet; a chasm appeared, a long canal exploding and running with supersonic speed from pole to pole.

And then the whole planet blew, a shattering, sparkling explosion of ice crystals, spinning out, catching the Helskan sun's rays in a myriad of sparkles and colors.

Out of that widening cloud came a single black speck, a single X-wing running with all speed, surfing on the very edge of an overpowering wave.

TWENTY-FIVE

Connection and Coincidence

"Oh, vocalize!" Luke heard C-3PO say to R2-D2 as he walked back to the room Lando had given him and Mara back on Dubrillion. He rounded the corner, coming in sight of the droids, just as C-3PO bonked R2-D2 on the dome.

R2-D2 responded with what should have been a long and single-noted "ooooo," but it came out as "oo . . . oo . . . oo . . . ee."

"He's just being stubborn, Master Luke," C-3PO insisted, and he moved to bonk R2-D2 again, but Luke, barely containing his smile, moved over and caught the protocol droid by the arm.

"I don't think Artoo has recovered from our flight through the cold and ice," Luke explained.

"Beeoo . . . ee . . . oo," R2-D2 agreed.

"I think he's got the hiccups," Luke added with a wink, and he headed away, straight for his room. The fight with the scattered Yuuzhan Vong forces was going quite well. Many had been destroyed with the planet, for many had swooped down in a foolish attempt to protect their home base and had not escaped the blast; and more importantly, the binding force that was the war coordinator was gone. Now the remaining enemy forces were no more than rogue squadrons, and Kyp Durron, among many, many others, including considerable firepower from the New Republic, was out on the hunt.

At least he could rest easy that the mop-up of the Praetorite Vong was in good hands, Luke thought as he entered the room. Mara wasn't there, and he had to work hard to suppress the urge to go and find her. She hadn't recovered from the ordeals of the past weeks, particularly from the spell that had come over her in the last battle. Her illness was winning now, Luke knew, and as far as Mara was concerned, her battle had to be a private thing. That pained Luke profoundly, the helplessness, standing by and watching the woman he loved so dearly fight against this inner monstrosity.

Luke turned his thoughts outward. He couldn't help in the private struggle, perhaps, but what about the more general fight? He held up a vial, one containing the molecular-transformation beetle they had pulled from Belkadan. Mara had felt within her a definite attraction for the thing, as if her disease had reached out to it. That sensitivity might have been misinterpreted, Luke realized. Mara might have been reacting to the fact that she merely felt sicker in the sick climate of the transformed Belkadan. Or it might have been well founded. Was it connection or coincidence that the disease within Mara and the others had shown up when it did, so near to an extragalactic invasion? Was it an inadvertent—or perhaps even purposeful—insinuation of some foreign disease into the galaxy by the Yuuzhan Vong?

Luke didn't know, but he intended to try, at least, to find out. If there was some way, any way, that he could help his beloved wife, then he had to try.

He bowed his head and closed his eyes, strengthening his resolve. He had so many important issues to attend, the resurrection of the Jedi Council not the least of them. He had to operate on so many levels now, as statesman, diplomat, warrior, scientist, and husband. Mara had talked seriously about flying away for a while, of going to Dagobah, perhaps, or some other wild and Force-filled place, where she could find

an even deeper level of meditation, an even deeper understanding of these things happening within her. Luke, of
course, had offered to go with her, but she had politely, but
firmly, refused.

This was her fight—this part of it, at least.

Luke blew a long and helpless sigh.

In a room down the hall, Leia Solo packed her belongings.
She, too, had so much work ahead of her, she knew. She had
seen these extragalactic aliens, the Yuuzhan Vong, up close,
and understood that the threat, though apparently ended on
any large scale, could not be ignored. There might be other
invasion forces, other war coordinators with even larger
forces at their disposal—and next time, they might not be fortunate to find such an enemy so unwittingly vulnerable beneath the ice crust of a watery world.

Leia appreciated how close they had come to complete
disaster, how easily, had they not found a way to destroy the
planet, the Praetorite Vong might have marched across the
galaxy, one sector at a time, with the New Republic never
really coordinating enough firepower to stop them, and with
the stubborn and often ignorant councilors of the New Republic never really understanding until it was too late that
they had to pay attention to this threat.

That would be Leia's job now, her unavoidable duty despite
her personal preference to stay out of it all. She had three
children who, though they had proven themselves quite capable, even heroic, surely needed her. She had a sister-in-law
battling in the fight of her life, and a brother who might need
her support.

And she had a grieving husband, a man devastated by the
loss of his dearest friend.

But wouldn't all of that be moot if the Yuuzhan Vong came
back, in stronger numbers and better prepared, and the New
Republic wasn't ready to meet them?

"Ambassador Leia," the woman whispered, not liking but

grudgingly accepting the seemingly inevitable title, one that the council would bestow upon her, declaring her to be an ambassador of Dubrillion and the nearby sectors, including the Helska system, of the Outer Rim.

She could only hope Borsk Fey'lya and his cronies would listen.

Halfway across the galaxy, another representative set about his latest task.

Nom Anor knew of the disaster of the Praetorite Vong. He heard the stories coming in from the Outer Rim, and that, combined with his inability to contact either Yomin Carr or Da'Gara, confirmed to him that the invasion force had been battered and scattered.

Now there were Yuuzhan Vong warriors running throughout the galaxy, and he had no way to control them. He had done his part for Da'Gara and the yammosk, had kept the main bulk of enemy warships paralyzed here at the Core and hardly turning their eyes to events at the Outer Rim. And still, the war coordinator, the Praetorite Vong, had failed.

At first, Nom Anor feared that his people might have underestimated their enemies, but then, as more complete reports of the truth of the disaster had rolled in, he came to understand that ill fate alone had ruined the day.

But it was not over, Nom Anor knew. Not at all. The Praetorite Vong was but a fraction of what his people could throw this way.

Now the Yuuzhan Vong executor went back to his work. He was on a small planet, a relatively unknown piece of real estate, but one with a brewing civil war and a mounting hatred for the New Republic.

He'd stir that brew.

TWENTY-SIX

Eulogy

The *Millennium Falcon* glided in quietly and slowly, the dead ball that had been Sernpidal wobbling before them, off balance, off its orbit.

Leia stood beside Han on the bridge, saying nothing, allowing him this moment of solitude and reflection.

And he needed it. He had spent the last days keeping himself too busy to face this inevitable moment, had tried to avoid it in the hopes that time would lessen the pain.

It hadn't. Not a bit. Looking down there, at the last place he had seen Chewbacca alive, Han could find no escape and no reprieve. Now he did think of his friend, fully. He pictured so many of the moments he had spent with Chewie, mostly expressions on the Wookiee's face, or a particular, peculiar howl, and no specific events. The events didn't seem important. Just the inflections in Chewie's voice, the looks he gave to Han, often argumentative, always with respect and honest love.

Han glanced over at Chewie's empty copilot seat, seeing his friend there again in his mind's eye, picturing him clearly, so vividly, and forcing it even deeper, focusing a mental image of Chewbacca so crystalline clear that he almost fostered the sudden belief that he could will the Wookiee back from the dead, that because he, Han, couldn't accept the loss, it couldn't be so.

But it was, and Chewie was gone, and Chewie wasn't coming back.

And those images continued: Chewie running back from the gun pod; Chewie chasing Anakin down the landing ramp on Coruscant after yet another misfiring of the repulsor coil; Chewie hoisting all three of Han's kids high into the air, not so many years ago, when they were not so little, just to prove that he could still do it. Han saw his favorite cap sitting under the copilot console, a cap Leia had given to him not long after the birth of the twins, emblazoned with the stitching *Congratulations, it's a BOTH!* on the front. How many times had Chewie stolen that old and ragged cap recently, plopping it on his furry head, stretching the band.

Han reached down and picked it up then, and turned it over, seeing the brownish blond hair of his Wookiee friend plastered inside.

All those memories drifting by, and always ending with the same, stark realization that there would be no more of them, that the book was closed, that those hairs on the cap were the last ones Chewie would ever put there.

With the typical protectiveness of a father and husband, Han's thoughts drifted to his children. He had caught them many times over the last couple of days blinking back tears, staring off into space, and he didn't have to ask them what they were thinking about. It was worse for Jaina and Jacen, he knew, and though that truth first surprised him, he came to understand it. Anakin was fifteen, a very personal and selfish age, and even with the added weight of guilt over Chewie's death hanging on his shoulders, the boy was too personally absorbed to fully appreciate the reality of the loss. The twins, though, had gone past that egocentric view of the universe, had a better-developed sense of empathy. And so Han had gone to his kids, all three, individually, and had told them all the comforting clichés that everyone heard through their youth whenever a loved one was lost.

How much emptier those words seemed to him now, coming from himself!

For a moment, after each session with his mourning kids, Han wanted to be the little one again, wanted a parent or a mentor to tell him all those comforting clichés, wanted the words to come from a wiser source than he.

He had that source, somewhat, in the person of the woman standing next to him, in his wonderful wife. Leia had loved Chewie as much as he had, and though she was not as often physically close to the Wookiee, and though she didn't have as many particular memories of Chewie as Han did, her grief was no less, he knew. And yet she had buried it within her, had put her own feelings back for now so that she could help Han attend to his.

He knew that.

"How close do you want to get?" Leia asked at length, and only then did Han tune in to the image on the screen before them and realize that Sernpidal had grown quite large. They hadn't come here to try to retrieve Chewie's body—of course, that task was beyond them, beyond anyone.

Han had come here, and Leia had readily agreed to it, because he needed this moment.

"What are we going to tell Chewie's family?" Han asked.

"The truth," Leia said. "That he died a hero."

"I never thought—" Han began quietly, his voice breaking apart.

Leia looked at him gently, allowed him the moment to compose himself.

"I had built this bubble around us," Han tried to explain. "Around all of us—you, me, Chewie, the kids, Luke, Mara, even Lando. Heck, even the stupid droids. We were all in it, you know? In it and safe, a cozy family."

"Invulnerable?" the ever perceptive Leia asked.

Han nodded. "Nothing could hurt us—could really hurt

us," he went on, and then his voice broke up and he just shook his head and blinked away the tears—and when that didn't work, he wiped them away—and stared out at wobbling Sernpidal. He knew that Leia understood, that he didn't have to say more. And even though it made no sense, she didn't disagree. This should have, logically, happened a long, long time ago, after all. And if not to Chewie, then certainly to one of the others, Han, perhaps, most of all. They had been living on the very edge of disaster for so very long, fighting battles, literally, for decades, running from bounty hunters and assassins. Even the first time Han and Leia had met, on the Death Star, of all places, and in the gallows of the place to boot! So many times, it seemed, one or more of them should have died.

And yet, in a strange way, that close flirting with death had only made Han think them all the more invulnerable. They could dodge any blaster, or piggyback on the side of an asteroid, or climb out a garbage chute, or . . .

But not anymore. Not now. The bubble of security was gone, so suddenly, blown apart by a diving moon.

"Even Mara," Han said, and Leia turned back to regard him, though he continued to stare straight ahead. "Her disease couldn't kill her," he went on. "I knew it wouldn't. Even with the reports of those other people dying, she'd live, because the others weren't in my bubble and she was. Mara was, and so she'd win out."

"She will," Leia insisted.

But Han wasn't so sure of that anymore, not by a long shot. Suddenly he got the dread feeling that Mara was indeed terminal, and the realization that those others in his bubble, most notably his kids, weren't exactly safe, either. With their efforts against the aliens, Jaina, Jacen, and Anakin had proven themselves worthy of the title Jedi Knight now, beyond anyone's questioning. They had moved beyond Han's control, and with or without that control, Han knew that they weren't safe anymore.

The bubble was gone.

The alien threat had been all but eradicated, so it seemed.

But to Han Solo, the galaxy suddenly seemed a more dangerous place by far.

If the system's primary was distressed by the events that had transpired on and about the fourth closest of its brood, it betrayed nothing to the naked eye. Saturating local space with golden radiance, the star was as unperturbed now as it was before the battle had begun. Only the conquered world had suffered, its punished surface revealed in the steady crawl of sunlight. Regions that had once been green, blue, or white appeared ash-gray or reddish-brown. Below banks of panicked clouds, smoke chimneyed from immolated cities and billowed from tracts of firestormed evergreen forests. Steam roiled from the superheated beds of glacier-fed lakes and shallow seas.

Deep within the planet's shroud of cinder and debris moved the warship most responsible for the devastation. The vessel was a massive ovoid of yorik coral, its scabrous black surface relieved in places by bands of smoother stuff, lustrous as volcanic glass. In the pits that dimpled the coarse stretches hid projectile launchers and plasma weapons. Other, more craterlike depressions housed the laser-gobbling dovin basals that both drove the vessel and shielded it from harm. From fore and aft extended bloodred and cobalt arms, to which asteroidlike fighters clung like barnacles. Smaller craft buzzed around it, some effecting repairs to battle-damaged areas, others keen on recharging depleted weapons systems, a few delivering plunder from the planet's scorched crust.

Farther removed from the battle floated a smaller vessel, black, as well, but faceted and polished smooth as a gemstone. Light pulsed through the ship at intervals, exciting one facet, then another, as if data were being conveyed from sector to sector.

From a roost in the underside of its angular snout, a gaunt figure, cross-legged on cushions, scanned the flotsam and jetsam a quirk of a gravitational drift had borne close to his ship: pieces of New Republic capital ships and starfighters, space-suited bodies in eerie repose, undetonated projectiles, the holed fuselage of a noncombat craft whose legend identified it as the *Penga Rift*.

In the near distance hung the blackened skeleton of a defense platform. Off to one side a ruined cruiser rolled end over end in a decaying orbit, surrendering its contents to vacuum like a burst pod scattering fine seeds.

Elsewhere a fleeing transport, snagged by the spike of a bloated capture vessel, was being tugged inexorably toward the bowels of the giant warship.

The seated figure beheld these sights without cheer or regret. Necessity had engineered the destruction. What had been done needed to be done.

An acolyte stood in the rear of the command roost, relaying updates as they were received by a slender, living device fastened to his right inner forearm by six insectile legs.

"Victory is ours, Eminence. Our air and ground forces have overwhelmed the principal population centers and a war coordinator has installed itself in the mantle." The acolyte glanced at the receiving villip on his arm, whose soft bioluminescent glow added appreciably to the roost's scant light. "Commander Tla's battle tactician is of the opinion that the astrogation charts and historical data stored here will prove valuable to our campaign."

The priest, Harrar, glanced at the warship. "Has the tactician made his feelings known to Commander Tla?"

The acolyte's hesitancy was answer enough, but Harrar suffered the verbal reply anyway.

"Our arrival does not please the commander, Eminence. He does not dismiss out of hand the need for sacrifice, but he asserts that the campaign has been successful thus far without the need for religious overseers. He fears that our presence will only confound his task."

"Commander Tla fails to grasp that we engage the enemy on different fronts," Harrar said. "Any opponent can be beaten into submission, but compliance is no guarantee that you have won him over to your beliefs."

"Shall I relay as much to the commander, Eminence?"

"It is not your place. Leave that to me."

Harrar, a male of middle years, rose and moved to the

lip of the roost's polygonal transparency, where he stood with three-fingered hands clasped at the small of his back—the missing digits having been offered in dedication ceremonies and ritual sacrifices, as a means of escalating himself. His tall slender frame was draped in supple fabrics of muted tones. A head cloth, patterned and significantly knotted, bound his long black tresses. The back of his neck showed vibrant markings etched into skin stretched taut by prominent vertebrae.

The planet turned beneath him.

"What is this world called?"

"Obroa-skai, Eminence."

"Obroa-skai," Harrar mused aloud. "What does the name signify?"

"The meaning is unknown at present. Though no doubt some explanation can be found among the captured data."

Harrar's right hand gestured in dismissal. "It's a dead issue."

A flash of weapons drew his eye to Obroa-skai's terminator, where a yorik coral gunship was angling into the light, spewing rear fire at a quartet of snub-nosed starfighters that had evidently chased it from the planet's dark side. The little X-wings were closing fast, thrusters ablaze and wingtips lancing energy beams at the larger ship. Harrar had heard that the New Republic pilots had become adept at foiling the dovin basals by altering the frequency and intensity of the laser bolts the fighters discharged. These four pursued the gunship with a single-mindedness born of thorough self-possession. Such fierce confidence spoke to qualities the Yuuzhan Vong would need to keep solidly in mind as the invasion advanced. Largely oblivious to nuance, the warrior caste would have to be taught to appreciate that survival figured as strongly in the enemy's beliefs as death figured in the beliefs of the Yuuzhan Vong.

The gunship had changed vector and was climbing now, seemingly intent on availing itself of the protection offered by Commander Tla's warship. But the four fighters were determined to have it. Breaking formation, they accelerated, ensnaring the gunship at the center of their wrath.

The X-wing pilots executed their attack with impressive precision. Laser bolts and brilliant pink torpedoes rained from them, taxing the abilities of the gunship's dovin basals. For every bolt and torpedo engulfed by the gravitic collapses the dovin basals fashioned, another penetrated, searing fissures in the assault craft and sending hunks of reddish-black yorik coral exploding in all directions. Stunned by relentless strikes, the gunship huddled inside its shields, hoping for a moment's respite, but the starfighters refused to grant it any quarter. Bursts of livid energy assailed the ship, shaking it off course. The dovin basals began to falter. With defenses hopelessly compromised, the larger ship diverted power to weapons and counterattacked.

In a desperate show of force, vengeful golden fire erupted from a dozen gun emplacements. But the starfighters were simply too quick and agile. They made pass after pass, raking fire across the gunship's suddenly vulnerable hull. Gouts of slagged flesh fountained from deep wounds and lasered trenches. The destruction of a plasma launcher sent a chain of explosions marching down the starboard side. Molten yorik coral streamed from the ship like a vapor trail. Shafts of blinding light began to pour from the core. The ship rolled over on its belly, shedding velocity. Then, jolted by a final paroxysm, it disappeared in a short-lived globe of fire.

It looked as if the X-wings might attempt to take the fight to the warship itself, but at the last moment the pilots turned tail. Salvos from the warship's weapons crisscrossed nearby space, but no missiles found their mark.

His scarified face a deeply shadowed mask, Harrar glanced over his shoulder at the acolyte. "Suggest to Commander Tla that his zealous gunners allow the little ones to escape," he said with incongruous composure. "After all, someone needs to live to speak of what happened here."

"The infidels fought well and died bravely," the acolyte risked remarking.

Harrar pivoted to face him fully, a bemused glint in his deeply set eyes. "Is that respect I hear?"

The acolyte nodded his head in deference. "Nothing more than an observation, Eminence. To earn my respect, they would have to embrace willingly the truth we bring them."

A herald of lesser station appeared in the roost, offering salute by snapping his fists to opposite shoulders. "*Belek tiu,* Eminence. I bring word that the captives have been gathered."

"How many?"

"Several hundred—of diverse aspect. Do you wish to oversee the selection for the sacrifice?"

Harrar squared his shoulders and adjusted the fall of his elegant robes. "I am most eager to do so."